They Came to Pick Tomatoes

The Rainbow

Book 3

Jacqueline Hendricks

This book is a work of fiction. The characters, incidents, and dialogue are drawn from the author's imagination and are not to be construed as real. Any resemblance to actual events or persons, living or dead is entirely coincidental.

ISBN 978-0-9914682-7-0(ebk)

ISBN 978-0-9914682-6-3 (pbk)

Cover Design - Rachel Manzo
Cover Photo - Ethan Hamilton

Author Photo – Sarah MacLaughlin

For Janet, Jenn, Jacqui and Vernie

Praise for The Shelter and The Dance:

I'm enchanted by the characters; even Jill's relationship with her parents and her friendship with Sadie. But, I MUST know how her love life turns out....Roberta

I loved reading *The Shelter.* It brings back so many memories of Kokomo [Indiana] and life during the sixties and seventies. Today, I started reading *The Dance* and I anticipate not being able to put this book down either. I gave you 5 stars, for the first book in the trilogy. …..Barbara

Just finished the first book. Loved it....things in the story sounded so familiar.... just finished book two.....loved it *The Dance* is a five star book...Better writing then Jackie Collins or Danielle Steel....It's a must read.....You will love it!!! But you must read book one first. Can't wait for book three...when is book three coming out? My husband is glad I'm done reading for now.....once I start a good book I can't put it down ... just remember I loved it....God will bless you....Marilyn

From the first few pages I was hooked on this book. Jill is a uniquely independent young woman with a rebellious streak. Her early adventures in sex, love and friendship drew me in to a new time and place, (1960's Indiana) but it was her development as a person and her insightful view of the changing world around her that kept me reading.

Wonderfully paced, thoughtfully written – this novel is so much more than the tale of a small town girl. Like all young people, Jill's early adult life is filled with triumphs and set-backs. Her experiences are so clearly articulated by the author I often felt as if I was right there laughing, crying and questioning everything with her. But her story takes us beyond the standard tales of love and heartbreak. Jill transforms as she is exposed to racism, inequality and injustice. She develops a social conscience, including her own personal sense of right and wrong. *They Came to Pick Tomatoes, The Shelter* is full of real life adventure, honest characters and an insightful critique of the times. Overall, a very enjoyable read. I highly recommend it...Terry

Hendricks tells the story of the United States coming of age in the late 50's and early 60's through the eyes of a mid-western girl who in turn is finding her way from childhood to adulthood. Hendricks is not afraid to address prejudice, racism, ignorance and naivety through the words and actions of her characters. Characters are well developed and the author avoids expected stereotypes. Hendricks also captures small town America's many hidden personalities. It is a good read and I look forward to the sequel...Susan

From the first chapter, *They Came to Pick Tomatoes* had my attention. The reader is drawn into the life of this 18 year old, her friends and her community. *The Shelter* covers that time in our life when we went from being the senior in high school to that first year in college. A time when we find ourselves no longer the senior, but one of a great many freshmen in a totally new environment. The author's description of her affair at the migrant camp formed the basis of her feelings with others. She grew up, not just physically, but emotionally. It made her closer than ever to her friends. I believe this book also was quite realistic in her relationship with those friends and her parents. The detail to description of those early events in Jill's life was excellent. Turning every page, I wanted more, certainly not an easy book to put down. To anyone of my generation, to anyone who grew up in the sixties, I highly recommend *They Came To Pick Tomatoes, The Shelter.* I would recommend it to anyone who remembers this time of their life, no matter what period, and can smile when looking back at it…Ed

Out of the shelter and into the storm goes Jill. *They Came To Pick Tomatoes, The Shelter's* young heroine faces what women of all generations face when the time comes to leave the safety of childhood behind, but in a time period of turbulence and change. Set in the 1960s, Jill's adventures not only instantly connect the reader to the universal struggles of growing up, but also of the unique struggle of the time period. Jill is a strong female protagonist whose gripping journey of self-discovery and discovery of the larger world will leave you waiting impatiently for the next book in this trilogy. I highly recommend this book. Kudos to Jacqueline Hendricks for crafting such an intriguing tale…Rachel

They Came to Pick Tomatoes, The Shelter is a very good read. I especially like the descriptions of the times and the place and the turmoil that most of us were going through during those years. Without doubt this captures the rock solid experience of growing up in the Midwest, as well as the ground shaking events of the world that were beginning to encroach on the idyllic times. This story of Jill coming of age is excellent and congratulations to the author. I think it is an engrossing read for just about anyone…M.Toledo

Thank you. I hope I have fulfilled your expectations. jh

They Came to Pick Tomatoes

The Rainbow

ᑳBook 3ᑲ

At the end of the rainbow
You'll find a pot of gold
At the end of a story
You'll find it's all been told

But our love has a treasure
Our hearts can't always spend
And it has a story without any end

At the end of a river
The water stops its flow
At the end of a highway
There's no place you can go

But just tell me you love me
And you are only mine
And our love will go on
Till the end of time

Till the end of time ...

Nat King Cole

Chapter 1

The morning sun shone in a crystal clear blue sky. Jill wore coverall's over her shorts and a tube top. She took a deep breath, smelling the freshly plowed dirt, "God's promise to the farmer," she repeated Luis' long ago summation. June 1, only the chickens rose earlier today than she did. She'd shared the early pink and yellow sunrise with the farmers' alarm clocks, cock-a-doodle-doo. The promise, always the promise of the new day, and this day, her promise was to get out the rotor-tiller and work on her garden. Her garden? First it had been Jack's garden, and slowly she helped. She started to direct, when she knew which vegetables and herbs she wanted for cooking. Yes, Hector, I like to grow and cook the vegetables not just wash them.

She pulled the rotor-tiller through each row in the small garden. Jack had been so helpful in getting a smaller model she could use. She liked the sinking squish of plowed soil under her boots, and the warm sun on her back.

School was over for another year. They had finished earlier than the city schools, as they still set their calendars to coordinate with farming. And here she was *farming*. The planting had to be done this week in order to have a full growing season. Maybe she could have started last week, but there was all the end of school paperwork and help with the Senior Week graduation activities. Yes, she had volunteered to be their class sponsor when they were freshman, and then stayed with them until the end, commencement. High School Commencement was her summer ten years ago 1960, at the migrant camp with Luis. But he had not called, not written since last month's birthday note to her and Luisa. Summer vacation, his invitation would come. Invitation? Their vacation plan, but for now, this early morning, her garden beckoned.

She visualized the abundance of vegetables and fruit that would emerge from the dark rich soil. Jack purchased fertilizer, and she would mix that in with her next rotor-tiller pass. The uneven strain of the steel blades jerked her arms, easier though than the mules of the pioneer women. She sank each foot into the newly plowed dirt, and laughed at her visualization of Jill Caitlin ankle-deep in Indiana. Had Mother Nature planted her in this Hoosier earth? The cornfields conspired as she slept? Sneaking in through the open windows and pollinating her brain? She fed her family and Sadie with the vegetables.

The seasons eased into one another around and around, a complete cycle. Another summer, but now, how different the summers would be...Dad had talked to Jack and she would be able to travel with abandon. Okay not freely, but easier. She could hear Sadie, "Oh, Miss Sarah B., just plant."

Her garden plot would yield a wide variety of fresh things and canable things. The weeds disappeared with each scoop of the rotor, but they would quickly reseed themselves faster than the lettuce and cucumbers, and then sprout before the musk melon and watermelon. The weeds would try to choke her vegetables; she heaved a sigh of despair. In one swoop she had gone from the bountiful harvest to fighting dastardly weeds. Hoeing? Yes, that would be in July, next month, no longer this cool early June morning temperature. What did Henry say, "If all the days in Indiana were like this, we'd have to build a fence to keep people out."

Planting the garden reminded her of Sadie's one and only attempt, a fiasco by anyone's definition. After planting the seeds and fertilizing, Sadie had done nothing else, no hoeing, no maintenance, and no weed killer. It became a jungle growth of tangled watermelon vines, ragweed, milkweed, buckhorns, beets and giant sunflowers. The friends took pictures in case Sadie felt the "plant a garden" guilt rise within her.

12

Smiling, holding up a large beet choked with weeds, Sadie had complained, "I don't even like beets, why did I plant them?"

The enlarged pictures hung in Sadie's kitchen. Michael shook his head that their acreage was farmed by someone else, "Not even a single tomato plant graces this backyard." And he pointed to the acre of their pine enclosed yard. "My grandfather is rolling over in his grave because we have no garden on this property."

Jill yanked the small tiller from the last row and turned off the engine. She'd converted grass and weeds into a twenty-five foot square of black-brown dirt in the center of her backyard. Smiling at her morning's work, she walked the short distance from the plot to the tool shed. As she unzipped her coveralls, she inspected flats of seedlings sprouting under the windows. The small ones were ready to plant. The garden shed was neat like everything Jack touched - spades and trowels hung symmetrically, watering cans stored on wood shelves, clay pots sorted by size.

"Time for coffee. Luis could you be in my kitchen fixing some L.O. Limited? Stop dreaming, Jill."

She closed the shed door and trudged in her dirt laden shoes to the porch steps. She scrapped them on the metal boot step then sat down and used a small putty knife to finish removing the mud. The phone rang. Her watch said 7:15, too early for Sadie, and too late for Lillian. Dad knows I'm alone, but he should be at work. She tugged off her boots, then ran through the screened porch, grabbing the receiver on the fourth ring.

"Jill?" Luis spoke.

"Yes." It had been two months since she'd heard his "Hasta luego," at the airport in Curaçao.

"Gringa, the Undersecretary of Commerce has invited me to Washington. My friend Jorge has only one more year in office, and then I can go back to doing other things. There will be a new director for the Agriculture Department. I need to be in the mountains right now, but...What are you doing for the next three days?"

"Hi Luis!"

"I'm not really interested in the Undersecretary, but you. You are the one Jankee I want to see."

"I'm fine. It's a clear day, not a cloud in the sky. Luisa's in Vacation Bible School. Jack is in Cleveland conducting a seminar." The early morning peace evaporated. Lightning strikes on a sunny day. Never in the same spot? Always in the same spot.

"Si. The conference begins tomorrow and lasts until Friday. The American flight from Indianapolis gets you into Washington at 2P.M. I'll be there at noon."

"Luis, I'm planting my garden. American Airlines? What are you asking?"

"I want to see you in D.C., your capital.

"Si, I know the place," she said.

"Gina has made the arrangements. Your flight number is 602. Write that down. We'll be staying in Arlington. The limousine is compliments of Señor Sam."

"Uncle Sam." She shook her head. Washington, D.C. But my garden...

"Gringa, I must go. Your United States, mañana. Adios."

She poured coffee from a Thermos. She'd filled the Thermos with the perked pot in order to keep it hot and save the flavor, but coffee from a Thermos reminded her of Henry and his work. She held the coffee mug and dialed Sadie's number, then plopped down at the kitchen table, "Sadie, he's so damned inconsiderate!"

"I'm asleep. What time is it? You know I don't keep your farmer hours!"

"Sadie, wake up! I read a magazine article by some psychologist and she said I'm having an anxiety attack."

"Let me understand this before I hang up on you. You have awakened me out of my most needed beauty sleep to tell me about a magazine article? You know I pay Hilda good money to keep my children quiet while I sleep..."

"It doesn't matter why I woke you up, just talk to me."

"What time are we doing drinks at the club, the pool is open."

"Not today. We don't have time to do that. I have to pack. You have to drive me to Indianapolis first thing in the morning. Luis makes me..."

"Stop right there. You won't get the adjective right. I haven't received a letter from your friends in Bogotá, so what is going on?"

Jill told Sadie of his invitation actually a command, but Sadie said, "That's him and you know it. Get used to it. Don't call me at these hours for shit you know. Sorry, you have me cussing first thing in the morning."

Sadie laughed as Jill explained her morning planting, then Sadie volunteered to come and plant the seeds. They both laughed at the

14

shared memory. Sadie said, "A trip to Washington is exactly what a woman who is having an affair needs. And you can visit Arlington Cemetery like you've been threatening to do for seven years."

ᘒᘓᘒ

The plane trip seemed quick. The ticket was just as he had said. She had shown the reservation desk her driver's license; they handed her the ticket, then directed her toward the gate. Sadie promised to be at the same place in three days. This slipping away had been easy, as Jack was in Cleveland at his conference, but she decided that Luis needed to give her more warning. It could have been inconvenient almost impossible and how awful not to be with him for three days. Henry had only said, "This is how it begins?"

What did that mean? She kept asking herself from Indianapolis. But now as the plane descended into National Airport, she answered Henry's question, no Dad, it began in the shed.

She disembarked. A young man dressed in a black jacket, white shirt and a black bowtie held up a sign that read "Jill Jones." They walked to a Lincoln Town car. As they drove towards Washington, D.C., each green and white sign by the highway named another place – the Capitol, Arlington Cemetery, Lincoln Memorial. She'd spent hours discussing the nation's capital with her students, but this was her first visit. Sadie asked her to come the few months when Michael was stationed at the Pentagon with the admonition to go to Hector's grave in Arlington. And Jill refused, "Not ready for that Sadie."

The hotel bellboy took her bags from the limousine driver who said, "Please take Mrs. Jones to Luis Ochoa's room, number 825."

The bellboy nodded, and they crossed the lobby, pink and maroon with the many subtle shades in between. Dark green plants matched the dark swatches in the rug. The lobby was filled with conventioneers wearing name tags on their business suits. A culture of professionals in the heart of power, yes, way beyond the cornfields. She could almost feel the beat, the pulse, the country. And the man she was meeting hated it so much. She and the bellboy walked to the elevator, leaving the buzzing conversations to the hushed whisk of elevator cables. She looked in the mirrored wall, and saw that her Hoosier wasn't showing and no mud on her shoes. She smiled.

Luis, wearing the hotel's white terry robe, opened the door. The bellboy set her bag down and waited, asking if they needed anything. Staring at Luis in the afternoon, no, she did not need anything else. Luis tipped the man, and then locked the door behind him. Fresh flowers and champagne waited on a glass-topped table. Thin rayon sheers curtained the patio sliding-glass doors and filtered the room's light. Jill parted the drapes and looked out at the Potomac River. The scent of his cologne filled the room. He walked to where she stood, hugged her tightly and kissed her, the taste of cigar. Yes, she was out of the cornfields, but the taste of Luis took her back to and in the middle of tomato fields.

Luis poured champagne. "Gringa, I have my first meeting in one hour. May I propose a toast to your safe arrival?"

"I feel as if I'm in some time machine. I don't see you, don't hear your voice for two months and in twenty-four hours," she touched his hand, "from Indiana to..." she squeezed his fingers, pulling them to her lips, "you."

She kissed his fingertips, then tipped her glass to his and took a big drink. The alcohol would calm the jitters. She would be sleeping with Luis all night, sharing the same bed. How many times since Curaçao had she wanted to do this very thing? Get in the bed, stay in the bed, wake up during the night to touch him and when the sun came up, to lie next to him. Señora Ochoa for a few days.

He put their glasses on the table and kissed her without allowing conversation. They moved from the table to the bed, not speaking. Him, this moment the same, in the shed, the green room, in Curaçao under the rhythmic wood slats. Luis's grip built the wall separating her from her farm life. His presence, touch, and taste surrounded their own special world like a brick fence.

As she eased from their love-making to a complete awareness of the room, the quiet music of the radio blended with her sense of satisfaction. When she walked into the hotel room, she had not remembered music. Now The Guess Who were singing, "American Woman..." the ceiling sparkled. She rubbed Luis's shoulder with her index finger. The creamy sheets were twisted in a roll at the foot of the king-size bed. Looking over her to the nightstand alarm clock, Luis jumped from the bed. He smiled slightly, then said, "The angel's mother, an angel herself, keeping me from ..." He slapped her gently on the butt. "They are singing your song, Gringa, American Woman, listen what I say...the English is not perfect, but having you, listen..." he laughed.

"No, it is your song, they are talking about what do you call us, Damn Jankees? Just say that instead of American Woman... Damn Jankees stay away from me...I got more important things to do...I don't need your war machine. I hope they are playing this on the West Wing Muzak."

"Señor Nixon...I hope he keeps buying Colombian coffee for his war machine."

She watched as he stood in front of the mirror. His husky body was a totally different shape than Jack's. There was not a slim muscle in Luis's cut. The salt and pepper hair covered his round chest, the body that fit hers as if made for her. Could she grab his arm and pull him back into bed? He shook his head as if answering her question. "Si, you were...the tiger in this bed." He walked from the bathroom and refilled their glasses. He stood before her like the winning bullfighter, "To my Gringa."

"Welcome to America from *your* American woman."

"I must go. Do you want to go to the White House for a special reception? I brought the tuxedo."

"Luis, you are...with President Nixon who won't end the Viet Nam War? No, hell no! I don't want to be near the White House with him in it."

"My Gringa," he laughed, "we threw tomatoes when he came to visit as Vice President."

"I worked so hard to defeat him."

"Politics? Jankee politics? You know what I think. This is supposed to be a place for tourists. You can find something to do? I'll leave you money. Don't get lost. Don't answer the phone. Don't use the phone unless I'm here," he said.

She thought she should say, "Yes, sir." He separated them as quickly as he had drawn them together. The way of Luis Ochoa as Sadie said.

He dressed in business clothes, a look that she had not seen, but more like the people in the lobby. He adjusted his tie under the starched white collar; combed his hair and moustache; and slipped on dress loafers over his dark socks. The double-breasted jacket of his suit was a summer weight light-gray. The silk handkerchief matched the navy and red silk tie. He pulled the long shirt sleeves down, barely visible at the edge of the coat sleeve. It all fit his bull-shape perfectly. He smiled as he caught her eye in the mirror, "London, Savile Row, Anderson and Sheppard. We'll go one day."

She had straightened out the sheet and pulled it up to her neck as he dressed. She was not ready to dress, not ready to leave the room, only to sit where they had been and smell his cologne on the sheets. He buttoned his jacket and snapped the lid closed on his briefcase. Turning he walked to the bed, yanked the sheet from her, "This is why…"

"Why what, Luis?"

"You're beautiful, Gringa." He shook his head slowly.

"Gracias, Señor Ochoa."

He reached with the back of his hand rubbing her breast, catching her nipple between his fingers, pinching her gently. He shook his head again, then walked to the dresser removing folded bills from his money clip. He placed two twenty dollar bills on the table, and then replaced the clip. Opening his briefcase and removing a leather case, he picked through several plastic cards, pulling one from the bunch and placing it on the money. "Here use this card to call Siddhartha from the *pay* telephone. You do want to call her and tell her about your Latin lover?" He laughed a low chuckle, walked to the bed, leaned over, and kissed the tip of her nose. "We'll have dinner later. I'll send the driver to pick you up. Everyone wants to meet with the Colombian, take him to dinner, but I have the only Jankee I want to have dinner with." He winked.

"Luis, I do want to see you in your tux."

"Handsome, Gringa," He looked at her flashing his cock-of-the-walk smile, then left.

She resisted the temptation to go through his luggage. Sadie would say yes, but she knew Luis was too private and she did not want to run into another gun or anything even close.

She curled under the sheets and closed her eyes. She was a million miles from the rotor-tiller as she woke to a knock on the door. The sun was setting. The clock said, 7P.M. She wrapped Luis's robe around her. The knock was more insistent. She peered through the small hole in the door, the limousine driver. He knocked again. Then asked, "Mrs. Jones?"

She opened the door a crack, the width of the chain guard, "Yes?"

"Mr. Ochoa wants you to meet him at Henri's at 8P.M. I am to take you. I'll be downstairs waiting."

The restaurant was all white: white linen table cloths, white uniformed waiters, with white towels on their arms, white napkins folded like sails, each table with a combination of white flowers in frosted glass vases. The crystal glasses and chandeliers sparkled. Couples sat in curved white leather banquettes chatting. Sitting at a private table for two, she and Luis talked and laughed. His face glowed in the candlelight from their centerpiece. He impressed her with his knowledge of Washington, no buildings taller than the Washington Monument, no thirteenth floors. He said, "The White House has a Lincoln Room, but do you think President and Mrs. Nixon use their green room like we used Siddhartha's green room?"

They laughed at the thought of the Nixon's doing any sexual act. He talked of his afternoon at the U.S. Commerce Department, letting her know Colombia needed the money of U.S. investments, but not the strings that always wrapped the money.

"With strings attached," she said.

"Si, American idiom." He smiled.

He ordered the wine from a long list; she recognized the light white Rheine of Germany, but only offered that she liked white. He ordered grilled salmon, then paused to confirm her choice of salad dressing.

He reached for her hand, twisting his gift to her, the emerald ring, allowing the candlelight to refract the light on the diamonds. She rubbed his gold wedding ring. Their conversation was about Luisa, school, her grades, mathematics.

"Spanish?" he asked.

"It isn't taught in the fourth grade at her school."

"You could teach her. You are the maestra, si?"

"And why do I say she should learn this language?"

"Her father is Colombian and she needs to be able to speak to him." He smiled and winked at her. "When will the school teach her Spanish?"

"In high school."

"You have school pictures?"

"I have one in my billfold, but I have our pictures from Curaçao."

She pulled the packet of pictures from her purse. They drank coffee and discussed the scenes in the pictures. He laughed when she told of Sadie saying Connie looked like the Dutch maid on the cleanser can. He said he would keep all the pictures, and the school picture.

"I will," he said, "put them with her mother's school pictures."

"You still have those high school prom pictures?"

"Si, in a very special place."

"Where?"

"You'll see." He tapped her finger with his.

"Luisa has not mentioned you to anyone," Jill said. He nodded, pursing his lips. "And," Jill continued, "asked if we would go to Mr. Ochoa's again?"

Luis explained he had another place in mind for August.

He ordered, "Bananas Foster for my gringa." When the waiter brought the brown sugar covered bananas to the table, he poured the rum sauce over the ice cream then lit it. Luis told her to eat it quickly before it melted. She tried to follow his directions.

"I've always said hot fudge sundaes are my favorite, but this was delicious, Luis."

He snipped the end of his cigar, "Let's go. I want to walk and smoke."

The sultry night in Georgetown was illuminated with store fronts and street lights. The driver said he would return to the same spot in an hour. Shops and boutiques, old townhouses with stoops leading down to brick sidewalks, lined the streets. She wanted to hug Luis and turned to him, "Luis..."

"Gringa," he stopped her sentence, "This is my birthday."

"Feliz Cupleaños, shall I sing?"

"Si," he smiled.

She quietly made it through the complete song in Spanish.

"Gracias. I like your accent. Puerto Rican?"

She stopped by a men's store window, "If it were open, I'd buy you..."

He turned her around to face him, stopping. Other people walked past them, young students, the flower children with their long hair held by leather beaded headbands, boys and girls looking the same, one accidentally bumped into Luis. His hair hung in long dark curls tied back with a bandana. The curls lay on his neck and shoulders. His eyes were dark, but he flashed a smile at the abrupt stop, the smile, and dimples, long and deep. He raised two fingers, making a v-sign and said, "Peace, brother," then backed up and walked around them.

"Such sadness on your pretty face. Why Gringa?"

"In America we say, 'It's a long story.'" She shook her head.

"Si, I understand. There is much for you to tell, but you are reluctant, why?"

"Hey! It's your birthday. We are together in Washington, D.C. My long story is personal, remember you said the shadow of death?"

He reached for her hand, "Gringa, I have missed much of your life, too much, I think. This will change. I want to know why singing a Spanish birthday song, caused this sadness." She squeezed his hand. Hesitating, he continued, "But when you are ready to tell the 'long story.' Si?"

"Si," she said.

"What present do you want to buy me?"

"Presents? Is that a Colombian birthday tradition?"

"No, it's Colombian to celebrate your birthday with a gringa. It's why I called you."

She laughed. Someone handed them a pamphlet on the "true revolution" with a hammer and sickle picture.

"Crazy Jankees. One revolution was not enough?" He dropped the brochure into a big green can that said, "Keep America Beautiful."

"I appreciate your happiness, but what if I hadn't come? How would you have celebrated your birthday?"

"Gringas are easy, when you have money. They smell money like bloodhounds. How long do you think it would take, if you left, before one of your gringa sisters came up to me?" He nodded to the sidewalk in front of them. Young women with scraggly hair, and political buttons on Army fatigues, tie-dyed dresses, Indian batik, long skirts, embroidered fringed vests and woven chokers with brightly colored beads. Jill looked down; her sundress was fitted at the top and short, slightly above her knees, in mint green with a white lace Peter Pan collar. There were four buttons down the front with hand-painted flowers in green and yellow. Did she look like the farmer's wife among this colorful group, most of them braless in see-through gauzy cotton?

"No, not these gringas, too young, too lost, too righteous," Luis answered her silent question. "Your face, Gringa, you have expressions that are like book pages, easy to…"

"Yes, Luis, I know. I have a hard time hiding my feelings. You hide all of it so well. Who are you?"

"Let's see, I'm 5' 11", I weigh eighty-eight kilos, m-m sometimes, I weigh ninety kilos. I was born June 2, 1930. I'm Colombian, a coffee farmer…Remember feel first, Gringa. Because it is

21

my birthday, I will allow you to ask *one* question, anything you want. Be careful, ask only for that which you want an answer. Honesty can be brutal."

"Just one question?"

"Si. And that was it." He laughed as she slapped his arm. She laced her arm through his, "You're not going to leave me? I think that is my question."

They stopped at the crosswalk of Wisconsin and M streets, several people stood next to them, the young hippies and the older dressed-for-dinner folks. Luis put his arm around her, leading her across the street. In the center of the street, he paused and looked down at her, "Jill, will you marry me?"

She turned her head. He smiled. When they stepped on the curb, she said, "Don't ask questions you don't want to know the answer to."

"As the French would say, touché, but I thought I was answering *your* question."

"I would never marry someone I don't know."

"Who is Jack Jones?"

Jill spoke, as if from a script, "He is an electrical engineer who works for Johnson Electronics. He grew up on a farm near Swayzee, Indiana. He graduated from DePauw University and received his master's in engineering from Purdue University in Lafayette, Indiana. The farthest west he's been from Indiana is Kansas City. He loves Indiana, loves his farm, his house, his wife, *your* daughter, and peach pie. He plays tennis, listens to classical music and likes to fish. He hates surprises and knows where he will be buried when he dies. He's learned to accept Sadie, and he and my mother are cut from the same cloth."

"Is that a Hoosier expression?" He arched one eyebrow.

"What do you know about Hoosiers?"

"Gringa, it is you. Indiana natives, si?" He touched her cheek with the side of his hand.

She nodded, "It means they are so similar the same material was used to make them. How about two beans from the same coffee bush?"

He chuckled, then stopped to look at a jewelry store window as the jeweler picked up the tiny velvet boxes from the window and rearranged the twisting display of watches. Luis talked to her reflection in the window, "You married your mother?"

Lightning, right to the same spot. Was she atoning for the guilt of having this man's baby? But he was here and she was here and they were a couple in…love. "Your degree must be in psychology?"

"I know my enemy."

"Human relationships are your enemy?"

"You already asked your question, perhaps next year on my birthday. Write this on your calendar, so you will remember." Smiling, his eyes sparkled, he was relaxed. "Our hour is up. I am ready to get my gringa birthday present." He winked, then bent and kissed the skin in front of her ear.

ᴦξᴦ

She awoke to his low voice, talking rapidly in Spanish. He sounded irritated, but his Spanish was much too fast for her to keep up. Listening discreetly to his responses required deliberate effort and when she figured out "order" and "kilograms" of verde "green," and General Foods, ICA, and Brazil two or three times, vehemently, then back to ICA, he was three sentences further into the conversation. She understood the angry tone and the argumentative answers to the caller. The natural conversational Spanish sounded like East Harlem at Hector's. He slammed the phone down. She looked at him pretending to be awakened. He rubbed her neck and the side of her face with the back of his hand. Could she purr?

His face was furrowed.

"I guess your birthday is over and you realized your true age?"

"Gringa, you are making a joke, but I cannot play. The Vice-President of the Federation is flying in to take my place. Politics, Gringa. You know about politics. You know about political wars. I spend too much time fighting fires, unfortunately, people get killed." He had not really addressed her, ranting, so she did not respond. People get killed. Hector was killed in a political war. Yes, Luis, I know, she answered to herself. Sadie and she would have to discuss Luis's political war.

"I am returning as soon as I can get a flight out of here. Do you want to stay? Do you want me to call and make a reservation for you? Can Siddhartha pick you up?"

He walked to the closet and removed a suit from the rack, then laid it in the garment bag that already had three neatly folded shirts. He glanced at her as he picked up his shoes and placed them in felt bags, and then wedged the leather squares into the bottom of his smaller leather tote. Opening the chest drawers he removed his black silk shorts and socks, packing them on top of the shoes. He walked into the bathroom.

She wanted to slow his departure, twenty-four hours was not enough. He seemed to be reacting as if moving on a moment's notice was normal. The source of pleasure, the affable Luis window shopping in Georgetown, now broke into a different stride. What happened in Colombia that just whisked him so urgently on such brief notice? He returned from the bathroom and stacked his toiletries bag on top of the underwear. He zipped up the tote, then the long "U" shaped zipper of the garment bag. He set the tote by the door and laid the garment bag on top of it, only his briefcase remained opened. He came to the edge of the bed, standing in front of her. He held her chin in his palm, "I apologize for my abruptness. You don't understand. I...Who is Luis Ochoa? I'll tell you." He raised his voice on the last phrase, and then said, "Luis Ochoa is a busy man!"

He instantly turned half away from her, his hand dropped to his side. The color drained from his face, his expression frozen, paralyzed as if something inside him had stopped. And yet he breathed deeply, taking a few brief hesitant steps toward the desk chair, then slumped down on the hard seat. His hands trembled, his recent urgency vanished as he shook his head like a small child refusing cough syrup, and then he bowed in prayer. He propped his forehead on one hand and crossed himself with the other whispering in Spanish, "Padre, Padre, perdóname porque he pecado..." (Father, Father, forgive me for I have sinned)

She watched him recede to another place, his shadow of death? He sat still, in supplication, holding his head in both hands. He had separated from her. She sat motionless on the edge of the bed waiting for him to look, to say, to ask...he continued to pray in a breathy whisper, repeating the Spanish, "Padre, Padre," then with another crossing of his chest, silence, eyes closed, head bowed.

Leaving Mexico City at the end of summer, twenty-one years ago, Luis said goodbye to his adopted family, "Uncle" Benedicto, short and round with a salt and pepper beard and "Aunt" Adelita the same height and weight as Benedicto, with her hair pulled into a tight bun. They both pleaded. Adelita held his hands as tears rolled down her cheeks, "Por favor, mi hijo." (please my son)

Benedicto never stopped asking, "Please don't go. You don't know this 'family.' You can stay with us as long as you need to. Please reconsider. We promised Mamacita to take care of you. She wants you to get your college education. Please."

As they drove to the train station, they had presented reasons for him to continue his education. They had been gracious and generous.

Luis responded, "You've been good to me, and I will not forget your kindness. I promise to return if I don't like the farm. But I must go now."

Benedicto hugged him, "Remember when God closes a door he opens a window. However, if you push open those closed doors, you may not like what is behind them."

And then Luis boarded the train for Veracruz.

His Uncle Ramos's farm felt like the right answer to his need to get away from the city. He would be working on the land and learning about a piece of his family he never knew he had.

From the Veracruz train station, he rode in a decrepit pick-up. The driver told him to sit with some laborers in the back of the truck. A young girl, maybe fifteen, sat in the cab. She kept turning around and staring at Luis. Her long black hair tangled in the hot wind. She hooked the strands behind her ears. Her skin was fair, white in comparison to the driver and laborers. Her eyes were hazel-green; Luis recognized the color from many years of looking in the mirror. As they bounced along she occasionally smiled. Luis looked from the teenager to his poorly clothed companions, banging with each road bump. They wore the leather sandals, ragged pants and stained shirts of peasant workers. They discussed a cock fight they had seen in Veracruz, laughing, recalling the strutting roosters and their owners. Several machetes rattled in the space formed by the wheel wells.

In the unrelenting gaze of the girl's face, he had a sense of being asked questions. The truck window kept a silent space between them.

They rode past fields of sugar cane and bananas. The other men referred to the "Cacique." (chief) Neither of them said Ramos's name. Their conversation excluded Luis, deliberately, he sensed. After they mentioned the cacique, they would glance quickly, and then punctuate the sentence with a cocked head toward Luis.

The city disappeared as the jungle overgrowth and mountainous climb swallowed them, a trip into the belly of the countryside. After what seemed like hours, the truck suddenly turned off the main highway onto a dirt road. It wound in a snake-like pattern until they passed two armed guards. They continued to a large clearing in heavy banana groves, pulling up in front of an ostentatious stucco ranch house, a hacienda. A matching stucco fence topped with wrought iron bars separated the main house from smaller quarters. The lesser houses were scattered under bent scraggly oak trees. Unkempt children played in the same dirt yard with chickens and dogs. A couple of squat women bent over outside ovens. Luis's fellow passengers grabbed the machetes and jumped from the truck, then headed toward the shacks. The driver yelled at Luis to stay.

The truck parked at the entrance of the ranch, clearly marked with a wrought iron arch. The driver yelled, "Get Out! Get Out!"

Luis jumped from the truck and grabbed the boxes of his books and belongings. He stacked them on the intricately laid ornate tile-covered road leading to the main house. The driveway encircled a three tiered water fountain that spouted and sprayed rhythmically. The girl leapt from the cab and rushed to help with the boxes.

"Buenos Dias, Luis. I'm your cousin, Papa said. I'm Maria! Your father was his brother. Your father died. I'm sorry. Come. You'll be living in here with my family." Her smile was inviting and comforting. Luis paused in the fresh country air. No more dusty city. The house was buried under palms, oaks and poinsettias.

A heavy wood gate with black iron hinges opened into a courtyard replete with flowers in large brightly painted clay pots. Purple and red bougainvillea draped the arched walkways that led to the rooms in the house. Screen doors opened on the terra cotta walk which surrounded the square-shaped garden. Concrete benches circled a small pool of goldfish. The center of the courtyard resembled a restaurant with wood tables and wrought iron chairs.

Luis followed his cousin down one walkway, then into a large room filled with dark heavy furniture. Native Indian artifacts, masks of carved wood and primitive stone tools decorated rough plastered walls. "Papa is away, he is busy," Maria said without further explanation, and followed with a downward glance.

His first weeks at the hacienda were idyllic. Maria introduced him to the horses, "We have a full stable of animals, some are used as work animals for hauling, others we use just for riding. I will take you on a tour of our ranch. Do you know how to ride?"

"It's been a few years, but yes, I know how. I want to see all of it and maybe you can tell me about the crops and the workers."

As they rode together for the first time, Maria pointed out the armed guards at regular posts, introducing Luis to these men who protected her father's farm. Maria explained, "Thieves try to take Papa's things, so we have this protection."

"What things? Bananas? Sugar cane? I haven't seen anything else. We have revolutionary armies in Colombia, is that a problem here?"

Maria did not answer, just "the glance" as he came to label the downward look when mentioning Ramos. Luis watched.

It had been good to transverse the farm by horse. After his first ride with Maria, he went to the stable, saddled his own horse and rode to escape the hacienda and to relax in the country.

He lived in a private section of the plantation home. His bedroom was located at one end of the house away from the courtyard and main living room, but close to the kitchen. He came to prefer the kitchen where the men gathered to talk with his Aunt Rebecca. She was short and heavy, no waist, like a bear. Her laughter filled the kitchen. She had a laughing response to almost everything, a chuckle even when nothing was funny. It helped to relax the ranch hands. Rebecca stayed in the kitchen all day monitoring the feeding of the large household. There were those who cooked and those who cleaned and those who supervised each group.

Rebecca loved to cook and asked, "Ah my son, please tell me your favorites." She hugged him tightly in their first meeting, "We are so glad you have come home, well to our home. Ramos has been so excited that you would be coming."

Every time he sat down to eat, she tousled his hair and called him, "mi hijo."(my son) The kitchen was warm and homey as they all shared stories of the farm, but none said the name Ramos except Rebecca. They never mentioned the cacique. They waited for him, but did not talk about his return. They shared glances like co-conspirators enjoying a moment without the boss.

He explored his new home from one end to the other. The main house sat in the center of a large banana grove. All the peasant labor lived in the same center section, but far removed from the hacienda. When Luis stopped to talk or observe the workers, they would pause and glance down. They audibly sighed in disgust, then a whispered, "Are you…are you his son?"

He asked Maria, "Why do they ask if I'm his son and why do they shake their heads in disgust?" She shook her head, and then said, "They don't like Papa. They are ungrateful indios. (Indians) They know nothing!"

Her haughty derision angered him, but he listened and watched. He did not however understand the Indians disgust with him. He did not know these men. He concluded in his first two weeks that Ramos had a great deal of money and there was something terribly wrong if his own father had no contact with a brother who was also a farmer.

Three weeks after Luis arrived, Ramos roared into the compound late at night. He burst into Luis's room, waking him from a deep sleep."Get up! Get up! Mi hijo. Come! Wake up, you can sleep after we have a drink to celebrate." He took a drink from a tequila bottle, "No glasses! Here take a drink!"

He welcomed his nephew with a big hug, and a clap on the back. Luis stared, then took a drink from the bottle. Ramos laughed, "Come, come, mi hijo, a big drink you're with Ramos now."

His bedside lamp was dim, but Luis's reflection stared at him holding out a bottle of tequila. Ramos was thicker through the middle, gray temples and furrows on his brow, a deep ridged "V" between his eyebrows. Their shoulders were the same width, height was the same, and the intense hazel-green eyes, first Maria and now Ramos. The older man shook his head and punched Luis's chest playfully, then boxed his ears as fathers do. In this instant of their meeting, Luis had been transformed from nephew to the son Ramos never had.

"No wonder your papa didn't send you before, he knew you looked more like me than him. Mi hijo, you've come to your roots. Here, drink to that!"

In the weeks that followed, Ramos insisted Luis work the cane fields as the Indians did. He told Luis the best way to learn the business of farming cane was to feel it cut; to cut it with machetes. And so Luis learned. The sharp stalks left their lines clearly marked on Luis's arms. In the evenings of the sugar harvest, Luis was cut and bleeding. He soaked his skin in salt water, then clear rinsing water and a topical cream prepared by the Indians on the farm. Ramos also provided him with a girl to bathe him, dress the cuts and rub his sore muscles. "A young man," Ramos informed him, "has needs that I can't meet. Just use her Luis and when you get tired of her tell me, I'll get you another one."

Ramos had shocked Luis from the moment he burst into his room, his crudeness, his mistreatment of Rebecca. He slapped her when her laugh irritated him. He ate at the head of the table. He belched loudly and used his sleeve instead of the napkin by his plate. He drank tequila from the bottle and smoked cigars. Ramos taught Luis about tobaccos and furnished him with the finest Havanas.

Luis learned all the parts of Ramos's business. Ramos started him in the fields. He spent the first year working in hard labor and in the office.

Luis worked side-by-side with men who hated him. They perceived Luis as Ramos, Jr. and called him "menor." (junior)

Luis retreated into his own space. He read and wrote letters, letters to Father Ibarra requesting books, to Mamacita asking of his son. He pleaded with Mamacita to tell him he could return home and to the coffee plantation. The bananas and sugar cane held no interest for him.

He hated the animosity of the Indian laborers and finally moved out of Ramos's house and into a small shack. Ramos viewed the move skeptically, stating, "Your judgment is lousy. Don't live close to those you own." Splitting a jug of tequila, the two had argued vociferously about the idea of slavery and ownership. Luis's move improved the lot of the workers. He coerced Ramos into remodeling the homes and installing electric pumps. Ramos submitted to some of these manipulations. And Ramos taught his nephew the business of running the farm; he introduced him to the local politicians, the local police and the art of making connections.

Luis's second year brought the end of any pleasantness between himself and his uncle. Maria's first derisive comments were nothing compared to the cruel actions of Ramos. Their relationship was raw and hateful, but Ramos wanted Luis to run the hacienda and run it as he did. He told Luis he would leave it all to him, and Luis must be ready to ride the bull or stab the bull as necessary.

Ramos came to Luis's shack late one night and rousted him from his sleep. Luis at first assumed Ramos wanted him to drink tequila with him, but he said, "Luis, now it is time for you to see how the bull is stabbed. We are going to the control center."

Luis's co-workers had spoken in whispers of the "cacique's casa." Luis knew it was another evil part of the devil's lair. He avoided the talk and Ramos's intimations. He heard of it as Ramos spoke in euphemisms, stating, "Ah Luis, I'm a busy man. They need me at the control center." And Ramos would leave the hacienda for an hour, then return ready to smoke and drink with Luis. Luis had recognized early not to ask Ramos questions about his comings and goings.

Ramos drove his jeep to a remote corner of the plantation, passing through all of what Luis had known as Ramos's property, then down a narrow road hidden in a thick unharvested banana grove. Luis had the eerie feeling that he was being watched as the jeep slowly eased through the verdant growth. In total darkness they reached a small clearing.

A clapboard building was squeezed between the tall fronds. The yellow light from inside illuminated the dark jungle walls. Two armed guards dressed in military fatigues stood by the front door. Luis sat silently. His uncle pulled up to the house. Ramos jumped out of the jeep and signaled Luis to follow him. They walked into the dimly lit interior. A generator echoed loudly against the wall of banana stalks. The building had two rooms. They entered a front room through an open doorway. Another military guard stood inside by a laborer Luis recognized as Jesus, who had worked the eastern plot. Ramos had identified it as section #2 in his books.

The man's shirt was stained with blood that dripped from his mouth and down to his chin. It had dried on his neck, one eye was swollen shut. Luis's stomach turned over. He wanted to run, to grab Ramos and say, "What the hell is this?" but he obediently followed Ramos into the interior room.

The second room contained only a desk and chair. A light bulb hung from a cord wrapped around a nail in the ceiling beam. It dimmed and brightened with the uneven motor of the generator. Millers and mosquitoes flew in the unscreened windows. Under the light, round shelled June bugs landed heavily on their backs. Their tiny legs twisted as their wings opened in a reverse push-up, struggling in a futile attempt to rise.

Ramos yelled for the laborer to be brought to him. Fear exuded from every part of the man's body. His open eye pleaded with Luis. Luis stood questioning in his head the purpose for this laborer's beating. The heavy handed smacking of the cacique did not compare to the Indian's condition. Luis kept swallowing and wiping the sweat from his face. The heavy drops rolled down his forehead onto his cheeks. The small room pushed in on his chest. His own eye hurt where the laborer's was torn and puffed. Luis glanced at Ramos. Ramos winked at Luis. Luis quickly turned from Ramos to the beaten man, who stared at him.

Luis twisted from one man's face to the other. Ramos shook his head, and then reached into the desk drawer. He withdrew a .44 caliber handgun. In a calm voice Ramos asked the laborer why he didn't want to work his job like he was told by his boss? The man pleaded, saying his wife had been very sick, trying to have a baby; he had stayed to take care of her. Ramos scoffed at the explanation, "You know I have no patience for lazy Indios. Ramos Ochoa is a busy man!" With the phrase, he shot the man three times. Bang! Bang! Bang! The sound rang in Luis's ears, he no longer heard the generator's churning, only the Bang! Bang! Bang! Again and again. Ramos casually placed the firearm back in the drawer. The man fell, twitching as his physical body adjusted to death, his one eye still staring at Luis.

Ramos walked from behind the desk. He stepped over the dead man's legs and spit on him. He looked at Luis with chilling dispassion, "Luis, I have no time for this trash. I'm a busy man. Comprende mi hijo?"

Luis rushed outside past the guards and vomited over and over. The black night smothered his spirit. His stomach cramped from the retching. He felt the furnace inside him, burning his skin; his clothes soaked with perspiration. He silently repeated his confessional prayer, Padre, Padre, perdóname porque he pecado…

His personal hell was disturbed by Ramos's commanding voice, "Come mi hijo, let's get the fuck out of here! I'm a busy man. This jeep is the only way out of here. I'm leaving! Get in or walk!" He laughed heartedly as he started the engine. Luis slipped into the seat next to him wiping the vomit on his sleeve. Luis rode vowing one day to avenge this death.

Ramos reached behind the seat and pulled out a big bottle of tequila. He took a gross gulp, then belched and handed the bottle to Luis, "It'll settle your stomach!"

Luis drank deeply, hoping the burning clear liquid would erase all that he had seen, would take him away from Ramos and Veracruz. Bang! Bang! Bang! He closed his eyes and promised himself that he must go to Mamacita's soon.

Jill now sat quietly, trying to anticipate his next move. Slowly he heaved an expansive sigh as if shaking some invisible weight from his shoulders. He looked up at her, meeting her eyes, then spoke, "Fear and innocence, Gringa, all over your face. I am okay, sometimes…the shadow of death…" He held out his hand.

She rose from sitting on the bed and bent down in front of his knees. She took both of his hands in hers, "Are you all right?"

"Si. I can't explain, you can't…" his voice was unusually soft.

"Please talk to me, ah-stay kay mar-tee nos say-paree. Si? I'll be here."

A limp smile curled one corner of his mouth, "You chop up the Spanish with a Puerto Rican accent. You're right, Gringa, but another time, another place." He reached and cupped his hand around the back of her neck, pulling her forehead to his mouth; he kissed it and then the tip of her nose. "It's a long story, Gringa."

"Last night you asked me to marry you. I did not get to say, 'yes.' But we must make time for these stories."

"Si. We will."

"Please hold me, feel first..." she said.

He squeezed her so tightly she heard his heart beating. Releasing her, he said that he must call for the driver.

"Luis, can I stay here in this room for a couple of days? I really want to see Washington, the tourist things."

"I will let the front desk know."

"Could you spray your cologne on the pillow and I will pretend I am sleeping with you."

He shook his head and laughed slightly. "Soon, my gringa, we will sleep together again."

ᘰξᘰ

She stayed her three days, visiting the Pentagon, but not knowing who to ask about her Air Force Colonel. They all wore dress uniforms. She was not sure how they knew how to get from one office to another, a confusing place, but she did have lunch in the basement's shopping area. She visited The Smithsonian with the Hope diamond and the American History museum, and walked around the tidal basin. She returned to her room exhausted and decided she must bring Luisa the next time. Amazing sights and feelings of power in the capital of the free world, home to the greatest democracy, she thought.

She now sat in a cab on her way to the airport stopping by Arlington Cemetery first. The torn plastic seat was so different than how she had come to the hotel. She kept the hotel key for a souvenir, her first time sleeping next to Luis all night. Asleep and relaxed it had been like sleeping with a bear. He took over the bed and subconsciously squeezed her tightly, then released her, turning over with his back to her. He did not cuddle or spoon. He slept and he hugged. And she wanted to do it again. She had said yes to marrying him, but what did that mean?

They drove along the Potomac heading for Arlington Cemetery. She had promised to say goodbye. Could she ever say goodbye? If she touched the white stone, traced his name, maybe. Oh, maybe not, maybe just drive to the airport. Luis left a message at the front desk apologizing for his abrupt departure. Luis. What would be the point Sadie, in going to this cemetery? To talk to a dead Hector, his lifeless face, buried with all the other war dead.

As the cab stopped in the unloading zone, she shook her head, is this a mistake? The driver turned to her, "Are you sure you want me to wait?"

"Yes, please, I won't be too long." She did not know how long it would take. Luis had given her plenty of money to pay for a cab, souvenirs, meals and museum fees.

The green cemetery seemed to stretch for miles, up hillsides dotted with trees to a large mansion. The symmetrical rows spread out geometrically no matter which way she looked it was a line of white head stones, names, dates, service, a cross or Star of David at the top. Posted signs asked visitors to respect the place with quiet as commercial airplanes roared over head. Passengers stepped from school buses and tour buses holding cameras, snapping pictures. Students waited impatiently for their teachers and tour guides to count them.

She walked slowly to the information center. The line stretched in front of her as tour groups of thirty or more stood in front of her. Her plan was to walk quickly to the chapel, to pray and then to talk with Hector in his resting place. The closer to the entrance the further she felt from the peace she wanted. Filled with tourists, chaos surrounded her, not solemnity. She shook her head realizing she had not come to his resting place. Hector. Was she ready to pray with him? He considered Luis swine. And now she was here because of Luis. Hector judged him without knowing him. I am not sure I know him either, but he is not swine.

Jill waited to get the information booklet behind tour groups, one behind the other. She turned away from the line. Yes, it was a mistake, time to leave and fly back to Indiana.

A young couple rushed past her. He was dressed in a military uniform, a pressed Army green uniform and looked eighteen, scrubbed, cropped hair, freckles on his nose; his girlfriend or maybe bride held tightly onto her soldier. Her sundress was as neat as his uniform – blue and white flowers, so different from the young people they had seen in Georgetown. Her strawberry blonde ponytail bounced as they ran.

The young man took pictures of his girlfriend with the Potomac River in the background, then she took one of him. He came up to Jill and asked if she would mind taking a picture of both of them. He gave Jill a brief lesson on how to use the one button instamatic.

33

Jill told them to stand close together and face the sun. They looked like two scared children, then she said, "Do you know what it means if you kiss a soldier at Arlington Cemetery?"

The young man said, "No." The girl shook her head.

"Well, kiss each other while I take your picture, and then I'll tell you." They kissed as dutiful soldiers, then walked back to Jill. She handed them the camera.

"Thank you, ma'am," the young boy spoke sheepishly, "Okay, what does it mean?"

"If you kiss a soldier at Arlington Cemetery, he'll never be killed in battle." Jill turned quickly and looked for her cab. Hector, I can't, not today. Using the back of her hand, she wiped her eyes.

ɤξɤ

"Henry, Jack called this morning," Lillian spoke as Henry and Luisa sat around the kitchen table. "He said he called the farmhouse, but no one answered. He wondered if we had talked to Jill. He said he called Sadie and she told him Jill went to the lake with Angie and her kids. Why didn't she tell us?"

Henry ate his pot roast and mashed potatoes. Luisa picked at her wilted lettuce salad. She had eaten the bacon bits, but left the limp leaves in the curdled vinegar dressing. Lillian had tried to get her to eat, but Luisa explained it felt funny on her tongue. Henry loved the salad and volunteered to eat Luisa's and his.

"Mom went to the lake with Angie?" she asked sadly.

"No, Honey, I don't think so. Henry when you finish eating would you mind driving out to the farm just to make sure everything is okay?" Henry looked at Lillian, then reached and grabbed Luisa's salad plate, putting it on top of his empty one. He took a bite winking at his granddaughter. Luisa took her index fingers and rubbed one across the other, indicating he had pulled one of Lillian's 'bad-table-manners' rules. "Henry, have you heard what I said?"

"Sure, Lil. Pass me the gravy. Please." He winked again at Luisa.

"Here Grandpa." Luisa picked up the gravy bowl in front of her grandmother's place, then handed it to Henry. He dipped a scoop of the thick brown, onion filled liquid onto his potatoes. Luisa continued, "Grandma, may I go to Mason's to play?"

34

"After you finish your dinner. You're just like your mother, eat like a bird and want to jump up and play, you don't give that food time to settle." Luisa looked at her grandma, then to her grandpa.

"Sure," Henry answered, shooing her from the table.

As Luisa stood, placing her crumpled napkin by her fork, Lillian spoke, "Yes, Luisa, but you play outside, so you can hear Grandpa when he whistles."

Henry finished his meal as Luisa scooted out the front door, the screen door slamming behind her. Lillian started clearing the plates from the table. He grabbed the meat platter and basket of uneaten biscuits, "Lillian save these, I'll eat them for breakfast. Put some strawberries on them, m-m, m-m, m-m."

"Henry, where is Jill?" Lillian demanded. Henry passed her coming and going, carrying silverware, plates, glasses, coffee cups, the food dishes from the table to the sink. Lillian searched her cabinet for empty jars, matching sizes to left-over food. She lined them up on the counter; the ingredients would make her Saturday night special – vegetable soup.

"At Angie's cottage you said," Henry answered, setting the large chuck bone into a plastic container that Lillian indicated.

"No," Lillian said, snapping the lid on the meat scraps.

"She's in Washington, D.C.," Henry stated matter-of-factly. He leaned against the counter crossing his arms. Lillian turned from the refrigerator where she rearranged other left-over's to make the latest additions fit.

She wrung her hands on the bottom of her apron, then stared at Henry, "You are kidding? No, you are not kidding."

"Lillian, you wash the dishes. I'll dry and we'll talk."

"This is not good is it?" The breeze blew in through the kitchen windows. The lace curtains rose gently from the windows.

"Jill is seeing Luisa's father," Henry rinsed the dishes with the hot water sprayer.

"What?! Oh, my, and you said it so calmly, and what? What are you talking about?"

"She's spending a few days with him."

"Why?" Lillian used the metal scrapper on the bottom of the big aluminum Dutch oven. "Henry, what are you saying?" Scrubbing the big pot was making her sweat. She wiped her forehead with her apron.

"As I understand it, the migrant man, Luis, got in touch with her last fall...at the beginning of the school year." He continued to explain the history of the relationship. "And now she is with him for a few days..."

"Jill's having an affair with Luisa's father?"

Henry nodded, then put the dried glasses on the cupboard shelf.

"And you don't care? She's committing sin and you...Oh Henry!" She rinsed the pan, then placed it in the drainer.

"What sin, Lil?" Henry said, drying the last pan.

"You know what sin, adultery!"

"Lillian, what *is* adultery?"

"Adultery is, well, when you have, you know a relationship with someone who is not your spouse, who is someone else's...oh my, my daughter is an adulteress."

"Is she?"

"Henry, how can you be so calm about this?"

"No, Lillian why are you so upset? These kinds of life hurdles are right up your alley. You and those Bridge ladies sit around and solve everyone's adultery problems."

"I'm in shock. My son-in-law, my granddaughter, what will happen to them? What am I going to say?"

"Nothing. You will say nothing. Your daughter is an adult, and she probably has no idea what she is doing, but when has she ever known?"

"I thought marrying Jack, she, he was older, but...why Henry, why an affair? I love Jack. He's been so good to Luisa."

Henry poured himself a large glass of iced tea, "She acted with heart Lillian. She always had a thing for that man. Luisa is *his* daughter, so when Luis contacted her she wanted to meet him and introduce him to Luisa, the best way she knew how. Luis had insisted then, on paying for his daughter, but Jill could not justify the money. I helped her do that."

"You're conspiring in adultery? How could you? What will God think of that?"

"God? Good god, Lillian. He gave us love and hormones, what a chemical mix, then He gave us choice. Jill makes choices that she lives with. I've made choices I live with. I married a woman who married me on the rebound. I live with that." He winked.

"How can I live with this?"

"Like you live with everything else, by saying things are 'just fine.'"

"My daughter is an adulteress," her voice softened. Responding irrationally to emotions was not the Lillian he knew.

"No, Lil, your daughter is *just fine*, I know you think she is all me, but she is strong and that's Kohlhass, you."

"No, Henry, your daughter is just like you. I'm going to call Luisa. When will Jack be back? I love Jack; he is such a good son-in-law." Lillian hung the wet wash rag on the faucet. She watered her African violets, then untied her apron, hanging it on the utility closet hook. She poured herself iced tea. The sticky June evening dictated some porch-swing time. Henry grabbed the Caylor paper and his glass of tea. They walked to the front porch.

"Did I," Lillian said, "do something wrong with Jill?"

"You mean did we have sex at the wrong time?"

"Henry hush! Luisa might hear you."

"Luisa is a block away. And no, you did nothing wrong. Jill rejects reason in matters of the heart and never plans on the consequences. Now granted, I, we have tried to give her direction, but she is headstrong and I guess we have Pop Havlicek to thank for that."

"Pop Havlicek? How about Henry Havlicek?"

Henry smiled, patting her knee.

Chapter 2

The July night air stood still. Jill sat in her screened porch imagining the tiny insects creating racket, in their bug symphony orchestra. They played a score of their own creation, legs rubbing against green scaly wings, tuning their tails, whistling, humming. Figaro in cricketese? She listened, protected from their physical bodies, but an audience for their music.

Her light gown did not feel thin enough in the heat. Last month in Washington, she slept naked next to Luis, but at home? She had to wear something. Jack insisted. What did Jack know about sleeping with a woman? After five years of marriage, Jack did not know her as Luis did. Sex had become like his lists, first, then second...third had possibilities, but no spontaneity. They had experimented some in their first year of marriage. Lying next to Jack, listening to him snore grated against her. What happened to the days of enjoying listening to William or Hector? She'd only spent one night with Luis in Washington, D.C. She'd said "yes" to his marriage proposal, every night sleeping next to him? Oh that was fantasy. *Her husband* snored upstairs.

She stared at the moon moving slowly across the starry night. The midnight scene reminded her of Sunday School felt bulletin boards. A piece of felt in a tree shape was stuck on a dark background, then two sheep and their shepherd. They could move the pieces wherever they wanted and they stuck as the teacher told the story. Put a piece on the material without glue and it stayed; to her child eyes she saw a miracle. She now looked at the white moon pressed on the black background. Could she take Luis like a felt shepherd and press him against the moon, then herself next to Luis? The moon would be above them, lighting their faces, the two of them alone, a miracle.

The humidity moistened her skin, a thin layer of dampness and sweat. She sipped ice water, then took an ice cube and rubbed it on her arms and face. She closed her eyes. Who was Luis sleeping with this night? Where was Luis sleeping? "Your Gringa sisters smell money like bloodhounds." My gringa sisters…obviously he's had some experience to make such a statement. Was he in his bed? In Cartagena? The mountains? A large, heavy wood bed with off-white sheets? She could curl up next to him, touching him as he slept, gently pushing the hair from his temples, relaxing his face.

After their short trip to Washington, D.C., no call, no letter from Bogotá, nothing. What was the crisis? Did he take care of it? When she was not forced to make choices, having the affair with Luis was easy. But August was three weeks away. Would he call or would he even keep his promise, or was it a threat? In the darkness she smiled. Hurry up August, time to see the Latin.

She thought of Madame Bovary, Hester Prynne, Anna Karenina, women who had had affairs. The affairs ended in disasters, children, angry divorces, wives devastated by their husband's philandering. Luis didn't qualify as a husband although, he considered himself married to her with his vow in the shed ten years ago.

He was back in her life, here to stay, allowing no means of escape from his demands. Oh, she did not even want to escape from him. He had asked her to marry him, but what exactly was that all about? A proposal in the middle of the street. I said, "Yes." Maybe I should have said, "Si." No, he said, "married to Jack," is a good thing, then why did he ask me? Jack, my choice to make my life stable, routine, normal, just like Henry and Lillian. Was it like taking out an insurance policy, if anything happens to Jack I have a second husband? Too morbid, too long.

Luis said I would not like his country, at least parts of it, the parts where he had to spend his time. Where would I live? Maybe I am living exactly where he wants me to live, but married to him and Jack? Is this his plan? A plan like Mrs. Ruberight said in Elliston, telling me I must have a plan. Oh yeah, my plans were always SNAFU's.(situation normal all fucked up)

Normal farm life had become…How did he find me? What birthday will I be able to ask that question? Oh, if I had only known he would find me and want me to be his wife, but Henry always says, "If we could predict the future, we'd all be millionaires."

Right now she wanted to go into the kitchen and call him, just to hear his voice, the way he said, "Gringa." It was 3A.M. in Cartagena. Only two hours of time zones separating them, but thousands of miles away. She could call and remind him that she had said, "Yes" to his proposal. She wanted to feel him, as he said, "feel first." Yes, close my eyes and feel him.

The window fans whirred in the background. On the porch the thick air smelled of newly mowed grass, Jack's evening work, and the manure from the Scott's hog farm down the road. Tonight the odor was tolerable. At these moments, Indiana was seductive like so many summer nights in her high school days. The night's forbidden wee hours would lure her to inch down her parents' creaky steps, gingerly open the screen door beneath their window and escape to freedom.

She, Sadie, Jim, and Michael would walk to the golf course and makeout on a blanket. Once they were soaked by the automatic sprinklers, and rolled around in the wet grass laughing. Henry had caught her creeping in the back door, but she had fumbled an excuse about getting a drink of ice water. Henry was groggy and told her to get some sleep.

Another late night date, the renegade friends drove to an abandoned stone quarry near Logansport. They sneaked underneath a fence, crawled on gravel and through bushes surrounding the water-filled pit. In the moonless night they stripped naked and slipped into the cold water, so deep they could only hang onto each other. A chorus of frogs and crickets provided a soundtrack. The teens laughed and splashed, a joy to skinny-dip in the forbidden lake, treading water looking at the stars, the four of them alone. She now chuckled at their lack of fear. Could she do it again? No, too old to crawl on gravel.

"Okay, Sadie," she said aloud. If Sadie said, "Let's go," she would. Dishonesty? It felt good and they did it. Maybe she could manage to be "married" to two men. I'll write my own book, Hester Prynne, only the moon will know.

"Honey, are you okay?" Jack tousled her hair.

"Sure, it's so goddamned hot, I wanted to get some ice water, then the porch, the moon, the crickets, lightening bugs, it was all too tempting."

He sat next to her, "Honey, your garden looks great this year."

"Thank you. I started a few days late, but the vegetables don't seem to have noticed." Jack was bearable; she could do this. She took Henry's advice – the best defense is a good offense. "Jack, the heat does something to me…"

"Besides cussing?"

She used her finger to slide down his tummy, stopping at the waistband of his pajamas. He pulled her onto his lap. One, two, three.

ﯦﯦﯦ

The early morning sun filtered through the lace curtains. Jill awoke to the scent of fresh coffee. She loved her bedroom. Grandma K.'s first quilt lay at the foot of the white iron bed. The pastel patches were stitched in a large double wedding ring design. She asked Lillian for it when Grandma Kohlhass died and the cousins divided up the heirlooms. She knew she would inherit other German mementoes when Lillian died, but not for a long time. She might be living in Colombia with no need for heirlooms.

The window fan sat on the large sill. The air smelled fresh coming through the fan. Maybe she would follow Jack's advice and take Luisa to Beau's cottage this week. A cool lake with Mary Ann? She shrugged, maybe not. The coffee smell and summer morning filled her bedroom.

Her favorite reading spot by the sunny window was an overstuffed chair covered with a flower print slipcover in the same colors as the quilt. Last night she left her book on the seat when she'd gone to bed. The book now rested on the small table next to the chair. Jack. Everything in its place. The glass of water she'd brought with her from the screened porch was no longer on the cleared nightstand. Jack. She and Jack had matching closets on both sides of the bedroom door. His doors were closed; hers open. Her clothes were smashed together on different size hangers, some for skirts others for blouses. Jack's neatly hung in some order only he understood.

She sat on the edge of the bed and slipped into her terry scuffs. She walked to the bathroom and smiled at her disheveled curls and slightly tanned face. As she brushed her teeth, she heard the phone ring. The clock on the shelf indicated 6:45. Luis knew 7A.M. Jack was still in the kitchen. During the summer she lay in the bed until almost time for him to leave. Their morning conversations were kept to a minimum, although he would call at 11A.M to find out if she had plans for the day. The schedule. When would he learn she did not do his lists? They had been married five years and he was still trying.

"Honey," Jack said, "Sadie is on the phone. She said not to be shocked about the early hour. I suppose she has made plans for your day. I'm leaving now, but will call at…"

"11A.M." they said it together.

Jack laughed. "Okay, Mrs. Jones, you have me figured out."

He did not see her roll her eyes.

Down the stairs and hallway through the kitchen door, to the phone; perhaps a letter from the Coffee Federation had arrived with her August travel plans. She poured a cup of coffee then picked up the receiver.

"You set your alarm wrong, Mrs. Fredericks?"

"Very funny, Señora Ochoa," Sadie said.

"Don't start so early Siddhartha. You see I'm awake at this time of day, but you are out of your element."

"I just decided that I want to go see my father."

"You woke up and said, 'Oh, this is a good day to see Mr. Stephanopoulos?' I don't think so. We do crazy things, but we have some reason…some something…"

"Michael said, 'It's time.' We have this conversation about once a year, usually around the holidays or Father's Day, should I or shouldn't I and I always get cold feet. You know all the reasons…"

Jill knew all the reasons; Sadie was right about that. She and her father spent years separated from each other. He had sent the perfunctory cards and money on all the right occasions, but Sadie's mother prevented the two of them from having a father-daughter relationship. Sadie decided when she grew up to re-introduce herself, but she married, had a baby, then another baby and another one. Sadie's mom jealously kept Sadie from knowing her father, ranting, "No 'count, no good." Sadie didn't really know because Emma Sue refused to allow

42

Sadie to write much more than a thank you note to her father. Sadie never saw pictures of her father, but Jill and Sadie assumed she had his coloring because her mother was translucent pale and had light eyes.

"I did that long lost father bullshit," Jill said, "with Jack and Hawk. You know it was awful. Plus your father had enough sense to get out while the gettin' was good. Henry tells you all the time how bright your father was to leave while he could and why hadn't he thought of that."

"I can see I have to remind Henry again that if intelligence and leaving are in fact corollaries, there must not be any Einsteins in his family tree."

"Dad is going to get you for that." Jill laughed.

"Really Jill, I am serious. *And* they are having an antique sale and street fair in Auburn. I just thought we could go wander for a week. Michael wants to go stay with his parents at the lake *and* take all the kids. Come on. We can do this. We haven't had a break like this for awhile, just the two of us."

"Once again with that infamous Siddhartha certainty, you are proposing to take me from the safety and security of this quaint little farm."

"Does that mean yes? Where is Luisa? I know she'd rather stay at Henry and Lillian's than on the farm. They have neighbors."

"Let me call Mom and see who is doing what with whom. Does Mr. Stephanopoulos have any idea what is about to happen to him?"

"Sort of."

"Explain."

"Remember, I wrote GM and they said he worked at a plant in Dearborn? Well, I wrote to the address they gave me. And this morning he called. Just like that. I snapped my fingers if you didn't hear. Our conversation, strange, strained kind of. We didn't get a rhythm, and kept interrupting each other. He asked if I could come to where he is because he hates Caylor. So I said a *friend* and I could drive up. He said, 'Great' and bring pictures of *his* grandchildren. There, we're invited."

"I'll call Mom and see. She hates it when I act wild with you. But Jack slept with the *perfect* wife so that should do him for a week."

"You didn't? I must know everything. Hurry and get your stuff organized. No comparison to the Colombian connection?"

"Hush. Different continents, Northern, Southern. Cold and hot, yeah, that's it, cold *and* hot."

They laughed as they hung up.

Indiana as part of the Northwest Territories was sold and settled. The Ordinance of 1785 specified the surveyed land be divided into counties each with thirty-six townships and in township number sixteen - a schoolhouse. These square redbrick buildings were abandoned as schools merged. On antique hunts Sadie insisted on searching all abandoned "number 16's" or farm sheds, looking for a treasure. She wanted only to find any piece or part of their original use.

They now drove off the main road. "I think we can climb through that fence over there and walk across the field to the school."

"Sadie, there are cows in that field."

"Cows are not going to bother us. Come on, Miss McDonald, don't pretend you don't live on a farm." Sadie led the way through the fence.

"Check out the no trespassing sign."

"Oh, Jill, we have ignored those signs for a long time. Forgive us our trespasses as we forgive those who trespass against us."

"Shameless in quoting the Bible. My shoes are covered in dirt and cow shit." Jill pulled up one foot and showed her. Sadie walked ahead, reaching the old school house with its broken door. She pushed her way in.

"Come on, another number 16!"

Jill always expected her to fall through the old wood floors, but she never did. Occasionally, Sadie would ask permission from the closest farm house. These out of the way impromptu calls produced the best "finds" – fire stoker, individual chalk boards, a paddle, a German grammar book printed in 1892.

They walked back to the car as one cow turned and let out a perfunctory moo.

"One old ruler and lots of cow shit. I swear Sadie, what I do for this friendship."

"What *you* do? I was ready to drive you to Benton Harbor in my drunken state, risk my great driving record, and then I woke-up with a crook in my neck for my generosity."

"You should have kept driving. I could have followed Luis and found out where he really went."

"He seems to have done quite well without you."

"Oh, Sadie, all these cornfields and tomato fields, has anything changed in ten years when we drove down these roads that night?"

"Uh-um, yes. I have a dusty ruler and three children." Sadie picked up the ruler and pointed it at Jill who shook her head.

When it came time to find antiques, Sadie knew no strangers. She talked to country folks whose property they walked through to get to an old barn or abandoned house. Jill watched and played the role of spoiler because Sadie did not know when she wore out her welcome. They picked through old family albums always looking for "Gramp Fredericks' people" and baseball cards for Mike's collection.

Sadie's Mercedes trunk and back seat were full. Indiana's little towns proved a treasure trove for antiques.

"If you don't stop Mrs. Fredericks, I will no longer have a place to sit. There is no space left in this car, a spinning wheel? Are you going to teach Claudine to make wool? I just don't get this obsession with dust and rust."

"It goes with the house. I have a place in mind on the second floor."

"You should've been a museum curator, look at this," Jill reached over the back seat, and plucked a half-painted kitchen utensil from the pile.

"Perfect on the kitchen wall…"

"No, there is some neurosis going on here, a Freudian reckoning with your past? You want to go back to your past and start again."

They had just crossed the Indiana-Michigan border heading for Coldwater, Michigan where Sadie had said the *best* antique shop was located. They were getting closer to Coldwater and much closer to Detroit and Sadie's rendezvous.

"No," Sadie turned to Jill and pushed the radio selection buttons, stabbing them as if to make her point, "that's not it. I just like the way these old things are put together, you know made to last forever. Those folks never heard of planned obsolescence." Sadie picked up the roadmap and handed it to Jill, a signal that Jill needed to figure out the next closest place to eat.

"It sounds like a topic your father might like to hear your views on. Cars and Detroit are the epitome of three year self-destruction."

"Don't bring it up unless we have to," Sadie said. She'd planned to arrive in Detroit in the evening and have lunch the following day with Mr. Stephanopoulos. The actual drive time from Caylor to

Detroit took five hours, but they had taken almost a week, staying in Angola at the Potawatomi Inn and leaving each day to explore some new area for old things. Sadie decided to take those five hours to drive back to Caylor, not to the Motor City.

Sadie called her father from the Inn. They arranged to meet over dinner instead of lunch. He said it would give them more time to drink and catch up. After hanging up, Jill warned Sadie again of the dangers of drinking at family reunions. Jill refused to referee a repeat performance like the one in Hawk's trailer. Sadie assured her it would be nothing like Florida.

Mr. Stephanopoulos had picked a sportsman's bar and restaurant close to Tiger Stadium. "It'll be easy to find, the atmosphere is casual and I know the owner. I'll introduce you to my buddies."

ꙦξꙦ

Sadie had been primping and pacing for two hours.

"Ah, the beautiful, thin rich bitch," Jill now said, looking up from the desk of their hotel room. Sadie stuck out her tongue, walking into the bathroom, closing the door behind her. When Sadie returned, Jill stopped teasing her, and assured her she looked like the perfect long lost daughter.

"Oh, god, Jill, part of me wants him to like me; part of me thinks who cares? I just want him to know that I know Emma Sue is neurotic and I can understand why he left us." She hesitated, "Well, I don't know why he left me, but I guess Emma Sue was too much."

"Possum Holler? Sadie, no one can take that for very long; we hid in your room for hours when we knew she was down in the kitchen. I mean a fur steering-wheel cover and all those weird little animal creatures hanging from her rearview mirror. She drove a Ford and worked for General Motors. Emma Sue, Sadie. It had everything to do with her and nothing to do with you. You're a little weird, but totally lovable."

Jill leaned back in the chair and stopped writing a postcard, a picture of the Lever Brothers Office in Hammond, Indiana printed in the '40's. Her friend Marcia Webster insisted Jill send her postcards from any road trips. She gave Jill a big hug if one were an antique card.

Sadie walked out of the bathroom, then surveyed herself in the full-length mirror. She wore a basic black sundress, mini-length. Sadie was dark from the sun. Her long legs looked even longer in the dress and black patent leather sandals. She tried on a red, black and white belt, then a gold one made of chains linked to faux coins that jangled as she arranged them across her stomach. Her hair was cut blunt at chin level. Now with eyeliner and mascara, "...Egyptian, Sadie, you look like Cleopatra."

"No, no, I want to be his daughter."

"Egypt is just across the Mediterranean from Greece; their ancestors were neighbors..."

She applied a brownish red lipstick, then smiled at her reflection, "Okay, Jill which belt?"

"Gold coins, he'll know right away how much you love money..."

Sadie undid the coin belt and put on the webbed conservative one, "There, now it'll take him longer to find out."

"Sadie, I don't think you ought to blame him for not being a part of your life. Remember, you were young when he left. I can't believe I'm agonizing all over again about lost parents."

Jill looked out the hotel window. The Detroit River was gray in the early evening hour. And on the far shore, Canada. She had not been to Canada, but they'd run out of week. Their schedule was to have dinner and drive back to Caylor. The sunset cast large rectangular shadows on the water. Detroit in a high rise hotel. Looking at the river and the commuters crossing in and out of Canada belied the idea of Detroit as the location for a terrible riot only three years earlier.

Canada was the "true north," Cynthia often argued at their inter-racial meetings, the only north where black people could escape to avoid persecution. It looked like Detroit, buildings, cars, streets. Detroit welcomed everyone now with a sign proclaiming the number of vehicles made thus far in 1970. They called themselves the Motor City, but at the moment it felt like the heart of Florida. Not another Hawk, she prayed to herself.

Sadie walked to where Jill stood at the large picture window, then hugged her and started crying, "I couldn't do this without you. You have always been my family, Jill. You have a secure family; it made you strong...."

"I'm feeling weak thinking of that crazy Hawk. We know nothing of your father. Let's make a decision now that if either one of us says, 'It's time to go,' we leave, no questions asked, okay?"

Sadie nodded.

"Wipe your eyes," Jill continued, "before your mascara makes you look like Rocky Raccoon. Let's go. We'll have a good time, and if we don't, we can cry all the way home."

ϒξϒ

The neighborhood was seedy, boarded up windows, broken glass stacked against empty businesses. How far away had the riot been? The racial tension was high in large cities, the newspapers called it the burning of America. But the five hour drive from Caylor to Detroit seemed like crossing a bridge from one era to another.

The bar was easy to find. Neon beer signs illuminated the small windows facing the street. Deep booths lined the walls and wood tables and chairs filled the long room. A restaurant length bar extended from one end to the other with TV's at both corners playing the Tigers baseball game. Dusty with smoke and filled with raucous men, a back room with a pool table was the liveliest area of the place.

When they walked past the barstools, the male patrons turned from their seats to look. Sadie, Jill thought, whenever, wherever, *they* stared. Almost immediately a man with dark curly hair receding at the temples walked up to them. He was a couple of inches taller than Sadie. From father to daughter, Jill played a matching game, the large dark eyes that twinkled when they saw each other, the narrow frame with long arms that ended in those square fingers that Sadie lamented as decidedly mannish. His thicker hands were covered with hair, and he wore a diamond pinkie. His mouth, his smile with the straight white teeth, the toasty brown complexion all were Sadie's. Mr. Stephanopoulos looked a lot like Sadie's son. Would he notice when he saw the pictures? Well the African ancestors did travel from their continent to the Greek Islands; it was a tradition to blend Greeks and Africans. The curly hair and olive skin of those north of the African continent had been pointed out in her sociology classes. Sadie did not have Steph's curls. The sleeves of his white shirt were rolled up, his pants were navy blue. Father and daughter hugged.

"Steph," Mr. Stephanopoulos said, reaching around Sadie's shoulder and shaking Jill's hand.

"Oh, Dad, this is my *friend*, Jill Jones."

They talked of their trip, finding the restaurant, and Detroit. He ordered them the specialty, pasta with white sauce, garlic bread, Caesars salad. He talked with a slight accent maybe from New York or maybe just Detroit. Soon other customers came to meet "Steph's daughter."

As the evening progressed, Jill regretted that such a kind friendly man had been denied her best friend. Sadie clung to him like creeping ivy wrapped around a chimney. The three talked effortlessly. Steph was amiable, bright and had a sense of humor like Henry's, teasing Sadie almost immediately about making a good catch with her husband. She and Sadie also teased each other from the moment they had walked into the place. Jill had said, "We've been a few places and met a few men, but this is our first Detroit 'shopping' trip. If the prices are good, we'll be back."

Sadie told her father to ignore Jill and that slight of Detroit and implication of shopping for more than antiques was out of line. Everyone laughed as the friends teased each other. Steph talked of his adopted home town, Detroit, his blue collar background, and then his promotion to management. Sadie laid her family pictures out on the table, telling a story with each one.

Steph asked about her wedding. She explained the rush to Las Vegas, then the surprise announcement to the senior Mrs. Fredericks who then retreated to her corner of what Sadie labeled their boxing ring. The two women had over the years made their peace even though the elder one occasionally cast a decidedly down-her-nose glance at Sadie. Jill watched as the father and daughter built their bridges; and waited for Hawk's fireworks, but Mr. Stephanopoulos was jovial and seemingly well-liked by everyone who came to their table to meet them. He also had pictures to show Sadie of her half-brother and half-sister. Sadie slightly resembled the brother; "Ari" who was twenty, eight years younger.

"The Workers of America," Jill labeled the men who appeared in beer commercials - fans at baseball and football games with rounded stomachs covered in pastel golf shirts, Tiger and Lion patches emblazoned on windbreakers. She defended her Chicago Bears against a barrage of boos. There was Gus with a fuzzy moustache and tattoos on his forearms; Jimbo, who was about 5'4" and called "Shorty Jimbo." He bought several beers for the men who beat him at pool.

Jill soaked up the lore and war stories of these men who escaped home from the mean streets of Detroit to the pleasure of each other's company. The men drank beer with peppermint schnapps chasers. The place exuded labor and unions, they talked of cars, the car companies, the president, the war, their drafted sons. Steph protected his guests from the leering beer drinkers. He explained for all interested parties, "This is my long lost daughter, see I told you road hogs I had one, and her best friend and they are both *married*. You can look, buy them a beer or two, but no touching!"

"Steph, you didn't mention the police protection," a middle-aged man spoke, seating himself next to Jill. He appeared to be forty or so, with vivid lines across his forehead, as if he spent much time frowning. His gray-brown wavy hair was combed away from his face.

"Sorry, Arnie, my daughter obviously, and her best friend Jill from wonderful fascinating Caylor, Indiana." He smiled broadly.

Arnie nodded at Sadie then Jill, "How do you do, lovely ladies from Hoosierdom. You did something right, Steph."

They all laughed.

"Arnie, is our police detective, now don't bore Jill with tales of the streets."

"No, no, I'd like hear about your work. I teach American history and we've been discussing the recent race riots in the country. Our country kids only know a couple of race definitions, Mexican and white."

"I don't want to…"

"No, no please do," Jill stopped him mid-sentence.

Arnie's furrowed frown lines reinforced his tales of the Detroit Police Department, robberies with shoot-outs and the riot three years earlier. He compared his job to sweeping back the ocean. "Middle class families flee from city neighborhoods to live in the suburbs. They leave houses and schools. I don't know what is going to happen to our great city or any urban area when everyone moves away."

Jill was impressed with his concern as well as the drama of peacekeeping.

"Those hippies," he continued, "stirring up all these kids that change is possible, not wanting to fight a war then burning their draft cards."

"Don't you think they are objecting to not being able to vote, but being asked to fight for a cause? What noble cause they want to know. Killing Asian people half way around the world?"

"You sound like one of those hippies."

"Oh, I would probably be out there if I weren't stuck on a farm, married taking care of my most important responsibility, my daughter. She is my noble cause. But I like the phrase, 'Give peace a chance.' I don't disagree with the peace movement."

"Free love and drugs, their motto, sex, drugs and rock 'n roll? I think it encourages all this drug use and then the mafia shows up with their supply, heroin, marijuana. And I'm out there trying to protect people from harm."

"Now that is a noble cause, but I teach teenagers, I answer questions about the war protests and flower children; they graduate and get drafted and must go fight. I lost one former student in the Tet Offensive. We had a memorial at school. I don't have easy answers, I lost my fiancé long ago in the very beginning of the war."

"I'm sorry to hear about those deaths, we've lost a few men from our department. It is dividing our nation. I understand about the not being able to vote, but these drugs…"

"From my cornfield protected kids there are no drugs at my country school near Caylor. We do battle the country school board's dress requirements, but listening to the Rolling Stones, or Jefferson Airplane are about as radical as we have it."

"It won't be long Jill, before you have the drug problem," he sighed. "The importers keep bringing the stuff in. It always starts in the cities, but sooner or later the small towns are affected." He shook his head, and then drank half a bottle of beer, a sad salute to another wave of his ocean. Detroit was a big urban ocean and she wanted to ask how he kept his spirits up in such overwhelming odds.

Many full beer bottles sat in front of them as each of Steph's friends bought a round of drinks for their friend and his daughter. Cold beer had become warm. Jill waited for any sign of change in behavior by Steph, but he kept smiling and touching his daughter's hands. She'd not heard Emma Sue's name.

"Sadie," Steph spoke quietly, "I wanted you to meet me as I am. These are the guys and this is my home away from home when I have the time. It's just me. I hope that we can try to start an adult relationship. I'm not good at sentimental, sappy stuff."

Jill stopped listening to the very personal conversation; Sadie would tell her what he had said. She now turned back to Arnie who had drunk the other half of his beer. "Heroin," she said, "now where did you say it comes from Arnie?"

"The guys are bringing it back from Nam along with an addiction that is being supplied by the Mafia. But the new kids on the block are from South America."

Jill stared, as Arnie lit a cigarette and offered her one, she shook her head and took a sip of beer, "South America?"

51

"Yeah, Colombia, Bolivia, Peru, these are the places that grow coca the stuff used to make cocaine or nose candy as the users call it."

"Nose candy?"

"Yes. Cocaine powder is inhaled through the nose."

Jill absently rubbed her nose.

"Jill," Sadie tapped Jill's fingers wrapped around a bottle of Pabst blue Ribbon, "we need to go. Steph is a working man and doesn't live real close. Are you ready?"

"This is your family reunion, but I have enjoyed meeting all these interesting folks. Maybe we can come again? It isn't that far if we don't go to every antique shop between here and Caylor."

"Okay, that's enough," Sadie said as Steph laughed.

In the parking lot the group hugged and said goodbye. Steph gave the directions back to the freeway and the directions to Indiana. The women had already decided to drive back to Caylor no matter what time they left. The night was humid and thick with summer. They stopped every hour for coffee.

"Sadie, you've dragged me down every back road in Indiana and to an emotional family reunion, could I just sleep for awhile?" Jill laid her head on the back of the front seat using a sweater for a pillow. Her eyes were closed as she talked.

"Right, like the night you let me sleep when we drove home from Chicago in the rain…"

"Chicago was your idea, Sadie. You wanted to see the Adler planetarium and communicate with the stars…Hey that's a good idea, let's pull over and communicate with the stars; I'll show you the constellations. You know I had a great teacher."

"Oh, yeah, the damn Colonel. Well, he wasn't so bad after you got to know him, and know him you did. But Jill, you were the one who wanted to have dinner at the French restaurant on the 95th floor of the Hancock Building and drink three bottles of wine, then drive home when I was beyond tired."

"And who embarrassed us in front of Reggie Jackson and half of the A's baseball team?"

"It wasn't my fault they parked their bus by the hotel," Sadie said.

"I loved your dad, what a character. I can see why he left your mom. She doesn't have a lighthearted bone in her body."

"I invited him to come to our house and meet his grandchildren. I told him I had plenty of room. Do you think he liked me?"

"He loved you. You could see how proud he was when he looked at you, when he introduced you. Now may I rest in peace?"

"What was Arnie saying about cocaine and Colombia?" Sadie asked.

"Oh, you heard that? Well, he said they are seeing heroin from France and cocaine powder from South America. I have plans to ask my favorite Colombian if he heard of such a thing. I thought coffee was their big crop."

ﻷﻶﻷ

Jill poured her second cup of coffee, took a cup of yogurt from the refrigerator, and looked through yesterday's "Caylor Fish Wrapper." She read the horoscope for Taurus and Gemini. This is the only thing this paper is good for. How does Dad read this garbage every day?

She walked to the back porch and started a load of clothes. The bright sun guaranteed she could hang the sheets to dry. Jack will be happy. He is content about the simplest things, hoeing weeds, cleaning Luisa's room while she was away. On mornings like this, Jill concluded, she loved her farm. She had the place to herself most days or shared them with Luisa. She began each summer vacation wanting to do "things and stuff" before school started in September. Jack suggested making a list. Anathema! Life stepped in the way of her best intentions.

Sadie had kidnapped Luisa, why? With all the others? But Sadie insisted they all entertained each other while they were at the lake. Luisa was a mini-babysitter for Mike, controlling him when possible. The phone rang. She shrugged, putting a clothes pin on the last corner of the sheet. Sadie? Begging for me to drive up to the lake for the day.

"Buenos Dias, Gringa! I tried to call last week…."

"Sadie and I went to Detroit."

"Why?"

"To meet Sadie's father."

"Another daughter not living with her father?"

"Different circumstances. It's a long story."

"Another?" Luis said.

"Luis," Jill scolded.

"Si, Gringa. August eighth through the twenty-third. You will be home in time to can your tomatoes. I know how much that means to you," he laughed.

"I hate it, but I have to do it."

"You want me to send someone to help?" He chuckled.

"Are coffee prices up?"

"Ah, you think I laugh only when I make money?"

"You seem to have a lot of money and you don't laugh much, so I don't think there is a connection. I wish I knew what made you happy. Coffee?"

"Of course, coffee and a good Cuban cigar *and* a nice naked gringa."

"Really? You left one in Washington, D.C., rather quickly."

"My business, Gringa."

"Coffee or money?"

"It's the same," Luis said. "We will vacation in Hawaii, try their Kona coffee. You will have fifteen days with your Señor Ochoa is that long enough?"

"It is not the time, Luis, but I will take the fifteen days. It is a typical day on my farm. My clothes are washed and drying on the clothesline. It's peaceful and I'm alone.."

"You like being alone?" he said.

"I like the farm without Jack."

"Another long story?"

"Nope. A short story; I am ready to change continents," she said.

"Not such a good day on the farm?"

"I think marrying Jack may have been a mistake."

"Are you feeling or rationalizing?"

"Feeling," Jill said.

"Marrying Jack was not a mistake; your disposition toward your marriage seems to be the mistake."

"Why are we having this conversation on the telephone? I'm sorry I even brought it up."

"Gringa, gringa, gringa…you are alone, I'm alone we can talk. I did not spend time with you in Washington as I wanted. My business is very demanding; I must always be many places at the same time, but I had wanted to be with you. Your long story of Hector, this man I know nothing of. I want to hold you and feel you talk of him. But now you talk of Jack. He is part of *our* picture, for now."

"Luis, I wake up at night and wish I could call you at two or three in the morning. I just want to hear your voice. I want to turn over in my bed and touch you. I can't do that, you can't do that, why? Jack."

"More than Jack," his voice dropped, and then he was silent.

"I want to see you as you say that. Is it me? I can't hold your hands."

"Never you. You never have to ask that again, Gringa. Next week, we will be together away from our farms."

"Luis, when I was in Detroit last week, I talked to a police detective who said Colombians were bringing cocaine into his city. Did you know that?"

"Damn Jankee federales, spreading rumors about Colombia. They never want to accept American deficiencies. But Señor Sam…I don't want to discuss this now or in Hawaii. Hawaii is a peaceful paradise and this is a repugnant subject."

Chapter 3

The sunlight brightened the scene of disarray as Jill packed for Hawaii. She pulled out each skirt, blouse, and shorts' combination before deciding. The "too worn or unfashionable" lay on the chair and bed. Hawaii? Warm ocean, soft sand beaches, perfect blue skies, romantic, sultry. Her thoughts sounded like a travel brochure. Dressy clothes for paradise? She took a cocktail dress, basic black chemise. A bikini that was not her, if she turned over too quickly her breasts fell out of the small olive and black triangles, but Sadie insisted. Skirts? Yes, mostly skirts. Luis would prefer skirts to shorts, but there'd be days and times for shorts. And the tiny underwear that Sadie said, "He'll like them Jill, not your Girl Scout panties that Jack never sees, you need lacy and black, yes."

"They are so tiny I might as well go pantiless."

"He'd love that, too. Try it." Sadie laughed.

She now tucked them discreetly into the side brocade pockets on her suitcase. She told Jack to stay out of the bedroom until she was finished. Finished? This for hiking? Or this for dancing? Dancing?

Maybe. In frustration she packed most items, easier to make a choice there. She clicked one suitcase closed and left to tackle Luisa's stuff. They were scheduled to stay on Maui, but Luis withheld any more details. After Curaçao, she confidently accepted his vagueness.

The last three weeks had gone fast and then slowly when she talked to Jack about what they would do. If the timing went smoothly, she assumed God approved, in a subtle way, her meeting Luis. But with any glitch, she doubted her affair. And this year Jack's annual fishing trip with Beau to northern Michigan conveniently came at the exact time as her trip to Hawaii. The only roughness in planning happened in Lillian's kitchen.

The Joneses had been walking out of the kitchen door when Henry asked about accommodations in Hawaii. Jill had thrown him a look, but as usual when he chided her, he ignored her and rattled on about a friend who owned a condominium. Insisting in August, he was sure the man, who also owned a lumberyard, would be happy to let Jill stay there. He grinned broadly, looked at Jack, and then momentarily met Jill's stare. Jill grabbed Jack's arm and said in her best, "Oh Henry" voice that she and Luisa would take their chance on a local hotel in Maui, "It is the off-season; it should be easy to find a room. We're staying in Lahaina. I want to find a local place, maybe a mansion home with rooms."

Henry raised one bushy eyebrow and shook his head. She accepted his resignation. Henry had been good about "the love thing," his term for her relationship with Luis. He led her to the edge of exposure, but unsuspicious Jack was basic, easy to please and easy to fool.

Now she viewed Luisa's clothes flung all over the bed. And in the middle sat the gray stuffed elephant Luis gave her in the school parking lot almost a year ago. Jill sat down and picked up the furry animal outlining the trunk and plastic button eyes. She had packed her "Charlie" away when she moved from Elliston to Caylor. Lillian asked her many times, "When are you going to the basement and sort all that high school stuff? You know Henry and I are thinking of retiring to Bradenton, one of these years. We have to clean out the basement, oh, clean out everything."

"I'll do it Mom. I'll get in the mood. And you are never leaving Caylor permanently. Dad can't keep his eye on me from Florida." But going through all the high school memorabilia scared her. The time was gone, but shifting through the pieces brought the past, no matter how ancient, quickly into focus, too quickly. So the papers, ticket stubs, dried flower bouquets and 45's sat in the darkness. She needed to know her history was there, but did not want to see it.

"Mom, are you finished? We are leaving soon. Sadie will be here in twenty minutes, Dad said," Luisa spoke coming into the room. "He showed me some wiggle worm he was going to use to catch my fish."

"I'm almost finished. Do you want to take your Charlie?"

"He wants to see the volcanoes, too."

Jill hugged her daughter, at nine and a half her head rested on Jill's chest. "We're on our way to Hawaii, Sweetie."

"Oh Mom, I'm so excited. Any secrets for me?"

"You never know," Jill said and tickled her daughter's chin.

She snapped the locks on the large American Tourister bag. "Well, you can carry Charlie and let him look out the window."

A horn honked. Sadie. Jill looked at her watch. 7A.M. Sadie on time first thing in the morning, it's a…. "Luisa, tell your father to come and get the bags." Jill turned off Luisa's window fan. Jack could close the window. She took one last trip to the bathroom inspecting the medicine cabinet.

Jack walked into Luisa's bedroom. He picked up their bags, carried them to the hall setting them by the door "It's finally here Luisa, time to see the actual volcanoes we saw in the library books."

"Oh, Daddy, I wish you could go with us."

"You'll have a great time. Be sure to have your mom take lots of pictures. I'll want to know everything." He grabbed her in his arms and hugged her, "I'm going to miss you, Pumpkin. Go tell Sadie your mom will be right there."

Luisa ran out. Jack turned to Jill and put his arm around her, hugging her. He whispered, "I'm going to miss you, too, but I'm happy you are taking Luisa all these places. Maybe one day we can all go somewhere, Washington, D.C. or someplace. Disneyland is going to open in Florida…"

"Jeezus, Jack, Florida…Another place, please. And, of course, I would just love to go fishing…"

"Back to the drawing board," he said, then leaned down and kissed her. He picked up the luggage.

Sadie leaned on her open car trunk, reminding Jill they had only two hours until she and Luisa boarded in Indianapolis for Los Angeles.

"Jack, are you going to miss your sweetie?"

"Which one, Sadie?"

"Only one of them is sweet, you know that Jack. The other one I'm sure, you would send on a slow boat to China."

"Sadie, that's enough," Jill scowled at her friend.

Jack smiled slightly and shook his head, "Honey, do you have your tickets?"

"They're on the dresser. I was saving them for last; I'll go get them."

"No, no," Jack dashed into the farmhouse. He quickly emerged carrying an envelope. "Here you go. This was the only thing on the dresser, but the return address says, 'National Coffee Federation, Bogotá, Colombia.' Where did you get this envelope?"

Sadie rolled her eyes, but Jack did not see her from outside the car, "Jack, I gave it to Jill filled with Green Stamps. I think she is saving for…"

"Stop Sadie. I gave them to Lillian."

"Actually, Michael is working with some Colombian coffee farmers trying to sell them farm equipment. Hey! We must go. We're running out of time."

"Bye, Daddy."

Jill hugged him and kissed him more warmly than usual. She said, "Be sure and bring home some fish and the stories of all the ones you couldn't handle."

"You, too, Honey." He waved as Jill rolled up the window. Sadie peeled out of the driveway, leaving a cloud of gravel dust. Jack stood on the front porch waving.

"Jeez-us to jeez-us, Jill, you didn't?" Sadie held up the envelope. Jill shook her head. Why did it feel like they were sixteen sneaking out on Henry?

Sadie took the country road to the main highway. They laughed nervously at first, then as the distance from Caylor increased, their anxiety decreased and they laughed as partners in crime.

Jill and Luisa had a brief layover in Los Angeles, but did not have to change airlines only planes. It helped that they were traveling west; the hours of flight were not lost in the day. Jill checked to make sure of the gate and boarding times before walking around the terminal. The structure allowed them to watch planes land. Luisa excitedly read the airline names on each plane.

The travelers had a certain "California look" about them. When she viewed the Californians, with their casual mismatched hippie clothes, long skirts and tie-dyed skirts with beads and cowbells, she thought of her cousin Klaus and the blond surfing persona, now noticeably replaced with scraggly hair. Klaus had moved to California after graduating, but was immediately drafted and spent the next two years touring other parts of the world before settling back in Pittsburgh to help run his father's business. Lillian kept up with all the family news. Klaus married and had a child or two; Jill couldn't remember his whole story.

Walking to their connecting flight, Luisa asked questions about the men with hair longer than hers and men in orange robes chanting in a foreign language. They watched the ambience of the new world, a counter-culture of love, barefoot travelers in patched blue jeans, fringed vests and rumpled t-shirts with political slogans. It bore no resemblance to their rural home.

"Oh Mom, I wish I could take pictures to show Darcie and Teresa. They would love the jeans with patches and pins, but the boys, some look like girls. I wonder what Dad and Grandpa would say?"

"I'm not sure they'd understand boys that look like girls, that's why they are in Indiana and we are on our way to someplace else."

"Mom, you need a long skirt."

"Where would I wear such a long skirt, all the way to my ankles? They look like members of an old-fashioned covered-wagon crew."

"I wonder if we can shop and buy all those things that Aunt Sadie likes. Remember in Curaçao? We bought lots of things for Aunt Sadie."

"No, we are not leaving the United States so we can't shop duty-free."

"I wish we were going to Curaçao again. I loved snorkeling with Papa and Caz."

Jill flinched before answering, "You liked that man, Papa?"

"He is different than Dad, but he says yes, oh, no, he says, 'si' when I ask him for ice cream, clothes, everything. And I love to hear him talk. I told Teresa…" Luisa stopped herself and looked at her mom.

"What did you say?"

"Oops, Mom. I just told her there was a…man we met who talked with an accent."

"That's all?"

"She asked about my necklace with the little seahorse and I…just explained a man took me snorkeling and I saw them and…"

"Teresa's mom would cross hot coals to know gossip about me. You know we went to Caylor High together?"

"Mom, that was the olden times. Her mom makes the best ice cream sandwiches, homemade. She showed us some pictures of you in school in her scrapbook. You looked funny. I like you better now, your hair, everything."

They found their seats and immediately Luisa leaned over and laid her head on Jill's lap. Jill stared out the window, stroking Luisa's hair absently. The plane roared to life and they were airborne over the Pacific Ocean. Luisa soon was asleep.

Jill had a silent dialogue with Sadie about the quick cover up of the "coffee federation" envelope; Luisa's reference to their trip to Curaçao with Luis; the innocent conversation with Teresa and her mom, Natalie, the nibby nose as she and Sadie always taunted her. Natalie had wanted to go to their high school parties, but the guys did not like her, too fat and too loud. She ended up married right after high school to the first boy who asked her out. She said yes to the date, then yes in the back seat at the drive-in. Seven months after her marriage she had a baby. Sadie and Jill added the drive-in story. Poor Sam Dobson, well, they deserved each other. He was no prize either, quiet, fat, pimples…she frowned at how judgmental they had all been.

Sam had become a cop, "a decent fellow," Henry said after they met at the Lion's lunches. And Natalie continued to gain weight. She recently had her fourth baby and seemed to gain twenty pounds with each. Natalie wore tent dresses, hiding pregnancy or weight? The only reason Luisa met Natalie was Jill and Jack's decision to send Luisa to school in town. When Luisa started kindergarten, it seemed easier to have Lillian and Henry two blocks away from Luisa's school than a long bus ride from the farm.

Jack took Luisa every morning on his way to Johnson Electronics which was thirty minutes from the farm or the school. Luisa and Jack established a non-mom dialogue in their commuting time. "We usually don't mention your name, Honey. I like that we talk just the two of us."

Luisa often talked to Jill of her conversations with Jack. Luisa had asked him why she had black hair because Jack had brown hair and her mother strawberry-blond. Luisa told Jack she had hair more like her Aunt Sadie's. Sadie and Jill had then discussed the hair color question and agreed that sooner rather than later Luisa would have to know the truth. Jill accepted the inevitability of that revelation. Luis's reappearance in her life had forced this conversation to take its place at the top of her priority list. Two weeks in Hawaii would provide time, a good time? The right time? Yes, an appropriate conversation among the three of them...

"Mrs. Jones?"

The voice took her from the ocean trance, "Yes," she answered the stewardess who handed her an envelope.

"This was in the captain's bag; he forgot until now. I'm so sorry. I hope the delay doesn't cause a problem. Do you need anything? A drink? Something for your sweet girl? Her hair is so pretty, the curls, like an angel."

"An angel when she sleeps. Thank you. No, I don't need anything."

Jill looked at the plain envelope. Now what Luis? She opened the unsealed white envelope with the American Airlines logo in the return address corner. The heavy stationery was printed like a Western Union telegram. "Jill" she could hear his voice as she read the type. "As you see your tickets only take you to Honolulu. A gringo, Andy Marshall, will meet you. I'll be waiting for my girls in Maui. Luis." The contents relaxed her. He organized the vacation time, but when the tickets came they only took her to Honolulu. She made her agenda with Luisa in mind, but Luis's plans...he would expect them to...oh, relax, Jill, we've only vacationed once together.

The landing afforded them a view of Diamond Head jutting into the turquoise sea and Pearl Harbor. Viewing the landmarks, goose bumps covered her arms. "You see the ship under the water?" Luisa nodded, "in 1941 when I wasn't born yet, a country, Japan decided to drop bombs on that harbor and sunk that ship."

"Mom, can we go there and see it?"

"I don't know if we will have time when we fly back from Maui."

Jill made a mental note to ask Luis about Colombia and WWII; her U.S. History books never mentioned it.

They exited the plane and were given the traditional leis. First-class, Jill thought, as Luisa patted the delicate petals. Luisa asked Jill for a grass skirt. In a grass skirt...would she look like a Hawaiian native? Jill wanted to take her picture with the pink and purple flowers around her face. Luisa moved farther away, a broad angle picture with an abundance of the courtyard tropical plants and bushes. The picture in the view finder was perfect, ready to snap; she felt a tap on her shoulder. Stopping mid-click, she turned to say something.

"Mrs. Jones, go stand with her I'll take the picture of you and Little Lou. Hurry because we don't have much time. I have to get your luggage and get you to the ranch on *his* time schedule." He winked at Jill.

Jill cocked her head. Impudent. She shrugged. "Andy Marshall? From Luis, no doubt." White skin permanently brick red from the sun; thin, shoulder length, sun-bleached brown hair, sea blue eyes with crow's feet. A cigarette seemed glued to his lip. Andy Marshall "the gringo." He wore an Hawaiian print shirt with a leather choker and medallion. What was it? The symbol, oh the harmony...

"The yin-yang, Mrs. Jones," he answered.

"Sorry for staring."

"Let's take the picture," he spoke, looking down at his gadgeted pilot's watch, "The time. You know him, obviously," he smirked, a dimple sunk in on one browned cheek. "Have you ridden in a helicopter? And Little Lou, she's not afraid to fly?"

"Mommy, who is that? Take my picture!" Luisa stood with her hands on her hips.

"Another one, ma'am?" Andy nodded toward Luisa and chuckled.

"Yes. Okay, Luisa. Thank you Mr. Marshall," Jill shook her head and handed the camera to Andy Marshall. She indicated where to push.

"Andy, ma'am, just Andy, always. No one has called me Marshall since the Army."

"Army?" Jill now stared intently at the scruffy new acquaintance. Maybe they were the same age.

"Yes. Special Forces," he spoke and the cigarette bounced with each word. "Go ma'am." He shooed her towards Luisa.

"Jill," she said, "only Jill."

"Mom?!"

Jill walked to stand with Luisa, but the Special Forces echoed in her ears.

"Jill, lighten up. Peace, happiness, you're in Hawaii...paradise...Smile, love is in the air." He smiled broadly, then winked.

63

Pearl Harbor and now this man in his khaki Bermuda shorts, military boots and cowboy hat with the Special Forces emblem embroidered on the crown. The hat was firmly molded flat on one side. Andy was solid, but slight. He had a large tattoo on his bicep that peeked out from under the short sleeve of the shirt. It looked like the emblem of the Special Forces again. Honolulu Airport teemed with military personnel. Many young men hustled by in their traveling uniforms, Navy, Army, Marines. The crowd reminded her of Germany, moving in and out of the Air Base with William and the Army Post with Michael and Sadie. All the branches seemed to be represented then and now. They carried the drab green canvas duffle bags and sported shaved heads.

Viet Nam occupied every headline and every newscast. She avoided those sensory reminders as much as she could and still teach current events, but this walk through the Honolulu airport overloaded her own capability to dismiss the memory of Hector's death. She followed one vet surrounded by more soldiers. They could've been taken from Hector's pictures of "the guys," the guys were right *here,* walking down the sunny concourse of Honolulu Airport.

Jill held Luisa's hand, trailing the fast-walking Andy to a small golf cart. The luggage recovery had not taken long. Andy said the inside of the helicopter did not have too much space. He drove them over several concrete runways oblivious to the busy overhead buzzing planes.

"Little Lou, are you ready to ride the whirly-bird?" Andy turned to Luisa who sat next to the suitcases on the back seat.

"Why do you say 'Little Lou?" My name is Luisa Jones."

"You look just like…" Andy started.

"Oh, Andy! What's that over there?" Jill said, pointing across his steering wheel at a long string of Quonset buildings.

"It's the private hangers for some of the flyboys. They have their own planes they fly on their off days." Andy took a cigarette from his mouth and tapped the ash on the rearview mirror, then spoke facing Jill, "You two look just like your pictures."

"What pictures?" Luisa asked, frowning.

"The ones…" Andy said.

"Andy," Jill interrupted, "how long does it take to get to Maui?"

"Not long, maybe forty-five minutes. A huge place you're going to. Whew! The money boys, they sure know how to put their acres together. I never wanted to own much property myself. I can't be tied down. Well, there it is ladies, your chariot to the islands of paradise." He pointed to the small rounded-nose helicopter. "We are going to have fun. Yoo-hoo! I love to fly helicopters, especially when I'm not fired upon."

When he gave them headsets to muffle the noise of the helicopter blades, the instant quiet became a canyon separating them. The small helicopter was built for four people, so Jill and Luisa sat in the back seats. Andy hand signaled with their "ears" on there would be no more talking until they landed.

They were buckled tightly and the four suitcases stored behind their seats. Luisa tried to look out both sides, back and forth, pointing first one way then another. Jill used sign language. She shared Luisa's excitement, playing a game of point and show with exaggerated facial expressions for emphasis. The helicopter ride stopped the military reminiscing at the airport, but the cavalier conversation of Andy Marshall and his "Little Lou" references would make the next two weeks tough. Why him, Luis? Oh, god, who are you Luis Ochoa? Surely Andy did not act this nonchalantly around "the boss." She should've told Luisa on the plane that Luis was meeting them. Now the helicopter noise drowned out all communication.

The black volcanic tops poked from the sea like Hershey kisses floating on blue shimmering silk. Hawaii, thousands of miles from Caylor. This distance? The farther the better. She could present Luisa with her "Papa" again. She did say she liked it because he said, "Si," to all of her requests. How to explain why he was here? It would have to come out. And "Little Lou?" She looked at the back of Andy's head, the long hair. Hector's first picture to her was the burr cut, the end of long hair. Luis had vowed in Washington that she would tell this long story. She had practiced dredging up the memories, but looking at Andy in the drab green hat...Hector – rode in helicopters, wore this dull color and the Special Forces emblem. Hector, maybe tell Luis first and get it over with. Tell what? Let Luis ask...

The ranch, as Andy referred to it, was a huge pineapple plantation, visible panoramically from both sides of the helicopter. White square buildings spread out in green clearings. Two large houses took shape out the window, one much larger than the other and separated by a jungle swath. A horse stable and fenced track was cut from another chunk of trees and bush. Three white cottages circled a half-moon shaped swimming pool; these were joined by sparkling white tiles geometrically placed on the grass. The helicopter suddenly dropped into a clearing onto an asphalt square entombed in dense natural walls of tropical trees, plants and shrubs. The chopper blades stopped, suddenly silence prevailed in thick air. Was it like that for Hector? No noise and dense humidity entombed by jungle?

Andy removed their headsets, and then took the suitcases, carrying them to a waiting golf cart. He explained they would be staying in the smaller of the two houses, asking if Jill noticed the difference as they descended. They climbed into the cart and whisked into a tunnel of overgrowth. The fragrant colorful forest of palms and monkey vines carried them to a whole new world.

"Mom, it looks like Tarzan. I wonder if there are monkeys."

"No monkeys Little Lou."

"We'll see lots of things, but I don't think Tarzan, Jane or monkeys," Jill said.

They quietly stopped in front of the smaller two-story white farm mansion. It was larger than most homes in Caylor. It could easily accommodate more than the three of them, or was it four with Andy? Raw jungle enveloped the residence on three sides. The residences had been built in the gentle mountain slope that rose sharply behind the smaller house. A gray mist provided a backdrop for dancing rainbows at its peak.

Luis now walked down the wide steps of the porch that extended across the front. Luisa looked at her mother, then back to Luis. She frowned at Jill.

"Mrs. Jones and her lovely daughter, welcome to Hawaii. Aloha." Luis held his arms invitingly. Jill walked to meet him. He wrapped an arm around her waist. She resisted kissing him. Luisa continued to look suspiciously.

"Hey, Lou, I'm outta here." Andy spoke as he strolled away, a gait with a slight limp. He lit a cigarette, clinked the lighter lid shut, then slid into the golf car. "Let you all get settled. Call as soon as you're ready to go." Andy quietly disappeared into the jungle tunnel shrouding the path. Another duplicate cart sat parked in the semi-circular driveway.

"Lou?" Jill eyed Luis curiously and knew where the "Little Lou" had come from. Luis shrugged. His acceptance of the maverick pilot surprised her. They stood on the wide steps next to their suitcases.

"Mr. Ochoa, is this your house, too?" Luisa pointed.

"No, Luisa. And please call me Papa." Luis glanced from Luisa to Jill.

"Are you on vacation, too, Papa?"

"Si."

"Why do you want to go on vacation with us?" She looked up, staring at his face.

"I enjoy the pleasure of your company, Luisa Jones." He squatted, making himself her height, "And who would make you heuvos the way you like?" He smiled at her. She looked at him, then to Jill and lifted her shoulders in the same shrug movement he had just done.

"This house," Jill said, "reminds me of Sadie's house in Georgia. Square, symmetrically exact." The lower level had sets of French doors that opened onto the long wood veranda. A Chinese woman, stood at one edge, watching. She was dressed in white, a tunic and long skirt with her hair cut short. Her face was expressionless.

"Your face, Gringa, I see the questions. Come, I'll show you to your rooms and give the history." Luis left the suitcases on the porch and nodded to the woman at the door who disappeared. He told of the first plantation cultivated in the 1800's by missionaries; the fortune that was made from pineapples and sugar, made them lose their love of preaching and saving souls in favor of capital accumulation. The owner built his son the second home which he occupied until he made his own fortune, then left and moved to his own island in French Polynesia. The scandal was that the son left his American wife and their five children to live with a Polynesian woman. Luis laughed at the story and shrugged as if it were a tall tale.

"Eventually," he said, "it came into the hands of my friend Chen Lau, who I call Kit, a Chinese merchant in Honolulu. He doesn't come here very often, 'no time, too busy make money, Señor,' he tells me. Kit has an even more beautiful place on Victoria Peak on Hong Kong Island. Perhaps, we'll go there next year."

The house was dominated by Chinese furniture, black lacquered tables, chairs and chests with thick brass hinges. Luis's story had taken them up a curved hardwood stairway and into a suite of rooms. Jill and Luisa's shared room had twin beds of the same black lacquer. Chinese porcelain figurines, jade sculptures, and free-standing large ginger jars decorated their suite. Vases filled with brilliant flowers sat on every flat surface Their sweet scents filled the space. The window-doors opened onto the wrap-around porch of the house's upper level.

Chinese servants moved silently as Luis played tour guide.

"Luis, I need to feed Luisa, get her into a bathtub and put her in bed. This has been a long day."

"No, Mom. I want to stay up."

"Tomorrow, we ride horses Luisa. Have you ridden a horse?" Luis said.

"No," Luisa looked at her mother for approval for this new experience. Jill nodded affirmatively.

Luis continued, "We start early and you will need to be rested. I hope the riding pants fit. I could only guess at your exact size."

Luisa clapped her hands, "Mom, horseback riding, Uncle Beau never lets me ride." She smiled and looked at Luis who had enjoyed her response, smiling with her. Luisa's clap brought a Chinese servant from somewhere, asking if he were needed. The small man with short black hair and white overcoat also smiled and bowed. Jill laughed, a tired punch drunk laugh, at the confusion. Luis ordered dinner for Luisa, and then explained the bath. The servant nodded and disappeared.

Luisa bounced on her twin bed. She jumped up and ran to the closets with their vented doors and inlaid pearl designs. She fingered the long tail of the pheasant sculpted into the wood. The black finish shone. She opened the doors and closed them, then walked to the bathroom. Jill prepared the bath.

"Luisa, it is past your bedtime. I know it seems early, but in Indiana it is 11P.M. and now I will reset my watch to Hawaiian time, young lady, while you take a bath, then get your jammies on."

"Mom…"

"No, this bathtub is amazing and you can trace the tiles with their pheasants and flowers. Come on. Your dinner should be ready when you get out."

The servant returned and addressed Luis in a whisper, indicating the food was ready for "young missy," and he asked where they would be served.

"Jill, it is warm enough she can eat in her pajamas downstairs."

"Sure, we'll be down in a moment."

She closed the bathroom door and walked to where he stood in the bedroom doorway. She hugged him and he squeezed her, then he kissed her on her nose and then deeply. He pulled away, "My tiger, you've returned. I'll be downstairs." He touched her cheek with the back of his hand, then turned and left. She inhaled deeply, his spicy cologne mingled with the island flowers, "Perfect."

Jill and Luisa walked downstairs through the large double doors to the front veranda. Luis motioned them to come and sit at a black wicker table set with a crystal pitcher of cold coconut punch and three frosted glasses.

"To paradise, now complete," Luis touched the edge of Jill's glass. The porch faced the open fields of the pineapple plantation. The house had been built up from the actual fields with a panoramic view of the jutting volcanic mountains on the horizon.

"It looks like everything I imagined, more so, really. Always more so, Señor Ochoa."

"Wait until we ride the horses, it gets more…picturesque."

ᴦᶾᴦ

Luisa slept soundly upstairs; the tropical breeze blew gently through sheer drapes. Jill had rubbed Luisa's hair soothing her to sleep in a strange bed, in a new environment. She had reassured her she would be sleeping in the bed next to her. Tinkling glass wind chimes outside their doors reminded her of her parents' front porch.

Jill and Luis now stood on the candlelit veranda embraced by the Maui night. The sliver C-shaped moon branded the inky sky, not like her imagined felt picture with a full moon. The smell of flowers in the vases and the bushes around the porch permeated their space; she had not accounted for a sense of smell in the felt scene. She leaned against the porch railing, counting stars and listening to swishing palm fronds. The velvet air balanced sea moisture and breeze. Her hair hung in gentle curls. A light gust moved palm fronds, the scratching soundtrack for the night. It teased Jill's hair and stirred Luis's cigar smoke. He put his cigar in the ash tray, then pulled her to him, "I know you like the taste of my cigar." He kissed her, his tongue and moustache burnished with that taste. She wanted more.

"Gringa, tomorrow I'm telling Luisa I'm her father."

She recoiled and extricated herself from his arms. He did not restrain her from pulling away.

"You don't want me to do this, but I cannot play a game of lies with my daughter. You say, 'a man of his words.' Honesty is what you demand in that statement. I will not be *dishonest* with her."

Jill walked away from him to the steps of the porch; she sat down staring at the sky, rearranging the felt pieces, now three people under one moon. She knew they could not go on living this lie, but the intersection of one marriage to the other. Luisa standing at the crossroads. A cold tear ran down her cheek. Paradise? No, not this decision. He had made it, she had made it, but to look at those innocent brown eyes and say what? How to explain a moment in a shed, a conception? He relit the cigar. She heard the long intake of breath, then the smell of smoke. Her face burned.

"Boss, you and Missy like a drink?"

Jill turned, glancing at his face, a half smile and no frown, waiting for her and then back at the servant.

"Anisette on ice. Missy?" Luis said.

She shrugged and turned back to the night sky.

"Bring Missy the same."

She bit her lips and tried to suppress the tears, the consequences. Didn't Henry say she must suffer the consequences of her behavior? Oh, Dad. It is so hard. My baby is going to cry and I am going to make her cry.

The houseboy left the drinks and disappeared. "Gringa, this is a perfect night in paradise. Come to your papa. You want to yell at me? You want to hit me? What? Make me disappear into the night?"

Her shoulders dropped. She stood and walked to the small table that held their drinks. "Will this help?" She drank it down, "You always win, don't you?"

"I told you that before, but Gringa you forget that my victory is not your loss. We are not enemies. You belong to me."

"I don't belong to anyone."

"Gringa, Gringa, Gringa, it is a decision *you* made. The most important decision you have ever made because the rest of them are mine and I am a responsible man, a man of his words."

"Who are you Luis? Who is it that I belong to?"

The houseboy had refilled her glass; she took another drink of the licorice flavored liqueur. She watched Luis blow smoke rings as he leaned against the railing and absently stroked his heavy moustache with his thumb. The smoke wafted around his head. The Latin on his veranda, dark, handsome, a stranger, yet she knew all the inches of his body. So close and yet so distant, physically known and emotionally a mystery. Impenetrable like the jungle enveloping the house.

He looked at the sparkling sawdust spread across the horizon as he spoke, "What do I do? Why do I love you of all the women I've known? A gringa, who can barely speak my native language? Who were my parents?"

"Good questions, or are they the answer? I just want to know who *you* are."

"You will and when you do, the questions won't be necessary; neither will the answers." He turned and stepped to where she sat. "I want to make love with you now. Come."

He grabbed her hand. She hated him, and heard Sadie's voice, about which adjective to use. He had dressed in the cotton drawstring pants that hung loosely on his hips with no shirt. He wore sandals. She recognized them as the water buffalo sandals that Sadie bought for them in Detroit, calling them "hippie" sandals. Luis's looked very worn. He effortlessly lifted her and threw her over his shoulder, a sack of potatoes, no a burlap bag of coffee beans. His bedroom opened onto the veranda. She fell gently onto his large bed. She tasted the licorice drink and the cigar. And him, thousands of miles and so many hours, the pleasure of one man's body, this man's body, paradise found.

ঌξঌ

She awoke in her own bed; the sheets were creamy cotton trimmed in silk print brocade. The piping around the cuffs of the pillowcase and sheet were royal blue; the blue matched the sheer coverlet of the twin beds. Lying in the silky bed, was she back in her fairytale princess green room? But how? Luis? In her bed? And not her nightgown? The royal blue matched the coverlet, but who put it on her? Where did it come from? She sat up on her elbows; I only drank that anisette with him, then what? As soon as her feet touched the Oriental rug, a tiny Chinese woman entered, carrying a silver tray with hot coffee and fresh flowers in a porcelain vase. She set it down on the end table, nodding.

"Jo son... so sorry, good morning, Missy," she spoke, then smiled, her eyes closed as her high cheek bones hid them. She nodded again, and then informed Jill her breakfast would be served on the front veranda whenever she was ready.

Filtered sun drenched the room. Luisa's bed was neatly made, the royal blue coverlet folded at the foot of the bed. The suitcases had been unpacked and sat stacked in the sitting room that led from their bedroom to the veranda outside their own set of French doors. She reached for her cup of coffee as the Chinese woman closed the door.

71

There was a note on the tray next to her coffee cup. She held it for a moment, then read:

Jill – I'm teaching Luisa to ride a horse. You had your lesson last night. We'll be back for lunch. Luis."

Last night, was it as satisfying as she remembered? Oh, god, Luis, are you telling her our secret? Is she crying? Does she understand?

She grabbed her duster and walked downstairs to the veranda. Breakfast was served. Jill finished her last bite of croissant when Andy came up the road in his golf cart.

"Hey, Mrs. Jones! Good morning. I just left the teacher and his student. I'm happy I'm not the student." Andy chuckled and bounced up the front steps. "Mind if I have some coffee?" he asked, sitting down across from her at the table. "The stuff they had at the stable tasted like horse shit."

Jill laughed, then spoke, "Sure, sure. Good morning to you, too. Join me. There are rolls everything, I guess. I sit here and these quick Chinese people bring things to me. They seem to have it all."

Andy still wore his cowboy hat, a pair of Bermuda shorts and a tight fitting t-shirt. He slouched down in the cushioned wicker chair. He removed a cigarette from his t-shirt pocket, tapped it on the face of his pilot's watch, then flipped it into his mouth, and lit it with the Zippo lighter. The stainless steel lighter had a Special Forces insignia on one side and a map of Viet Nam engraved on the other. He sucked forcefully on the tobacco and offered Jill one. She shook her head. A houseboy appeared with a porcelain ashtray.

"These ga...Chinese are great. I have to remember to say Chinese and not gook, although they look alike. Chinese people live all over Viet Nam especially in Saigon."

"When were you in Viet Nam?"

"Officially or unofficially?"

Jill cocked her head.

He continued, "Two tours, Mrs. Jones..."

"Jill, please," she said, "I don't want to think about being *Mrs.* Jones right now."

Andy raised one eyebrow, speaking, "Two tours, Jill. 1963 and I turned right around and went back in 1964. I took a small piece of shrapnel in my thigh," he pulled up his shorts' leg and showed her a long scar that looked like jaggedly torn newspaper. "It wouldn't look so bad, but a medic had to stitch it for me as the ground was shaking with mortar shells..." Andy paused and closed his eyes, "He did a great job considering," he traced down the smooth flesh that joined the lines of raised skin, "Medics always did a great job for us. How old are you Jill?"

"Twenty-eight. Why?"

"You look at me," he snuffed out the tiny end of the cigarette deliberately back and forth smashing the black ashes in the clean white china dish. "But you're looking at someone else. I call it the military widow look. They are always trying to make you into the dead man's image. I get it a lot because of the military everywhere on the islands. Their men go and don't come back. Zap!" He snapped his fingers. "They want you to be his replacement."

The houseboy appeared, "Boss, you need something? More coffee? Missy?"

"No, thank you," Jill answered, dismissing the servant, then chuckled at their efficiency. "You must be careful around here; they are very attentive."

"Jill, are you a military widow?"

"No...no, not really, no. Well, maybe...well, sort of. Special Forces?"

"Yeah, they sent us to all these places where Americans weren't supposed to go, told the American people we were advisors. Advisors? I had my boots on and carried a gun. Hard to advise a rice paddy. I could not write my family. We just went in, stripped, no noise, no knowledge, then we came out, well some of us came out. Hey, Lou said I should pick you up and take you to the stable and if you want to ride, he said dress accordingly."

"Why do you call him Lou?"

"It's his name."

"Oh. Let me change. I'll be right back." Jill stood and placed her napkin on the table. What did her face look like? Luis felt it. Andy noticed. She opened the screen door. Special Forces. 1963. Special Forces. 1963. Medics. Special Forces. She grabbed the railing, then ran up the stairs, but the words chased her, beat her, and stayed with her as she changed from her robe and nightgown to jeans and t-shirt.

"That was quick," Andy rose from the chair. "I guess you know that when he speaks, we don't have much leeway." Andy laughed and Jill joined him, releasing the tension that Andy's presence caused.

73

He drove with a cigarette hanging from his mouth. His casual appearance was exactly like the pictures Hector had sent of his Army buddies.

"You know how to ride, Jill? The places to go around here can be more dangerous than some mine fields."

"M-m a long time ago at 'Y' camp, I was taught how to mount, dismount that basic stuff."

"Where do you live in Indiana?"

"You knew Indiana? Caylor, but what else did he tell you?"

"Ah, Jill, he pays me well. Ask him." He smiled at her, and then took a long puff of his cigarette.

And the boundary was drawn.

They drove through a thick jungle then onto a perfectly manicured road with stately palms lining each side of the white crunchy pathway. They came to a fork in the road. One way led to the larger plantation home. The Georgian columns and square two stories looked as if Scarlett O'Hara would dash out the front door, holding layers of lace flounce.

Andy turned onto another path that took them directly to a long white stable. The distinct odor of horses interjected itself with the sweet smell of sandalwood. Luis and Luisa rode in the open grassy field behind the wood barns. Luisa shrieked when she saw Jill. Luis barked at her and she sat still on a very large black horse. The horse also stopped still when Luis yelled. Jill stepped out of the car and took her camera from her purse. She snapped shots of Luisa, but avoided any pictures of Luis, knowing he would inspect all the returned film besides watching her take them.

Jill put the camera back into her bag and leaned against the wood railing. Luis had tied a bandana around his forehead and tied one around Luisa's. He wore jeans and cowboy boots that looked much like the ones Jill remembered from the migrant camp. No plaid shirt, instead a brightly flowered Hawaiian print clung to his sweaty chest. Luisa wore the leather crotched riding pants Luis provided. Luisa also wore cowboy boots and a flowered shirt, a copy of Luis's. So that is why he wanted to know her size, she thought. Father and daughter smiled at each other as the riding lesson continued. Luis shouted orders and Luisa followed them. Teacher and student rode parallel, then Luisa by herself as he inspected.

"Walk him all the way to the end; then turn him around. I'll be right here. Show your mom what you've learned while she slept." Luis rode over to the fence where Jill and Andy stood as Luisa rode slowly.

"Gringa, I think we have a vaquera.(cowgirl) No fear, good timing and horse sense." He reined in his horse and held out his hand, "Come, you can ride with me." Jill crawled between the fence slats and placed one foot in the stirrup. Luis reached for her hand and pulled her swiftly into the saddle. He inched forward as she squeezed tightly against him.

"Meet Hurricane," Luis said.

"Don't I get my own horse?"

"Next time. I don't want you to get saddle sore. You are a gringa after all."

She tried to pinch him on his leg, but his jeans were too tight. He laughed and used the end of the reins to gently slap her leg. "Whoa, Gringa, you cannot hurt the teacher. Who will teach your daughter to ride?" He laughed, riding closer to Luisa as she pulled on the reins to turn her horse. When they had seen Luisa handling her horse, Luis took them away from the track and down a path away from the stable just out of sight of Andy and Luisa. He pulled up the reins on his horse, stopping in the thickness of jungle hibiscus. Luis was sweaty from his morning workout. He turned half-way around in the saddle. His wet shirt pressed against her, as he kissed her. He smelled of sweat, the body odor of the shed. She hugged him closely and prolonged his kiss.

"Buenos Dias, Gringa. Did you sleep well?" He chuckled mischievously.

"It wasn't the anisette, was it? And how did I get in my bed? And who put my nightgown on? Where did it come from?"

"Too many questions. You slept well? You look rested. I've said nothing to Luisa. I thought that would be your first question."

"Maybe together?"

"Perhaps. This saddle doesn't bother you?" his eyes sparkled and danced.

"Ah, yes, I must develop those Luis sex 'calluses' all over again. These flowers are the orchids they use to make the leis."

The private grove of jungle foliage was thick with bright reds and yellows, so perfect that they seemed artificial. Jill did not recognize any of the drooping green bushes and spindly tropical trees except the palms. Some looked delicate and others smelled sweet and delicious like all the lotions she bought to soften her skin.

"Orchids. Here," he plucked one from the tree and she put it behind her ear, "and another one for Señorita Ochoa. She'll want to look like her mother."

"But dressed like her father."

He smiled, "The size was just right."

They rode the short distance back to the stables. Luis grabbed the reins from Luisa and led her horse back to the stalls where two Chinese boys worked cleaning and freshening the straw in the individual pens. Luis jumped down from his horse, turning the reins over to the stable boy and then helped Jill down. He walked to Luisa who talked non-stop starting each sentence with "And then Mom."

They returned to the guest house in their golf carts. Luis told them of his schedule for the day. He had to shower and change, but he would take them to the beach, a short walk to snack stands and beach stores. He excused himself from the beach outing explaining he and Andy had to go somewhere, but would return later in the afternoon to pick them up.

ૐ

Jill looked in the full-length mirror at her shape in the tiny bikini. "M-m, passable." She patted her round tummy, the kangaroo pooch from carrying Luisa. Hector had called it that and loved patting her constantly; reminding her he was going to fill it with more babies. Oh god, it must be Andy triggering all these memories. She reached for her lace cover jacket. It would protect her until she lay in the sun; eyes closed, soaking up the warmth and ocean mist on the beach. Hawaii. It seemed like a dream and she feared waking up and being back with Jack at the farm.

Luis stood in the doorway watching her as she put things in a beach bag of "things to do." She had a book, *The Confessions of Nat Turner* that she'd wanted to read in preparation for her students, suntan oil and a tube of nose cover for Luisa, a small bag of change and her driver's license.

"You're going to a public beach in that?"

She looked in the mirror again. "I don't look good enough for the public beach?"

"Come here, Gringa."

She walked to where he stood. He closed the door behind him and braced it closed with his heel and kissed her, sliding his hand down her back. The bikini came off easily as he sucked on her breasts and rubbed between her legs. He laid her on the thick Oriental carpeting his feet pressed against the door. He separated her legs and was in her. She managed to whisper, "Luisa?"

"She's with Andy. We have a few minutes. I want you now, Gringa."

"Little Lou, what about this? You can blow it up and float, but your mom will have to hold onto you. We can't have you floating out to sea."

Andy and Luisa rummaged through a walk-in beach toy closet. It resembled a store at the beach -surf boards, fold-up chairs, umbrellas, plastic buckets, small shovels, air mattresses, inner tubes, boogie boards of Styrofoam, snorkeling masks, life jackets in various sizes, tanks for scuba diving, air pumps for the many inflatable toys and rafts.

"Yes, bring two, then Mom and I can float together. Andy why do you keep calling me Little Lou?"

"Because you look just like Lou."

"Lou?"

"You know, your father."

"My father's name is Jack!"

"Your father is upstairs with your mom, and his name is not Jack."

"My father is in Indiana and his name is Jack. Quit saying Papa is…"

"See you said it yourself. Papa, you call him. I call him Lou and you're Little Lou…Now what else?" Andy turned back to sorting through beach toys. "Let's take the boogie board. I'll give you a quick lesson." He talked to an empty space. Luisa had rushed out of the "beach store" and was heading toward the house. Andy ran to the door and called after her."Hey! Little Lou! We got to load this stuff into the jeep. Come back here." But Luisa ignored him racing to the mansion.

Luis took her swiftly. She trembled from her shoulders to her toes. He shook his head and smiled as she clamped her legs around his back. "No time." He slapped her butt, "We must go. Our time is up. Change the look on your face. Andy will know what you've done."

"Okay, I'll pull myself back together, but I think it's what *you* did. How did I get up here last night and dressed in that strange silk gown? Nothing I packed."

"Chinese tea. And dressing you was primo, almost as good as undressing you. Now we really have to go."

"Chinese tea? Primo?"

"Si. Special herbs to help you relax and sleep. Primo? Outstanding." He pulled her to her feet and she retied the strings on the bikini and put the cover-up on while she walked to the bathroom. Luis had just finished buckling his belt when Luisa burst into the room.

She glared at Luis stopping long enough to say, "Who are you?" and ran past him into the bathroom. "Mom, my father is Jack, right? Andy said that man," and she pointed at Luis, "Papa, is my father. He's not my father! Jack is my father! Oh, Mommy."

She started to cry, and Jill bent down to hug her. Luis walked to the bathroom door. Jill squeezed Luisa to her and sat down on the toilet holding her daughter on her lap, soothing her, patting her, hugging her.

"Jill…" Luis said.

"Get out of here!"

"Jill, stop," Luis walked in and sat down on a lacquered chest used to store dry towels and wash cloths. "I'm not leaving here. Luisa…"

"Mom, Jack is my daddy…" Luisa burrowed closer to Jill's chest, pressing hard on Jill's breasts and covering half of her face on the lace coverlet.

Luis flinched, then spoke, "No…" Two letters "n" and "o" resonated as if thunder had clapped. No.No.No.No.

Jill stared. Luis stared back at her. Jill kissed the top of Luisa's head. "No Luis, not…"

He slowly shook his head.

"Angel," Jill whispered to Luisa. Oh god, he was going to do this and now, right now. Luis sat barely moving his hands on his thighs. Luisa was warm against Jill's skin, too warm as the sweat sealed them. Luisa's tears dripped with the moisture in the humid air and perspiration. Jill closed her eyes. God, help us, then she said, "Lo, Jack is…"

"I am your father, Luisa." The air jelled.

Jill pinched her lips together.

"Mommy…" Luisa squeezed her tighter and moved, pressing harder on Jill. Jill pulled a tissue from a wood lacquered box sitting on the toilet's tank. She wiped Luisa's tears.

"Angel, Luis," Jill paused as Luisa looked up; the mahogany eyes begged. The tears filled her black lashes. "…is…your father. Now she knows Luis." Jill looked from daughter to father. "May I please be alone with her? You should go talk to that out of line Andy Marshall!"

He rose and stood beside mother and daughter. He patted Luisa's long loose hair. Luisa watched him with an arm tightly clasped around Jill. He reached over and pried her loose. Luisa's chest heaved reflexively. Luis wedged his arm around her small frame. Luisa released her hold on her mother, then Luis lifted her into his arms and carried her to the bed. They sat quietly; his large arms encircled her while he stroked her tiny shoulders. She trembled as a baby rabbit separated from its mother.

Slowly Luisa's breathing normalized. Jill walked to the doorway of the bathroom, staring at the interlocking silence of father and daughter like a human zipper, teeth fitting neatly with each breath loop. She recognized the healing of hurt; Henry had held her many times in this same protective way, the strength of reassurance. Henry's presence made so much of her life possible; no one could hurt her as long as Henry held her.

"Luisa, your mother and I met each other ten years ago when I worked not far from your farm. She was eighteen and worked as a teacher, she told you this. We met, but we could not be married. She went to college and I…"

The door to the bedroom was wide open, but Andy Marshall knocked before speaking, "Lou, we have to be on the other side of this island shortly."

"Si," Luis stood abruptly, but continued to hold Luisa in his arms.

Andy looked at Luisa, "Let's go Little Lou." He held out his hand.

Luis shot a direct look at Andy, "Luisa!"

Andy jumped back, holding up two hands, "Yes, boss."

"Luis," Jill said walking into the bedroom, "maybe we should stay here…"

"No, Mommy," Luisa squirmed in Luis's arms. He set her down and she walked to Jill. "I want to go to the beach."

"Andy, take Luisa to the jeep; we will be down in a moment."

Andy grabbed the beach bag Jill had left by the door, "Come, lit...Luisa. I'll show you what I found."

Luis stood at the door, closing it after they left, then turned to face Jill, "Gringa, it was time."

"Maybe. She'll have questions. I have questions."

"Si?"

"Explaining Jack. What do I say? And who will be there when she falls? And what if it's you she wants? What do I say? 'We have to wait until he calls?'"

"My daughter can call me anytime. Any...time. I will be there *if* she falls."

"And Jack?"

"Jack is *your* husband, you can explain that. Now we must go. Maui has wonderful beaches. Come, you'll see their value."

Jill inched toward the door. Luis pulled her next to him, kissing her nose, then hugging her. "Gringa, you don't know Luis Ochoa, but I do. You must trust me."

"Or not."

"Or not?" He gently slapped her butt, "Damn hard-headed Jankee."

Chapter 4

The days' boundaries blended like the shades in a watercolor painting. They rode horses along mountain ridges, the asphalt ended, but the island slopes continued. The turquoise sea crashed on the black volcanic rocks below them. They drove the jeep to waterfalls buried deep in jungles and twisted back and forth on the road to the volcano park. Nineteenth century missionary homes in Lahaina provided the history of the early white settlers and whalers. Jill took pictures and bought postcards for her American History class and one for Marcia Webster. Andy taught Luisa to use a boogie board. Sadie had demanded souvenirs so they bought a crystal pineapple decorated with gold and old framed whaling pictures. Jill knew Sadie would find nooks and alcoves to show off her Hawaiian gifts. A restaurant built over the ocean had the best broiled Ahi. Jill ordered fish at almost every dinner, the freshness and closeness to the ocean made it delicious.

Her mental calendar clicked off Monday, then Friday, then Tuesday each day glorious in and of itself, each one in the house of the rich merchant with his impeccable servant staff. If they left for the day, their clothes were washed, ironed and hung in the closet. The flowers were fresh and when she asked for it, the special tea. Jill woke up in creamy silk gowns that she wanted to keep, but seemed to be part of the house, the bedroom.

Luis appeared familiar with the hospitality. He checked in each morning with a particular older man and in hushed voices they went through the list of needs of the guests. The staff asked for their preferences for breakfast and dinner. Hearing one of these conversations, Luisa spoke up early in their visit.

"Papa, I love shrimp, peeling the shells and dipping them in sauce…"

"Si, I will let them know, young missy wants shrimp." He patted her head and winked.

Luis made the house schedule based on their plans. Jill assumed this was part personal hotel for Luis's friend Kit and his visiting business clients. Luis never said anything about Kit's business or their personal relationship. Jill waited for a moment to ask about what had happened to Luis in Washington, D.C., but it didn't come. She weighed the joy of relaxing in a faraway place, to the turmoil of recollection, and joy won every time. Luis had not mentioned Hector.

Jill and Luisa talked of Jack and Luis. Jill reminded Luisa she had been their flower girl and asked her to recall that day, at least the pictures. "You were my daughter when I met Jack. He adopted you right after we married."

And then an attempt at the biology of where babies come from, how couples have a special relationship to make a baby. "It is what happened between Luis and me."

Luisa listened to all the information, not crying or questioning. Jill thought her acceptance came from an innate communication comfort with Luis. Was biology trumping five years of interaction with Jack? She didn't know, but planned on spending part of the flight home discussing how to go on as if…it would be a long flight. She was proud of her daughter navigating the explanation of the two relationships.

Jill managed to send one postcard of a missionary home to Marcia and one to Sadie, but had written in coded terms not knowing when, if or who would possibly read it.

Dear S.

The time has gone too fast, some people make things very exciting, too exciting. Si? You can go so far and then you step on a land mine, like the volcanoes, you never know when they will erupt.

82

Day 13 ended, but like the Hawaiian horizon, difficult to know where and when. The fourteenth day, Jill now thought, waking up...the day before the end. Alone in the silk gown between the silk sheets, she stretched, staring at the satin tenting that hung in folds over the French doors. Could she make a drape like that over her bedroom window? Oh yeah she needed French doors and a second story veranda. Home. Indiana. Visions of cornfields creeped up on her, no longer days, but hours.

She had not talked of Hector for the entire time, but she'd adjusted to Andy's constant presence, even to his stories of gook-kills and jungle raids, of the CIA and their insistence on using certain Special Forces troops for their deepest, most insane missions. "Insanity" was Andy's constant adjective.

She wove the cloth of the place and time of Hector's death. It looked dark green almost black velvet, invisible, a feeling of wet and fear with silence, but silence that was a noisy nature habitat, sounds for a Puerto Rican from the city that were totally alien. Shrieks and squawks completely incongruous to all he knew. There was breathing, of his platoon, of his best friend, his back-up, but there was also breathing of the enemy. Their breathing was all the same, the human sound of inhaling and exhaling, the fearful intake, impossible to discern from Vietnamese and American, but they were all there, waiting for the slip, the tiny blip that was different than the rest of the chorus. In Mother Nature's stomach, raining, dripping water, they were unable to sneeze or to wipe sweat from their eyebrows and noses, unable to flinch. The salty rivulets dripped onto already moist upper lips, an excruciatingly slow drip as a stalactite in some underground cavern, wet, waiting, rigid, building. Waiting. Then it all happened. No referee blew his whistle, no green flag waved, but they scrambled, and there was death. In the pit of Mother Nature's digestive track, thick black gunk, leaf remains, insects and mud, she took them; the mother reclaiming her children, children no longer whole as they had been on birth dates eighteen, nineteen, twenty years earlier.

The sun now blazed through the sheers of her bedroom. Mother Nature in all her brightness, the morning sun. A new day dawning...Had one shiny ray penetrated where he died?

Luis had taken Luisa for an early morning ride, a ritual on this vacation. Could she stay in bed and not pack, ever? She lay still, knowing the Chinese servant would bring her coffee as soon as she turned or stretched. In the stillness she heard footsteps, heavier than the servants who made scant noise. Her door opened wide. She sat up, "Luis!"

"I left Luisa with Andy," he strode into the room, "at the stables. She wanted to say adios to Gaucho. I wish I could ship that horse to your farm. But she couldn't take care of him, could she?"

"M-m, no, I guess not. 'Oh yeah, Jack, meet Gaucho a gift from Luis Ochoa.'"

He smiled, "Si. And you are still in bed? I thought you had to pack suitcases." He looked at the empty luggage still sitting next to the chair where the servants had placed it. "I told them you wanted the bags..." He pushed her head slightly back and looked at her face, "Are you listening to your Señor Ochoa?"

"Luis, I want to stay in Hawaii."

"Si. Should I make arrangements with Kit? Maybe you can teach the Chinese servants more English."

"No, with you, here, us." She reached and grabbed his wrist that still held a handful of her hair; she eased his hand to her mouth, then kissed his palm.

He pulled his hand from her, "Gringa, Gringa, Gringa...pack your suitcases. I am taking you out tonight. We are going dancing and dining. You will get to dance with your papa. I promised you I would one night at the migrant camp. Andy said 'yes' to playing cards with Luisa, some military game. I forget..."

"War," she said.

"The tango, have you done that?" Luis was strong; he could easily throw her across the floor.

"No, I haven't done the tango, but maybe we should just do..." she touched his flowered-print shirt on his tummy.

He laughed, and then plopped down on the bed, boots and all, he lay next to her. The narrow bed allowed them to lie wedged on their sides. "Do this, Gringa? I cannot have my way with you in this tiny bed. Jack would fit in this bed with you?"

"No," she answered. Luis smirked.

"Gringa, all of our vacations will have a beginning and an end," he used his index finger to outline her face, "It is a complete package. I accept this even though lying next to you is incomparable. Just like this." He hugged her tightly; they almost fit in the bed.

ᴙξᴙ

The thatched roof and torches were Hawaiian, but the band had a Latin flavor and the menu featured a few Spanish bean and rice entrées. They had shared a mai tai and Jill wore the paper umbrella behind her ear. She bought an Hawaiian print sarong and now wore it tightly wrapped around her. When Luis suggested they find a club to go dance, she was suspicious, but he had done exactly that. They left Andy and Luisa in the middle of War with Andy promising to teach her "21" and Luisa asking if they could all live in Hawaii forever. Luis promised he would consult her mother to find out the "parameters" of Luisa's request. And Jill reminded both of them that Luisa needed to go to bed at nine o'clock. Luisa frowned as Jill spoke, "Tomorrow we have a long flight and a time change, so nine will actually be one in the morning. Maybe eight..."

"No, Mom. Papa keep her out dancing."

"I will do my best, Señorita Ochoa." He laughed.

Now the music, rum, candlelight, and cha-cha beat connected like the tiny orchids of her lei. The restaurant had provided leis. Luis relaxed, in the ambience of the music and festivity. He wore his casual drawstring pants and Hawaiian print shirt and for the first time an emerald and onyx ring. He had a gold neck chain that was visible when he twisted during their dancing. Jill had not seen him wear jewelry except the gold band he always wore. Tonight he also had substituted his diving watch for a thin gold watch. There was nothing ostentatious about the jewelry and he wore it comfortably, but she was curious. She always wore the emerald ring he had sent her and her wedding ring from Jack. She hated the diamond Jack had given her for an engagement ring and tossed it in the bottom of her jewelry box soon after they married. He ignored her rant on diamonds and she resented that he hadn't listened to her and bought it anyway.

The dance floor had a few other couples; two celebrated marriages –a young couple's honeymoon and the anniversary celebrants, "twenty-five years," the bandleader announced. The bald-headed husband had no rhythm, but swirled his mumu draped Mrs., laughing and drinking. Jill touched Luis's chest. The curled hairs were moist. She smiled, and spoke, as they danced two steps up, two steps back, cha-cha-cha.

"Luis, I feel like I'm in heaven, but angels don't sweat." She laughed and pushed off his chest, turning her back to him, two steps back, cha-cha-cha.

The music ended. He grabbed her, then threw her backward in a tango-like toss.

"You do this like a professional..." she said. He stood her up, straight. She caught her breath, grasping his shoulders, "Where, Luis?"

He smiled, "In Mar del Plata, Argentina." His eyes danced.

"Don't tell me, Eva Peron?"

"There are many more women than Eva Peron in Argentina."

The dark-haired lead singer, a golden brown muscular man, who wore a flower print wrap-skirt and four leis around his thick neck, started the first chords of the newlywed requests, "You're my soul and my heart's inspiration..."

Luis kept her on the dance floor as the rhythm slowed. He hugged her close and kissed her lightly on the nose. His habit tickled her nose with his moustache. She smiled and squeezed him closer. Luis whispered in her ear, "Te amo." (I love you)

"Si, Señor Ochoa, te deseo." (I want you)

He smiled. "You are beautiful, Gringa."

"It's the mai-tais and island band, you've lost your perspective."

"I thought you were beautiful from your first day at the migrant camp. The sun shone on your hair, it looked like spun gold. An angel, you don't remember?"

"I do, but I didn't think you saw me. You were unloading baskets and yelling at some men with equipment. I thought, 'Who is that?'"

"I caught the maestra in the corner of my eye and said, 'Quien es?" (Who is that)

"'You're my soul and my heart's inspiration, without you baby what good am I?'" the band sang the song's hook.

"Gringa, you are my inspiration. I love you."

"You will have forgotten this in the morning," she said, shaking her head.

"You avoid the expression of love. Say it, 'Te amo.'"

Jill dropped her head. He put one hand under chin, lifting her face. She closed her eyes. He stopped dancing, grabbed her hand, then led her to the back porch of the restaurant. They used the short wood stairway to the beach.

"'You're all I got to get me by....'" the song continued.

Jill cringed, was this like choosing a switch for Grandma Caitlin to whip her with? No, she wasn't five and she hadn't done anything wrong. The feeling was easy enough to say to William, he knew Viet Nam and accepted her loss of Hector. Love for him was better if it didn't involve commitment, as Sadie said, "I tell them both I love them, love is a feeling not a commitment."

But with Luis the feeling of love 'yes,' but she knew he asked more than that. Commitment, why did it seem so scary? She wanted him, to stay with him, to love him. She shook her head. Hector said the same thing that I always used sarcasm to cover my feelings, but I finally made the commitment....

The night was dark and soft like a black kitten's underbelly. The waves broke in small light ripples, the restaurant's torch lights reflected on the water and the band's music rolled through the scene. Heavenly Maui. The sand was in her shoes as they entered the shadows beyond the lights. Luis now released her hand and stepped away from her, walking completely around her. He examined each inch as if buying a slab of beef from the butcher. The sea air mingled with a smoky barbecue odor, a luau. How could anyone not fall in love here? It would be simple. Say it, Gringa, she coaxed herself.

"Gringa, I want to know and I want to know now, this night can last as long as it takes."

"Know what, Luis?" She kicked the sand, then slipped off her sandals.

"This," he paused and measured the air with his arm, "distance you make when it is time to feel with your heart." He walked slowly backward, facing her. She glanced at him, the eyes, those damn green eyes staring, recording her movements.

"I could ask the same of you," she stopped, putting her hands on her hips, the shoes rested on her skirt.

"Si, but they don't work in opposition with me. I feel intensely, and for you...it has not stopped in ten years. From the time we sat on bushel baskets in the rain, I knew what I felt. You remember?"

She nodded.

He continued, "And how did you feel?"

"Scared, but drawn, like a moth to the fire," she answered slowly.

"Love?" He raised an eyebrow.

"I didn't know you." She stared at her toes; the sand was cool. She touched his tummy.

"Now?"

"Do I now? It is no different," she said. He kept his eyes on her face.

"It is another hurdle. But your entire body responds to me from your eyes to your breasts," he took his index finger and made a figure eight, circling one breast, then the other. He traced the space between her breasts to her navel, stopping at her crotch. "Your body does not hide from Luis Ochoa, I feel it with this," he extended his index fingers to her lips. "All of it," he quickly slid from her mouth to her hips, "all of it, responds to your Papito. Say it. Tell me what you feel."

She stared at him silently, but the noisy chatter of... "I want to stay with you in Hawaii...I...Luis..." she looked at the ocean.

Like lightning he quickly backed away from her, "It's that man!" he yelled, "I've waited fourteen days for your long story, but you are silent, you now turn away. Tell me."

"What man?"

"Hector Andujar! Special Forces, 1963. Laos. Killed in Action. An action that no one knew about, not even you. You were told Pleiku, Viet Nam. All of you. Always Pleiku, a lie by your United States government, but it wasn't there. He ... he is standing here in this space and when we are naked our skin pressed," he forced his hands together, palm-to-palm, "skin-to-skin, he squeezes in this space, squeezes between us!"

Jill turned away from him and walked toward the ocean. The water swirled around her toes, then her shins. She stepped deeper. The waves rushed from under her heels, the balls of her feet, and toes, creating a depression where the bottom of the sea had been flat. The water drenched her hemline; a wave smacked her stomach soaking her whole dress. She stood still, but the water pushed her chest.

Special Forces 1963. Hector Andujar. Special Forces. Killed in Action, Pleiku, 1963. She had read the notice at the apartment in New York. The Secretary of the Army...Killed in Action.

And the sea crushed and pulled her, soaking her again and again. The rum and angered green eyes ripped open the wound. Seven years reduced to yesterday, to now. And she walked further, deeper into wet blackness. The waves splashed her face and left salty residue that mixed with her tears. Her hair tips now drenched in the water, the paper umbrella fell out and drifted aimlessly until the ocean swallowed it. Her leis floated on the surface. The salty warmth bathed her, pulling and pushing as the waves came and rolled back out. Some came over her face. To swim or to walk or to drop to her knees and let the Pacific take her? She stopped and the Pacific Ocean held her.

Slowly the water became the water; there was no water in her felt picture. She turned her back to the blackness and stumbled toward the beach and the light of the torches. Luis stood still, away from the breaking waves. When the water circled her waist, she turned and stared out at the inkiness of merged sea and sky. The moon shone slightly on the water, a half moon. She laid her arms on the undulating surface, palms up. "God help me." She had tried at Arlington Cemetery, looking at the rows and rows of white marble headstones, but couldn't acknowledge that the earth housed *his* body. Now she stood in the ocean that connected her to the South China Sea to the country where he last felt life. She whispered across the sea, across time, "Goodbye, Hector Andujar."

One foot in front of the other her dress dripping, her lips salty, the ocean pulling at her ankles, she ran and increased her pace, reaching Luis as he walked along the beach. "Luis," she reached for his hand. They walked along the beach, not speaking. The band's music glided in tandem with the breeze. She shivered in her wet clothes. Luis put his arm around her.

"Luis, you left me in Caylor. I thought I would never see you again. You said I couldn't go with you; we had our own roads to travel. I had my daughter. She was your daughter and I named her after you. She was my only connection to you. Hector stopped seeing me when I told him her name." She shook her head

He hugged her, "Jill, I am sorry for this pain. I know it is your long story, but you may stop."

"No, I want to say it, so I don't have to say it again, and you will know. My heart was broken: no you, no Hector, gone because of you, a phantom in my life. Then he came back. Hector supported me, loved me, wanted me, and we made plans to marry, but there was Viet Nam. So many things all fighting what *I* wanted. I am not a fortune teller. I did not know you were in my future. I don't know now that I will ever see you again when we leave Hawaii. Love?" She paused, thinking of the answer to that question, "I'm thousands of miles from my home and my husband, I said 'yes' when you asked me to marry you, isn't that enough?"

He stared, holding her face in his hands, "No Gringa, it is not enough."

Jill met his eyes, looked down, looked at him, then looked away. She took a deep breath, "I love you, Luis," and with the release of air and emotion she sank in his arms, more than a feeling, a commitment.

He squeezed her, "I know, Gringa."

The ocean whispered on the cool sand. The constant breeze dried her hair as he rested his cheek against her limp curls.

"I promised *our* daughter," Luis spoke slightly louder than the sea, "I would talk to you of living happily ever after in this tropical paradise. She has blossomed in the islands. Horses? I can see that our next vacation must include horseback riding. But you know, Gringa, to stop our lives and stay here is impossible. My business and my government demand my presence all over the world. You say, 'Who are you Luis Ochoa?' That *is* who I am. A salesman, a farmer, an emissary for the president of Colombia and the National Coffee Federation, and like my friend Kit, I, too, am busy making money."

They sat down finding smooth stones among the black jagged rocks. The water endlessly rinsed the tiny holes of the lava, depositing sand.

"Luis, we have a saying, 'all work and no play makes for a dull man.'"

"Si. Are you saying I'm dull?"

"No, I'm saying you must do other things than work all the time."

"Other things?" He lifted one eyebrow.

"To relax. Sitting here at the beach, listening to the water, you are relaxed. You lie in bed and smoke a cigar and talk. You are relaxed."

"Si. Do I do these things in Colombia?"

"Who do you lay in bed with while you smoke your cigar?"

"In Hawaii, with my gringa."

"No, when you are in Colombia?"

"When you come to Colombia, I'll relax with you and have my absinthe on ice."

"Let's go!" Jill stood and jumped from their perch on the rocks. "I'm tired of this. I'd rather play War with Luisa; I have a half a chance of winning." Jill reached the flat sand surface and quickly walked toward the lights of the restaurant. He ran up behind her, then yanked her all the way around.

"Carmen!" he yelled, "Is that what you want? Cecilia! Is that better? Christina! You want more? Juanita! Milagros! Guadalupe!

90

Socorro! Esperanza! Marie Elena! Constanza! Dolores! Sophia!" His face flushed as the names rushed out, sizzling in the black night like bacon in an iron skillet, "And the ones with no names! The cunts! I fucked them because they were there!" His nostrils flared, his neck veins were visible. He turned away from her, then faced her, kicking sand, opening his hands, clenching his fists, reaching toward her, then abruptly reversing his movement. He stopped. His shirt clung to his broad back in sweat saturated swatches. The cotton rolled with his breathing. He half-turned, the breeze caught the wet shirt, ballooning the front and tail.

The women. There they were, names and more names. How long did that cover? The last six months or the last ten years? She curled her toes into the sand. He passed close to her; she reached for his arm, but caught his sleeve, then spoke, "And only *one* daughter?"

He stopped and looked directly in her face not speaking. The ocean came within inches of their feet. She slid her hand down his arm to his hand. He squeezed tightly…"One daughter." He paused, then in a breathy voice spoke, "One son."

He looked down at the sand, then at her eyes, the intensity locked onto her like a cat stalking a bird. "Two," he inhaled deliberately, then slowly exhaled, "…women. Lourdes and Jill." He wrapped his arms around her and squeezed her in a hug that crushed her into his chest. He released her gradually from his embrace.

"Absinthe and ice, Señor Ochoa?"

"No, absinthe is illegal in the United States. I have something else I want you to try in the jeep, Primo."

Luis paid the bill and they walked holding hands, looking disheveled in partially drying clothes sugar-coated with beach sand. Jill carried her shoes and small purse in one hand; her lei slightly tattered still hung around her neck.

"Mrs. Jones, I would like to take you dancing again, another night, another place, another country?"

"We look like we did the *last* tango," Jill said, then laughed. He shook his head and laughed with her.

They eased into the jeep and Luis reached under the driver's seat pulling out a small wood box. He handed it to her. It was completely smooth on all sides with a small inlaid design of the same yin-yang as Andy Marshall's medallion. The design was fashioned in onyx and mother-of-pearl. It appeared to have no means of opening, only seamless sides, bottom and top.

"Gringa, have you ever smoked cigarettes?"

"Sadie and I tried them and she ended up smoking them for a year or two, but I only shared with her when she made me."

"Well, open the box."

She struggled trying to figure out how to do it, "Right. This is a trick."

"Slide the side," and she did as instructed and a small sliver came out of the box then the lid lifted off revealing two rows of perfectly rolled cigarettes. "Take one out, Gringa." He smiled at her halting moves, "Smell it, Gringa." She sniffed it, turning up her nose at the new scent. "Primo," he said.

"Primo? You said that was the name of my Chinese tea?"

"No, dressing you in a silk nightgown was outstanding. So too, this. Now these cigarettes are smoked slightly different than regular cigarettes. When you inhale, you hold your breath, you'll want to cough and cough. Try not to. But we have plenty of cigarettes; you should be able to figure this out. Oh, one more instruction, reach under your seat and get the bottle of tequila it will help you not to cough."

She did as he told her. He stopped the jeep to light the joint. He took a long puff and handed her the cigarette. She inhaled then suppressed a cough.

"Breathe in. Don't cough. Take another breath."

Her lungs burnt and felt as if they would burst, then she coughed and coughed. He took the joint from her, "Drink the tequila!" She sipped the clear liquid. It burned all the way to her stomach and she turned up her nose, pursed her lip, then wiped tears from her eyes.

"Luis, are you trying to poison me?" she gasped still trying to catch her breath from coughing.

"No, no, Gringa. Here try this again."

"Again?! Tell my daughter I loved her until the end."

He laughed, "I will let her know. Now take another hit..."

Her second attempt was better and she needed only a small sip of the tequila. By the time they reached the plantation house, they had finished the joint. And the marijuana relaxed her. She laughed and tried not to, but could not stop. Luis laughed with her. They pulled into the front driveway. Luis took the box, but left the tequila.

"Primo, primo, primo, like cream o' ....wheato?" Jill giggled hysterically at her rhyming.

"No, not cream of wheat. But we must talk quietly so the Chinese servants won't know we're here. Catch your breath, Gringa."

She put her finger to her mouth, "Shish-shish, no Chinese," and giggled, "Shish-shish, no Chinese, no-no, shu-shee, Japanese." She burst out laughing. He reached around her face and kept her in a loose hammer-lock covering her mouth. She put her hands on his forearm, yanking, trying to uncover her mouth. He shook his head; she tried to nod in the squirming. He released her and she whispered, "Primo, primo, primo, I feel magnifico, co-co," biting her lips, holding her mouth tightly closed in an attempt to control her laugh. Luis shook his head. She put her index finger over her mouth and used her other hand to cross her heart, then held up three fingers as in the Girl Scout pledge.

Luis spoke in her ear, "You are no Señor Frost." He smiled, shaking his head.

She grabbed his arm, stood perfectly still and recited.

"A dented spider like a snowdrop white
"On a white Heal-all,"

She hesitated and shrugged. He encouraged her to continue. He crossed his arms on his chest and listened.

"holding up a moth
"Like a white piece of lifeless satin cloth –
"Saw ever curious eye so strange a sight?"

Again she paused and dramatically cocked her head as if addressing an audience with the question,

"The blue Brunella every child's delight?
"What brought the kindred spider to that height?"

Raising her hand to emphasize the height and twisted her mouth as if asking herself this question, and then continued,

"(Make we no thesis of the miller's plight.)"

As she started the next line, Luis spoke with her,

"What but design of darkness and of night?

"Design, design! Do I use the word aright?" She held both arms out with her palms up.

"Gringa, you use Señor Frost very well. 'In White.' He sent that version to a friend. Very good, yes design, it is all about the details."

"Design, design, I have designs on Señor Ochoa, no the details, sir, I have details." She reached and grabbed his crotch. He smiled and held her hand, forcing her to rub the front of his body. He said, "Design, design, you use your hand aright?"

"Si," she answered, and giggled. She untied his drawstring pants. They loosened and she reached inside them. He removed her arm, retied his pants and pulled her up the front porch steps.

"What Señor Ochoa, you can't take your own medicine," and she let out a muted laugh, then said, "Shish-shish, no Chinese."

They eased through the French doors into his bedroom. He closed the doors behind them and turned on the light closest to his bed. The Chinese lantern design created a golden glow, then he went to the heavy teak door leading to the hallway and bolted it with the lock that went into the door jamb and floor. The servants understood the secure lock. They would not knock or initiate any service until he unlocked it. Jill followed him, throwing her purse toward a chair. She untied the side bow of her wrap-around sarong. Luis opened the wood box and lit another joint. He held it out for her. She sucked in the burning irritating smoke and took a follow-up gulp of air. He poured her some water from a silver pitcher on the coffee table.

"Here," he said, "cold water; it is better than the tequila."

She drank the full glass hardly stopping for air. He slid open the doors on a massive hutch. Inside were a turntable and an extensive record collection. He selected a jazz album by Grant Green, "Carryin' On." The music was soothing. She unfastened her strapless bra and tossed it toward a chair. She left on her panties. Her lei covered her nipples as she did a hula move to the jazz beat. She yanked on Luis's pants which fell easily from his hips. She unbuttoned his shirt, fingering his gold chain, the yin-yang again only in brushed gold. She used her lei to brush his chest hairs. She twisted as the charmed cobra emerging from his basket, then she squatted in front of him burying her face in his crotch. He laced his fingers through her hair rhythmically pushing her head. She shook loose from his grasp, and stood up, pulling him to the bed.

94

"Come," she spoke, then laughed, "come, what a word, come, is it spelled differently? K-U-M...come...I want to have my way with you."

ʏξʏ

Luis had patted her until she had fallen asleep rubbing her as she lay in the crook of his arm. He had dressed her with a gown from his chest of drawers, her body as limp as a ragdoll. He had turned out the light, unlocked the door, and stealthily carried her to bed. Luisa slept soundly, but the Chinese servants had not heard him, or if so had not acknowledged his movements. Returning to his room, he had locked the door and called David. Luis explained that the primo deal was completed and instructed his son to arrange a shipping date, docking in Seattle. David had assured him the last bags of green beans were in his warehouse in Buenaventura ready for roasting. They would be shipped to New Orleans before his return. "Papa, Abedi called, they're meeting in Abu Dhabi next month. He said all the attorneys will meet two days before the principals to complete the bank charter."

"You called Rome..."

"Mr. Angotti said he would meet with you there and you can fly together ahead of the meeting."

"David, if Jill and Luisa need to come..."

"Yes, Papa, when you make that decision, I have them learning English, now, and I have been looking for a safe location for the orphanage."

"Si, adios."

Now he sat on the edge of the bed and opened the nightstand, removing a cigar box and then behind it his .44 caliber gun. He lit the cigar and checked the gun's cartridges. Click, there was a bullet, click, yes, click all the chambers were full. Holding the safety latch open, he absently spun the cold chamber, the death messenger. The darkened room invited his descent into the tunnel of termination, a slide he prevented in his women's presence. But they slept, and his mind refused to embrace Morpheus. Goddamned marijuana, I know better. It had been fifteen years, but a few puffs of hemp and it came back, not came, rushed like some goddamned tsunami. She always wants to know who, would she ever understand? Maybe one day, but not this day; I have hurt her enough already.

Laredo, Texas; Veracruz, Monterrey, like the train…click, click, clickety-clack, don't look back. A goddamned nursery rhyme. How do you stop a train? The silver bullet. Click, click, clickety-clack, clickety-clack, don't look back, he had repeated it over and over again, but it didn't stop, it was dark then…the night silence broken by the whistle and the clickety-clack, steel on steel, silver in blackness, a small bullet in a black chamber…

In the early afternoon as the train from Mexico City pulled into the Veracruz station, Luis stood on the platform waiting. The afternoon was warm, only fourteen hours since Luis had left the hacienda. Luis felt the bull strength in their embrace, the feeling of hugging oneself. Luis bent to retrieve his uncle's suitcase. Had they found Manuel's body? Rebecca would be crying, angry because Luis would return to discover his best friend's death. Luis saw them all as he spoke to Ramos, "Welcome back, Compa. (buddy) Rebecca said to keep you here for a couple of days, let you enjoy yourself in case the news was bad."

"Ah, it is time to celebrate not cry mi hijo.(my son) *Our* bananas will fill the boats in the harbor and head for America. Rebecca is right, though, two days in the city will be good. I want some rat poison, tequila at Margarita's and maybe some Margarita, too." He laughed, then started to cough. He coughed and spit loudly. He reached into his pocket and pulled out two cigars.

ᴦξᴦ

Luis had met Manuel when they had harvested cane, competing for stalks and plots. Manuel was short, feisty, steady, ready to fight. He had a bushy moustache and scars everywhere, the souvenirs from his battles with people and the land. He stood like an ironwood tree – gnarled and disfigured, but tough, the layers of scars like bark; his body told a story. Luis had had to beat him down on their first encounter, working rows at the cane harvest. Manuel had missed Luis's arm by a fraction of an inch on one swipe of Manuel's machete. Luis viewed it as a deliberate assault because so many of the laborers hated him. They had drawn blood, swollen eyes and bruised faces, but their friendship had begun.

Manuel and Luis talked as much as two laconic men talk. They smoked Ramos's cigars, shared many liters of tequila and competed in the fields like members of the same team. Manuel talked of his past in

96

pieces. He began to paint the picture of the United States that Luis would eventually buy – a land of opportunity, "lots of money in those United States." Manuel had explained the Bracero Program, that Mexican workers were well received. Manuel gave Luis the names of people and places. They dreamed aloud of the desire to leave, but as time and liquor worked on them, Manuel told Luis of his inability to go anywhere near the U.S. It was the goal for the two of them, but Manuel drunkenly confessed that he had killed a man at one U.S. job site, "another bracero." Manuel had run as far as he could, ending up with Ramos. Manuel had also left the U.S. silently in the night, hitching a train ride south. Luis had listened carefully to Manuel, taking mental notes of how to find work, the details of leaving swiftly, discreetly.

Luis waited until the right moment, and the clickety-clack, clickety-clack; twenty-four hours from one death to the next, the unstoppable train, silver in the blackness.

Luis now twisted the barrel, releasing the ammunition chamber from the pistol, then flipping it back. He held the small safety and spun the rounds. All six chambers carried a silver bullet, click-click, click-click, click-click, faster, click-click-click almost the clickety-clack.

Manuel was Robert Frost's "Silas, The hired man…nothing to look backward to with pride, and nothing to look forward to with hope, so now and never any different." And in the end, as Silas, Manuel was "dead." Maybe he was dead before he came to Ramos's.

First, it had been Manuel. Luis had spent too many drunken conversations with him. Maybe Luis had said something, then forgotten it in his own alcoholic numbness. It was Wednesday, June 16, 1954 at 10P.M., the very moment before he was scheduled to leave for the drive to Veracruz to pick up Ramos. Luis put a pillow over Manuel's face. Manuel was too drunk to fight and died a calm painless death. Luis had then left, taking all his belongings that would fit in one suitcase. He jumped in the truck and headed for the city. Ramos was returning from Mexico City. He had sought a political favor to guarantee that the bananas growing on his plantation shipped to the United States for the best price. The competition was stiff in Mexico City, but Ramos Ochoa had influence in many circles where those decisions were made.

Rebecca made Luis pick up her husband. She told Luis he was the only person who could control the radical, violent Ramos.

"I brought a change of clothes," Luis spoke to the uncle as they made their way toward the truck, "I figured you were ready to visit a few of the putas." (whores) Luis paused as the uncle held the match to light his cigar.

"You know me mi hijo. Tequila and chochito,(pussy) they make the world go 'round."

When Ramos said, my son, Luis clenched his fist; he was not this man's son. Luis hated this man more than anyone he had ever met. It revolted him that he looked just like his uncle, even the shape of their square thick hands. Luis wished sometimes he could rip off his own face, so he would no longer resemble this evil person. Each tortured day with Ramos became worse than the day before. The hacienda had become a living hell. The uncle reviled all that was good and decent. He murdered men for no reason. He beat workers to perform better. Bending over in the cane field, planting rantoon for ten hours, twelve hours, fourteen hours; it was never enough.

Luis was from the line of conquistadores, proud Spaniards who led their country at the request of the King, royal blood. The labor of Ramos's hacienda disgraced the Ochoa name. There was no compassion. Luis hated his inability to stop Ramos. Ramos constantly cajoled his nephew into imitating his behavior. Luis fought many fights, occasionally with machetes over a bottle of tequila because he was the "son." Luis had no interest in beating a person just because he could. Ramos had perfected anger. He dared people to stand up to him and when they were ready to burst with rage, the bully with the power to kill them, did. Luis was a prisoner, marking time, and he had vowed to kill the devil who was his jailor.

Margarita's Cantina was lit with bare low wattage bulbs hanging from dangling wires. It smelled of stale smoke, urine, musty water and beer. Men relieved themselves in the corners and on the outside walls. From these bars, Ramos recruited men who were desperate, out of work and had nowhere to go but a dirt pit bar. It was a place like Margarita's where Ramos picked up Manuel, literally had thrown him into the back of the truck. Manuel had passed out and Ramos paid the bill for the alcohol and drove the drunken man to the hacienda. Luis now thought of Manuel's lifeless form under the sheet of his bed. Devoid of life. Manuel had no life even when breathing. He existed to use a machete, to stir cooking cane, a human machine.

Ramos liked the poor women that hung around the doors, the poorest of whores who waited for someone to buy them a drink or to buy them. Ramos insisted that young barely pubescent girls be made available to him. They could not be more than twelve or thirteen years old, but Ramos's money bought him someone's younger sister for the right price. He liked the older whores, but only to perform oral sex as he drank. The dirt-floored cantinas provided the freedom for his gutter performances. Luis now sat in the front row seat of Ramos's last show. Ramos followed a script of disgusting scenes each more despicable than the last.

"Luis, you want a puta to suck you? It goes just right with the rat poison. Vamos a culiar!" (Let's go fuck) Ramos spoke to a dark-haired wide-eyed girl who had just been brought in by her brother. She wore no shoes and a dress, a size too big, decorated with red, brown and black flowers on the skirt, not a little girl dress. She had painted dark lines on her upper and lower eyelids; her lipstick was dark red as if she sneaked into her mother's cosmetics. She nodded hesitatingly. Puta, a terrible epithet for the child. Luis gave her several pesos and said, "Vete! Andole vete!" (Go, get out)

Ramos stared at his nephew. "What? You sent my amusement away?"

"Later, Compa, later. Use the other one," Luis spoke, pointing to a woman who leaned from another table toward the man with the money.

Ramos signaled the woman to come over to his table. She was heavily made up with bright red painted cheeks and long dark hair twisted with some red and yellow ribbon. Her dress hung loose, exposing the top half of her breasts. She, too, was barefoot. Thick lines surrounded her black eyes. Brass bangle bracelets clinked on her dark arms. Her scarlet nails were chipped. She smiled at Ramos's invitation, exposing a toothless grin. Ramos laughed and coaxed her to smile again.

"Mi hijo look at the mouth, built for the pinga."(dick) Ramos laughed and gestured for the woman to get on her knees as he unbuttoned his fly. Letting his penis hang outside. Ramos reached from a stack of pesos on the table and pushed them one at a time into space between her breasts and her dress. He spread his legs and leaned back in his chair, chugging a glass full of tequila. He pointed to his penis and opened his mouth wide to show the woman. He pulled her close to his crotch and pushed her head as she took his penis in her mouth.

Luis smoked a cigar and drank absinthe, the extract from wormwood. He watched the smoke rings dissolve into the foggy light of more smoke, but he listened to Ramos grunting in his drunken speech and turned the page of the script with him. Luis knew when Ramos had reached the right page; his cue and so he waited. Ramos entered the last scene in the bête noir. He would become irrational, ready to throw chairs, take punches, rage, the Ochoa temper. Hector Ochoa had always controlled it, but Ramos Ochoa championed and relished the anger. Ramos's actions defined this moment as if he read his own script.

Ramos stood, pulling his penis from the woman's mouth, then said, "Bitch, you ever been pissed on. Show me your titties! I must piss!" The woman slowly pulled her dress exposing her nipples; some of the pesos fell to the ground. She went to reach for them, but Ramos grabbed her hair, and yelled, "Sit, show me those tittties, bitch!" She held each side of her dress in her hands.

"Yeah that's a good bitch..." Ramos spoke, and relieved himself, splashing her face, the breasts, the money. His intoxication made it impossible for him to aim. Some of the men who had been watching now came towards the Ochoas. They cursed the pig. Finally, Ramos started his rage, grabbing the table and dumping it. He retrieved the bottle of tequila before it slid from the table. The woman quickly scooted under another table.

Luis in one deft move reached under his uncle's chin and pulled him by the head out of the bar. When they reached the truck, Luis threw him onto the seat and grabbed the tequila bottle slinging it toward the ground. He jumped into the driver's seat. Ramos slurred, "Where are we going? I was starting..."

"Shut up Ramos!"

"Shut up? Do you know who you are talking to?"

"A fucking drunk!" Luis shouted at the uncle for the first time in five years.

"I can play fucking drunk! Is that what you want? To play with an old man, mi hijo?"

"I'm not your son and I have nothing to say to a drunken bastard!"

"A bastard? You son of a whore! Did your old man tell you that?"

"Shut up Ramos! Before I kill you!"

"No, he didn't tell you your mama worked in a dirt cantina, just like that one," Ramos made a limp undirected gesture with his hand, "that I pissed on her just like that fucking slut. No. Your old man felt sorry for her and dragged her to that damn coffee farm."

Luis clenched the steering wheel on the truck. He had never known his mother; never seen her, his father had said she died when Luis was born, their only child. Luis heaved slowly; he felt the heat, the charge like a river of fire, filling every part of him. His hands burned with the grip of the wheel.

"The slut, a quarterone," Ramos continued, "couldn't take the country life," he slurred and driveled as he talked, taking a swipe at his leaking chin. "She left you and your old man...the most exquisite white-negra flesh...one-eighth, as if that drop....like gold brandy in firelight, Magdalena...She stole a mule...back to Caracas where she could make more money as a whore, a common slut for a mama and you end up looking like me..." his last words were garbled, then he nodded off to sleep. His head hit the side window.

A common slut for a mama, Magdalena, she had a name, a common slut, rode a mule. Luis drove away from town into a thick overgrowth. He followed the dirt road he had carefully chosen at dawn when he had arrived in Veracruz. Luis inched the truck deep into the overarching bushes. The jungle brush closed in around the truck, slapping at the windshield and doors. Luis buried the vehicle into the tangle.

Now invisible from the dirt road, he turned off the ignition, reached under the seat, and then removed the .44 revolver that Ramos preferred when killing his victims. Luis whispered in his uncle's ear, "Ramos, you evil bastard, I have no time. I am a busy man," He repeated it slowly, "I...am...a...busy...man." He pulled Ramos' eyelids open and stared at the green that was his green. Luis held them open for a second, then let the man's head flop on his chest. Luis put the gun to Ramos's temple and pulled the trigger once, then once again. "For you and for all those you killed. You may now piss on the devil." Luis crossed himself.

Luis emptied Ramos's pockets, taking all of his money, and jumped out of the truck. He grabbed his suitcase and flung the keys and gun into the bushes. He headed toward the main road, turning around for one last look back at the sarcophagus of the devil. The pitch black jungle was still, having consumed the truck and the dead.

When the sun rose, Luis boarded the train heading north to Monterrey miles away from Veracruz out of his Mexican Hell. Clickety-clack, the rhythmic swaying of the coach sliding on steel rails. He had killed two men in twenty-four hours. He tried to judge his behavior in terms of Papa Ochoa. His father had been a gentle man, spending his life with his campesinos, the peasant laborers. It had been the system, but Papa Ochoa lived in a time of divisions. Divisions between workers and landowners, conservatives and liberals, coffee growers and city dwellers, but in all the separations he had bridged the two.

Mamacita's husband was attacked by bandits as he returned back from the city to his hacienda. His injury left him unable to work or think clearly. She was a young mother and there was Papa Ochoa, resourceful, quiet as the earth he walked, dependable, responsible. He took over the running of the big place in the mountains. The campesinos worked hard for him and always returned to help during the harvest. He was more than overseer.

"Invaluable," Mamacita had constantly reminded Luis, "He kept our people on the land when they were urged to join the bandits. When they thought of going to the city he kept them at 'Saldana.'" Saldana, he repeated the name in his reverie, Saldana, the hacienda. What was? Who was? Mamacita wrote saying only to stay where he was.

Clickety-clack clickety-clack, the train's rhythm, removing him from the murder. Murder? No, it was an abscess that burst, now things would be good. Good? Evil? Good or evil? Where was the dividing line? When did black become gray become white? The world was better without Ramos, would be better when the news was relayed. The indios could be released from their bondage. Ramos was evil. The Bible said only God could judge a man. God would judge, had judged Ramos's soul. Luis had sent God that evil soul. Was it good what Luis had done? Had he played God, or had he played into the will of God? He shuddered with the weight of that decision. Wasn't Judas only an instrument of God's will?

Luis prayed silently, nodding slowly with the train. "God, you have Manuel now; he belonged with you. He struggled long enough; my departure would have caused his torture. No, no more suffering. I sent him home to You. God forgive me for I have sinned...make me humble...please God, let me feel Your strength to know I have done good...and let me find love...I leave this hell of darkness, this evil...let me feel love, Amen."

Clickety-clack. His body felt cold, then numb. He stared at his knee, but did not feel his knee. He took off his jacket, rolled it, and wedged it between the window and his shoulder. To Monterrey, el Norte...miles, countries from David, from Mamacita, from Colombia....

Now he clicked the revolver's chamber, and placed the weapon back in the drawer. He turned off the music, closed the cabinet, laid out the shirt he wanted ironed, and unlocked the door. "'Who are you, Luis Ochoa?'"

ᴙξᴙ

When they stood by the helicopter, waiting for Andy to load the luggage, Luis handed Jill a business card. "You may call this number, if I do not answer, whoever does will know exactly how to reach me." He bent down and hugged Luisa. Jill wished she could take a picture of the two of them. She memorized the embrace.

Luis stood, he leaned and whispered, "Marijuana agrees with you." He smiled.

"How did you know Laos? And Andujar?"

"Don't ever make the mistake of underestimating your Señor Ochoa. I have no tolerance for mistakes. Adios." He touched her arm with his index finger, then pinched her nose between his knuckles.

Chapter 5

Jill stared at the kitchen calendar. For two weeks in August no marks, no appointments, nothing, a blank calendar. Actually too many events to put in such tiny squares…two full weeks with Luis. She could fill in those squares; no leave them blank except for her memories. She now wrote "can tomatoes" with a long arrow extending through three days. There was stillness this morning in her kitchen, no Chinese servants, waiting for her to blink. The view? No mountains with misty rainbows dancing at the peaks, only the Indiana agriculture. Dark emerald corn stalks ribboned the fields. Mr. Titus, the farmer who rented the acres closest to their property, had left one section in weeds; their jagged, irregular shape smacked against the straight green that rose to the same height as polished troops waiting a general's inspection, the march of August's army.

Jill opened the window over the kitchen sink. Sadie would be marching out to the farm if Jill did not make time in a white square to talk of Hawaii, Luis. There was so much… but Sadie kept saying, "No more snippets, I know Jack is standing right there listening, but I want each piece of the story, not the *Reader's Digest* version."

Jill sipped iced tea. She had to can the damn tomatoes and go to the first teachers' meeting, oh jeez not the superintendent's admonitions again. Linda Crawford had called begging for 45's to play at their class reunion. 1970. Had it really been ten years? The request put sorting through her high school memorabilia at the top of her things to do. Okay Sadie, not the top. Maybe both things at once. Sadie could help sort, but what day?

The white calendar's squares, twenty-third, leave Hawaii, arrive Indiana. Jack happy to see his returning family. Luisa only slightly uncomfortable with her first, "Hi, Daddy!" Her quick glance at Jill, who nodded. Honesty, words, but the feelings? Nowhere to put them where they would stay.

And her first night sleeping with Jack, thank goodness Jack was happy with the steps, one, two three. The natural movements she had with Luis, Jack referred to as her "tropic magic." "No!" She wanted to scream, "It is my lover, my love. My Latin." But she adjusted. Sadie's voice reminded her, "Rise to the occasion, Miss Sarah B." Would marijuana make a difference? Oh, yeah, Jack you want to smoke some of this with me? She shook her head at the thought.

The hardest part of seeing Luis was leaving, her heart hurt and objected to being packed into the structured day. Luis had opened up the days; they all connected with his presence in each one. Now they were empty, like Christmas afternoon with nothing left, but used wrapping paper and empty boxes.

The twenty-fourth box - push, push herself into this day, back into the square. The first squares were difficult, but she knew slowly she would get into her routine. When school started, the students would get her on the track, the train of calendar squares, like so many boxcars would roll along on steel gauge rails.

She filled a colander with fresh tomatoes, walked to the sink, and then let the water splash over them. The water splattered and cleaned the skins. They came to pick tomatoes. He came to pick tomatoes. She removed the telephone from the hook, back home again in Indiana, and dialed Lillian's number.

"Okay Mom, I'm ready. Tell Dad to get the cobwebs off my stuff. Sadie and I are coming over to be sweet sixteen, seventeen and eighteen all over again."

"Great news, Honey. I'll tell him. I think he wishes you two were always sixteen."

She planned the visit to Lillian's basement and those years when it was important to go steady, wear the satin prom dress with the long white gloves and dance to an endless stack of 45's. The wa-wa-watusi. Jill shook her head, remembering Sadie and her trying to learn that crazy step with T.J. So many memories to share with her classmates in ten years, but this last year with Luis's return, what could she say? "I went to Curaçao for Spring Break and Hawaii for two weeks this summer."

And yes this is my husband, Jack, Jack meet...I thought he was so cute and here's Creighton who wanted to eat my box, you know Step Three, the step that scares you? Oh yeah and Heidi who helped me through American History. I hated it in high school and majored in it at State. Yeah, ten years, things have changed, a few pounds, an affair with a Latin lover. Viet Nam? We have lost a few in that horrible war, Leslie Matchett, Carroll Davis, Joe Burns, the flooring contractor's son. And Dave Bromley, killed himself, no one knew why, well maybe someone will at the reunion. One night to catch up on ten years. I hope Marie Elena Zambrano comes, she kept telling me, "No," all last semester. I must call and remind her.

ﻉﻍﻉ

Lillian's basement was dimly lit, musty and dusty. The concrete blocks and limestone walls felt moist and smelled of mildew. Henry ran a dehumidifier to help with the excess moisture. The ground level windows were small. Bare electric bulbs hung from the floor joists and created shadows in the already dark crevices. Lillian had set up a card table and Henry brought empty boxes to separate trash from keepsakes. Lillian showed the friends which boxes and corners contained Jill's things, then left them.

"Sadie, where do we start? I think you need to look through the records and pick out the ones we liked best."

Jill's portable record player was thick with dust. She popped the snaps on the side speakers and handed Sadie the cord. Sadie, stood on her chair and swayed trying to get the plug in a reconverted light socket. Jill dusted the spindle converter and slid it over the narrow metal record changer, then flipped the speed from 33⅓ to 45. She removed an inch stack of records from their storage box, then pushed the "on" button, suddenly Billy Bland, "Let the Little Girl Dance" filled the basement. The Havlicek cellar became four years of high school all over again as the women danced and laughed. The records changed, and eventually the 45's were sorted; their conversation had traveled from Caylor to Colombia.

"Okay, Jill, Los Angeles. What was it like?" Sadie refolded the program from the high school play, *Our Town*.

"Hippies or flower children walked all over the place, even some Jesus freaks and those orange robes…"

"Oh, yeah the Hare Krishna. Michael and I saw them in New York."

"Sadie, I think we need to invest in those long skirts; they cover a multitude of things."

Sadie handed her another 45, "Play this as you tell me what next."

Jill looked at the record label, "Oh you would pick this one, 'Theme from a Summer Place.' …where it may rain or storm, da-da, and my heart is free. I want to go back to that summer place right now."

"You're here now so continue…Okay, leave LA, arrive…"

"Honolulu. Definitely a summer place. And there was Andy and his helicopter." Jill described the former Special Forces pilot and explained how he knew of Hector, "Well not exactly Hector, himself, but the activities of the CIA and the use of Special Forces. He told me they were in and out of places, places the U.S. government never talked about, and never let anyone know."

"I told you, I told you. They probably lied to you; maybe Hector is just missing, like so many others. They don't want to admit they didn't bring their bodies home, just lied to us. You know the stories Michael has told us about the communications he saw. None of it good. God, I hope they end that war. It just seems to get worse every day. Our generation!"

"I know they lied on the paperwork I read in New York because Luis told me Hector had died in Laos."

Sadie stopped sorting and stared at Jill. "What?! How could that be? A Colombian citizen knowing the truth about an American soldier? You didn't ask him twenty questions? Your usual."

"He told me when we were in the middle of an oh-so tense interaction. But I did bring it up right before we left. He said 'don't underestimate your Señor Ochoa.' Luis is more than we have any idea. I mean we were staying in some Chinese merchant's house, more hotel than house and we stayed in the secondary home. You'll see in the pictures. Luis and he are good friends. I never saw the man."

Sadie cocked her head, "Never saw the man? Very strange."

"A true confession story?" Jill asked then Sadie nodded.

"Of course, I want to know every detail."

"Okay," Jill smiled, "My last night...I...we...smoked marijuana."

Sadie's eyes grew large, "What the hell do you know about smoking anything?"

Jill continued, "Sadie, what happened to our world of matching sweaters and skirts? All those clothes and people seemed so important. Now this..." She held up her emerald ring. The symbol they both used when thinking of Luis.

"So different, Jill? It's just another ring. The only thing missing is the angora. You still can't figure out what to do with the men in your life. We spent hours listening to 45's, talking about guys, and wrapping angora around the class rings to match our outfits. Remember?"

"They were the center of our universe."

Sadie laughed, "Duh, Miss Brighter-than-everyone-else."

Jill chuckled and turned off the record player.

The afternoon ended. They climbed the stairs to Lillian's kitchen and some butterscotch pie. They'd picked the records, cried, but mostly laughed and left Henry's trash can full.

"Henry will be so mad he missed this golden opportunity to tease both of us sitting at his kitchen table. I just know he had a thousand questions about Hawaii," Sadie said.

"Siddhartha, do you know something you want to share?" Lillian said.

"No, Mom, nothing, she knows nothing. Oh yeah, grass skirts and luaus."

"You two spent too much time in the basement; you are acting just like you did in high school."

They all laughed.

In the hot afternoon Lillian's yard blazed with all her brightly blooming flower beds. The friends walked to their cars. Sadie hugged Jill, "When do you see the Latin again? Too bad he doesn't still pick tomatoes. You could drive out to McKinnsey's. He'd be out there. Hot

August afternoon, I know you think about that with every tomato you touch."

"People do the picking for him now. Coffee beans. At least I have a phone number I can call. Ring, ring, 'Luis, please come and pick some tomatoes.'" Jill stopped and stared at the street, Catalpa, Caylor, Indiana. "Sadie, I feel a million miles from him. Did I really just spend fifteen days in Hawaii? Sometimes we fought as if we could kill each other," Jill shuddered. "He has a look,'" she narrowed her eyes and imitated Luis's frown, "that makes you think he could tear someone apart, piece by piece."

"You were scared?" Sadie stared at Jill.

"I don't like it, but I'm more afraid that he'll get angry and not see me again. And that really would tear me apart."

"Yeah, that's my favorite from Michael. 'Mental cruelty, my dear, much worse than physical cruelty. So think about it before you do anything.' He gives me that in a sinister Bella Lugosi voice. But he's right. Oh well, you're," Sadie waved her arm to encompass the street, then sang, "Back home again in Indiana."

She laughed as Jill reached to put her hand over her mouth. "And," Sadie continued, "now we have to figure out how to make the right impression on the Class of '60. Our senior cords?"

Jill shook her head, thinking of Jim's name in a heart.

Sadie laughed, honking as she drove away. Jill struggled with a box of canned bread and butter pickles that were sitting on the ground by her car door, a gift from Lillian. Jill wedged them on the floor behind the driver's seat. Lillian had given her three boxes "For Jack," Lillian had specified. Jack, Jill thought, why had she and Sadie spent the whole afternoon and not talked much about Jack?

Jill kicked off her sandals and walked barefoot in her parents' backyard. The grassy living carpet created without a loom bent under her soles, soft, slick and warm all at the same time. The familiar smell of Lillian's flowers and the grass took her back to so many summers of Hide and Seek, Kick the Can, tea parties with her dolls. A limestone flower box encircled a water fountain. A gray molded-concrete cherub held a large pot that poured water into the first shell shaped tier; water gurgled down to a larger second shell-shaped tier. Henry had given it to Lillian last summer, "Just because," he'd said. Lillian planted orange, pink, white impatiens and geraniums now a circle of colorful ribbons hugging the massive tree trunk.

Henry and Lillian worked to make the area peaceful. Near the garage Henry had created a shaded alcove with a wrought iron table and chairs. Lillian made cushions for the hard seats. A grape arbor full of dark purple fruit extended along the property line, separating the Riley's backyard from the Havlicek's. It smelled sweet. Lillian used the grapes for homemade juice and jelly.

The locusts buzzed; one after the other, they took turns as if saying, "It's your time to make a racket." They marked summer's end. A summer that had forever altered Luisa's future. She bent over and picked up Luisa's sandals abandoned next to the huge sycamore tree that shaded most of the yard. She must have tossed them on her way to Mason's. Jill spent time on their flight home, answering her questions. Jill assured her that nothing had changed; they would still live at the farm; she was not leaving Jack; Luisa would start school in September at her same school; they were not moving with Luis. Jill made the assurances, but did not know if she could guarantee any of those things.

Closing her eyes, she took a deep breath – roses and grapes. She tried to summon up Luis, to share the August heat of Indiana. Call him? He had given her the number, but phone calls to Colombia? There would be no way to explain that to Jack. She would have to go to Sadie's. No, she must learn to adjust to his absence. His absence? The thought brought the emptiness. Her return to Jack was easy, suspicionless Jack. He would never make a good Sherlock Holmes; he had no clues. He had told them all-the-ones-that-got-away stories, but managed to fill one section of the freezer with his catch. Jill now stood by the fountain letting a stream of water run through her fingers.

"Jill, come and help me with this last box of pickles." Lillian called from the back screen door.

Jill slipped on her sandals, then headed towards the house. The tomatoes and vinegar scents filled the kitchen.

"Mom, don't forget tomorrow is fish dinner at our house. Don't bring anything. Jack is coming home early, so let's say six."

"Wait, let me check my calendar. Let's see tomorrow is the twenty-sixth, I have a Bridge club in the afternoon, but what time?"

August twenty-six, had Luis thought about that? Silly thought.

"Six, Mom, see you then."

"Are you sure you don't want a peach pie, I know that's Jack's…"

"Nothing. Gotta go…"

"Will Siddhartha and that wonderful family of hers be there?"

As the screen door slammed, Jill yelled, "No, and I'm driving by Mason's to pick up Luisa."

The twenty-sixth, the numbers always come back to me. Do other people do this? Okay, does Luis do this? Can he recall the numbers? Will he? Oh, jeez, Jack is coming home early…I wish I could call Luis and say, "Happy Anniversary!" But he said the telephone number was for Luisa.

ᴙξᴙ

They ate dinner in the dining room. Henry volunteered to help with the dishes. After Luisa cleared the dishes, Jack took Luisa and Lillian to the backyard to show them his garden flowers. The mums needed something; he had asked his mother-in-law, she of the green thumb, to help him.

Jill and her father now stood by the sink washing, rinsing and drying. The others moved from the garden to the barn; Jack leading the way. She stared as if watching a silent movie. Luisa would show her grandma where she intended to house her horse. After Hawaii the subject of having her own horse was the only one her daughter discussed. Luis had promised that if Luisa could talk her mother into it, the horse would come. She agreed to call and see about the cost of hay, 4-H, shodding, the veterinarian, and the saddle. It seemed like a big investment, even though money with Luis would not be a problem. She considered the time required and decided to convince Luisa a dog would be a better pet and save horse riding for their vacations.

"So Princess, where is your precocious mind as you stare out there, at the same barn, in the same field that you've been staring at for the last six years?" Henry spoke scrubbing with the S.O.S. pad on the aluminum pan Jack had used to fry his fish.

"I was right there," she pointed at the barn, "watching Jack open the door…."

"Hawaii. Did you see a grass shack on the beach where the barn door is?"

"Scrub," Jill said.

"It was a good trip for you. Jack's fish stories didn't cover up your experience. Your face is lit up like a pumpkin on Halloween."

"Dad, it's your age, senility; your eyes are playing tricks on you. They do all kinds of things with glasses and surgery…"

111

"Nope, Miss Sass, I've been looking at your face much too long not to know. You're in love, Princess. Jack didn't notice?"

"How would he? He has a freezer full of fish, a garden full of vegetables, two bushels of tomatoes for me to can, and mums that don't grow fat enough." Jill hung her wet dish towel on a rack. She opened a drawer and pulled out a clean dry one. She shook it open twisted it and then took a swing at Henry.

"The things," Henry said, sidestepping to avoid Jill's use of the towel as a switch, "always the things. Is that how you do it?"

"I don't know how I do it, Dad. I'm not sure I do, 'do it' and mostly today I don't even care if I cover it up. We told Luisa the truth." She sat down at the kitchen table and sipped a glass of tea.

Henry whistled, then spoke as he took a seat opposite her at the table, "Her reaction? She seems good, happy."

"I know she is happy because I told her I wouldn't divorce Jack and I wasn't marrying Luis. She didn't want me to be like Emma Sue. She's heard Sadie and I talk about all her husbands. *And* I said I would look into caring for and feeding a horse."

"Princess, are you okay with this arrangement? It seems to me you're operating somewhere between reality and fantasy. One of those is going to get the better of you."

They both heard the knock at the door and in silence shrugged their shoulders. Jill stood and walked to a window that looked out on the front yard. A blue van with Mooney Florist inscribed on the side was parked in her driveway.

"Company, Princess? Too late for fish, but the peach cobbler…"

"I don't know…" she spoke, walking to the front screen door. A teenager with a baseball cap inscribed with the same emblem as the van stood with a long white box under one arm.

"Mrs. Jones? I sure hope so. I've been up and down this road and this looked like the only place with people."

"Yes, I'm Mrs. Jones."

"These are for you," he said, handing her the box. He quickly turned from the door.

Henry came from the kitchen and met her glance. He shook his head, then spoke, "And what have we here, Princess? Looks like those boxes roses come in." He chuckled and put his arm around her, "Roses? You getting roses from a secret admirer?"

"Maybe you should go to the barn with the rest of them."

112

They walked into the kitchen.

"And miss the prima donna's performance, not on your life. Like I said, fantasy or reality." He threw his head back, laughing heartily.

"Stop." Jill put the box on the table and untied the scarlet ribbon tied loosely around the box. She ran her hand down the shiny white cardboard, then slowly opened the lid.

"Come on, come on you're making an old man have apoplexy," Henry spoke, picking up one end of the box. The lid came off and Henry continued, "M-m-m-m, Princess, someone spent a bundle. White roses." Henry talked as Jill removed a small card that was wedged in among the lacy green ferns and thorned stems. "I bought Lillian a few for our anniversary, set me back some. Let's see, how many are in this box…"

She read the card in silence, "Design, design! Do I use the aright? August 26, 1960. Always in August."

"Twenty-six of them, Princess, must've bought all they had. Read the card. Who is it from? I don't think this is the work of an *engineer*." Henry poured himself some iced tea from the pitcher on the table, then sat.

"Dad, you know what the card says?"

"I give up. Read it to me."

She read it and he shook his head, looked at her, "Again, please." She repeated the quote.

"Now do you know what it means?" She asked.

He told the story of how he made her look him straight in the eye and repeat the memorized poem as she practiced. "Lord knows why you picked that obscure poem…" Henry said.

"It was short…"

"Yeah, yeah, I should've thought of that, always, you always tried to do less work so you could see boys more," he laughed.

Jill kissed him on top of his head. She placed the big bouquet into a hand-painted porcelain vase. Tiny Lilly-of-the-valley flowers danced on the china sides, Grandma Kohlhass's. She glanced out the window as she filled the vase with water. "Dad, they are coming back from the barn, what am I going to say? Help!" She set the vase in the middle of the table and threw the box away.

Henry held up his hand, shook his head, then said, "Nope, this is your bailiwick, somewhere between fantasy and reality."

Jill smelled each rose. August 26, 1960, and thought of the heat and dry straw, sweat and tomatoes, rotten tomatoes, dirt, a long time

113

ago, but the smell took her back to the shed. Now she buried her face in the roses, took a deep breath and held it.

Jack walked in talking about bushels of beans, numbers and pounds how many would be put in the freezer, how many would be canned, "I figure we will have all we need," he stopped in the kitchen doorway, "...Jill, fresh roses? Where in the world did those come from? I saw the florist van, but I figured he was lost. They're for you? You have a secret admirer?"

"Right, Jack," Henry said and winked at Jill, "just what I said."

"I guess so. I don't have too many clues who they came from. Obviously, they didn't come from you. I thought maybe you were welcoming me home."

"Roses. Is there a card?"

"Yes, Jack. Here maybe you know something I don't."

Jack read the card and held it as if rereading. Luisa tried to take it, but he held on. Henry grabbed Luisa's hand and Lillian's hand and asked them to go to the porch swing.

Jack looked from the card to Jill, then frowned, "Strange message. And you knew they weren't from me. Ten years ago today, I didn't even know you. You were eighteen, is that the summer you had that horrible boyfriend you told me about? Jim?"

"Yes, this is the day I told him to go fly a kite."

"You remember *that* date? Interesting, after all this time you remember the date you broke up with your old boyfriend. Don't you find that strange?" He threw the card on the table.

"Not really. I remember a lot of dates that have significance for me in my life, like the day I met you...April 10, 1964."

"But we married. I am your husband; it would make sense that you remember the day I met you. But what is the quote. 'Design, design! Do I use the word aright?' What is this about?"

"It is a line from a poem I memorized in high school. It's by Robert Frost. I learned it right after I memorized, 'On the eighteenth of April in seventy-five, hardly a man is now alive who remembers that famous day and year and the midnight ride of Paul Revere.' I'm thinking if I recited that poem for Jim some time. I don't know. But he hated me to quote poetry; he said I sounded like a snob. God, I hate him. No, he didn't do this. Roses are too classy for that jerk, puke, really. I'll call Sadie tomorrow and see if she has any clues. Jack, it is our class reunion on Saturday, maybe someone will tell me."

"Let's go through that day again. August twenty-sixth, maybe I'm missing something."

"The county fair. Sadie and I wore our senior cords for the last time. I rode the Ferris wheel with Jim, hating him, knowing we were going to break-up. Sadie and I chugged cherry sloe gin and went to a party, a wild party. I was drunk, not walking very well. I told him, I forget what name I called him. He accused me of loving Mexicans only he didn't use that word; he called them a racist name. He grabbed me and held me off the ground, cussing and threatening to hit me. Michael and Sadie came to my rescue. Michael wrapped an arm around Jim, and Sadie pulled me to my car."

Jack hugged her, "I'm sorry Honey, I made you go through that again. Let's go back to secret admirer. You did have some strange friends from high school. Where did Lillian and Henry disappear to?"

ᴙξᴙ

The stove was covered in large pots; some held empty quart Ball jars sterilizing in boiling water; two Dutch ovens bubbled with cooking tomatoes. Jill scrapped the sides of the pan and smelled the steam – creamy tomato soup. She held the tongs and slowly grabbed the lip of the hot jars and placed them gently on linen towels spread out on the counter top. The sealing lids and closing rings were boiling in another pan. She took out six jars and put six more into boiling water. Her apron was covered in tomato stains. She had tied her hair under a bandana, but the tendrils curled up as she cooked in the stuffy kitchen. The windows were open and the fan whirred around her legs, rearranging the hot thick air from one place to another. The sink contained a colander filled with tomatoes, waiting to be boiled. She walked from pot, to sink, to countertop doing several processes at once. She heard the phone ring, but decided to let Luisa answer it. When Luisa did not call her, she continued canning the tomato harvest. Three bushel baskets still sat on the back porch.

"Mom, Papa is on the phone," Luisa spoke from the doorway. "I told him you were canning tomatoes and that I couldn't go in the kitchen, but he said I could come and tell you *he* was on the phone."

"Yes, Luisa, let me turn the heat down. What else did he say?"

"He asked if I had started school and if not what I was doing with my time. And to send him the pictures you took of me in Hawaii, and when could he send Gaucho." Luisa put her hands together as if praying to Jill, then walked into the kitchen and opened the refrigerator, pulling out a pitcher of Kool-Aid. She poured a glass, then left, pointing to the phone hanging on the wall, "Say yes, Mom!"

Jill sat on the kitchen stool she kept by the phone. Jack's list hung by the phone, no mention of calls from Luis. She smiled, then drank a big swallow of iced tea. She had debated about calling him, wanting to tell him about the class reunion, but he said the phone number was for his daughter's use. And her need to talk had nothing to do with Luisa. "Luis, I apologize for taking so long, it is the tomato harvest. I was just looking out my window at my tomato plants and thought could you just come and pick my tomatoes and I'd rush out and grab you and take you to my tool shed."

"Straw in your shed?"

"No, concrete, I'd have to find a blanket," Jill said.

"Si, go on. We are in the shed..."

"I'd leave the rest up to you; you seem to know what to do in empty sheds."

"The tomatoes inspired you?" Luis asked.

"Yes, and Hawaii and Washington, D.C. and the green room."

He chuckled. "Gringa, I apologize for not calling before to see how your return flight and homecoming were."

"Luisa had many questions and I told Jack that I had explained to her that she was not his biological daughter."

"And what did he say?"

"He wanted to know why I had told her and I explained that she asked questions about the way children look like their parents, but she did not look like him and just a little like me."

"Was he satisfied with this answer?"

"He objected saying she was too young to have to consider this adult interaction. I told him she seemed to accept it okay. He said, 'Okay, Honey, I'll trust your judgment on this.'"

"Your parameters? Jack sounds like a reasonable man. Did you get the roses, Gringa?"

"Reasonable you say in one breath and in the next ask me about *the* roses. Oh, gracias, Señor Ochoa, *so* thoughtful."

"'In White' for my gringa."

"Are you able to have a long conversation? I need to talk to you and I'm sure you are not coming to Caylor anytime soon."

"No, no time soon. I'm in Vancouver, British Columbia, then on to Toronto. Do I need to stop and see my gringa?"

"Your presence has already done enough damage. Canada is a better place for you."

"You speak in sarcasm. I have not presented myself to Caylor for a year."

"Luis, you speak with a forked-tongue."

"Jankee idiom. Say what you have to say."

The roses lasted almost a week. As she grabbed the stems to trash the bouquet, the wilted petals had fallen all over the table. Twenty-six buds of beauty, had they really caused so many problems? Jack kept asking, "Who?" And she presented new theories, thinking with each suggestion of Henry's "fantasy" remark.

The night of the class reunion came. They went alone, but as soon as they parked, Jill met Sandy Fortune with her husband, a handsome Italian man with big blue eyes. She and Sadie had discussed how short dumpy Sandy had landed such a man. Sadie and she bumped into each other in the parking lot with a quick greeting. Then person after person from the Class of '60 stopped and talked. The former classmates surprised her, some were heavier, thinner, balding, totally made-over from the Caylor High School of the late fifties. Linda pointed to the people dancing to Jill's 45's and said thank you. Sadie had disappeared, but came back with two cold PBR's, then proposed a toast, "To the old, may it long endure."

"Jack?" Jill asked, then touched the neck of Sadie's bottle.

Jack came up behind her, "A toast to me, I like it. Sadie, who sent the roses?"

"I tried to go through the Secret Admirers, but I don't know anyone who really was interested in your sweet wife, Jack." Sadie shrugged, "Except for her long-time steady, but I'm sure he hates her now, having a Colom…Mexican child and all."

"Sadie!" Jill said, "Let's go, and see some more of our crazy classmates. Come on Jack, I'll introduce you to my past."

The beer, the "remember-when's," the music and always another cold beer. She laughed until she cried with old friends. Outside the Country Club ballroom, she met Creighton, Greg Baxter and Heidi and shared a marijuana cigarette. Jack asked why she smelled like cigarettes. She shook her head and said he should have noticed that many of her friends were smoking. She also told herself she would never bring him again.

Her new old friends from the Interracial Club laughed with her and pointed out people she knew who had changed dramatically. The farther she drifted from Jack the more fun she had. Sadie and Michael danced and laughed together. Creighton reminded her she still owed him a pair of panties, still disgusting she thought, but she did like smoking marijuana with him. He made her laugh. Jimmy Van Lue invited everyone to his parents' house for a pool party afterwards and swimming suits were optional.

She wanted the night to go on and on, then suddenly there was Jim. She quickly scanned the crowd to find Sadie, but as usual when she wanted or needed her best friend, she'd disappeared. Jim was heavier than ten years earlier. His hair was longer, but not long enough to be stylish, as if he were trying to be more modern. He smiled all those white teeth shown in the same boyish grin. He asked her to dance just as Jack's voice came from behind her, "White roses? You sent *my* wife white roses?!"

Jim pulled her, muttering, "Who's the crazy old man?"

"My husband, you creep…" She jerked away from him.

Jim firmly held her arm and dragged her toward the dance floor, saying their song played and she was going to dance with him for old times' sake. He turned and yelled over his shoulder to Jack, "You don't mind, do you, *old* man? I think she owes me that. I'm the one that busted that sweet cherry." He threw his head back and laughed, not seeing Jack make a step toward him and Jill. Jill turned, yanked away from Jim just as Jack punched Jim's jaw. Jim stood still, staring at Jack; he pulled his fist up to swing. Bam! Jack punched him in the stomach. Sadie ran up. Jill was screaming Jack's name. Michael came from a crowd and grabbed Jack. Sadie put her arm around Jill's shoulders. Jim fell to his knees, throwing up on the dance floor. Their song played over the speakers, "to know, know, know him is to love, love, love him …and I do and I do…"

Jill ended her story, Luis spoke, "Gringa, there is much in that story, marijuana, swimming without clothes, but who is this Jim? Jim who?"

"Jim Bancroft," she answered softly.

"I know of Jack and Hector Andujar. Jim Bancroft, he was in the picture with you and Sadie. You hiss when you pronounce his name. You hated him, Gringa, but I don't know why."

"He is stupid, racist trash!"

"I understand basura. Where does Jim Bancroft live now?"

"In St. Louis, Missouri. He is some sort of manager at the Brown Shoe Company. They must like jerks in Missouri. It is a good place for him, 250 miles from me. He has a wife. I was surprised someone married that ignorant…"

"Gringa, we have drunk men fighting at Carnival and often over women. However, here they often shoot each other before they finish. And Señor Bancroft, what happened to him?"

"I don't know, and I don't care."

"You've heard the last of him. And the next time I give you roses, I'll be looking in your angel face. You have my *word* on that, si? Now explain forked-tongue."

"You say something, but mean something else, or you say something and don't mean it at all."

"What did I say? Perhaps you misunderstood."

"I ask to go with you, then you remind me that Luisa is better off in Indiana than with you in Colombia, that we both are. I have that part correct?"

"Si. You understand, although you keep asking me the same question, so I wonder if you truly understand? And do I mean something else?"

"When you send flowers to the house, it causes problems that threaten my marriage, my marriage that is the foundation of living in Indiana with Luisa. The marriage that makes your daughter's life normal. The marriage you labeled 'good' when we were in Curaçao."

"Parameters, again. Gringa, can you fly to Toronto tomorrow?"

"Luis…yes, if you promise to keep me and never let me out of your sight."

"Italy next month, Rome. Will the school let you go?"

"So tempting, almost as good as having you in my shed."

"Jill, when you go with me as you say to 'not be out of my sight,' you must decide that this is exactly what you want. You must not have any desire to go back to Indiana, ever. And the number you have for me…use it whenever *you* need me. For Luisa, but also for you, when you want to speak to your Papito. You said 2A.M. to hear my voice, si?"

"Yes."

"You will speak to my assistant, Gina, she knows where I am and she knows of you. I mean this, but you must tell her *when* you want me to call you back, the marriage, your parameters, your time zone. You understand?"

"But…you're a busy man…"

119

"Gringa, don't ever say that to me again! Whenever you need me, you must call me."

She hung up, alone in the emptiness of her kitchen, filled with the smell of tomatoes. Goddamned tomatoes. Toronto. Rome. Leave Indiana forever. Reality. Fantasy.

Part 2

Chapter 6

Lillian sat on the front porch swing sewing tiny pre-cut patches together, stacks of precisely cut squares three inches tall. Each stack was color coordinated. Jill walked out from the screen door, carrying iced tea. She set the tea on the small wicker table that also held an embroidery scissors and a spool of thread. Lillian took tiny stitches to connect an orange square to a peach print. She pushed absently on the wood floor, swaying slightly in the hot afternoon. Next to her wide lap lay completed squares in the same orange-peach pattern.

The summer afternoon, the quilt patches were different colors, but still the same scene. If Jill had left for years and came back blindfolded, she could have guessed "July" when seeing Lillian like this. It was July 1975, but it could have been July 1970 or July 1960 or July 1950. Lillian in her world of cotton patches, no, Jill said to herself, I cannot, am not....Jill sat down, then sorted through the patches, remembering some of her old clothes, the dress for Freshman autumn prom, Easter, when? Sixth Grade?

"Mom, you're not using this yellow print? I hated that dress. Don't put it on my quilt."

"You looked so sweet in that yellow dress, Jill, at least until you managed to stain it with chocolate ice cream."

"I didn't stain it, Maxwell chased me and the ice cream sort of…ended up on the dress." They both laughed at the long ago incident.

"Mom, that has been, let me see, I was six, twenty-seven years ago. The material will be worn out before it gets on the quilt." Jill picked up more pieces from Lillian's miniature bushel basket she used for storage. "Why do you keep all these old patches? Are you ever going to use all of them? Luisa starts high school in two months; she'll have her first prom dress. Should I save the extra material for your patches?"

"'Waste not, want not.' How many times have I reminded you to save things? Young people today don't know how hard we had it. Everyone used to work together to help each other. Nowadays, it's just throw away. Throw away bottles, cans, clothes. No one appreciates anything." She paused to pick through her stack matching print patch to solid color patch. "Women change husbands as if they were replacing shelf paper; out with the old, in with the new."

Jill had heard this lecture many times. It usually came when she was in high school asking for new shoes or a new purse.

Lillian continued, "There is no pulling together for the long haul. I can't understand why it's all changed so much. My parents were married sixty-two years until your grandma died, used the same dishes her parents gave her for a wedding present." She stopped swaying and sewing as she pressed a hand-sewn seam with her fingers, then surveyed the match.

Jill tossed the patches she had been examining back into the box, "Mom, I'm thinking about divorcing Jack."

Lillian's eyes shifted from the patch to Jill. She lay the patch down gently on her lap. Jill picked up a peach print and beige satin square, then spoke, "Here Mom, use these colors together and make a patch. It will coordinate with my soon to be peach bedroom."

"What do you care about making a coordinated patch for your bedroom? You just threw out your husband. Who will sleep in that peach bedroom? Explain to me Jill Caitlin Jones what the dickens you are talking about. I suppose you already mentioned this nonsense to Henry?"

"I've talked to you about Jack for ten years. I was just sitting here watching you, thinking, I don't want to sit on that damned farm…"

"Jill, don't use that language…"

"…sitting, making patches…with Jack….oh God, Mom, I can't do it."

"Sure you can. Bloom where you are planted. You can do anything you set your mind to…"

"Well, I don't want to set my mind to this. I don't love him…well; I do love him, but like a…good dog. He's a friend, helps me…no, he is a great helper. He does everything I ask him. But I can't stay on that farm pretending…."

"You just called your husband a dog! It's *that man* you go see. He's done this to you. I knew you couldn't have two men in your life. I have been telling Henry since you both started this, for five or six years now, well, I've been saying God does not approve of adultery. I don't care about the modern interpretations, adultery is what it is. You can't hide sin from the good Lord, I told Henry. And here you are…" Lillian scooped up the finished patches, forming another stack. She opened a large Red Wing shoe box and laid the pieces on other completed pieces in the same shades of peach and orange.

"Mom, you can't blame Luis. He hasn't asked me to divorce Jack. He hasn't asked me to leave my husband, nothing. I just don't want to be married to Jack, anymore."

"You haven't thought of Luisa or you wouldn't talk like this. She loves Jack."

"She also loves Luis, *her* father."

"Ha!" Lillian pointed her small bird-shaped scissors at Jill, "I knew it was that man! You know a bird in the hand is worth two in the bush. That man lives a long ways from here, a long ways…" her voice trailed off. She dropped her hand back into her lap, as she looked away from Jill and across the porch to the street.

The streets were thickly shadowed from the leaf-laden big trees. Luis was miles away, but Jill now had the sense that at any moment he could come and take her and Luisa. In the last five years, she had learned that his power and influence went much further than Cartagena, much farther than South America. He seemingly knew people from all the continents. Luisa and she had been to Australia, Hong Kong, Italy, Greece, and Rome for Spring Break and summer vacations for two weeks.

Her school had instituted mini-sabbaticals if a week away could be justified. Thank goodness for Don who talked the principal into giving her the time, "for her history class, WWII." She'd gone to Italy and met Luis and Mr. Angotti. Five days and no fights, no Luisa. Mr. Angotti had shown them villas for sale in Tuscany. Luis had reminded her they looked like the homes of princesses. They were solid and majestic on the rolling green hills covered in vineyards. She agreed with Mr. Angotti that it seemed like a good investment.

"Renovate and restore, Señor Ochoa," he kept repeating. They saw homes that had been restored and renovated. Jill agreed with Mr. Angotti, and then the telephone calls to Gina. She hinted he was in a different time zone and would have to be awakened in order to receive Jill's call. The pieces of his life and business were closely guarded, but like a determined dandelion something would poke through a crack in his protective shield. She knew Lillian's anxiety and in many ways over the years; it had been hers as well.

"Mom, I'm not leaving Jack. I just want to. Maybe like these patches, he'll come in handy."

"That was mean-spirited, after all that man has done for you, made you a decent woman..."

"I hate it when you say that! No man made *me* a goddamned decent woman! I am a decent woman, period!" Jill jumped up, then walked into the house, grabbing her purse from the hall chair. The screen door slammed as she ran down the steps.

"Jill..." Lillian cleared off her lap and stood from the swing, "call me."

Jill paused with her hand on the car door, "Luisa and I are going to Molly's this weekend. No telephones up there. I can't talk to you anyway, you never understand me. I'm sorry you didn't have another son, maybe your life would have been better!" She jumped in the car and took off too quickly from the curb.

Henry walked out of the front door, as Jill's car rounded the corner, "Where did she go Lil? I wanted to ask her something."

"She went home, I guess. She says she's thinking of divorcing Jack. Your daughter."

"She's talked of doing that for ten years."

"You sound like her," Lillian said.

"But why did she leave? I told her I wanted to talk to her. It's not like her to leave, and not say goodbye to me."

"Oh your mother's Irish came out, Henry."

"Why?" He walked over to where Jill had sat and plopped down on the cushion, causing the patches to fall to the ground.

"I told her what I thought," Lillian bent over and picked up the scattered material, "she's never liked what I thought. She likes to do whatever she wants and not think about anyone, but herself. Leave Jack? What the dickens? And what about Luisa? Not one thought about Luisa. I don't understand, she's not a mother, she's..."

"Lillian, she's not like you, but neither is she selfish. She does think of people other than herself. She's made a wonderful life for her daughter and I expect she will continue to do so as long as necessary. Jack was just not what she expected and it's been hard for her. But she will do whatever is best for Luisa. I'd bet my seat on the heavenly choir on that."

"Oh, Henry, the way you sing they gave that seat away a long time ago."

ᴕξᴕ

The narrow asphalt road was lined on both sides with trees. The sun penetrated between large maple, sycamore and willow trees; the bright beams flashed on the windshield as they drove. Indiana's back roads were a transportation network from the past. The whole country had divided highways, but when Jill turned from paved road to gravel it was the same as it'd been fifteen years ago driving to Benton Harbor. The trees formed a thick natural tunnel. With the uneven ruts of stone, her car shuddered and rattled. The lake was surrounded by woods, but cottages sat on cleared squares of grass connected to the water's edge.

The gravel road continued, but Jill abruptly turned onto the two parallel concrete tracks of Molly's long driveway. Molly invited her to the cottage each summer after the pier was installed in June. The invitation stood until September. A handcrafted model of Molly's lake home served as a mailbox and the only driveway marker.

The cottage had no phone and no television. Mail was the only way to get a message to her. "Do Drop Inn," the white three-story frame house, sat atop a grassy terraced yard. It faced the calm lake, wide enough that binoculars were needed to see houses on the opposite side. Jill had been there when a thunderstorm brewed and caused the surface to be covered in white caps, with waves splashing against Molly's seawall.

Jill parked next to Molly's big blue station wagon. The car's back door was open and two air mattresses hung precariously on the bumper. There was a trail of inner tubes and swim fins to the side door, a door that led to a concrete block storage area under the deck. Jill and Luisa climbed three wide steps to the patio door and walked through the open sliding glass door. Molly sat at a Formica topped table in the middle of the large kitchen. Molly was frumpy, the victim of her own great cooking. Her dark hair was chopped short, a pixie which made her round face look fatter. She had slightly bulged blue-eyes. Her tan was varied dark and light shades from wearing different sundresses and swimsuits. She rarely sat still to sunbathe, staying instead, in the kitchen or laundry room. Molly held Jeremy wedged between her thick thighs. Jeremy was Molly's six year old nephew. Always Molly had her own two teenagers and "extras" as she called the contingent that came throughout the summer.

The cottage consisted of an upstairs with four large bedrooms, the middle floor with a large deck outside and the kitchen and family room, and the lower floor that could be used for sleeping among the stored lake toys. Molly posted rules for every room, and then yelled that her teenagers were illiterate. Anyone in wet swimwear was required to eat on the back patio, but the cushions on the kitchen chairs were often wet. Bring your own snacks. All damp towels were to be hung on the clothesline. Molly harped about these rules to anyone who would listen. Her oldest son would laugh and say, "Ah, Ma, give it a rest."

The kitchen smelled of sloppy Joes. Molly smiled as Jill and Luisa walked in, carrying sacks of groceries. Molly motioned toward a cleared space on the counter, and then finished tying the strings of Jeremy's bright orange life jacket.

"Hi, Sweetie," Jill said, bending over to kiss Molly's cheek, then Jeremy's, "I'm so happy to be here. We have more things, so we'll make a couple more trips."

"Sure, honey, you know I'm always glad when an adult walks through my door. There is only so much teenage I can take. Do you want a beer or lemonade? I'll fix it."

"Beer. Lemonade." Luisa and Jill said at once, then laughed.

Jill sent Luisa out to the car as she removed a glass from Molly's freezer. Luisa brought in the last bag of groceries, grabbed her lemonade and headed toward the stairs that led to the bedrooms.

"Luisa, put your mom's stuff in my bedroom, we'll split the twin beds," Molly said to Jill, then back to Luisa, "and you'll have to squeeze in…"

"I know Molly, I know," Luisa answered.

Jill sat down and sipped the icy beer, the first sip, the coldest sip always brought Hector's memory. "I needed this so much. I get...I didn't bring beer. I don't usually drink..."

"Stop, Jill, don't start that, my kitchen is yours. But why, though? Why did you want to get away? I have asked you since Memorial Day to come up. It isn't any hotter or muggier than the rest of the weekends."

"No, not hotter. It is just, oh, I wanted to talk to you. I'm thinking of divorcing Jack."

"Divorce Jack? I am not surprised, but why now? The big 'D,' huh? Something happen I should know about?" Molly drank her beer in one hand and stirred a large aluminum kettle with the other. She filled the ladle and brought it to Jill to taste. Jill nodded and gave the thumbs up.

Molly did not know of Luis. She returned the spoon to the holder, dripping ketchup sauce on the stove. She sipped the beer and wiped the spot with her apron. "Okay, Jill Jones, you're not talking. Do I have to ask questions? You are the one who always asks the questions. Tell me, is it another man? Oh, I know it isn't that, that only happens on soap operas."

"Yes," Jill spoke haltingly, "for the last six years."

Molly turned down the gas burner and plopped into the chrome chair. Her eyes asked, as she placed the beer on the table. In short interrupted thoughts Jill told Molly of Luis. Molly patted Jill's knee. When Jill finished the story, she drank the last of the beer. Molly jumped up and opened two more bottles.

"Jill, Luisa...she is starting high school, her whole support...her life...."

"Of course, Molly, it's like running into a wall as the song says, 'too high I can't get over it, so deep...'"

"And you want to, Honey?"

"Molly, I'll have to buy more beer."

"Shush, that rule is only for those alcoholics that think this is a damn tavern. We have to discuss this over beer." She picked up her bottle and tapped the edge of Jill's.

Molly had been divorced for several years. The settlement included alimony and the cottage. Jill had met her at school where they both worked. Molly was the school secretary. They had become friends through their mutual mission activities in the church. Molly's sweetness and good heart earned her the accolade "salt-of-the-earth" from Jill and

Sadie. Luisa and Molly's daughter, Jan, were the same age. The girls planned all their church outings together.

The cottage's niche in the woods created privacy and total darkness. It was Friday night, and the frogs belched their low gurgled croaks. Jill listened to their loud song from Molly's kitchen. The bugs smacked against the screen. She and Molly washed and dried dishes. Luisa and Jan walked in followed by Dean and two of his friends. Jan had long straight blonde hair with big green eyes. She had freckles across her nose and tanned skin. As the two girls stood together, Jill thought of Mo. Why Mo? The blonde hair and suntan? Maybe or maybe Mo was thinking of her. Grandma Caitlin had said when you think of someone who isn't with you, it's because they are thinking of you.

Dean, Molly's oldest teenager, was now trying to reach around Molly to get a bag of potato chips lying on the counter. Dean and his friends were dressed in jeans, t-shirts and sneakers. Jill teased them for getting out of their swim trunks. They reminded her of the Beach Boys with their scraggly bleached blond hair and suntanned faces.

"Mom," Jan spoke, "Dean is going into town. Can Luisa and I go?"

"What will you do in town?" Molly asked looking at each of her children's faces.

"Ma, I'm not taking them into town with me. It's like taking sand to the beach," Dean said, shaking his head at the girls.

"Mom, tell him, tell him he has to," Jan said.

"Luisa," Jill turned from the cabinet where she had placed a dried glass, "I think you better stay here with Molly and me."

Molly said, "Thanks, Jill. No girls in town."

"Thanks, Ma," Dean said, then grinned mockingly at Luisa and Jan.

"Now skedaddle, out! Out! Jill, do you want to get out the cookies you made?"

"Yes, Mom!" Luisa said, grabbing the big Tupperware tub. Luisa and Jan walked out of the kitchen to the front of the house. The couches and tables were arranged to look at the lake. The boys followed, begging for chocolate chip cookies.

"Spray yourself with OFF! if you go out," Molly yelled after all of them, then turned to Jill, "The mosquitoes have been little vampires this year, look!" Molly held out one arm that was covered with red bumps.

"Molly, how do you stay calm in all this craziness?"

"The kids are easy; it's dealing with Stanley that destroys me, even after being divorced for six years. I still hear the rumors of Stanley and student nurses. His weakness from the very beginning of medical school."

"Yeah, I had that long ago when I was engaged to a doctor. I hate the feeling of jealousy, really it still erupts occasionally even with Luis. He lives away and I don't know and my head starts traveling down a road of suspicion. He hates it and tells me, 'No need to feel that way.'"

When all the dishes were done and the kitchen swept, Jill realized the kitchen was cleaner than she had ever seen it. The house was quiet. The boys had left; Jeremy slept and Luisa and Jan had disappeared upstairs to their bedroom to listen to records.

"Jill, you are so lucky to have found Jack; he is such a devoted husband and you have him wrapped around your finger. How do you do that?"

"I don't bother him too much. And I let him enjoy the things he loves like gardening and fishing. Jack made the decision to be married and he doesn't want to make it again. Resolve, 'I hold these truths to be…' resolve – boring resolve in his whole attitude about life."

"He's a great father to Luisa. And he doesn't look at any other women."

Jill sighed. "You're right he loves Luisa."

"You say that as if it is wrong. What's going on here? Jack is a decent man. It is a rare quality. You should count your blessings."

"Yes, Lillian. He is an anchor and I'm sinking. Some days it takes everything I have to drive to the farm after work. Everything. Was Stanley any good in bed? Sadie tells me that's the key. Sadie, mother of three, she spends enough time there."

They laughed. Molly spoke, "Yeah when he wanted to be. I think he was always having an affair. Luisa's father? He ruined you for Jack, huh?"

"Maybe, maybe Hector. I tried, I have tried. It seemed so right at the time and maybe it still is. Sometimes I feel like I have been in some Broadway play and every night it is the same script, the same lines and now I'm tired. I want to change leading men, I want to change scripts, I want, no, I don't want to play act. I want something real."

"Sweetie, I'd think a long time before divorcing such a good, decent guy like Jack. You don't know what is going to happen in the long run. Sometimes what you think is going to happen doesn't."

"The Lillian in me listens to that same voice and keeps me on the farm. I wish you had a phone. I had a fight with her before I came up here, over this same stuff. I know you're both right, but I flew off the handle at Lillian." Jill let out a breath and shook her head.

ช๕ช

The morning was clear. The humidity percolated up from the grass. Jill stared at herself in the mirror. Her body glistened with the heat and moisture. She wore her bright blue two-piece, not quite a bikini. "Beautiful," Luis had said in Belize. Belize had been their last vacation, spring break 1975. She wrote about all of them in a journal. Their sixth Spring Break and she still didn't know much about Luis Ochoa. Who was he? Perhaps the mystery is what ruined her for Jack. She wanted to turn the page, but he avoided the most pointed questions. She'd learned to stop asking because he became annoyed at the same questions. Yes, in six years she had learned to almost accept his non-answers.

There was a knock on the partially opened door, Luisa walked in, "The Belize suit." She smiled at Jill.

"Shish."

"Mom, Jan went to put gas in the boat, do you want to swim with me?"

They left the cottage through the front upstairs' bedroom. The sliding doors opened onto wide wood stairs that led down to the main deck of the house. Water toys were scattered on the deck and the terrace. Luisa picked up two partially inflated rafts. She handed one to Jill, then quickly grabbed it from her.

"I know you're getting old Mom, and out of air; I'll blow yours up."

"Old? I'll race you to the diving platform anytime you think you're ready!"

"Now!"

They dropped the air mattresses, ran to the pier, then jumped into the fresh cool water. They swam the fifty feet to the wooden float. It rested at an angle on empty fifty-five gallon drums. The ladder hung from one side of the white wood. Luisa beat Jill slightly. She grabbed the edge of the platform and eased onto her back, laughing.

"Mom, remember when we raced last summer?"

132

"I beat you then, Miss Smarty-Pants."

"I know, that is what I was thinking. I'm bigger, big enough to beat you. Wait till Papa sees me. What will he say?"

"You want to see your papa?"

The mention of Luis caused Jill to shiver all over again. They rarely talked about him. The subject was their secret. Jill opened her eyes to make sure no one was in earshot.

"Mom, who is Papa? I mean really. He says he is a farmer. I wonder if he drives a tractor like Uncle Beau? He said coffee farming. But there are no coffee farms in Indiana. Don't you wonder about him on a tractor and in a barn?"

"I think he has laborers that work his farms and coffee is a crop that is planted and harvested by hand, on the sides of steep mountains. It requires a certain elevation and protection, so no tractors for your papa. I know he travels on a helicopter from where he lives in Cartagena to his farms. He doesn't say much more to me than you, maybe even more to you."

"Why do you love him? And you love Dad. How? I don't understand."

"At fourteen you can't understand completely, but I want you to."

The roar of the outboard motor muted their conversation. The boat came directly toward the deck, then cut away, making an arc of water that drenched them. Luisa jumped, yelling at Jan and Dean who were coming directly at the raft again. Just as they approached, Dean turned off the engine and they floated silently next to the raft which was rocking in the waves created by the two sweeps past.

"I'm sorry, Mrs. Jones," Dean looked at Jill from behind the steering wheel, "I had to get Luisa back. She and Jan sprayed me last time. Come on Luisa we're skiing from the pier."

The quiet returned and so, too, Luisa's unanswered question. Yes, she loved Jack. Oh jeez, love what a word, so many different ways and kinds of love. Jack loved her daily to the point of numbness and acceptance like the grandfather clock in her hallway. It was dependable, but she rarely noticed it anymore, the exquisite carved wood, ornate brass hands and moving dial face. She'd even grown so used to the loud ticking, she no longer heard it. Jack, what did he say to her last? Had she even heard him?

Jack took care of her, asked what she would fix for dinner and pulled meat from the freezer or retrieved canned vegetables from the basement storage. He kept her car clean and serviced, and the washer and dryer always worked. He changed every burnt out light bulb. Dependable Jack! But Luis sent enough money to buy another farm if she wanted one, or a new washer and dryer, or a new car. Lillian never mentioned the money, but she had to know that Luisa was getting experience as a world traveler, the kind of lesson she would not get in her classroom. Luisa had been places most of her friends only heard of in geography class.

Jill talked of her trips to some of her faculty friends. After the orientation meeting in late August, everyone asked what each had done during vacation. And now she was less than a month away from the next trip. Luis rarely told them where they were going or where they would meet him. Sometimes he would appear magically next to them on the plane, other times he would be at the airport when they arrived or a driver would be waiting for them. She never planned that part of the itinerary. Jack's itinerary was always the same – Sheboygan, Wisconsin, and so was the company – Beau, a farmer, Rick Harlow, a used car salesman and beer drinker extraordinaire, Crab Maxwell, no one ever called him Thomas except his secretary, "Law Offices of Thomas Maxwell," and Jack, an engineer. In ten years no changes to the same boring itinerary.

But Luisa, she answered to her absent daughter, there is the love of your father, Papa. How to explain the love of Luis? He made love with passion and forcefulness, and when he looked at her first thing in the morning or as he finished making love, just as Grandma Caitlin had said, she saw his soul, his feelings. She shivered now in the heat of the sun.

When she looked at Jack many more mornings than Luis, she saw nothing. Would the presence of Luis Ochoa diminish if she spent twenty-four hour days with him, week after week, months at a time? She fantasized about building a life with him. What did Henry remind her? Somewhere between reality and fantasy? Luis intimated there would be a "when" not an "if." He had a plan, but where she fit in was an ongoing question that was answered with a "not yet." He had deep reservations about pulling Luisa from her family and her life in Indiana. She knew he had been sent from his home and that act alone had made a difference in his life, one he mulled over with her. He occasionally said he had to do that to meet her, but expressed the pain he felt leaving his land and his home.

A spray of cool lake water startled her. She sat up as Luisa whizzed past on the water-skis, laughing and waving. Jill could almost hear her say, "Look Mom, one hand."

ᴦ§ᴦ

The weekend was over too quickly. Jill and Luisa honked as they drove away from the Do Drop Inn. The woods soon hid the house from view.

"I always feel so much better after a couple of days around the water. I hope Luis picks a spot next to the ocean this year," Jill said, turning from the concrete tracks to the gravel road.

"Where are we going? I need to call Papa and tell him I am going to church camp the first week in August. Jan and I planned our week. I get to go to Sr. High Institute this year. All the boys…"

"Don't mention that part to your papa. He'll plan our trip for sure that week," Jill said.

"I hope Grandma remembered to pick up my application at church this morning. I have to have it turned in this week along with the money."

"I'm sure your grandma will remember and grandpa will be happy to remind her."

"Mom, can we stop there on the way home? We go by Caylor first, please?"

"Sure, I need to apologize to Mom anyway."

Jill pulled out onto the main highway, rolled her window half-way up and signaled Luisa to do the same. When Luisa was finished, Jill turned off the radio, "When I was your age, Luisa…"

"Not another one of those lectures, 'boys at church camp,' by Jill Havlicek…" Luisa paused and laughed.

"Aren't you full of sass, it must be the 'teenage' Molly fusses about. No, not a lecture, but yesterday you asked about the men in my life…"

"Mom, other mothers don't have two men in their lives at once."

"I don't know about other women, but I will try to explain mine. One of them is home with me; I know where he is twenty-four hours a day. He loves you and makes sure we are both taken care of.

135

The other one…he loves you, too. He provides plenty of money to take care of your needs, but we can't be together. He won't tell me why."

"What does he say?"

"We can't be with him. He is too far from your grandpa and grandma, too far from our home."

"Grandma says 'home is where your heart is.' Where's your heart, Mom?"

"Aren't you being all grown up?" How could she tell Luisa her heart was in South America? Jill continued, "It isn't so easy. Sometimes your heart says one thing and you can't use it for decision making."

"Clear as mud, Mom, maybe when I'm older, right?" Luisa reached over and turned on the radio.

They drove down U.S. 31 headed south. Luisa kept pushing the buttons of the car radio. She found a station she liked and laid her head back on the seat, closing her eyes. The angel at fourteen she still had a sweet baby face, but when she was angry her face became that of Luis Ochoa. She rarely let her anger control her, although Jill had seen her let go with fury at one of Dean's friends. Luisa did not say what the boy said or did, but Dean told him to get out of the house. Jill had seen the face as Luisa stood in the kitchen door, watching the boy walk out the back door. Luisa had one hand clenched as if she wanted to punch the kid. In the quick glance before comforting her, Jill had said, "Luis's daughter."

The big rough hand-painted signs advertising O'Brian's Orchard sprang up like milkweed along the rusted barbed wire fences. "Fresh Green beans," "Fresh Peaches," "Melons," "Sweet Corn – yellow or white," "Sorghum," "Tomatoes." She slowed down and drove onto the crunchy highway shoulder, then into the dusty gravel parking lot. Several cars and trucks were parked by the entrance. She pulled into a spot by a miniature red barn marked with a "For Sale" sign. A cute tool shed for Jack; maybe a summer project for him. Something to do while they were on vacation with Luis. Luisa woke up with the gravel pinging underneath the car.

"O'Brian's, Mom?"

"Yes, I want to get some things. You sleeping or coming in?"

They both walked into the reconverted barn to be met with competing smells of strawberries, peaches and corn on the cob. Large metal scoops jutted out of open burlap bags filled with rice, beans, and coffee. She smiled at the words "Imported from Colombia" printed on the bag. Jill grabbed a basket and started sorting through the apples.

Luisa came to her, holding long strings of red licorice and a bag of sunflower seeds.

"Mom, when will you tell Dad about Papa?"

Jill shook open a brown paper sack and put handfuls of green beans into it. She told Luisa to pick out two quarts of blueberries.

Luisa talked, walking toward the large wood table of berries in their wood baskets, "Don't try to get out of this. I want to go to Colombia to see Papa."

When Luisa came back, she squeezed the berries next to a ten pound bag of potatoes in Jill's cart.

"When, Mom?"

"I can't tell Jack," Jill said, tapping a musk melon, "not yet."

"Am I Colombian? My mom is American and my papa is Colombian, so what am I?"

"Now that is a good question for your papa. Here help me with this bushel of peaches."

Jill showed the man behind the counter her produce. He was middle-aged with a farmer's tan. He wore a green apron over a short-sleeved plaid shirt. He nodded and smiled as he weighed her green beans. His forehead was white where his hat protected him from the sun. His arms and face were like Henry's, the color of permanently baked brown. Henry was mostly retired now, but he stayed brown all year. Mr. O'Brian called a teenage boy to help Jill with the bushel of peaches.

"We grew 'em right behind the barn. Best peaches in Indiana. I know Benton Harbor says they sell the best peaches, Michigan peaches, but I swear by these Hoosier specials. They make great pie, and great for canning. Come back and see us now."

Jill left telling him she would have her husband drive up and take a look at the red barn outside. Jill followed the teen-age boy to her car where Luisa stood with the trunk open. As Jill bent over the trunk, Luisa said, "Mom, Aunt Sadie just pulled in here."

"She comes here sometimes to get fresh vegetables. You know she has no garden. We'll have to tell her how nice the lake was."

Jill stood up, slamming the trunk. She turned around to watch as Sadie's four-wheel screeched to a stop. Michael jumped out of the passenger side. Sadie slammed the driver's door and ran towards Jill. Michael came to Luisa, and hugged her, "Bad news, Lo."

Sadie held out both arms, then hugged Jill, "Sweetie, Lillian and Henry were killed! Only hours ago...On their way home from church...a rig, oh you know all those lights they run, trying to get by

Caylor...oh, god, Sweetie," and she stopped talking, but sniffled and wiped her eyes.

Jill clung to Sadie and they cried, pressed together. Jill sobbed, against Sadie's chest. The long and short of it, her dad's description, Dad. No, no, "No Sadie, no, not them! Why? Coming home from church? No, those lights are on the by-pass, not home from church, no. Are you wrong?"

Sadie patted Jill's hair, stroking her softly, as tears covered her cheeks, "They must have been on their way to Henry's favorite cafeteria on the by-pass, Lorraine's."

"Mom and Dad... Sadie?" Jill said and pulled away from Sadie. They walked to Luisa and hugged her. Luisa squeezed her mom, whispering "Not Grandma and Grandpa," she repeated their names as she took each breath. Sadie embraced both of them speaking, "Jill, Michael's going to drive your car. I drove 100 miles an hour to get to Molly's, but I missed you. Let's go. Jack's at your mom's."

She heard the four wheeler's door slam and noticed a box of Kleenex on her lap. Jill pulled one out as Sadie slid in the driver's seat. Luisa leaned from the back seat and patted her mom's shoulder.

"Mom and Dad? Sadie," Jill reached for Sadie's arm, "not Henry. No, no." Her whole body tightened. She swallowed and swallowed, but her throat had closed and she cried. Her face burned; she rolled down the window and let the wind tangle her hair. She closed her eyes to the whipping strands and imagined the truck hitting Henry and Lillian's big Buick. How fast was the truck speeding, trying to beat a red light? She heard the crash and clenched her fists and screamed, "No! Not Dad! Stop! Stop!" Jill slammed her hand on the dashboard. "No, Sadie, tell me..." Sadie patted her hand.

Sadie talked, but the wind drowned out her voice. The slap of air beat her. Jill was filled with the present, but only sat and cried about the past. The vacations, the long talks, "Sadie, who will I talk to? Who? He was the only one who listened, who knew. Oh, Sadie. What am I going to do without him?"

Sadie responded through her own tears, "You know he was like the Dad I never had. He was my dad, too. We'll just have to try harder to be there for each other, to help each other and to think what Henry would say. I loved them so much. Oh, their house, their love, home to me, too. Lillian put up with us when we were naughty. Remember when we decided to make a cake only we didn't know you needed a recipe?"

"Recipe? We didn't know the word."

"There was flour and sugar everywhere and how many eggs did you use? She only scolded us a little bit and cleaned up the oven."

"All that burnt dough and the dried eggs on the cabinet...Sadie...no Mom to call and say, 'Can you pick up Luisa? Can we come to dinner? I don't feel like cooking.' And she would call Jack and invite him, so he would think it was her idea, not me being her spoiled baby.'"

"She made us know the meaning of 'lady-like. Now you girls sit there and act lady-like.'"

"Sadie, she really made you and Mom act good?" Luisa asked.

"Every Wednesday, for church children's choir. We had practice," Jill said.

"And we hated going."

Jill shook her head and blew her nose, "But Luisa, we could have earned our angel wings when we were in that Wednesday Wonderful choir."

"Wonderful? No, we endured and smiled on Sunday mornings when we had to sing," Sadie said.

"Yeah, Honey, our only saving grace was Sadie and I couldn't carry a tune."

"Luisa, your mother can sing. I'm tone deaf."

"As soon as we passed being cute, Mom didn't make us go anymore. I think that ole Miss Higgenbottom, the choir director, called her to encourage us to quit."

The drive to Caylor seemed short. At the moment Jill adjusted to the comfort zone in Sadie's car, they drove up in front of Lillian and Henry's house.

Jill and Luisa walked up the porch and were besieged with Jack's brothers, sisters-in-law and the cousins. Henry and Lillian's house contained everyone, but no one. All these people needed to leave so Henry and Lillian could come home.

Jill hugged and cried her way into the kitchen. Jack answered sympathy calls on the telephone, but dropped the phone and held her. Patting her hair not speaking, he did not let go of her, hugging her in silence. When Jill had come through the swinging door, Henry's minister rose from the kitchen table. Reverend Bradstreet with his fat arms and fatter stomach waited to hug her. Friar Bradstreet, she and Sadie had nicknamed him. He was all round, short, bald, and a connoisseur of church potlucks. Jill cried until her breath came in spasms. Jill pushed away from Jack and took a Kleenex from Sadie.

Reverend Bradstreet put his arm around her shoulder, "God now has two of the very best people in His home."

Sadie fixed them iced tea, but insisted Michael go get some vodka for them. He objected saying the liquor stores were closed on Sunday. Sadie said, "Michael, go to your mom's; she has more liquor than the liquor store."

Jack talked on the phone with the mortuary for the cremation instructions. Henry had specified that he and Lillian should be cremated.

"I came from dust and I will join my Maker the same way. I want you to think of me every time you have to clean up, 'that damn Henry! Dust everywhere!'" Henry had repeated this description of his demise many times.

Jack made the provisions calmly in the chaotic middle of too many people and too many things. Jack held his arm around Luisa.

Jill always dismissed all the talk of his preparations to meet "the grim reaper," now he had done just what he said. No, no, she shook her head and walked out of the kitchen. Each room became a kaleidoscope of peoples' distorted faces and Lillian's furniture and lamps, swirling colors of light, then the phone ringing and the door bell, the wind chimes from the front porch. She leaned against the wedding wall, feeling the same as when she exited the Tilt-a-Whirl at the county fair. The stairs...she climbed a few steps and sat down. She bent her head between two of the oak balusters, grabbing the carved wood, she cried.

People brought food, but why to Lillian's kitchen? Lillian was going to come in any moment and cook, yes, she would bring her garden vegetables in the scoop of her apron. She would fuss about all these people in her kitchen. Jill closed her eyes and heard Henry's truck pull up. She knew it was Henry coming from work. No, it was Sunday. Henry wasn't coming to his house ever again.

Jill ambled outside to the porch swing. The box of patches sat on the table. She rubbed the top of the shoe box, "Mom, I'm sorry," she started, "so sorry."

Sadie walked out to the porch and handed Jill a glass of iced tea, then sat next to her. Jill picked up a quilt square and used it for a handkerchief.

"Sadie, I can't take it here anymore. Could we leave? And just go somewhere? I feel like they're here, but they aren't. I feel like they are going to drive up and Dad is going to say 'What the Sam Hill are all these people doing at my house?' I don't. I can't be here. Let me check on my baby." Jill stood up and started toward the screen door.

"Yeah, whatever you want to do, *whatever*. I'll tell Michael. Jack can handle all these things. It is what he does best."

They took the vodka, two cups, a small cooler of ice and drove to the park. The park had no phones, no messengers of condolence. Sylvan Park and Sylvan Creek were a rustic combination of shaded trails and open grassy fields. The crooked creek meandered between a thick stand of black walnut trees and towering maples. A red covered bridge had been built over the tiny creek. How many times had she and Sadie come to this place to talk and solve what seemed like all the world's problems? The friends now walked along a narrow path by the splashing and chatting creek, the soothing sound of water on rocks.

"Jill, do you want me to call Luis? I think he would want to know. God, I wish Henry had met him. I think he'd be pleased to know the strength of the man who captured your heart."

"Can I just wish him here? But no one knows, only Dad and ...Oh Sadie, I don't want Dad to be gone. Why? Why? He was so healthy. All that work on those houses kept him strong. Mom's mom lived to be 90. Mom should be here. She had so many years left. Why Sadie? Why? Tell me the reason, please."

"There is no answer, but he is here with us, his presence. He loved the park, this corner of the world. He brought us here and we played in the creek catching crawdads and tadpoles. He swung us as high as we wanted on the swings and caught us at the end of the curly-que slide. Yeah, Henry's here. And he's here in us, we always say, 'As Henry would say.' He put that in us, all the Hoosier philosophy. What would he say now? He went 'to take his seat on the heavenly choir' and 'how much better it sounds already?'"

Jill had to laugh through her tears with her best friend. "You're right Sadie. He would be having a good time with both of us reduced to tears. He would be in shock that we were crying. I think he figured us for a couple of hedonists and that we missed our calling. We should've run a brothel."

"See, I told you, he is coming right out of your mouth."

"Do I sound like him?" Jill asked.

"You always have. It is just now, we'll have to rely on you."

The squirrels rummaged through the grass as the women threw pebbles into the creek, watching the small ripples. The ducks gathered quickly, diving for the pieces. Sadie said, "Sorry ducks, no bread around here only vodka." They walked, kicked sticks and reminisced.

"Jill, will you be okay, now? Do you want to go the farm? Or back to Lillian's?"

"I'll be okay. What did Dad say? 'Chin up and keep going'? I'm okay for the moment. Take me to Mom's."

The house had cleared. The kitchen was filled with food. Jack greeted them, "Are you okay, Honey?"

Jill nodded.

Sadie said, "Jack, we've talked. It's a hole in our hearts that only time and each other can heal, if ever. They were like my parents, too. So much better than Emma Sue. A Mom and Dad who loved me like I was their own daughter." Sadie hugged them both and left. "Jill, I will call whoever I think needs to know."

Jack handed Jill a list with the time of the memorial service and the cremation process. She sat down at the kitchen table across from Luisa. She held her hand and spoke words that ran together through her tears.

"They will call and see if we want to see them before their bodies are cremated. You can make that decision and if you want viewing at the memorial service and the church."

The basic facts cemented the deaths. Jack's pronouncements smacked against the spiritual presence of Henry and Lillian. His cold details slowly brought the reality of death back to Jill.

"The memorial service," Jack said, "will be next Sunday. It should be time enough for everyone to get here. Henry's sisters will have to come from Florida. Your brothers thought that was good. But, Honey, if you want something else…"

"No, Jack, you do this fine, just keep organizing. I can't think about it. I don't want to. I'm going to take Luisa back to the farm. I don't want to stay here any longer." One call to Colombia, oh, she wanted to do that, but…no, from Sadie's. She would go tomorrow and make the call with her.

Chapter 7

Jill knelt on a green velvet pad lining the church's oak railing, a small bent shape in the cavernous church sanctuary. Two-story floor to ceiling stained glass windows dominated one side, allowing the muted shades of light to illuminate the quiet space. Serenity filled every inch. Jill prayed at the altar, asking God to help her accept what had happened. Her thick and swollen eyes hurt from crying. A large black straw hat hid her face. Sadie convinced her to wear the borrowed hat to prevent anyone from seeing her sadness. The service had gone smoothly. They sang Henry's favorite hymns, "This is my song, O God of all the nations, a song of peace for lands afar and mine. This is my home the country where my heart is….other hearts in other lands are beating with hopes and dreams as true and high as mine…Oh Lord."

And "A Mighty Fortress," the song repeated over and over as she prayed. The soloist's baritone voice had given her cold chills as Miss Higgenbottom played on the organ.

Oh, Dad, so many others whose hearts beat, I wish you could have met him, to hear him, to know his heart, not just my heart, to know that he loves me. Are you listening, Dad? Can you see me? Your spirit is here. You haven't left me yet, say something, let me know. I'm lost. I need you. Do you know that? I tried to hear the words, "A bulwark never failing..." My faith isn't as strong as yours. You were my bulwark, now what, Dad? They say you are with Mom and you are at peace with God. I need you here with me.

She stopped. Luis will never know him. She shuddered and wiped her face with a damp Kleenex. "A bulwark never failing..." A bulwark never failing? How to be that strong to never fail. I need to be strong.

Luisa walked from the pew, then the few steps to where Jill prayed and placed her hand on Jill's shoulder. The wood of the old church floor creaked with her movement. "Mom, do you want me to stay here with you? Everyone else has gone downstairs to the reception; I think Aunt Sadie is trying to organize all of that."

"I want to be alone for a while longer, angel. Please tell your dad and Sadie, I'll be down soon." Her chest shook with each gasp.

"Yes, soon. Aunt Sadie will be here to get you, if she thinks you've been alone too long."

Luisa stood and walked away from the altar. Jill heard her daughter's footsteps on the squeaky wood, then a pause in her walking and then silence. The sanctuary entombed her, a creak, and another creak. She tried to pull the silence into her head, to create internal peace, but couldn't. She squeezed the wood railing, "Please God, please give me the strength to open my eyes tomorrow and the next day and the day after that. Please help me...I need the bulwark."

"Jill," Luis whispered.

She squeezed the rail, bending her head closer toward the gold oak with their dull brass hinges. A twinge caught her from shoulder to ear and then she smelled Luis's spicy cologne. He knelt next to her. She laid her hand on his arm, and squeezed gently, then tighter. A flesh and blood Luis. He embraced her, kissing each cheek, then held her tightly. Jill trembled and cried. A mighty fortress, a bulwark never failing... she clung to him and blinked tears that refused to stop. Dad, did you send him?

The afternoon light radiated through the stained glass illuminating one side of his face. He turned looking over his shoulder to the balcony, then all the way to the dark shadows at the back of the church. As his attention returned to her face, the sun struck his green eyes, slicing across the penetrating stare, "Is there a private place? Where no one…"

He abruptly stood, then pulled her up quickly. She led him to one side of the sanctuary and a small door that opened into the choirs' storage room. They slipped in and closed the door. Dusty shafts of colored sunlight lit the cluttered quiet space. Gold and white satin robes hung in an open closet. A scent of lemony furniture polish permeated the room. The folding chairs held hymnals. Felt banners in purple, green, red, gold and white drooped haphazardly from free-standing poles. A baby grand piano was partially covered in purple flannel quilting. Luis sat on the quilt covered piano stool.

"Luis, I thought you wouldn't, couldn't …" she held his shoulders.

"I was able to come. I wanted to be here for you, even if I can be of little help. These are your people, this is your town and these United States are a very inhospitable place. But you know I am here for you and Luisa. I saw her as I walked in. She said that you needed me."

"Can you stay?"

"No, I must return almost immediately."

"You came all this way for such a short time?"

"I combined business with this personal trip. I had avoided the business, but your call…." He nodded toward the outside of the church, "…it was a sign."

She looked toward his nod, but saw only the stained glass scene of Jesus praying at Gethsemane. "I wish you had known my dad. He was the man in my life. And my mother, she never understood, but she accepted me and loved me unconditionally. Oh Luis, I feel lost. I thought I would always have them to take care of me and now…"

"And now me, Gringa. You know money is available…"

"I don't think about the money. I just want…oh, it always comes to this," she sighed and shook her head.

"To what?"

"To us. It is impossible. You live a million miles from me. You can't live here. I can't live there. I hate it. I'm tired of living this lie."

"It's not a lie. It is the circumstance of our life. Between us there is no lie." He frowned. "What do you want me to do? We can only stay here for a moment before you will be missed. I told Luisa to keep Siddhartha busy while I talked to you."

"Tell me we can be together. I just said goodbye to my mom and dad. I want so much for Luisa to have us together. I don't think I could have lived the life I've lived, including meeting you if not for them. Now Luis, now, please think about this."

He held her tightly. As he kissed her, her hat fell to the floor. She tasted the cigar and felt his mustache, the comfort of holding him, the assurance encircled her.

"Luisa starts high school, a very important time."

"Are there no high schools in Colombia?"

"Si. English speaking schools? Not many. We will be together for two weeks. Let's talk about all of this then, together, as you say. I have a surprise for you, but together. I think it is time to plan our time, *together* for a month or two in the summer. Luisa must begin to know much more about the world in which she is growing up."

"Months?"

"Si. Your school vacation is three months."

"Jack?"

"As I've said before *your* husband. You say together. He is not included in that term?"

She shook her head.

"I must go," Luis said.

"I love you," she squeezed his hand tightly, as if holding it could keep him.

He stood and she slid from his lap. "Si. Hasta que la muerte nos separe… Te amo. Now I must leave. We will meet next month, as always, in August. I will find my way out." He bent down, retrieved her hat, handed it to her, and then kissed the tip of her nose, "We'll talk, and call me anytime. I wanted to hold you, to feel." He embraced her tightly, then turned and opened the door cautiously and left.

ᴙξᴙ

The dark blue Lincoln idled across from the church. A twenty-ish man with military-cut light reddish-brown hair sat tapping his fingers on the steering wheel as if keeping time to a song that only he could hear. Luis opened the passenger's door and slid onto the leather seat. This slightly tan, young man said he was twenty-six, but looked eighteen, Raymond Sandy.

"The church resembles a fortress," the younger man spoke over the hum of the air conditioner, "is it to keep people in or out?"

Luis turned the dashboard vent to blow directly on his face. The wide cushioned seats of the Lincoln absorbed the rough country roads that took them out of Caylor toward the airbase, Grissom Air Force Base. Raymond Sandy explained it used to be called Bunker Hill, maybe Luis remembered that name. The blue road sign said 400W.

"Señor Sandy, continue to 450 West, then turn south."

"Not the way to the air base, Mr. Ochoa."

"Si, a short detour. I may never see this place again, but it has much meaning for me."

The heavy green weeds of the drainage ditch slapped against the car. Luis pressed the power window button; the glass retracted into the door and the humid July afternoon blasted into the car as if opening an oven door.

"Mr. Ochoa, this is why they install air condition…"

"I want to hear this place," Luis spoke softly.

The flap-flap-flap of milkweed hitting steel and the ping-ping-ping of gravel, the soundtrack of those migrant days. The hot wind rushed across his face. Luis took off his tie and unbuttoned the top buttons of his shirt. He closed his eyes and took a deep breath. Raymond Sandy automatically lowered the rest of the windows ratcheting up the heat and the volume of the country's sounds.

The red barn appeared on the horizon. The large black letters were chipped and bleached, but readable, "McKinnsey." The cow's picture still visible in the washed-out paint. Luis smiled slightly. The fields stretched in both directions, tomato plants, rambling vines, row after row.

"Mr. Ochoa, you've been here before?"

"You know everything about me, Señor Sandy," Luis said not looking at Raymond Sandy, "or is your CIA (Central Intelligence Agency) not so efficient to know this piece?" Luis chuckled, then lit his cigar. "Cuban, Señor Sandy, in your United States, do you want one?" Raymond Sandy shook his head.

"Slow down," he commanded through a puff of smoke. The tiny shed was now only see-through rotted slats. Hollyhocks and sunflowers wove in and out of each rough crack, a tapestry of plant stems and clapboard. A broken rusted tractor appeared to hold up one wall. Luis shook his head, "Ah, young man, destiny, the invisible contract more trenchant than prison shackles. What a difference traveling this road has made. I borrow from Señor Frost."

"I'm familiar with Robert Frost. I have traveled many roads not taken, including this one. I am not familiar with this flat Indiana farmland or these country roads, although my sister spent some time here at college in Elliston. I remember driving…"

"When?"

"Let's see, she graduated in 1964. It's been awhile. Where to Mr. Ochoa?"

Luis pointed to a road sign. 1964 was when Jill graduated. The CIA did not know this either. "When it says 250 North, turn right. You will hit Highway 31, then north to Señor Sam's air base."

"This farmland all looks the same. We call these mid-western states fly-over country." Sandy chuckled at his characterization.

"Flying over such rich farmland, dirt that produces food to feed your American citizens. And you say 'National interests,' what could be more in your interest than this land?" Luis turned away from the youngster, staring at the green foliage that extended as far as they could see, so accessible. His mountains were fly-over country, the only way to get to certain places. His land was the reason for riding in a car with a boy from the CIA.

Raymond Sandy, it was probably not even his Christian name. Christian? These basura had no Christian in them, no souls, amoral predators. They lived in the shadows destroying governments, assassinating leaders, Chile, Señor Allende what a good man, and Señor Mosaddeq in Iran. They will political rivers to change course, "American Interests" and "National Security" were the euphemisms for their treachery. Did these United States even know their interests? A democracy that destroys democracy in the name of profit? Ah, si, the capitalism, the great American financial institutions. Unable to tame the jungles of Ho Chi Minh, but they fell in love with drug money, another financial institution. Their banks now filled with cash, cocaine or heroin on every dollar bill.

Luis had delayed this conversation for months. "They" the elusive they of their nether world called, contacted, and called again. Were there any roads they did not travel to pursue their national security interests? They had clandestinely called on Jorge. The revolutionary guerillas set up the labs to process their coca leaves. They paid for the right to use the land or killed the owners and took the land. The DEA (Drug Enforcement Agency) wanted to catch them, ruining whose cash supply? Señor Sandy's, or Bank of America's? But Luis had to get some relief for his section of the cordilleras, Colombia's mountains, so graceful, so inaccessible. And Saldana under constant protection, more soldiers to protect the hacienda, more weapons, more defenses.

Coffee takes too long to develop in the richest tradition of Colombia. Each week brought some new problem, more costly than the last. Death. Too many were dying in the mountains; the rivers filled with dead bodies. Raymond Sandy could stop some of the madness. They would train between coca fields and coffee bushes. Let them be the first line of defense for Saldana, keep the guerillas from trying to recruit his campesinos. His father had been so good at maintaining the balance.

The eight hours from Caylor on the small Beechcraft Baron to Miami with only one stop eviscerated the men. They faced each other in the four small leather seats behind the pilot. They argued, negotiated, compromised then struck a deal. They called it "the meeting." When Raymond Sandy shook his hand on the runway, Luis sensed respect from the young man.

There were those who took U.S. Government aid, USAID (US Agency for International Development), or their World Bank, loans provided to assist farmers in their development of cash crops. There were those who took U.S. Government aid as payment in kind. They allowed the U.S. Government agents to use their jungle properties as training camps for soldiers who would be deployed for secret military operations deep in Central America. And there were those who did both.

Luis would play these government agents. DEA? No, they were unsophisticated cowboys. The CIA and their special forces trained to work in the jungle unseen, denying every mission? Yes, they, Raymond Sandy, promised to protect him in all his dealings. His coffee would be defended where need be. It was not his first experience at the game board of international chess. Chess, Luisa must practice this game with him, next month. Jill seemed to keep her in adolescence, not enough Spanish and not nearly enough world politics.

Luis left Miami. The sea stretched under him. In a few hours he would be home.

Twenty years ago, 1955, creeping and crawling from Veracruz to Monterrey to get in those United Sates by train. Would he have believed the story then if told, one day…one day Señor Ochoa, you will be *ushered* through United States Government Customs Agents to board your own Lear Jet after a meeting with another government agent, a representative from the CIA? No, he would have accused the fortune teller of insanity.

In 1955, Monterrey, Mexico had been exactly as Manuel described it. The place was teeming with peasant laborers, standing in lines to vie for the limited openings in the bracero program. Luis had paid a few people and soon stood at the front table talking to the contractors. He answered the first question in English. They paused from their paperwork to eye the Colombian. They asked his place of birth, "Mexico City," he had answered. The gringo contractors, he quickly learned, needed English speaking laborers to help with the Immigration Service papers. One interviewer asked where he had learned English. Luis had spoken haltingly; the foreign tongue had become rusty in its non-use. He had had no need for it at Ramos's hacienda.

The interviewer introduced himself as Mr. Martinez, a stocky man with silver gray hair, long side burns and a large red mole on his nose. Mr. Martinez took Luis into an office and asked him to have a seat, then Martinez paced around and around looking at Luis.

"Ah, yes, Señor Ochoa, correct?"

Luis stared at the nervous man and said nothing.

"We," Martinez continued, "have a need for bilingual workers to help transport, but mostly to work with our members, the landowners. We pay better, well actually you earn a percent of the fee on the labor that you can deliver. You would work back and forth across the border, but only seasonally. You understand two months or forty-five days at a time? We don't have braceros in the U.S. too long. Señor Ochoa, you have a birth certificate?"

"No, Señor Martinez."

"We'll arrange for that in order to ensure your safe entry and exit. Are you interested?"

Luis had not decided if this were good fortune or bad to be advanced so quickly into the program. Reluctantly he answered, "Si, Señor Martinez. Please explain exactly what is expected of me and how much I will be paid."

They had their meeting. Luis secured not only a higher wage, but also a position for which others wanted to bribe him for preferred treatment. The first contracts were in East Texas to pick cotton. Luis became a crew chief, but the bigger picture, the Bracero Program, he found unsettling. Once again a powerful group was taking advantage of the economic hardship of another group. In the first year of his bracero experience, he was in and then out of the United States. He hated the yo-yo program. Every time he reentered into Mexico, he worried if the

150

federales would be waiting to arrest him or at least ask questions about Ramos Ochoa. But nothing.

The United States Government used the laborers until they were done with them like spent casings, then shipped them back to Mexico to wait for the next call.

To make money in the United States one had to stay in the United States. Forty-five days was not enough time, and the Mexican government kept part of his wages. One year of the bracero program convinced Luis he must do something different. He would end his connection to the program and do as others had done.

Luis had chosen Nuevo Laredo as the beginning of the jump. He made inquiries. He could not return to Colombia, and he could not go back to Veracruz. At the border town, he could cross with a coyote's help.

Luis now flew over the turquoise sea, shimmering like a woman's silk scarf in a breeze. The pilot announced they would be arriving in Cartagena on time. Home, an impossible destination on that starry night in Laredo. He had never heard of the CIA, or Lear jets, or his little gringa, and never fathomed the money, more money than.... Oh Jill, I have come so far and returned. I had wanted to find you that lonely night and did not even know you.

"Say, Ochoa," the coyote spoke in the Texas darkness. Jose, he said his name was Jose. They were all named Jose or Jesus, a transportation business without correct names. "Where," Jose continued, "did you learn to fish?"

The firelight illuminated Jose's high cheek bones, shiny forehead, smooth face and the glint in his eyes. He'd told Luis he was part Indian. His teeth were broken and chiseled, his hands tough and used like the soles of good boots.

The coyotes were always available for a few dollars to escort the desperate into the United States, el Norte. It was considered the haven. Even now, as he sat in the comfort of his own plane, he too, had looked again to the United States for a haven. Father Ibarra had told him, "Luis, you belong to a vast interconnecting community." And so he sat eating fish long ago in the moonless night with a coyote, listening for the rumbling, then the whistling of the train. They were a quarter mile from where they were to jump the Missouri-Pacific train that would take them north of Laredo. It would carry him deeper into the United States, avoiding the border and the agents.

"How long do we have?" Luis asked Jose.

151

"Not too long," Jose cocked his head listening. "I have enjoyed your company, Ochoa."

Company? It had been only a couple of days, but Luis had many coyotes to pick from and his Jose had strong shoulders and honest eyes. He stood straight, ramrod steel. Life at the border should have beaten him to the shape of a cane chair, but Jose stared people directly in the eye.

"Where you come from Ochoa?"

"Veracruz."

In the distance they heard the train whistle, the only train that left this late from the Laredo yard. Most were scheduled for the daylight hours to avoid this illegal riding.

"Great fish," the coyote spoke, "I didn't realize the Rio Bravo could grow something this tasty." The whistle sounded, louder, closer. "Señor," Jose stood and threw the fish into the fire, "it is time."

They started to jog toward the steel-clack, Jose said, "We'll run until we are going as fast as the train. It is slow still, but grab the ladder and pull yourself up the side. Crawl along the top of the car until you find the open door, drop over the side, swing into the box," his directions were now coming between breaths of air, "Do it as quickly as you can because it will pick up speed quickly. Good Luck in San Antone."

"I will always remember your help. Jose, if…"

"One favor Ochoa…."

"Si?" Luis spoke as the train's large lights illuminated the scrub brush.

"Sometime when you see a man in trouble, help him." It was the last time Luis heard his voice. He knew Jose had not heard him say, "Consider it done." The sound was deafening, but he ran and ran. In the end with one swift reach, he held the steel ladder.

Coyotes, Luis now stared at the horizon – blue sea, white sky, CIA agents, the Farm Labor Act, all doing the same thing, conducting foreigners who were needed for national interests in and out of these United States, a porous border when need be. Raymond Sandy, CIA; or Jose, coyote, they made it easy to move across the border. He shook his head, ah Jose. Had it been twenty years? Father Ibarra had spoken to Luis in the quiet voice of empty classrooms and silent cathedrals. Much of what Father had said made little sense to the seventeen-year-old that spent most of the time being homesick, although Luis had carefully listened.

Now the priest's husky low voice repeated itself, "Man's longing for himself, to be free, to be independent, to have a better life, the drive to risk his life for another place. You are driven Luis Ochoa. You'll join those before you, and you'll make a tread in the path for someone to follow."

How did he know? Father Ibarra had cautioned against dismissing any parts of experience no matter how small. "These parts," the priest explained, "will be important at the least expected moment."

ᴦξᴦ

It had been three weeks since Henry and Lillian had died. She'd written Mo at the last address from her Christmas card, but she had no idea how long it would take to find her. Then Mo had called and said she would be in Chicago; could Jill come and meet her? Jill hung up the receiver having said "yes." It would be so good to see her. All these years they had promised to see, to meet, to spend time together, but something always came up. Maybe a weekend in Chicago would be a nice change? Luisa would be at church camp. She could drop her off at the lake cottage retreat, then drive two more hours into Chicago.

Mo had said Stewart would be in meetings during the days. They could shop and talk. Talk. Mo had said the word in a tone that meant only one thing – there was news of her father she wanted to share. The colonel, she would have to remember to call him. Sadie always said, "The Captain," in a mocking tone. The captain, the colonel, the professor, it had been ten years, one husband and Luis. Her life had changed. Mo had written of new women in and then out of William's life, never staying long.

Chicago. The drive had been simple. She now drove around the block to find parking. Chicago kept growing and growing. So many new landmarks she needed to come more often, but now her travel plans included Luis and Chicago was not on his agenda. She wedged her car into the place the attendant indicated and handed him the keys.

She walked onto bustling Michigan Avenue. In Los Angeles she had seen her first hippies, now Chicago had long-haired men in platform shoes. Bob Dylan sang, "The times they are a-changin'." Chicago defined this song; Caylor was stuck in the 1950's, just the way they wanted it. Flower children? They had all been invited to San Francisco and too many from Caylor had died in Viet Nam and others had come home changed. She would listen to Mo's take on the end of

153

the war and in turn what the colonel thought as Mo always said, "Well, the colonel says…"

Jill called on the hotel's house phone. Mo let out a whoop, then instructed Jill to come up to the room. The paneled and mirrored elevator eliminated any discomfort of riding up twenty-six stories to the top of the hotel. When the doors opened, she was met by security officers. Mo also stood with them.

"You're here!" Mo hugged her, then looked at her, then hugged her again. Mo escorted Jill down the hall and into a suite of rooms. She closed the door behind them, then immediately put her fingers to her lips. "I know you have questions, but I can't answer them here. We'll go for lunch, then walk to the park. My father taught me well." Mo winked at Jill.

"And me," Jill laughed.

"You took a different course from him than me," Mo teased her with a big smile. "We have much to catch up on. I am sorry about your parents. They were so good to me at school. If it hadn't been for your mother's care packages, I think we would have starved some days. And, of course, I want to know 'the between the lines' of your letters. I also think you have had some between the sheets. I need to know the details. Is that your new theme song, 'Me and Mrs. Jones, we got a thing going on…'"

Jill crossed her index fingers indicating that Mo was insinuating misbehavior.

Mo laughed, "I am a terrible writer, so I don't blame you for not giving me more details. You never seem to tell me the whole story. The affair Mrs. Jones. I want to know all about…"

"Luisa's father, Luis."

"Amazing he found you after ten years, how did he know where to find you…"

"Mo, I don't know how he knows much of what he tells me."

"Father has had questions about this man. I told him you never say much. He's always had a special 'interest' in your well-being. I tell him the best thing you did for your well-being is discovering that hanging out with," and she leaned into Jill's ear and whispered, "a spy," she pulled away from Jill "was detrimental to emotional health."

They left the hotel and walked along Michigan Avenue. Mo had made reservations at one of Stewart's favorite Chicago restaurants. He'd been happy to be home for a few days. Jill told Mo of her love of

Chicago as the big city in her life when growing up in Caylor. In eighth grade they'd had a field trip to the Natural History Museum and she had fallen in love with the city that day. But now she'd seen so many other cities, she was no longer sure. Florence, Italy moved into first place.

They ate lunch as Mo explained, "Stewart is involved in negotiating the return of the Viet Nam prisoners of war. Mr. Kissinger decided to keep it all hush-hush. Stewart knows that part of the world, we've been assigned there for the last umpteen years."

Jill watched Mo, older, but so much more attractive -her frosted blonde hair and make-up made her glow. Maybe her marriage had added the sparkle.

"How is Stewart? I mean do you like being married and traveling?"

"Oh, it is what it is, you know I like to be in charge, but visiting with foreign dignitaries...I have to wait on Stewart to set the tone, subservient me. You can imagine me biting my tongue." They both shook their heads and chuckled.

"Jill, tell me of Cynthia. Do you ever see her?" Mo spoke as she dipped her fork in her salad bowl.

"She has three children, each with his or her own strong personality. Exactly as you would expect from Cynthia. She practices law part-time filing lawsuits on the behalf of her favorite causes, a class action suit against the garbage collection department in Kokomo. She keeps me posted at our Interracial Club meetings, but she really hasn't changed. And she did marry the best looking man in Caylor. Have you ever seen pictures?"

"No. I occasionally get a Christmas card from her, but it is a picture of the kids usually. She probably doesn't want me to lust over her man." Mo laughed.

"I try to contain myself when he is around. What about Armentria?" Jill said.

"Moved to Boston, I think. Somewhere on the East Coast."

"If you ever hear from her, please send me her address. I would love to write her, she was such a comfort to me in the days after finding out I was pregnant. Just plain acceptance, a gift from God, I think. Everything else was a challenge."

Mo reached and patted her hand. "She's what? Fourteen, now? We graduated...eleven years ago. Amazing. More wine?"

They ordered more and drank more.

"Mo, what about Christian? He was just entering high school. He had so much confidence at your wedding. I'm sure he must be on the board of some corporation by now."

"He finished high school, then went to Virginia to school, VMI, wanted to join the service, follow Dad, but then something happened."

"Something?"

"Dad talked to him and tried to figure out something and that's all I know, something. He does send a postcard every once in awhile from some faraway place. Oh listen to me, I have been to so many faraway places, not a good reference point. Have you been to Rome?"

"Yes, I managed to escape the cornfields. Luis and I toured Tuscany. He was looking at villas for a possible investment. So amazing, old and full of character. I imagined who had lived there and the circumstances of building those huge homes on mountain tops."

"If you ever land in one, let me know. I'm coming to visit."

They ate salad and bread sticks and kept drinking wine. Jill sat in awe, listening as Mo described state dinners at the White House and foreign attachés in the ambassador residences. The farm, Caylor, so simple, but Luis had been showing her the world, not at American Embassies, but as a tourist. Jill realized that she and Mo could have met if they had only known and kept in better contact with each other. She laughed now as Mo described spilling red wine on some foreign minister's bitchy wife.

Mo said, "Oh she was mad about it, but I just..." she paused, smiled, and then waved at someone over Jill's shoulder. Jill had just turned around when William came to the table.

"Mo!" Jill said.

"Shish," Mo said, "Hi, Dad! Here she is, our little country girl."

"Ah, Jill, a sunrise of intoxication in my darkest hour."

He was grayer, still slender, and handsome. He smiled broadly and graciously joined them.

Jill watched father and daughter talk easily. Mo no longer showed any animosity. Jill recalled the sharp barbs Mo often flung at William, but she now seemed happy well-adjusted. Perhaps her marriage had given her stability, although her lifestyle was a whirlwind of countries and crises. Mo had always been strong; she and Stewart must have found an anchor in each other.

"Jill," William spoke, "a penny for your thoughts."

"Marriage. But have you lost your touch? I was thinking what a strong marriage Mo and Stewart must have to make it."

156

"I have never done well in the institution," he winked at Jill, "but you, Mrs. Jones; you've been married how long?"

"Ten years." Jill looked down, then reached for her wine glass.

"May I propose...no, let's see if they have some white German wine."

"Cut the..." Jill said and looked at William.

"Jill," Mo said, "Stewart and I have developed signals to pull ourselves out of and away from situations. Otherwise we'd drown."

William sat back, glancing between the friends. He chuckled at their antics.

Jill heard the chuckle and it was fifteen years ago, the first time when he met them at the dorm. She glanced at him and lifted her glass to touch his.

William said, "May I see a picture of your daughter? I've been assured she has grown more beautiful...like her mother, age is becoming." He nodded, then saluted her with his wine glass.

The waiter brought the wine menu and William ordered saying deliberately, "Light, White...Rheine." He winked at Jill, "For old times, as they say. And her father approves of his angelic daughter?"

She had not mentioned Luis and did not want to discuss him with William. She really had not wanted to discuss anything with William, but the charm, the rogue, the temptation, not lost or even diminished in ten years.

"Luis Ochoa," she blurted, then wished she had kept the name to herself.

"Yes, Luis Ochoa of Colombia. Don't punish yourself, I see your face. I remember his name from what, fourteen years ago. Who is your Luis Ochoa?"

How did he know Colombia? Had she written that to Mo. No. And he had said it with deliberate sarcasm as if he could recite chapter and verse from a dossier. Jill stared at Mo, who immediately feigned innocence, holding up her hand, shaking her head and swearing her non-complicity.

William poured the white German Rheine wine into Jill's glass and his. Mo put her hand over her glass blocking his pouring. "Mo has said nothing, Jill. She is your loyal friend much to my chagrin. We talked long and deep that summer. Bodensee. I often think of those items on our plate, the what-if's that so destroyed your appetite. Now you've been dining on all that Indiana farm food, agreeable?"

He watched her and she knew that he could see exactly what life was like in Caylor with Jack.

The lunch ended. They walked slowly to the park by Lake Michigan. The sail boats wove independent paths across the blue water. The sweltering heat diminished with the cool air from the water. The beach was filled with children and swimmers wading into the shallow water. Mo looked at her watch. She excused herself, explaining she had less than an hour to get ready for tea, then dinner with the Percivals of Hong Kong and London.

"Dad, would you mind entertaining Jill this evening? I know she wouldn't enjoy a stiff night with those absolutely snooty Brits."

William smiled and assured both women that he would be more than pleased to be Jill's host for the evening. "Mo, it would be my pleasure to insure Mrs. Jones has a brief respite from the dullness of country life and give her an exquisite memory to take back to the cornfields."

"William, I can watch a movie in my room."

"Absolutely not. We're in Chicago, jazz clubs, new musicians so much better than the clubs in Indianapolis. It is warm and we can sit outside."

"Perfect, Dad. She needs to have some night life, a long way from Caylor and sadness. Promise me you won't say anything to make her sad."

"Scout's honor," William held up his hand in the three finger scout salute.

Mo had managed what Jill thought was impossible, an evening out with William. Why? He must have talked her into it for some reason.

Before Mo left to go with the Percivals, she whispered in Jill's ear, "You'll be fine. He wanted so much to talk to you, begged." She shrugged and walked away.

When Jill and William returned to her room in order to change for the evening, she had a message from Mo. Mo and Stewart laughed so much over tea with the Percivals that Mo insisted Jill and William join them for drinks. Jill turned to William who nodded an agreement. She changed her clothes and they left to join Mo and her British friends.

Harry Percival was a natural comedian, joking about the House of Lords and referring to his own penis as a privy member. They had not been in the least proper British as Jill imagined all those with such accents.

After dinner William whispered in her ear, "Time to go to an afterhours jazz club." And they went. Laughing, then earnestness, an emotional teeter-totter of feelings, up then down and tears as she told him of the accident and the pain of the last month. He held her, but did not cross any boundaries of intimacy.

"An officer and a gentleman and promise to my daughter in exchange for this…" he paused and held her hand, then used his index finger to brush her cheek.

He continued, "I hope we can be friends, not sure how to do that with you, but I want you to know I have no hidden plan to infiltrate your life. I want to stay in touch one way or another."

"Oh, spy-like so no one knows?"

"No, friend-like, a call at the appropriate time to say, 'Hi Jill how are you and Luisa? Plans for the summer?' That sort of thing."

"As in call my house and talk?" She shook her head, "I think through Mo is best. She is good about letting me know how to get in touch."

"So be it." He winked.

He was easy to talk to. She'd forgotten how much talking to him had always comforted her. He walked her to her room, and left with a hug and brief kiss on her cheek, and a promise to meet for breakfast.

They went to an early Sunday brunch, after the second glass of champagne he stared intently. He shifted in his seat and drank the last of his champagne. "Now that the war has quickly ended, the military is taking a much closer look at the MIA's."

"War talk? Not for breakfast, please."

"Actually the war is over and now the pieces are being examined. Preparation for the next one." He shook his head. "Hector was never classified as an MIA and his remains were identified and returned. Identified? How did anyone know it was him? Tags. Teeth. Witnesses. However his particular mission had been kept a secret by the CIA…"

"I thought that was your employer."

"At some level, which is why I was able to verify…"

"Why?" she said.

"For you. You can close that part of your life. I've read the record."

"Should I thank you?"

He shrugged, "No, I did it for me. I thought he was the reason you married Mr. Jones, and the reason that for all these years you have never called or tried to get in touch. I did not allow myself to believe that you did not want to be with me, only that you loved him."

"William, you know it had nothing to do with Hector and everything to do with a very well placed Colonel, someone who feels more at home in a plane than firmly planted in one place. Mo, I'm sure told you, I had lost hope for Hector. I've been to Arlington Cemetery. I was at the Pentagon, looked for you actually, but such a confusing place. They were all Captains or Colonels, or Generals, so many bars and stars, but no you. I made my peace in the Pacific Ocean. I loved him. People we have loved affect us for the rest of our lives, they don't just go away, and they don't die leaving us nothing."

"I loved you... maybe still do." He touched her hand.

She placed her hand on top of his, "And as Sadie told me, love is a feeling not a commitment. What we had was feeling, you could not commit. I enjoyed it all, but your job...you told me that was your commitment."

He nodded, "Yes, you're right. But what a feeling we had."

She shook her head and smiled.

"So now tell me...Luisa's father, Mr. Ochoa..." William said.

"You've been investigating him also? You have no boundaries! You say friends and then... What are you looking for? And why? Never mind! Never mind! Never mind!" She jumped up, threw her napkin on the table, and with a red face rushed from the restaurant.

She paced in the hotel lobby, why William, why? You begged Mo, for *this*? She returned, only he had the answers.

William arched an eyebrow, graciously stood and helped her with her chair.

He continued talking not missing a beat. "...He's the director of a large agency in Colombia, one that receives hefty payments from the United States government. Foreign businesses and the men who run them, those that get checks from Uncle Sam are...watched."

"And so you spy on him?"

"No, I teach at UC Santa Cruz."

"Not so innocent, Colonel Cunningham. You aren't telling me this because Luis heads the National Coffee Federation."

"Jill, you accuse me unjustly. I will conclude with these final words, so we may enjoy our moment of taboo. I will always be here for you, *and* all that I represent...Be careful."

160

"Of you?"

He laughed. "Yes, touché. Shall we order coffee to keep your Colombian in business?" When they set the two cups on the table, he smelled it deliberately, "Ah, the fine smell of Colombia."

She sipped hers. Putting his cup down, he said, "You might want to read the stock market section of the *Indianapolis Star*."

"I'll bite, why?"

"The coffee futures. If you look at the numbers long enough, they will begin to talk to you."

They walked to the lobby and waited while the valet brought her car. She stood by the door and then he kissed her. Ten years. His same soft lips took her into him.

She shook her head, "An officer *or* a gentleman?"

He chuckled, lightly touching her under her chin.

Henry liked to remind her if she didn't know where she was going it didn't matter what road she took to get there. She drove home from Chicago, she knew the roads. But home? Home was where she wanted to go to be with Luis. Which road? Coffee futures? William stirring the pot. Stop. Yes, that will be the letter you so want, the one that says stop.

Her road now south on Interstate 65, she passed the exits for Valparaiso, Frankfort, and at the exit for Indiana 26 and Lafayette she headed east to Caylor.

Coffee futures? Is that the exquisite memory? Is that the reason for begging Mo to see her? In a week she and Luis would be together, she would ask him about coffee futures. Home. Heart. Luis. Who are you, Luis? And if I knew, what? Would I want you less? Would I want to stay in Indiana? She smelled Luis and heard his voice. She shivered, then suddenly warmed, thinking of him. And not to think of him? No, it doesn't matter, he is who he is. And Luisa and I belong to him. What? For better? For worse? For unknown?

Chapter 8

The glow of fluorescent light illuminated storage shelves and Jill. She stood in her cool damp basement as the dehumidifier hummed. The slightly musty odor and shadows offered comfort in her self-imposed exile. She sorted Ball jars, checking dates and pulling the oldest ones to the front. "Not that many left from last year," she sighed.

Jack had installed metal shelves and attached labels, "Fruit, Vegetables, Tomatoes, Whole, Sauce, Juice." It was neat an orderly like a damn grocery shelf. Oh, why wasn't she grateful for his organizational skills?

Jack was stopping at Lillian's to pick up her canned goods and bring them here, to her shelves. Three weeks and she still could not go near her parents' house. Lillian had jelly, juice, applesauce, so many more vegetables. Oh, Mom, I'm not you, these few pints and quarts don't compare to your shelves. Jill sat down on an old bar stool and pulled the Kleenex from her jeans pocket. She put her dust cloth on top of a jar of pears.

"Mom," Luisa called down the stairs, "Papa is on the phone."

She looked at her watch, 4P.M. Jack wouldn't be home for a couple of hours. She pulled the metal chain to turn out the light.

"My little gringa, ¿Cómo estás? (how are you) You've been in my thoughts every day. Are you ready to travel?"

"Si, more than ready, everywhere I look, everything I touch…I want to pick up the phone and call my dad. It is so hard, and why? I don't understand why."

"Death is a part of life. A passing. Their souls are now with our heavenly Father. Bodies turn to dust, the earth, our source of life, again and again. I did pray for them and you. At the church, Luisa asked for a special trip. Your tickets will be arriving at Siddhartha's soon. We'll be together and we'll talk."

"I only want you to hold me and tell me…maybe it is time to leave Indiana, forever, as you said."

"Your flight is two hours and the rest will be a surprise. For my women, two weeks with Papa Ochoa."

"Two weeks, may I do more? Close my eyes and every time I open them, you are there."

He chuckled, "Ah, my gringa, always trying to figure out your surprise. Call your Siddhartha. Te amo." (I love you)

She hung up, cheered at just the sound of his voice, the accent. She couldn't tell him about Chicago, Mo, the exquisite memory or coffee futures.

"Lo, I'm going back to the basement."

"Where did Papa say we are going? I suppose a surprise, right? He didn't make you sadder did he?"

"No, he makes me…feel better. I have work to do down here."

She took the last step into the basement. A wave of sadness swept over her as she stared at the Ball jars. Mostly Henry was with her, a phone call away. Dad's alive and well and sitting in his office musing over a blueprint. She held her breath now, biting her lips, trying to hold back tears. They ran down her cheeks, but the personal conversation did not stop. Mom, see how hard I'm working? Organizing canned vegetables and fruit? Some day you'll return, right? We'll see each other, and I can tell you all that you've missed. Please, Dad. Mom.

Jack had worked to make the last few weeks easier to bear. His consistency was comforting. He protected her from intrusive sympathizers and seemed to understand her need to be alone. She managed to go to Vicksburg and pick up her tickets. He didn't ask where she was going, but she told him they were flying to South Carolina and renting a car, just to drive wherever and stop whenever.

He questioned her return to the South, "You made me promise to stop you if you wanted to venture south of the Mason-Dixon line. So I am fulfilling my promise, Mrs. Jones."

"We'll enjoy the scenery and not interact with the locals."

"Promise you won't call and complain if some miscreant decides to talk to you."

She smiled and nodded. "I'll do my best to keep miscreants at bay." She saw Luis's face and stuck "miscreant" under an imagined police head shot.

Jack met with a realtor, her brothers wanted to sell her parents' house as quickly as possible. He called an auctioneer making an appointment to view what was marketable in the house. Jill knew she had to go there to save the things that meant the most to her, but every time she thought of it, she cried. She shook her head attempting to stop the thoughts - the wedding wall of pictures, her mom's chest of drawers and closet filled with dresses ready to be worn to Tuesday's Bridge Club; her jewelry that coordinated with each outfit, purses and shoes; Henry's empty suits where a body should have been. Maxwell and Mathias had taken the stuff they wanted right after the memorial service.

Sadie concluded that some of the antique pieces had "money written all over them." Jill decided to store those things in their barn until she could look at them without crying. Sadie volunteered to have it all packed, moved and stored by the time Jill returned from her two week vacation. "A couple of teenagers, some spending money, and the packing will be done."

Jill could then sort at her leisure.

ᴙξᴙ

Jack left with Beau for the fishing trip, and Sadie now drove them to the airport.

"Where are we going, I mean what does the ticket say?" Luisa said,

Sadie handed the National Coffee Federation envelope to Jill, "You are flying to Charleston, South Carolina."

"We knew that part, Lo."

"But he said an island, an island all to ourselves, that's what Papa said."

"He did? You know more than me. But we often fly one place and end up somewhere else. I'm sure it will be 'an island all to ourselves,' although, I wouldn't mind spending time in Charleston. Your grandma used to talk about the handsome antebellum homes. Remember she had that book on her coffee table in the den?"

"Jill, I am so glad you are getting out of Caylor. And I will have that house all packed away. I just want you to enjoy every minute of your vacation." Sadie laughed, "And I'm sure you will. Latin lover and all..."

"Stop Sadie, think of the children," and she put her hands over Luisa's ears.

"Mom, I'm fourteen, I know what a Latin Lover is. I watch *I Love Lucy* reruns. Desi is from Cuba. And Chico on *Chico and the Man* is so cute."

"Oh, your daughter is so grown up Miss Country Cornfield."

The threesome had gone shopping because Luisa and Sadie insisted Jill needed to buy something new to wear on her vacation.

"A new bikini? Sadie, maybe I'm getting too old for that sexy look."

"Come on, you're with your best friend. No secrets. Buy the navy one, the daisy print maybe it will make him think you're innocent." Sadie laughed.

Jill bought the daisy print wrap to wear to and from the beach and a basic sundress in lavender and mint green that was made like an apron.

"Perfect, Jill, easy to take off and it will look great with your sandals. When you unpack you are going to say thank you Sadie, and I will say you are welcome. Luis only sees you a few times a year and you need to look special. Not that school teachery style you wear most of the time."

Sadie insisted they go to the Country Club pool "to get some color" and to have their summer cocktails.

Jill was there, but not there. Life marched in lock step, one day after the other, the sun rose, the sun set. The locusts started their August racket and she too, now in concert with August, off to join Luis on their "own island."

165

With the suffocating sadness, when all she could do was get dressed and breathe, she hadn't managed to subscribe to *The Indianapolis Star*. She knew nothing about coffee futures. Perhaps she would ask him anyway and see how he reacted, look for a tiny opening to his life. Unlike Jack who had a picture window for easy viewing, Luis had a brick wall, twelve inches thick, like the gun storage building in Charleston to keep everyone out during the war. Impenetrable? Almost. Her questioning occasionally could elicit a glimpse of something. Yes, bring up coffee futures and then watch and listen.

She boarded the plane with much anticipation and excitement as they flew to his "world." For the moment, the squid like grip of Caylor's streets, houses, and stores loosened its hold on her. She cut each encompassing arm and floated free. To Charleston...the elegant southern city of brick homes built by slave laborers.

They exited the plane and walked toward the baggage area. A driver resembling James at Sadie's in Georgia, held a sign with "Mrs. Jones" written on it. He was dressed in black and wore black leather gloves. He had an ear to ear smile. She waved; at least it wasn't that damn Andy Marshall.

The car moved slowly through Charleston.

"What's wrong, Mom?" Luisa looked at her. They were now almost the same height.

"The South, it doesn't change. Cynthia was right, there is much work to be done."

"What work?"

"The civil rights activists, T.J. and the others..." she stopped, staring at the Grecian-columned homes with the large verandahs, majestic in their aging. "Slaves built those elegant mansions," she could hear Cynthia reminding her, "We could all live in mansions, if we had free labor to cut the timber, fashion the iron and build them."

"Mom, T.J.? Who is that? You've lost me."

"A college friend who spent his summer working in the South."

"Charleston? South Charleston?"

"No, *The* South, the Confederate South. You've studied the Civil War. 110 years ago and dramatic changes occurred, but some things still seem very much the same. It is those things that irritate me. I see them and I wonder when will they ever change?"

The elegant homes facing the sea reminded her of the ultimate romance, Rhett Butler-Scarlett O'Hara. Scarlett made a dress from the curtains of her plantation "Tara," in order to impress Rhett in

Charleston. Jill wanted to ask the driver to stop and let her walk along the seawall. And to visit the slave market where human flesh had been auctioned like so many cows and hogs at the 4-H Fair.

"Mom, this South talk is making you sad again. Let's think of Papa and a happy vacation, because he always takes us on great vacations. Think how much fun we had shopping in Hong Kong, and eating shrimp with their eyes and antennae looking at us, and snakes in jars, oh and the ducks hanging with the flies on them."

Luisa squeezed her hand, and continued to talk non-stop as they traveled through Charleston's streets. She reminisced about the trips with Luis, "And now Mom, we are going to our next adventure. I'm so excited. Papa always makes you happy, and sometimes..."

"Sometimes?"

"Sometimes, what do you say? Grandma Caitlin comes out."

Jill had tried to keep Luisa's excitement in check, their secret, but each year as it had become more comfortable, the containment was more difficult. When they returned from Hong Kong, Luisa had slipped and referred to "Papa," Jill quickly said, "Papason, the name of our guide."

It seemed almost true. Hector said, "It's hard to improve on the truth." But the truth could be partial or whole. Now they sat in a limousine headed to another rendezvous. Luisa had two fathers, so different in so many ways. Luis traveled extensively and Jack stayed home. Luis took her to faraway places. He lived in another country. Luisa had asked if she could go home with him. He deflected, but said one day she could come and stay. He qualified his invitation, explaining that staying at his home was beyond her mother's "parameters."

She stood by her word in their pillow talks and phone conversations. His suggestion that Luisa stay with him caused her to shudder with an unknown sense of fear that perhaps one day he would actually take her with him. Luisa might be smitten by the money and the life in another world so different than the archaic Caylor. How could a small farm in Indiana compare to the world stage? It couldn't, and so she insisted on her parameters, even though, she too, wanted to go and see him. She saw the same seduction between Luis and Luisa. He presented a world of travel, expensive hotels, and regal dinners. Luisa became enchanted, listening and sharing the sights of his vacation choices. Jill allowed herself to be drawn into the tales of foreign state dinners and political alliances made on yachts in the Mediterranean Sea. She fought the Siren song, but not very well, often begging to be taken along. Saying goodbye to him hurt in places she did not know she had until he pinched her nose and she kissed his fingertips. But they said farewell, always as if they would see each other the next day.

They now turned toward the harbor, pulling up to the gate of the U.S. Naval Base. The driver stopped at a gated entrance while a military security guard dressed in white from his hat to his shoes made a telephone call. He hung up and told them to proceed. They drove a short distance to a wooden dock that seemed to extend for miles. Moored to metal hooks, the size of small cars, were U.S. Navy ships, gray massive behemoths separated by wooden boardwalk roads. A variety of Navy ships were tied with rope as large as tree trunks. We're driving over water? Each pier was big enough for two cars to pass each other.

They parked and waited, until a crew of three men wearing formal white military-type uniforms walked quickly to the limousine. The driver met them, opened the trunk, unloaded the luggage, then opened the passenger door, and helped Jill and Luisa out of the car. One military-clad man walked to greet them. In a heavy accent he said, "Good evening, Señora Ochoa and Señorita Ochoa. Please follow."

Luisa stared wide-eyed in all directions. Navy ships spouted, steamed, and bristled with movement. Sailors moved quickly along the decks. The small entourage walked past the large ships and down a wood labyrinth to a few smaller craft. Jill held Luisa's hand tightly. What now, Luis?

Following the immaculately dressed foreigner in his white polished shoes, they reached their destination. A narrow gangplank was lowered, then the small group stepped from the board street to a gently rocking yacht. The white boat seemed small compared to the gray Navy ships, but Jill thought maybe half a football field length. Longer? It reminded her of James Bond movies as if she were in fact part of some Hollywood creation. The guide interrupted her tinsel town fantasy, directing them to walk down a small stairway to a closed compartment door.

The door opened and there in the middle of the room, dressed in white, an open shirt, his drawstring pants and sandals, Luis talked quietly to a man wearing a butler's uniform. The teak paneled living room was lit from a small wall of windows. One end was a large mirror that had two doors on either side with two downward steps. Luis rushed to them, opening his arms for a big hug.

"Ah, mis muchachas de Mayo,(my girls of May) Welcome! No problems?" His effervescence caught Jill off guard. She reeled from the entire greeting, starting with the crew outside the yacht.

"Hi, Papa."

"Luis, what is this? I mean is this your boat?"

"You did not see the name, 'Papa's Place'? Oh, Gringa, why do you always question your Señor Ochoa? Let me pour champagne to celebrate your arrival. Then a tour and perhaps, a question or two." He filled two champagne glasses from a chilled bottle in a silver urn. He graciously handed 7-Up to Luisa.

"Papa, I think you did it. Mom is finally smiling."

"And angel, I have only just begun."

French doors opened onto an outer deck. They walked outside into peach twilight as the yacht slowly pulled away from Charleston Harbor. The houses she had wanted to see were black shadows against the gold orange sky.

Luis's world, could it be held here in his arms? Jill closed her eyes, his arms a mighty fortress in a yacht, leaving the pain on shore.

"Say farewell to America, Jankees! You are being kidnapped by El Campesino."

"The farmer? Right, Papa?"

"You see, Jill, she is learning Spanish. A toast…May our days *together* be as splendid as this sunset."

"Oh yes, Papa. You are making Mom happy."

They drank and stood silently as the lights of Charleston twinkled slowly awake and the bright red ball became flat. Jill put her arm around Luisa's shoulders. Luis put his arm around Jill's waist. The sea breeze enveloped them.

The butler came onto the deck asking if they needed more champagne.

"There seem to be several people working on this yacht," Jill spoke, then sipped her champagne.

"Si, they are paid to do whatever we ask them. Unfortunately, they only speak Greek. The captain knows some English and his son Demetri has attended New York University. Are you ready to walk around and try your sea legs? You'll get used to it."

"Luis, this boat is so big."

"One hundred seventy-two feet long and thirty feet at the beam."

"The beam?"

169

"The widest part of the ship."

"Sailor?"

"No, pirate."

She shook her head and smiled. He continued, "There are six staterooms two adjoining," he winked at Jill. "I think Mitsos usually has more than three guests. I see your face, Mitsos is a business associate."

"Are we the only ones on here that don't work?"

"Si."

Jill wanted to keep the conversation light and jovial; his matter of fact tone pronouncing Mitsos' name meant he did not want any more questions. When he was miles from his business, he laughed, teased, played with them as if no one was watching, he could "dance." But where was the "away" from his business? It seemed the places they visited had pieces of something he had to do either for Colombia for his coffee farm or…the missing "Who is Luis Ochoa?" piece.

Mr. Angotti, the Italian banker, appeared to have no interest in coffee or Colombia, only investments in many countries. When Jill had been around both of them in Florence, they often spoke in Italian. Even in Italian, though, she could tell that the relationship was respectful and successful. They smoked Cuban cigars together and agreed on the wine.

The Greek crew prepared and served dinner. Jill thought they could have invited several more people to dine with them at the spacious mahogany table in the formal dining room. They ate from china plates, crystal glasses and heavy sterling silverware. The chairs were upholstered in rose satin. One wall with doors on each side was a bar with a complete liquor cabinet backed by mirrors. It gave the dining room an illusion of being much larger. Another wall was half curtained with a buffet cabinet under the curtain. Champagne chilled in the silver bucket on the buffet. Luis had been right in his assessment of the gentle rocking. The china dishes were unusually heavy, "seaworthy" Luis explained. The wood table had a small ridge around the edge "to prevent sliding in case of tumultuous seas."

Demetri came in after dinner. "Hello, Señor and Señora Ochoa and Señorita. I am Demetri and my English is being improved by talking to you." He bowed slightly.

He looked as if he could have walked off a postcard of Grecian Art. He was olive-skinned with curly black hair and sparkling black eyes that lit up his entire face. Jill smiled, as he explained he worked for his father in the summer. The craft was to be available at all times for

170

one to twelve guests. He did not know the owner, but his father did. The owner, as far as he knew, never used this particular yacht. He kept it for American business friends. Demetri said, "I am so happy to have Americans aboard, please, to correct my English."

Luisa listened attentively, giggled, then smiled broadly when Demetri looked directly at her. Luis frowned at Luisa's giggle, then sternly eyed the young man.

Luisa asked, "Is there a radio or music tapes?"

"Luisa, we are too far to get a radio signal, but I have a cassette tape player and American tapes in my room. Earth Wind and Fire, Bruce Springsteen, Aerosmith. Señor Ochoa, may I take Luisa to listen to music?" Demetri walked to the door.

"No, I think she will stay here with us." Luis flashed a look of consternation at the Greek teenager.

"Oh, Papa, where am I going to go? As you said we are kidnapped. Mom?"

"Demetri, perhaps you could get your tape player and come back and sit outside with Luisa."

When he had left the room, Luis stared at his angel. Could a mirror have reflected his image better? In resoluteness, they were equally endowed. He smiled slightly, walking with them to a glassed-in sitting deck with double doors that opened onto an outside sun deck.

"Luisa, you don't know that young man. Strange men for my daughter? It is out of the question. You roll your eyes when I talk to you?"

"Papa, this is my vacation, too. And besides I know the difference between a strange man and someone trying to be friendly. Mom?"

"Luis, we can watch them, the walls are glass. I'm sure Demetri is a well-mannered young man…"

"He's Greek!"

"Yes Luis, and you are Colombian. Are you being…?"

Luis stared from the miniature Ochoa to Jill. He breathed deeply, his nostrils flared, then his shoulders dropped. He sighed, and lit his cigar, "Gringa, do you want to walk on the deck?"

"Should we wait for Demetri to return?"

"I'm sure he is a 'well-mannered' young man. Besides it is only a short walk to the bow."

The blackness surrounded them from the sea to the horizon. The evening was balmy tempered by a slightly cooler sea breeze. The flickering stars pierced the black velvet. She pointed out constellations to Luis. William, the star gazer, she shivered at the thought. Coffee futures? No, not now on this wonderful peaceful night.

"Gringa, are you cold? We can go in or do you need a sweater?"

"No, no. I just remember my first lesson in star gazing, a bitterly cold Indiana night. When I think of it, I shiver, clear but freezing. My best star gazing was with Sadie at the Planetarium in Chicago." She related the tale of Sadie and herself. When the lights went out, she grabbed for Sadie's hand, but ended up with the man's hand sitting next to her. The stranger patted her hand, then she realized what she had done.

"A strange man, in a dark room, held your hand?" Luis asked pointedly.

"Well, yes, but for just a moment. I was embarrassed. Sadie teased me, unmercifully."

"Now I see why my daughter is so anxious to go with a strange young man," he said. She placed her hand on Luis's holding the rail of the yacht; he had calmed down. They stood at the front of the yacht. The water splashed the sides of the boat while the soothing winds and rhythmic hum of the engines enveloped them. When they had moved out of sight of the back deck, he held her and kissed her. With his moustache on her upper lip, she tasted the familiar cigar.

"Do you remember when you did that the first time?" she said.

"Of course. You were scared, but it didn't take you long to figure out you liked it," he smiled.

"Shish. I don't want my daughter to think I was too brazen."

"Oh? I thought you were the one who wants her to be honest? Did you want me when we rode in the truck?"

"M-m maybe, you scared me. You still scare me."

"What does that mean? You think I will throw you overboard?"

"No, I just don't know who you are."

"What does *that* mean? You know where I live. You know my name. You know I'm a farmer and you know what I do for you when we are alone."

"And that's who you are?"

"It is complex; people are not simple definitions, even Jack. Each time we are together you learn more about me. You know I have a friend named Mitsos, and another named Kit, and Señor Angotti. So you can say, 'I know who Luis Ochoa is, he is a man with friends.' Gringa, I brought two books for you to read on our vacation. Both will help you understand your Señor Ochoa. Actually three, a Spanish-English dictionary because one of the books is written in Spanish. And I will be here to answer questions, for you."

Jill shook her head. He was an enigma, but he was right. She flushed at the mention of his prowess. All the sex she and Jack shared, but never the passion she had with this Colombian coffee farmer. He smelled of the distinctive cologne he always wore. She reached to touch the outside of his pants. He tossed his cigar and grabbed her forcefully, pressing against her breasts. He kissed her. Touching bodies, their action and reaction to each other deafened Luisa's soft call. She and Demetri walked towards them. Spotting them, Luis whispered, "Now your daughter knows." Jill gently slapped his shoulder.

ᛣᚨᛣ

Morning broke over the Atlantic Ocean. Jill rose early, her "farmer's hours," as Sadie derisively tagged them. The blue sea turned steel gray against a pink and lavender dawn. She had checked on her teenager who was doing an exact imitation of her father, sleeping very soundly. From a side door, a crew member appeared with a pot of coffee and juice. The gentle wind, the smooth encompassing breeze, the smell of the sea permeated all her parts. What was Sadie saying about "the therapeutic nature of water, negative ions and moisture in your hair and skin?"

Now she was coddled in a cocoon of sea air filaments. The ship headed easterly and maybe north. Once again she knew Luis had picked the perfect remedy for her malaise. She remembered the great things her Mom and Dad had said about their Caribbean cruise for their 25th Anniversary. When she mentioned the years and celebration to Jack, he flatly rejected the notion of seven days on a cruise ship. His bass fishing boat was as big a ship as he wanted to board.

Jill teased, "I may spend my anniversary with someone else." Now her reverie was interrupted by the man who was taking her on a cruise on their almost Fifteenth Anniversary, would they make it to their Twenty-fifth? Luisa would be twenty-four.

"Gringa, are you enjoying your coffee? Come here, I have something 100% Colombian for you." His especially low before-breakfast-baritone voice enticed and seduced her. She followed him to his stateroom just off the deck where she sat. The sea, the Siren song, she untied her robe.

He laughed, "Oh, will you take advantage of El Campesino?"

"Si, Señor Ochoa. A dark rich robust Colombian would be perfect."

From her waist to her toes, she warmed at his presence, his taking. So many self-imposed inhibitions, her defenses against the mechanical Jack, were unleashed on the creamy elegant sheets in the stateroom bed.

Lying next to him, she absently pulled his salt and pepper chest hairs and traced the long scar that almost precisely divided his body in half. He feigned pain at her touch while he drank his coffee. "Gringa, do you learn these things on the farm in Indiana? Or is this the way Hoosier women are raised?"

"No, you tell me when you learned to be the quintessential Latin Lover?"

"Quintessential?"

"Yes, perfect."

"Why I do what I do well? It is in my genes. I inherited it. Who is Luis Ochoa? Hm-mm and how did he come to be...so Latin? I read a book, *How to be a Latin Lover*, by Kevin Fitzpatrick." He laughed, and laughed.

She shook her head, but he had tickled himself and kept laughing heartily. He paused to sip his coffee, but tears came to his eyes from his joke. She smiled, a relaxed Luis Ochoa. When he stopped, he spoke hoarsely, "While I was waiting for the United States Immigration to deport me...in the waiting room...copies for everyone." He shook his head and tousled her hair, "Now you know, Gringa, I learned it in a book."

"Bracero? Were you in the Bracero Program? I wrote a term paper about it for Dr. Busching's sociology class. You said it at the migrant camp, remember?"

He nodded, "Goddamned Jankee slave program. I'll write the paper for you. Let's start, page one, paragraph one. Do you want to write this down? I'm sure young Demetri can find you some paper."

San Antonio, Texas offered some consolation for migrant workers. They lived in clusters and warned each other if the Immigration Service started hunting braceros to send back. Luis learned his first lesson and escaped the sweeps. When the harvest brokering began, he went with a group to Arkansas, Illinois and Michigan. He was gone most of his second summer and fall. Returning to San Antonio, he wrote to Mamacita to tell her of his residence. He rented a mailbox and waited to hear from this precious link to his homeland.

The winter took many of the braceros back to families in Mexico. Luis stayed and sought employment locally. His greatest asset, English, helped him land a lawn maintenance job with the local country club. He was assigned caretaking duties for the tennis courts and occasionally would caddie. His intensity served him well; he watched, listened and learned. Waiting on and serving rich Texans was an education in American culture that fascinated him. He developed a taste for expensive food which he was served in the kitchen by the Mexican cooks.

"Luis, *you*, you waited on people?"

"Ah, Gringa, questions. You always have questions. There is much to tell and I haven't told the best part. I have done *many* things."

At the tennis court, Luis watched the paid professional work with the wealthy, honing their skills. He grabbed his first racquet at age twenty-seven. His strength was an asset, but it took much practice to channel the power. The club pro liked the Colombian's determination and stamina. He knew that Luis planned only to work during the winter months, then would go on the road. Luis tried to explain his love of the farms and back breaking work in the fields with the migrant camps. "It was not a day worth living," his father had told him, "unless your hands held dirt, touched plants, and trod the source of life. A man should hurt at the end of the day; the shoulders should be sore so the woman can rub them, the stomach aching so the woman can soothe it with dinner." His father always insisted on a woman's role as man's caretaker.

"Luis, your father? You've never mentioned him, except you said his name was Hector."

"He left when I was fifteen, to go to Caracas. He told me Mamacita wanted him to go. He did not return to Saldana until I was in Texas. We thought he had been killed by jungle guerillas or thieves. When Mamacita wrote to say he had returned, she also said he was very sick and died soon after he returned. I think he came home to die. The mountains, Gringa."

"I am so sorry. This whole trip has been about my sadness, but your sadness, your pain, Luis, you're sharing only this piece."

175

"No," he whispered, shaking his head, "Not now. One day when we are growing old *together*, we can talk of your Señor Ochoa's pain."

"Old together? I will think about that. Please tell me the rest of the 'many things' you have done."

"The pro worked with me trying to break into me. See Gringa, you are not the only one with this question. He said I had potential. He did not know me, but he did not want me to join the migrant trek. It seemed a waste of talent, promise, my 'potential' he kept calling it. The pro kept thinking that there must be a price that could be paid to get me to sacrifice the migratory trip. He connived and schemed until he was able to present an offer. As in the *Godfather*, an offer I couldn't refuse. An older woman, a tennis student, lived in a mansion on the outskirts of town. Her husband was a Congressman in Washington. He had extended absences from the house and the woman was looking for a trustworthy general maintenance man, bilingual to work with the other help."

"How old was this older woman, Luis?"

"How do you know I worked for her?"

"Money, you like it too much."

Luis laughed, "Gringa, why do you ask who I am and you know already?"

"The house was two-stories and twenty-two rooms surrounded by rolling fields. There were horses, a tennis court, a pool and acres of grass and shrubbery to be maintained. But my new boss wanted companionship, to be available on many levels."

"A gigolo? That's what you were? How disgusting!"

"Si. Some Jankee women paid for what you get free."

Jill slapped his arm. He laughed and pulled her to him, kissing her.

"Luis, is this a true story or something you saw at the movies?"

"When you see the movie, Gringa, tell me. Maybe I should make a movie. You want to be my co-star or should I find another gringa?"

"Who would play the San Antonio boss?"

"She was tall, thin, with short blond hair…Lauren Bacall."

"That's enough!"

The light camaraderie was interrupted by a knock on the door.

"Señor Ochoa, we will be docking in one hour at St. Georges."

"Gracias. Jill, we will be here for a few days. The ship's crew has business with…business. Tell Luisa to pack all her things, so the crew can transport them."

"Luis, where are we? St. Georges does not ring a bell."

"Bermuda. Do you think if I wired Jack a ransom note he would come and pick you up in Bermuda?"

"No, I'm sure he would tell you to keep me, but send him his daughter…"

"Send him *my* daughter?!" His brow furrowed, the perfect "V" between his eyebrows. She closed her eyes and sought a peaceful repose. Deep breath, Jill, sea air. Inhale. His passion once again ruining the moment. Passion created their best moments of interaction as often as destroying them. For every trip they took, she knew it would come, the volatility. No matter how much she and Sadie discussed and analyzed where all the instant rage came from, she was still surprised and smitten with his first "Luis lightning strike."

"Luis, you have to accept the facts of our lives…"

"I have to accept very little that I don't like. I change situations to meet my needs and this too will change. Don't *ever* refer to Luisa as Jack's daughter!"

"Luis, he adopted her and if you have any notion that that is going to change, we need to talk and sooner rather than later. I'll go wake *your* daughter and make sure she has her bags packed." She walked out of the state room, submitting to him? No, not today, not this morning on the azure sea of Bermuda. Bermuda?

Jill found Luisa awake and excited about the "gorgeous" Demetri with the accent that was "awesome." Her excitement reminded Jill of her own teenage summers when boys were the only part of life that mattered. Luisa's happiness erased the harangue she had just heard from Luis. And for a while, she had totally forgotten her best friend, grief. Dealing with two Ochoa's was all encompassing.

"I suggest you limit your references to Demetri with your papa."

"Mom, I think you need to face-up to him. You always tell Dad exactly what you think, what you are going to do and what you did. Papa doesn't have a wife, that's why he acts like this."

"Oh, thank you Dr. Freud." They both giggled.

Bermuda. Luis explained that they would be there two maybe three days. He reserved rooms at a home converted to a small hotel.

Breakfast was part of the reservation, but the other meals were at local restaurants. He told Jill they would do whatever she wanted.

"Gringa, you might want to make a note, but for the next few days in Bermuda, your wish is my command," he chuckled.

She immediately bought a book of what to see and do in Bermuda. The first day they took the tourist bus and she picked places as they drove by them. She made a note that Church Bay was a good place to go snorkeling. The quaint houses, they were told, had roofs that allowed for the collection of rainwater in basement cisterns as there was no source of fresh water on the island. Their boutique hotel had a tennis court, but no pool. The ocean was everywhere and she wanted to go to the beach to think, read and perhaps swim.

Each morning Luis walked down to the marina to check on their departure; upon his return, he and Luisa played tennis. Three days turned to five days. Luis took the opportunity to teach Luisa some pointers on tennis. Jack and she had been playing for a long time, so Luisa enjoyed challenging her papa on the court. She was a good match for him considering the differences in their strengths. Luis told Jill to make sure Luisa receives professional tennis lessons. He knew something could be arranged through Siddhartha and her Country Club.

After a shower and change of clothes they both waited for Jill to explain the "game plan" as they came to call it. On the third day when it seemed that their stay might be extended, Luis came back to say that Demetri asked if he could go snorkeling with them. Luisa said, "Yes, of course, tell him yes, Papa!"

Luis frowned and looked at Jill, "Parameters, Señora Ochoa?" he had asked.

She said, "Sure," reminding him that he would be chaperoning them underwater. So they went. Jill found a place in the shade where she could read and hear the gentle waves. She spread her beach towels and removed one of the books that Luis had given her, *Colombia: The Political Dimensions of Change* by Robert Dix. She immediately looked in the index to see if she saw his name. No Luis Ochoa, no, National Coffee Federation, yes, Colombian Coffee Growers Federation, okay, question two. She started with those entries, but then was drawn to Chapter Thirteen almost the end of the book, "La Violencia."

Why do they always give feminine articles to horrible acts of men, la guillotine, and war itself, la Guerra? It must be the machismo of Latin men. Oh, yeah, la Luis. She shook her head, then used the book for a pillow until Luis came up and dripped water on her. She sat up, "Where are Luisa and Demetri?"

"Still swimming with the fishes. I told them twenty more minutes, then time to get out of the water. And you are swimming with Señor Dix, I see." He picked up the book.

"Luis, I did not find your name in the index, are you sure you want me to read the book?"

"Si, I am in the book. You must find me."

"Good thing I started with Chapter Thirteen, 'La Violencia.' I read a couple of chapters and it was hard to comprehend that so many people are at war with each other, like our Civil War. I didn't want to read it here, in this tranquil lagoon where everything seems so right with the world. Let's walk down to the water and check on them."

He helped her up and put on his straw hat and sunglasses. She wrapped her sarong around her, to avoid the sun. "I hear my mother's voice telling me that I burn easily and to stay out of the sun. Luis, you never talk of your mother, only Mamacita, a woman who would have been your mother-in-law."

"It is a difficult subject for me, Gringa. I grew up with one story told repeatedly, then my uncle, Ramos, told another." Luis gritted his teeth, "I don't know which is the true version. When I asked, Mamacita didn't want to confirm what he said, but didn't deny it either."

The water was cool on her feet. The sun warmed her, but she kept covered. Soon Luisa and Demetri emerged from the clear water carrying their snorkel masks and tubes.

"We need to go get some lunch. It looked like some funky beach places not far from here," she said, holding Luis's hand.

"With Demetri?"

"Yes, Luis. He is…"

"Well-mannered," Luis mocked her description.

"So, Luis what were the stories? My mom had an interesting story, coming from small town Indiana and all."

"Later, Gringa. I must chaperone young Señor Demetri. And right now, I am walking with the best mother, the mother of my daughter, a hard-headed Jankee." He bent down and kissed her quickly. He had deflected her question, but in such a gentle manner. Had Mother Nature's ocean, sand, and warm afternoon cast a spell on him?

ᴚξᴚ

When Demetri welcomed them onboard for their departure, he indicated they would only be stopping to refuel before heading for Georgetown in the Cayman Islands their destination.

Each morning she sat on the deck reading Colombian history as her family slept. The picture being painted was of two or three groups of people who controlled everything contrasted to poor campesinos who struggled every day to survive. How did Luis navigate that dichotomy? And would he answer if she asked?

The whole idea of discussing politics with him intrigued her, but also scared her. Maybe next time, not this time, or when she had finished the book. Her sparring partner, Henry, was gone; she needed to talk to someone about the elections and Republican policies. Nixon just resigned, so politically, America survived his presidency. Viet Nam had come to an end, even though the remains of those missing in action were in dispute. She cried knowing that there would be no more debating around her mom's kitchen table. Could Luis? She would have to tell him how important politics were to her.

Her second book from Luis, she had managed to translate the title, *Open Veins of Latin America*. It would take awhile for her to translate the whole book, but she wanted to be more fluent to have a regular conversation with him in his native language. Politics in Spanish? Maybe.

As the days at sea progressed, Demetri's constant interest in Luisa made Luis the nervous father.

"This is not your best performance, Luis. The girl is interested in boys and it is going to get worse before it gets better."

"Jankee idiom! What are you saying?" his serious tone had now lost some of its intimidation.

"She will begin dating boys. She will begin to fill out like a woman and…"

"That's enough. I will take her to Cartagena, where I can keep these hungry dogs away from her."

"How long can you keep her locked up? No, Luis, it just doesn't work like that."

"Not in America, but in my home…" he said.

"She lives in my home, remember…"

"Si, I am thinking it may be time for her to…come"

"Ask her."

Jill mostly slept to the engines' constant humming, but she woke and quietly slipped outside to the balmy tropic air of the Caribbean. Luis snored heavily, occasionally coughing. Smoking all those cigars could not be good for him. He played tennis, snorkeled, rode horses. She wanted him to be healthy. Their conversation in the church reinforced her hope that one day they would be married. And he had said "grow old together."

She stared at the distant twinkling lights of an island. They competed with the sky's canvas. The horizon of sea and night sky met somewhere out there. She shook her head; not wanting to leave him, the yacht, an empty sea and the mysteries of an unknown horizon.

Dad for you, I'm here and she sang, "A month of nights, a year of days; Octobers drifting into Mays; I set my sail when the tide comes in, and I just cast my fate to the wind," a dream, let the boat take us wherever. Where was this magnificent yacht going?

"I shift my course along the breeze; Won't sail up wind on memories; the empty sky is my best friend…" How many times had she heard Henry hum the tune?

Going home to Jack, vacation after vacation became oppressive. She needed to talk to Luisa. The older Jack grew, the less he demanded or wanted sex from her. Henry had been right; he had told her not to marry an older man. Luis was older, forty-five; he had lived a tougher life, back-breaking migrant work. Climbing the mountains in Colombia. Luis wore his years well. Jack would be fifty-four in December, a big difference in those eight years of her two men. Yes, Dad, Jack is too old. If he were younger…no, really he is not for me. Was I so desperate to be married that I settled? I didn't know my fate.

"I shift my course along the breeze…won't sail up wind on memories…the empty sky is my best friend…da-da-ta-da-da."

The yacht moved effortlessly through the calm dark Atlantic with the rhythmic splashing of water against hull. And her song provided the soundtrack on the night. "I shift my course along the breeze…The empty sky is my best friend...And I just cast my fate to the wind…" Damn cornfields. I don't want to go back.

Luis came and stood with her on the deck watching the yellow gold moon turn cream as it rose to become full and shimmering on the ocean.

"I thought you were asleep," Jill whispered.

"I turned to touch you and it was only empty space."

"The night, the tropics, oh Luis, the sea and wind."

"Si, I listened to you sing that song...Cast Your Fate to the Wind. Please more..."

She sang softly, "There never was, there couldn't be... a place in time for men like me, Who'd drink the dark and laugh at day...And let their wildest dreams blow away...my father used to sing that song all the time."

"Gringa, you have a soft sweet voice almost a whisper when you sing, full of love."

"One of his favorites. He loved to travel and never was able to do it enough."

He held her hand, pulling it to his lips. The moon inched higher on the horizon.

"Luis, do you know what it means if you kiss a gringa in the light of the full moon on a yacht in the Atlantic?"

"Tell me."

"Kiss me first."

He held her and kissed her, then slid his hand down her back grabbing her butt and pushing it against him, "Now I know, it means you can have your way with the gringa."

She nodded. "I think that is exactly right...Or maybe it means I can have my way with a Colombian coffee farmer in the middle of the Bermuda Triangle...Or maybe it means two people from very different worlds can create love forever."

"I think *that* is exactly the right meaning, my beautiful Gringa, glowing in moonlight, my Nyx, the Greek goddess of night."

ϓξϓ

Seven days aboard the ship. Jill relaxed, napped, ate well and soaked up the sun and conversations with her Ochoas. They played Monopoly, a set made for the owner as all the nomenclatures were place names in Greece. Luis's intensity was counter-balanced by Luisa's luck. Jill played the role of moderator and jester. "Luis, it's just a game."

Luis and Luisa played Chess every day. She listened as he talked. Reading Colombian political history demanded a quiet spot away from the Chess game, but she overheard some of their conversation.

"Luisa, whenever you move your knight or bishop, you must always think a couple of moves ahead, for example, if I move this pawn then what will you do? Or if I move my knight, what will you do? This is called strategy, planning your moves. Entiendes?" (understand)

"Papa, do you have a strategy for Mom?"

The Chess teacher paused staring at his daughter who stared back.

"I have a plan for everything I do."

"Are you going to marry her?"

"She is already married."

"Did you ever ask her?"

"Si."

"Well, did she say 'no'?"

"No."

"Papa you make this hard. Did she say 'yes'?"

"Si."

"What are you going to do?"

"In Chess, in business, in love, you never tell anyone your strategy, Luisa, never."

Luisa stood up, "Chess lesson is over Papa, I need to go to the galley and get something to eat."

Jill put down her book and went into the bathroom to change into her bikini. As she walked by the door to the stateroom there was a knock. Luis answered. She heard Demetri's voice.

"Señor Ochoa, we've received word that a tropical depression is forming off the coast of West Africa. Captain Papademetriou would like to talk to you about docking times."

When he came back from seeing the captain, he sat on the deck, staring at the sea. The butler brought him his preferred absinthe on ice. He sipped it and smoked his cigar. He seemed to be in another place as he blew smoke rings. Jill wanted to ask, but waited. His business had not permeated the entire vacation; he had relaxed for most of the two weeks.

Luisa rubbed suntan oil on her mom's back. The sun set as they headed west and south. They were able to watch it sink into the ocean. The tranquility was broken only by the rhythmical hum of the engines.

"Mom, the galley is so interesting. A kitchen, but its fixtures are locked into place. The cook showed me how each worked when the waves or swells were huge."

"The cook may want to charge extra for seaboard cooking classes," Luis turned to face them seating himself next to Jill.

"Papa, he is very nice. I laughed with him. I taught him English, well, English words. I taught him to say, 'Have a safe trip.' Demetri helped me with translating."

ΥξΥ

Quiet settled over the yacht. Jill slept to the constant sound of the engine's humming and Luis's snoring. When both stopped, she woke up and felt for Luis, he was not in the bed. She rose and walked outside in the moonlight, the yacht rocked slowly. The water's slap—slap-slap against the side of the boat broke the night's stillness. Another boat with few lights approached the yacht. One blinked a signal, then another signal. The second boat floated parallel to hers, but on the opposite side. Suddenly many men appeared from out of the hull and jumped to her yacht. She bent down and inched along the portholes to hide from view. She thought of her favorite sleuth, Nancy Drew, who was always getting into forbidden things.

Soon the Greek crew started hauling large wood crates from the hull of the yacht, passing these crates to the workers on the other ship. They were quick and quiet. The men seemed intent on what they were doing. Her concentration was broken when Luis knelt beside her, and put his hand over her mouth, keeping her from speaking. He signaled her to return inside.

The moon shone through the window of their stateroom. The reassuring purr of the engines started and set the yacht in motion. Luis kissed her. When she tried to speak, he placed his finger on her lips. They held each other tightly, then made love in the sultry night. No locusts, no crickets, nor mosquitoes only the whirring engine in the starry Caribbean darkness.

"Luis, was she good?" she whispered.

"Who was good, whom?"

"You know the one in Texas?"

Luis chuckled softly, "You just had your way with your papa and you are jealous of another gringa and so long ago?"

"Stop. Was she good?"

"You thought your Latin lover had only puta chochinas?"

"Puta chocinas?"

"Dirty whores."

"No, well just her, was she good? Did she please you in bed?"

"Gringa, gringa, gringa, you make a mistake. It is irrelevant," and his icy response ended the intimate moment.

They crossed through the Windward Passage in the early pre-dawn hours.

ཡξཡ

As they ate breakfast, their last meal on board. Luisa rubbed her finger on the silver fork; she put her napkin on her lap and drank her orange juice. "Mom...Demetri asked if he could write me when he gets to New York."

Luis put his coffee down, frowning, "What did you say, Luisa?"

She paused from taking her first bite, "Oh, Papa."

"What did you tell him Luisa?" Luis said.

"I said I was only fourteen, and I would have to ask my parents."

"What else did you say?" Luis placed both elbows on the table, leaned forward and stared at her.

"Papa, can I give him my address?"

"I am one step away from throwing young Demetri over the side of this ship! Jill, you may make this decision because I have no tolerance for it." He leaned back from the table and looked directly at Jill.

"When I was in the eighth grade, I had a pen pal from Tasmania. It was educational, writing to each other about our separate countries. How can I deny my daughter an opportunity to meet a young man from another country?"

Holding up his fork, pointing it at Luisa, "If you both do this, remember that I take no responsibility," he shook the fork back and forth as if the fork said, 'no,' "for the outcome. None. And don't call Papa and ask for help when you realize you've made a mistake."

Luisa jumped up from the table, hugged her papa, and kissed him on the cheek.

The bitter sweetness of the Ochoa family, Jill knew, was so right between them all, but so short-lived, always.

185

They spent their last night together in Georgetown. A last supper she thought as they sat in the hotel's elegant dining room with linen tablecloths, fresh flowers and candlelight, Luis looked at Jill and took a drink from a wine glass. "Together?...Si, together. Gringa, we shall now discuss your request."

He pulled some snapshots from his pocket, "Villa della Principessa, it is in Tuscany. It will be ready to live in next summer..."

Luisa and Jill looked at the pictures of the three-story perfectly square stone mansion. The paint had been sun washed revealing the pastel colors of sunset - pink, peach, cream and gold. It had a large front yard that led down to a stone and wrought iron fence. The back yard was manicured with several small patios and alcoves for sitting, a double stone stairway led from the back of the house to the yard. The chipped paint of the window frames and aged walls were characteristics she had seen five years ago when she traveled to Rome with him.

"Amazing, Luis. Did we see this one?"

"No, Gringa. Señor Angotti found this close to the small city of Lucca. He is having it renovated inside and out. It will be ready next spring. I had planned to show you then, but I wanted to cheer you now. Villa della Principessa, home for a princess. I want you two to spend next summer in your Italian home."

Jill whispered, "My surprise."

"Si."

"Coffee Futures?" She stared directly at his eyes and squeezed her napkin. There William, I said it.

He paused, cocking his head towards her, "No... I sold my interest in a bank. From the book? Coffee futures?"

"Mom, a whole summer in Italy. Oh, Papa, is this true? Our own special place?"

"Si, you like it?"

"I love it, Papa."

"And you, Gringa?"

"Luis, really? You're like some goddamned genie! Make a wish!"

He smirked, "I told you that Gringa, or should I say Grandma Caitlin, when we arrived in Bermuda. Genies grant three wishes, you have two more?"

"A whole summer in Italy? Three months?" Jill said, "June? July? August?" No garden, a two-week fishing trip, no church camp for Luisa, a full summer. "Jeezus H. Christ, *a* whole summer?"

How could they plan for so many days away from the farm? 'I have to accept very little that I don't like.'

"No, Gringa, *all* the summers in Italy. Siddhartha can come and visit you, help you fill it with European antiques, although Señor Angotti assures me there is much that can be used inside. This is *your* house, and we will all be...*together*."

"Together?" her face burned. She took a drink of water. "Together, do you use the word aright?"

"Si. I use the word, 'aright.' As they say in Chess, 'Check,' Gringa."

Chapter 9

The light snow melted as soon as it hit the windshield, only headlight beams from oncoming cars shattered the darkness. The four wheel drive vehicle was steady on the wet pavement. Jill sat silently on the passenger's side. Luisa lay asleep in the back seat. Thanksgiving with the Joneses in Swayzee now disappeared behind them with night's black velvet drape.

"Honey, I know this was hard for you. I watched you. Your effort was admirable, but I'm not going to put you through family again at Christmas," Jack spoke, as he reached over and rubbed her leg.

"Oh, we're not going to have Christmas this year? That would be good. I keep thinking of Dad complaining that he wasn't born to carve turkey. And Mom's cranberry sauce, it tasted better when she made it. I used her recipe...Oh, Jack, I *have* to do Christmas. I have to accept their deaths."

"No, Honey, not this year. Lillian always told me that I should take you places because you love to travel. I asked some of the guys at work and they said Disneyworld is a great place to take your family."

"Disneyworld, Orlando, Florida, how far is that from Ocala?"

"Disneyworld, not Ocala, not Hawk Jones. If we have time, I may drive there by myself to see him."

"You would do that to yourself?"

"He is my father; I have a duty to stay in touch. I'm sure he doesn't know about Lillian. He would probably like to know that."

"Jeezus Jack, the man is an ogre. And…what about Luisa? Have you talked to her?"

"Of course, I talked to her first. Are any decisions made without her approval?" he glanced over his shoulder and nodded slightly. "You'd think she was the CEO of this family, but she was easy on this one. She hates to see you like this. She never knows what to say. So what do you say to going to Florida for Christmas? It wouldn't feel like Christmas with palm trees and summer weather."

"I don't know. It might be good to get away from here." Not another holiday dinner with Mary Ann, who looked at each inch of Jill, from the emerald ring which she always commented on, to her "Oh, where are you going this year on *your* vacation?"

Jill wanted to scream, "Luisa's father decides where I go on my vacations, Luisa's father bought this ring, this bracelet from Curaçao, Luisa's father, Mary Ann! He bought us a villa in Italy!" But she smiled and let Mary Ann's probing innuendoes go unanswered.

Jack massaged her shoulder. She stuffed her hands in her coat pockets and stared out the windows. Sparkling pieces of snow rushed at their headlights. "Shooting stars" Henry had named them as they drove on these kinds of wintry nights. She'd sat on the armrest with her head resting on Henry's shoulder. Dad are you there? Where did these snowflakes come from? You didn't tell me how to have Christmas without you and Mom. The four-wheel vibrated on the icy rough pavement. The tires audibly scratched the etched surface.

"I asked at work to take two weeks instead of one. We can do Christmas Eve in Swayzee and leave Christmas day for Florida. Luisa can open her presents before we leave," Jack looked over at her.

"You think of all the details, don't you?" Jill glanced at him, then back to the window. Melted flakes collected in beads of water, trickled down the side of the glass and then onto the window's chrome frame. The road was narrow and infrequently traveled. Jack easily navigated the poorly marked country roads. The roadside drainage ditches were filled with drifted snow.

I know, Mom, my husband is trying to take your advice. Yes, a decent man, a good husband, "Okay, Jack. I'll go," she heard herself answer. "I'm ready to leave winter for awhile. Mom was right. I do feel better when I know I am going to go somewhere."

"Did you hear Beau say he put a bid in on old man McKinnsey's farm? I remember hearing you say that is where you worked your high school summers. I guess McKinnsey, the old man anyway, is ready to retire and move to Florida. The son has rented out most of the acres, but now wants to sell them because he makes his money at the grain elevator, and on the Board of Trade in Chicago. He is quite a gambler."

"Coffee futures?" Jill said it, and then stopped.

"No, Jill, pork bellies? Where in the world did that come from, coffee futures?"

"Oh, when I was in Chicago seeing Mo last summer, someone was talking about the Chicago Board of Trade and I listened. But when you said gambling, Board of Trade, it made me think of coffee futures. We talk about Wall Street in my senior honors class."

She turned and used the window to distract her present from the past, swirling with Lillian and Henry and now Luis and coffee futures and McKinnsey's farm. She drew triangles on her steamed window and hummed Cast Your Fate to the Wind.

ᚱᚵᚱ

The three weeks of the pre-holiday season were filled with activities for school, Jack's work Christmas party, church, and the annual Interracial Club exchange. Luisa had been picked for freshman cheerleading. Her practices and games kept Jill traveling to and from each part of the holiday season. She prepared refrigerator sugar cookies at the church kitchen, made it to the second half of Luisa's games, home to grade papers and finally, Christmas shopping for Jack's family.

She volunteered at church to spend two Saturdays in December boxing up donated canned goods for those in need. Bitsy and she bought toys for the children invited to the Interracial Club party. Luis could buy villas in Italy; he could buy toys for these children. At some point she had asked or told him that she did this every year. He reminded her the money was for Luisa. She told him… "To whom much is given, of him

190

much will be required," quoting the Bible. He had paused, then said, "For Luisa... and for all of *your* good deeds."

Her December calendar was fully marked with each activity taking a space, including the trip to Indianapolis with Luisa to see *The Nutcracker*. It looked like the advent calendars she had cherished as a little girl.

The most time-consuming activity was addressing Christmas cards. Lillian and Henry received cards from all over the country, people who did not know of their deaths. With each card the sadness consumed her, but she knew Lillian would want her to answer each and every one.

Jack addressed many of the envelopes, but she wrote the notes. Each year they seemed to have more friends than the year before. Jack told her it was a sign of life well-lived. Being busy kept her from dwelling in the dark place of her first Christmas without them. When Christmas arrived, she would be in Florida, sunshine and Mickey Mouse shaped lollipops at Disneyworld. It would not be Christmas at all. The Joneses had decided to do their family exchange the Sunday before Christmas, permitting her and Jack to leave for Florida on the twenty-second. Now they would be in Florida on Christmas Eve, spinning around in the Magic tea cups or the Jungle ride.

The church scheduled caroling for the week before Christmas. She and Luisa volunteered to stay at the church with the women's group and make hot chocolate and chili for the carolers when they came back from visiting nursing homes and shut-ins. Singing and laughing with her church friends was a bright spot. She checked off another day on the calendar, only a few more days and they would be headed south.

Today's date, Friday, the last day of school. She took a drink of coffee and went to the hall closet to get her coat. The phone rang just as she tied the coat's belt. She put on her hat and went back into the kitchen. One more sip of coffee and she picked up the phone.

"Jill?"

"Sadie, I'm ready to walk..."

"Good, I'm glad you didn't leave yet."

"I'm all bundled up and ready to walk out the door, I'll call you when I get home."

"No, don't call, come over here after school and bring Luisa."

"Jack took her long ago. She has cheerleading after school..."

"Okay, I'll keep this box from the National Coffee Federation until after Christmas."

"What!?"

"Yes, Sweetie. UPS just dropped it at my door. I can't stand it. I want to open it now."

"No, you nosey hussy. I'll be over and if one peep hole is cut, I'll…"

"Sorry, no threats. I hold all the cards in this game of two husbands one wife."

ϏξϏ

Jill watched the clock. The hands did not move any faster for her or her students. They talked quietly in her afternoon classes. She sorted through the shelves and closet trying to get organized for her return from vacation -a stack of papers that students had not picked up; library books that needed to be returned to the school library; tattered bulletin board cut-outs that were no longer usable. The Department Chairman wanted her to complete a check list of her progress in her American History and world geography classes. She'd finished during her last period, conference period.

She now stopped by his office before heading into the teacher's lounge.

"Well, Jill, I hope you have a safe trip."

"Thank you, Don. I'm glad to be leaving the winter for awhile."

"I hope you don't like it too much and get lost on the beach."

"That would be nice, wouldn't it? I don't think my husband would allow that."

"How is Jack?"

"Looking forward to some pro-am tennis tournament that is going on while we are down there."

"He still owes me a tennis date. Remind him, please. And I wish both of you a Merry Christmas and your pretty daughter."

"Thank you."

"Hey, Jill, this is Christmas. Cheer-up. You look tired. Have you been doing too many extra activities?"

"I tried to be real busy these last three weeks, so I wouldn't have to think of my first Christmas without Mom and Dad."

"I know it is tough. I miss Henry myself. He was such a lovable gruff character. He told me I had a lifetime guarantee when he built my house, promised me the house would outlast both of us."

192

"I'm sure that's true. Homeowners only called because they wanted another room added, never because something was wrong. I remember when he'd have me out there working. He wanted only perfection and kept referring to me as 'child labor.' My friend Sadie and I always tried to quit, but he wouldn't let us take more than just a break."

"He reminded me of your 'child labor' tendencies when he was talking to me about how you were working out."

"He did?"

"Yep, said I must keep on you if I wanted to get the job done, but you'd be good. Guaranteed it as a matter of fact."

Jill wiped a tear that formed and forced a smile. Henry had been her biggest cheerleader even when she wasn't around.

"Stop crying. I know, let me tell you his favorite joke. He always started, 'Hey Don, you're a school teacher, let me tell you this one'...About the teacher who couldn't get anywhere with one of his students. He asked the kid how many days of the week started with 't.' Two, today and tomorrow, then he asked the kid how many seconds in a year? Twelve. January Second, February Second. Then he asked him how many 'd's' in reindeer?"

They both said together "365" and sang, "Rudolph the Red-nosed Reindeer, dee-dee-dee-dee." And they laughed at Henry's old corny joke.

Don said, "Yeah, he sure liked to tell a joke. You'll be okay. My father died when I was in high school, had a heart attack lifting a bale of hay. Always bragged about how he could, and bam! Died right in the barn. Like your dad, he was a helluva man."

"I'm sorry. I didn't mean to bring out this sadness. I'm really okay, probably more tired right now than sad. I have many things to do before we leave. And I need to get out of here. Luisa is waiting."

"Sure, sure. See you next year. Soak up some sun for me."

She pulled on her hat and adjusted it to cover her ears and hang to one side. She put on her gloves and walked the same hallway as that afternoon when Luis pulled into the parking lot. In five years, she thought of him at the end of every school day. She heard the car drive up and the door slam, and saw her trunk full of ball jars; each day the same twinge, when the school door closed behind her, locking itself. Today a blast of icy air burned her eyes, destroying her summer fantasy. She tied her neck scarf tighter as a frigid gust blew between her legs, only slightly protected with cut-off thermal undershorts. Yeah, Don, can I get lost on a beach?

She drove to Caylor High School to pick up Luisa. The facility filled her with ghosts of long ago. Two of her former classmates taught there and Luisa now had one of them for an English teacher. When she had gone to Parents' Night, she and Jack walked down all those familiar halls. They climbed the worn marble stairs with their deep grooves from years of use. Now she waited patiently for her little cheerleader. She looked at Luisa and thought her so young, but remembered how old and grown up Sadie and she perceived themselves as freshmen. Luisa jumped in the warm car.

"Mom, can we give Cathy a ride home? She lives on the way."

"We aren't going home. We are on our way to Sadie's, but if we don't take her, how will she get home?"

"Her dad was supposed to pick her up, but didn't come. Luisa whispered, "Please Mom, I'll tell you about her dad later..." Luisa winked at Jill and pointed at Cathy so only Jill could see.

"Okay, it's Christmas."

"Thanks, Mom," Luisa leaned over and kissed her cheek. Luisa motioned for Cathy to get in the car. "Mom, this is my friend Cathy Bancroft. Cathy this is my mom, Mrs. Jones."

"How do you do Cathy? Which Bancroft are you? I used to go to school with a Jim Bancroft."

"Oh, he was my uncle, my dad's younger brother."

"Harrington Bancroft, Harry. I remember pictures. He was in the Army the whole time, so you're Harry's daughter?"

"Mrs. Jones, did you know my Uncle Jimmy was killed in a car crash a couple of months ago?"

"No, I never heard about it. Was it in the Caylor paper?"

"He was killed in St. Louis. Dad went to the funeral, well Mom and Dad, but Dad didn't get along with Uncle Jimmy. Dad said they are not sure if it was an accident or not. He drove off a bridge and his car went into the river. Mrs. Jones you are so lucky to be going to Disneyworld. I wish I could go."

"Uh-huh."

"Mom, are you alright? You look funny."

"Oh, yeah, I'm fine. Cathy now where do you live?"

"1216 Lindsey. Right by the used furniture store, Bailey's."

"Sure, I know exactly where that is."

They stopped in front of Bailey's.

194

"Nice to have met you, Mrs. Jones. Merry Christmas and Happy New Year."

Cathy closed the door and Luisa turned immediately to Jill, "Her dad is a drunk, Mom. He says he is coming to pick her up and never shows up. I feel sorry for her. She is always asking for rides. She doesn't have to stay after school, but waits, hoping someone will take her home. Her dad sounds like a jerk."

"Aren't you the little gossip. But her 'Uncle Jimmy' was a jerk, too. It is a sad story, but Jim was fond of alcohol himself. Let's talk about something more cheerful, and I don't mind taking her home, if she can wait. You know some days, I'm late."

"I'm so glad Dad is getting you a new car, so my friends won't have to ride in this old clunker."

"We aren't at your Aunt Sadie's and you already are talking like her. There is nothing wrong with this car. It starts, and the heater works, and it takes your friends home."

"Mom, this car is old and tired and the radio died last month. It's embarrassing. At least Dad has a decent four-wheel."

"Pray tell, where does this come from? Your grandmother didn't give you this champagne taste and not me or Jack. I'll blame Sadie. She thinks the same way."

"Papa would not want me to be picked up in an old car like this. You should buy a Buick like Grandpa's car."

"Oh, your papa, is that it? Speaking of the devil, Sadie said we have something at her house from him."

"All right, Mom. He gets me the best things!"

"It's not a horse."

"I wonder Mom, does he know we are going to Florida? I hope so because maybe he could come. You only seem happy when he is around."

"Yes, he knows we're going."

ﺭﺥﺭ

Sadie's house had been selected for the Caylor Christmas Tour of Homes, a tour sponsored by the YWCA to raise money for their ongoing activities. Sadie and Michael liked it that their home was open to the public. Two weeks before the tour, one of the local florists decorated all the rooms on the first floor and put electric candles in every window of the house. With Sadie's eclectic collection of antiques and the florists' fantasy designs, she ended up with two Christmas trees, one in the living room and another in the sun porch they used for a family room. Sadie shook her head reaffirming that always in her house everything came in twos.

Now as Jill pulled into the large semi-circular driveway in the late afternoon, the house was illuminated with all the tiny electric window candles. The huge white pines that stood sentry for so many years in front of the house glowed with hundreds of tiny flickering lights. Each year Michael had to hire a tree surgeon to decorate them. Vicksburg had become a Christmas house.

Jill rang the bell, then walked in the front door with the huge pine wreath. This year Sadie had picked one from the florist's options that was all green boughs with white decorations. Tiny angels, birds, satin balls and silver strands of ribbon danced among the twisted branches. Jill decided this was her favorite wreath so far. She leaned in and smelled the pine.

Sadie had cinnamon and nutmeg cooking in a spice pot. The aroma combined with the bayberry candles burning in the living room, foyer and sun room. Jill took a deep breath. It smelled like Christmas spice everywhere. The electric candles and Christmas lights in each room reminded Jill of an English home in a Charles Dickens' novel. Sometimes, like at this very moment, Jill was convinced the house was a museum. The basement was the most modern space and Luisa usually escaped to the TV, a pinball machine and pool table with Mike and his friends. Michael put in a juke box and on occasion Jill and Sadie would play their old favorite 45's from high school.

"Sadie, we're here." Jill called to her as Kate toddled toward them dragging a long red satin ribbon. Jill picked her up and walked to the kitchen.

The Messiah was playing somewhere; it came through on one of the intercom speakers. Michael installed the system to keep track of everyone in the big place. Sadie said, "He just wants to keep track of me. Doesn't he know I'm always trying to hide from all of them?"

Sadie walked from the kitchen with a cup of coffee and a roll of chocolate chip cookie dough, "Here, Sweetie. Your favorites, Colombian coffee straight from the man's mountains and raw cookie dough." Sadie hugged Jill and Kate together. "I see you found your baby. Sure you don't want another? You're not too old you know, women are having babies, later and later. I think I read in *McCall's* almost forty…"

"Well, I have some time. We are only thirty-two, so you could have another, too. No. Stop suggesting the impossible. I'll just have the coffee, not another baby." Jill looked around the hall as they walked to the kitchen. "Always a new knick-knack in some alcove or shelf and now vintage Christmas decorations. Every time I come here I feel like the kid in the candy store, one of these and one of those."

"My house is your house. You can take whatever you want. Michael might even pay you to take some of it."

"I need to ask him about shipping it to Italy," Jill said.

"Come on. Sit with me and talk. You don't have to rush do you? I want to fix Irish coffee. I wrote down the original recipe last month when we were in San Francisco."

"I told Jack I might be late because I was stopping here. He's really been especially sweet this month, sweeter than his usual. But Sadie, I just heard some shocking news. Jim Bancroft was killed in a car crash two months ago. Did you know? No, I know, if you knew, I would know. What a shock! Yes, let's do Irish coffee."

Jill sat down at the comfortable table and pulled the holiday napkin from the wicker holder in the middle of the table. She held Kate and took off her hat and coat, balancing the little girl on her lap.

"Aunt Jill, will Santa come to your house? Have you been good?"

"Here, share a cookie with her. And get her to drink the milk in her cup." Sadie put a small plastic cup with handles in front of Jill.

Jill took the red ribbon and tied it around Kate into a big bow. "Santa doesn't need to come to my house because I won't be home, but for your mom, here…Merry Christmas, Sadie." She put Kate in the booster seat next to her.

Each window in Sadie's kitchen wall of windows had a small candle and half-way up she had hung small Christmas wreaths. Sadie mixed the Canadian blend whiskey in the white porcelain mugs with a hand painted Christmas tree on the side. She dropped a dollop of whipped cream on the top and sprinkled it with a nutmeg. Luisa had already ducked down to the basement.

"Here's to us," Sadie handed Jill her coffee and proposed a toast.

"And to all of our Christmases past."

"Yeah, like New York…" Sadie said.

197

"Stop, Sadie that was New Year's anyway. And you really want to talk T.J.?" Sadie shook her head. "You know how hard it is not going by Henry and Lillian's? How can it really be Christmas without going to Mom and Dad's? All their Christmas decorations are still out in the barn boxed up and labeled with Mom's handwriting. Maybe next year."

"You are lucky the house sold so quickly, you won't have to go by and see an empty house where love and lights should have been."

"Drive down Catalpa? I almost did when I took Cathy Bancroft home today, one of these times, I will forget."

"Hey, hey, I don't want to cry yet. Tell me more about Jim Bancroft," Sadie said.

Jill told Sadie the story she had just heard from his niece. They speculated on the accidental death and why there had been no mention of it in the local paper. Sadie said, "Michael may know. He is always running into people we went to school with. He's at the Country Club playing gin and drinking gin with some of the guys in the Stag Bar, no ladies allowed."

Sadie fixed them a second Irish coffee. Luisa had come upstairs to ask about her present and to say Mike was not letting her play pinball. Sadie told her to follow her into the library where she had put the box earlier that morning. Luisa carried the box into the kitchen. Jill stirred the whipped cream into the hot coffee.

"Sadie, this Irish coffee is so good."

"The coffee was *my* present from Señor Ochoa."

"I kind of like it when the Irish and the Colombians mix it up," Jill said.

"Curaçao. I remember."

"And every other place we've been."

"Look at the postmark on the box before Luisa opens it. You know I was all over the box, trying to figure out what was in it," Sadie said.

"New Orleans? Weird." Jill shook her head, "He is such a mystery. Jeezus, will I ever know what makes him tick?"

"Oh, let's just open the presents. We are going to spend a lot of our lives trying to figure him out. We know he has money and that's a good thing. Okay?" Sadie said.

Jill opened the box, "A sweet little 'the best things come in small boxes' for you Luisa."

Luisa pulled the red satin ribbon off the gold paper and opened a blue velvet covered box, "Oh Mom, it's beautiful. Look!" She held up

198

a gold necklace with a small pearl pendant on it. She opened a second smaller box, "Oh Mom, pearl earrings, but they are pierced. How did he know I want my ears pierced? Please Mom, now we have to get them done. Look! Aren't they perfect? Let's go tomorrow. I want them pierced. Please?"

"We'll see. Maybe when we get home from Florida. Open your card. I want to see what he says."

"Open your card, Mom. I want to see what he says to you."

Luisa opened the card that was decorated with angels, all with dark hair, all children. She opened it and read,

"Dear Luisa, I wish you a Merry Christmas, Feliz Navidad. The money is for your trip to Florida.

I love you, my own Christmas angel, Papa.

"Mom, it is a $100 bill! Whoopee! Disneyworld, here I come."

"Okay Jill, open your box. I can't stand it. I walked by the library twenty times trying to think of some way to open the box and you wouldn't know."

Jill slipped the gold ribbon off the black box. She lifted the lid and unsealed the paper sticker on the tissue paper. She pulled out a bracelet, a chain of tiny links each with an emerald mounted in it, an exact replica of the Villa della Principessa dangled from the clasp. "Oh, Sadie, it is gorgeous. Here fasten it on me."

"Open your card!"

The card had a water color picture of red and white roses decorating a Christmas tree. Printed on the front with gold embossed lettering, "Feliz Navidad."

Gringa,
Green as the palms of Bermuda,
Gold as the sunset on the azure sea
A reminder of our past
And a token for our future.

Your own Señor Frost – Luis

When Jill finished reading she handed the card to Sadie who was refilling their coffee cups. Jill turned her bracelet by the table's candle, letting the light reflect off the tiny stones. "Sadie, it's so expensive. How will I explain this to Jack?"

The phone rang in several places at once, but Sadie did not answer, knowing Mike would pick it up in the basement.

"We'll think of something. We've done emerald rings, and a tennis pro, now a bracelet. 'Gosh, Miss Best Friend, I think you are so

199

special, I just had to buy you a token of my love and friendship.' See how easy that was?"

"Mom!" Mike's voice called to her through the intercom speaker, "Pick up the phone." Sadie reached for the old fashioned phone in the kitchen. She placed the ear piece on the cord to her ear; and talked into the horn shaped mouth piece. The large wood box had a metal crank that no longer functioned. Michael had it remodeled for her, making it work with the modern phone system.

"Yes?"

"Siddhartha, is Jill there?"

"Yes, as you said, I corralled her here this afternoon. Punctual, I might add. The coffee, Luis, it is superb. I wish we could get this stuff in Caylor."

"You did," he chuckled.

"Thank you. Hold on while I call the woman who is wearing her Christmas present and dreaming of summers in Italy on this cold winter day."

Sadie shooed Jill to the library phone. It sat on a presidential size desk. Sadie had been using the desk's top to wrap presents. Jill adjusted to the semidarkness and unburied the phone from a blanket of red Santa Claus paper.

"Hi, Luis, Thank you and Feliz Navidad."

Bayberry scent seemed to come from the paneled walls. Two large paned windows were on each side of a bricked fireplace. A gas log burned and added a golden glow to the dark room. The book lined walls were illuminated by the electric candles in each window pane.

"Gringa, you're radiant. In the firelight?"

"Are you standing outside the window?"

"No, I remember the library from my visit, large fireplace between two very tall windows and surrounded by Christmas trees."

"All the details except the wrapping paper, ribbons, sparkles, tissue paper and unassembled boxes. And thank you, Papito."

She heard him softly chuckle. "You say 'Papito' to me from 3,000 miles, but looking at you in gold and emeralds, the princess. I can't resist, I must reduce the distance. I will join you in Florida."

"Luis, I'm going with Jack. You know that. What are you really saying? Jack would not understand a Colombian sleeping in his room."

"He can have his own room, Gringa."

"No."

"Siddhartha knows the details. We've talked. Ask her."

200

"Perhaps you and Sadie will share the same room. Oh that's right, she isn't going to Florida. No, Luis. You in an adjoining room? Jack walks out and you pass each other in the hall? Share a bathroom? Your toothbrush on my vanity? No. You can't see, but I am shaking my head. No, Luis."

"My hard-headed Jankee, I will see you in Florida. I have to conduct interviews for another pilot. Andy has arranged appointments. And of course your presence made it the perfect time. It is your Christmas present. Shall I wear a red ribbon?"

"No..." Jill heaved audibly, "Si. Wear the ribbon. Si. Come to Florida. Si! Si! Si!" She pushed away the paper in front of her, a roll of ribbon unraveled and fell to the floor, a plastic tube of glitter bounced on her, then spilled on the carpet under her feet. She brushed the glitter which became enmeshed in the rug.

"Gringa, Gringa, Gringa, think about what I am going to tell you. Think about it when you drink your coffee, when you drive to Florida. Think about it as you touch your bracelet. Think about it when you brush your teeth and kiss our daughter goodnight...you... *belong...* to me. Siddhartha will explain my travel plans. Adios."

Jill whispered "adios" to the dial tone and returned the phone to its hidden place under the trimmings. She sat in the big swivel chair, turning it around and propping her legs on the desk. She stared at the tiny electric flames of the window candles and out to Sadie's lawn. The tall pines' Christmas lights flickered through their snow dusted branches. She absently fingered the bracelet. "Joined together forever, Luis? Jack, my friend from Colombia, Luisa's father actually, will be sleeping with us. You don't mind getting a room somewhere else do you? No. I didn't think so. Oh, Dad, where are you? You said I did 'best' in boys. But this is so hard. I feel like I'm getting an 'F.'"

The door opened a crack, then completely as Sadie walked in, "Gringa, look at you, sparkles everywhere. Happy New Year!" Jill made another feeble attempt to dust them from her dress and the thick carpet. "Okay," Sadie continued, "I will tell you the details. It will be ever so tricky. I get to be the appointment secretary."

"Sadie, you actually conspired? Does it ever occur to you people that I'm married. And no one even suggests I get divorced. We all just act like that this bullshit should go on and on!"

Sadie switched to a southern accent, "Why, my, oh, my, Miss Church, at Christmas? Next you will be using the good Lord's name in vain. It's the holidays. You are just not feeling like yourself." Sadie put her arm through Jill's elbow, pulling her from the desk chair.

"Sorry about the glitter."

"Now you know that is why the good Lord made vacuum cleaners and Hilda to use to them."

"Was I bad in my other life, Sadie? And now I'm blessed with a zany best friend, a Latin lover and a feckless husband?"

"No, I was wrong, it isn't Miss Church. It is Miss Sarah B. Yes, it was your other life. We were sitting in the Roman Emperor's throne room, he was your husband, when you said to me, see I was your handmaiden, 'Sadie,' you whispered, 'I want that Roman soldier over there, the dark one.' Smash! The Emperor, your husband, smacked you into eternal life. And now here we are. You're right."

Jill laughed and hugged her friend, "Okay, you win, but how do I explain a Colombian coffee farmer will be sharing my room?"

"Michael's client?"

"Right. No Sadie, do better."

"Anyway, Michael's home now. He said he didn't know about Jim and as soon as you get off the phone he is going to call Harry Bancroft. He met him a few times when he came home on leave. Come, let's talk husbands, Florida, Colombian coffee farmers. I want you to stay with us for dinner. Come."

They worked in the kitchen getting dinner ready. The cookies came out of the oven and the cheeseburger meatloaf went in, next to the baked potatoes.

Jill chopped vegetables for salad, then called Jack, "Yes, Honey, I know I haven't packed and we leave in two days. But I'm bringing you dinner and I want to show you what Sadie gave me." She shook her wrist. Sadie smiled and shook her head, mouthing the word, "tramp."

Jill hung up, "Yes, a deceitful tramp. I need another Irish coffee."

"Steph called. He and his wife are coming down the Friday after Christmas, something about their kids leaving on Christmas night. My first Christmas with him, I am so excited. Jill in the pantry, are jars of Lillian's homemade applesauce, would you please pick one? Don't cry. Let's just remember her and Pops when we say grace. You can do it, go get it."

As Jill walked back into the kitchen, Michael was leaning against the cabinet drinking a beer. "Hey, it's the little farm girl with multiple husbands."

"Shish Michael, the children. Very funny."

Michael laughed, "Come on give me a hug. And your daughter is seriously beating Mike at pinball."

"Jill, listen to the Jim Bancroft story. Tell her, Honey."

Michael took a drink of his beer and spoke, "His car went out of control over a bridge. He landed in the Missouri River, trapped inside, he drowned. It was in the morning on his way to work, so Harry was almost sure he was sober. They found a gun in the seat next to him, Harry said that maybe he ran himself off the road. Harry did say the gun part surprised him because Jim always insisted he did not want any guns around his kids. He said it was all really freaky; the police ruled it suicide. And they did not want to put any of the story in the Caylor paper and let the local small town gossips have a field day with the news. Harry didn't say much more except Jim's widow, Janet, has already married someone else. He wished us all a Merry Christmas."

"Michael that story is bizarre."

"Oh, yeah, like most things that go on around here. We are headed to Florida, for a few days after her father leaves." Michael looked at Sadie, "Yes, she doesn't want her best friend to be alone during the holidays. Really? I guess having one's husband and daughter with the masses of humanity at Disneyworld is being alone." He laughed.

As their conversation rambled on, the dinner came out of the oven, the table was set, and the children were called. Michael told them that he was seriously considering an offer Caterpillar had made to him, "A promotion and a raise, but much more time on the road. I guess life is just a series of trade-offs. I haven't decided if Sadie likes me here or gone."

"You know I like you here, except on the days that end in 'y,' seriously, let me say I have the best husband in the world," Sadie said, lifting her glass of wine to toast Michael.

"Agreed. Michael, here's to you." Jill raised her glass, "Thanks for always helping us find our way through the fun house."

"Jill, I am looking forward to meeting the coffee farmer. With Caterpillar, I will be given the South American territory. He knows people, right?"

"He seems to know a lot of people. I've only met a few. But I'm sure he would introduce you to the ones he knows, I think. Honest to god, I don't know, but we can always ask. Henry said, 'It never hurts to ask.'"

Chapter 10

The tiny round light bulbs were spiked and sprouted at the end of long brushed aluminum gold tubes in an exploding starburst effect. The chandelier dominated the space below a curved ceiling. Tiny twinkle lights poked through the sand colored dome. It reminded Michael of the planetarium his Eighth Grade science teacher, Mr. Patterson, had tried to create when they studied constellations. The vaulted curvature had an excessive splattering of pierced light holes. It enchanted Sadie. Why did his wife like such an ostentatious splash of brightness? "Eclectic," she had told him. It also lit the restaurant with the best stone crabs this side of Miami and that was enough reason for him to choose it.

His wife had made arrangements to meet the mysterious Latin here. The man who used Michael's home as a message service and clearing house for his affair with Sadie's best friend, now sat across from him. The waiter suggested an aperitif. Michael ordered martinis for him and Sadie. Luis ordered Stoli with lemon juice.

Luis relaxed comfortably filling the white French Provincial chair, "Louis XVI imitation," Michael noted. The chairs and tables were the only French Provincial pieces in the restaurant. Eclectic. The formally dressed waiters shuffled quietly, emptying ash trays with each flick of ashes. Luis had declined smoking his cigar, suggesting that they move to the attached outdoor bar after their meal.

The restaurant opened on one side to the beach and fifty feet further west, the Gulf of Mexico. The glass prisms of ornate wind chimes clinked in the gentle Gulf breeze. The tinkling of ice cubes in crystal goblets blended with silverware tapping against china plates in the crowded dining room. Winter, and the snowbirds had come to Florida. A hidden music system played Ray Coniff's Christmas carols. The smell of the ocean and balmy temperature from the evening breeze had dispelled any notion Michael had of Christmas. From a complete holiday home, to St. Petersburg, Florida, the season had changed in spite of Christmas wreaths hanging on the restaurant's walls.

Luis reminded Michael, of well, he was not sure. He looked typically Latin, golden brown, dark, slightly curled hair and a heavy moustache. Michael hated to label anyone "typical." His hair was not fashionably long like his own, nor were his clothes the psychedelic mod, bell-bottom look that dominated the current gentlemen's fashion magazines. Luis's casual open shirt was silk and fit his broad chest. He had left the first couple of buttons undone. Was this because of the temperature or the machismo that Latin men tried to suppress in order to focus attention to it? Michael had accepted this attention or suppression in meetings from corporate headquarters in Illinois to international meetings in Caracas and Buenos Aires.

Luis's linen jacket looked like Savile Row or probably Hong Kong, natural bone buttons, full shoulders, a loose cut chest, and a pressed champagne colored silk handkerchief that peeked perfectly from the upper breast pocket. His dress spoke, screamed class. Michael appreciated classic dressing, his trips to New York and Montreal and a year in Germany had given him an opportunity to see and shop in the most fashionable haberdasheries, yeah even the name, haberdasheries, Ltd., oozed class. Caylor was strictly bib overalls and flannel shirt country. Luis's linen pants were not the suit's pants, but with a flax blend the nubs matched the silk handkerchief, slightly darker, only slightly, the warp a subtle match to the shirt and jacket. No socks, though, dressed for dinner and no socks. It *was* Florida. Michael had to give him that. Gucci loafers, Belleair Country Club, Florida blue bloods.

The comfort of the shirt, the jacket, the front double tucked pants, Luis was comfortable with the gringos as Michael knew Latins called him and Sadie. Okay, Sadie did not look like the typical, oh that word again, gringo, but she acted the part. She teased Luis and he responded to her femininity. Where did the charm come from? A cliché? Latin charm? Michael knew this was the characteristic of salesmen. They possessed a unique sense of people, the response to a look, the proper probing question that was not offensive, yet enabled the questioner to elicit the desired response and allowed the customer to feel as though they had some control of the buying process.

Yes, he and Luis shared that. Luis was at least a salesman, but the eyebrow that raised, and the serious sweep across the eyes, green eyes. Luis's eyes enchanted his wife, she had told him that, but they hid as well as they exposed.

"He owned coffee plantations in Colombia," was Sadie and Jill's explanation, "a coffee farmer." It was where the great coffee Sadie served came from, some mountains by Medellin, "Luis's farm," she assured him. And as Luis talked of beans, picking and roasting, Michael was fascinated by and curious because there was more to all of the women's coffee farm chatter. They all knew, Jill and Sadie and Michael had sat around the kitchen table and discussed the possibilities, many times, speculated actually on who Luis Ochoa was. But they ended all discussions with the same conclusion, none of them knew.

Sadie had said, "Meet him, Michael, judge for yourself. You are a good judge of character, what do you always tell me? 'You can't shit a shitter.'"

Michael met him; they now cracked crab legs together and sat exchanging political positions on the conflict in Viet Nam. Michael was pleased the war had come to a close; he had lost some friends there. But Michael regretted that the ending was ambiguous.

Luis spewed his anti-American epithets about "police actions" in other countries, trying to control what and who needed to be free. The sarcasm when he used the words, "land of the free" was raw and sharp. There was nothing ambiguous in Luis's arguments. He described the CIA as the truly American foreign police, using countries and their leaders as pawns in an international chess game with the Soviet Union.

Michael liked Luis's passion. He was not neutral on any subject; he just chose the ones to shoot with his intensity in Sadie or Michael's direction. Michael responded in kind. As the dinner progressed, Michael grew to respect the strength of their dinner guest.

Michael knew Luis controlled much of Luis's space, but saw that he respected him. Did it emanate from Sadie and Jill's introduction? When the topic of investments percolated to the top of their animated discussion, Luis listened to Michael. Luis leaned back in the chair and absently used his thumb to rub the gold band on his left hand. Strange, a gold band on an unmarried man. Most of the salesman, including himself, did not wear their marriage symbols.

"Drugs, actually, Med-Wicke, in my own backyard, Indianapolis. I think the mafia has the illicit drug business safely in hand. Great profits, but they are not listed on the exchange. The computer challengers in the Silicon Valley will give IBM headaches, I think. Anyway, I've invested on both sides. Armonk and Santa Clara, East Coast –West Coast. My father refuses to rearrange his portfolio and stays with the family business – glass. My grandfather was the horse trader in the family. He lucked into the early oil boom in Texas, cashed in, and then played the markets from Chicago to New York. He taught me about ticker tape when I was trying to digest two plus two, but his passion, farming. He relaxed behind the wheel of his tractor. Always talked of the dirt and life. He farmed a lot of corn."

"Tomatoes?"

"Some, rotating crops."

Luis sat still concentrating on Michael's litany. His face serious, the sweep Michael observed across the eyes. Michael was curious, but any question at the moment would be intrusive. "Luis, you promised a cigar. Let's enjoy the moonlight over St. Pete and then I must go. Mike has tomorrow planned. My wife has *your* day planned." Michael winked at Sadie who returned the wink with a scowl for the blatant allusion to the rendezvous she had planned for Jill and Luis.

"Si. She and Jill seem to be quite the team when it comes to planning and speculation. What was your term, horse trading?" Luis stood, putting a hundred dollar bill in the check presenter and pulling two cigars from his pocket, "Cuban. You don't mind do you? You are almost in their backyard."

Michael accepted the contraband, having been offered the same in the corporate president's office at a Christmas sales seminar last year. The aluminum cylinder was pale yellow. Michael glanced around, then followed Sadie and Luis outside. Aramis, he's wearing Aramis, Michael noted as the breeze brushed the trio. They crossed through the arched opening to the expansive Italian Renaissance-inspired patio. Large urns with vines and bright flowers sat in the corners. The patio's chunky concrete balusters had been strung with tiny flickering Christmas lights. Eclectic, Michael reminded himself. He puffed the cigar and inhaled the sea breeze. The best of Florida, he had concluded long ago, was summer in winter.

"Drugs, you say Michael? In Mexico, they are cheap. They transport everyone's. Southeast Asian, Hawaiian, South American. Transportation, now that is an investment. I live by the sea. I use the shipping lanes like your Mack Trucks use the highways. I'm always looking for the best deal, the least extortion. Coffee is cheap, but transportation, getting the products to their market...with the volatile oil prices. It is a headache, seasick, perhaps." Luis viewed the sea, the "means," not the soothing balm they were experiencing, hearing the gentle slap of waves.

"Our merchant marines are dwindling. They seemed to have priced themselves out of the market. I can see a day when all American ports will be filled with non-American flag ships." Michael paused at the essence of what he was describing and shook his head at the absurdity of having only foreign vessels in American ports.

The threesome leaned against the waist high concrete rail that separated the patio from the beach. In the distance people strolled at the Gulf's edge. The width of the concrete and its flat scratchy surface from years of salt water buffeting provided a seat for Sadie between the two men. She wore bellbottoms and platform shoes that made her the same height as Luis. Michael loved her long legs, her model-shape, that he teased her was like a boy's shape, but in her clothes she carried his moneyed status well. She insisted on larger than necessary diamonds and aquamarines, she was at once understated and expansive.

People turned to look at his wife because she was attractive, not drop-dead gorgeous, but alluring, one look was not enough for most people, men or women. At first glance, Michael knew that they determined her ethnicity ("foreign or domestic", he teased her), then the package, her hair more stylish and fashionable than all the other parts. At the moment her dark hair was parted simply down the middle, but hung perfectly straight to the center of her back. Michael adored her at these moments. She was graceful and appealing. Really, he admitted, he adored her period, but she had evolved, responding as Henry used to constantly remind him, to his money as if "she were born into it." He chuckled when he told people his mother-in-law was from Possum Holler, Tennessee.

"Michael, I want to walk back to the hotel."

"I'm not sure how safe it is…"

"I can escort her the short distance," Luis said.

Michael heard Sadie's choice which meant she was walking, and debate was futile. Luis did not want his wife, Michael sensed from the moment they seated themselves around the dinner table, when Luis assisted her with her chair. Nothing. Michael had watched men react to his wife for fifteen years, from the young punks at the Army posts to the men at the business conventions. He recognized immediately which ones undressed her and those who were merely intrigued and those who were intimidated by her presence. But Luis had obviously, no interest. He respected her, listened to her attentively, and laughed at her descriptions of Jill and their antics. Michael sensed a partnership in a conspiracy which he also accepted as a play in which he had a walk-on part.

Jack was not Michael's kind of man. No golf, no country club, no gin rummy with the boys, no drinking. Yeah, Sadie called his friends "the road hogs," but they were like him. Jack was a farmer once removed, but removed to an even more settled life. Yes, the threesome had laughed around the kitchen table over Jack.

And for the first time, he observed Luis's reaction to the mention of Jill. Luis loved her, now he saw that, a certain smile in his eyes, unconscious rubbing of the gold band when Jill's name was mentioned, and the push to extend the replay of any story involving Jill. "And then what did you do?" he had asked Sadie, probing for more details. The animation was inconsistent with the business Luis.

"You don't mind, Luis? She can be reckless with offered kindness and courtesy."

"I've broken horses and trained Dobermans, a walk on the beach with Jill's best friend is manageable," Luis said.

"Thanks, Luis, but comparing me to wild horses and dogs…No, I can navigate two blocks on the beach by myself."

"Well, Luis, there you go," Michael kissed his wife and hastily left the two of them. Michael mused about the cantankerous side of Sadie when the martinis kicked in.

ᚱξᚱ

Thick moss covered oak, bald cypress and long needled pines rose from soggy marshland and lined the white highway stretching west in front of the car. Jack had rented the car for Jill to drive to St. Petersburg. It had been easy to escape Jack's vacation. He needed to go see Hawk and she wanted to see Henry's sisters in Bradenton. He'd headed north and east toward Ocala and they planned to rendezvous in two days to return to Indiana. Sadie had promised Jack she would take care of his Mrs. He had agreed to the two friends spending their final two days at the beach. Luisa demanded some time by the ocean, but Orlando was landlocked. She and Luisa were off to stay in Sadie's suite at the Don Caesar right on the Gulf beach. She did not want to squander the scarce moments with Luis so she drove down in the cool pre-dawn.

Luisa slept peacefully stretched out in the back seat. Jill sipped the coffee she'd bought at the convenience store outside of Orlando. She'd ordered the large size and hoped she could make it to St. Petersburg without stopping. She also couldn't keep the thought of being with Luis in two hours from consuming her. He had come to interview pilots. Andy would be with him, a couple of his "buddies from Nam," were living in Florida and Luis wanted to talk to them. Why didn't he hire Colombians? He did not elaborate. She accepted that the interview process was more information about his business than he usually imparted.

She also wanted to talk to him about this jack-in-the-box visit, just popping up in her life. She turned the radio on, but no station played anything she liked. The hypnotic lines on the highway overtook her thoughts. Luis we have to stop seeing each other. No, that won't work, the pain of even thinking it, no. Luis, we, okay me, I have to stop this. I must stop and work at my marriage. Oh, no, hell no, I can't say that, don't want to. Sorry Mom, you said wrong and deceitful, that's probably true, but it is my choice, my consequence. Okay, Plan B, Luis, when Luisa gets out of school in June, and we head off to Italy, we can return to Cartagena instead of Caylor. Oh yeah, that will go over real well. She drank coffee as the sky lightened behind her.

Looking in the rearview mirror, Luisa was completely covered under the beach towels. My daughter does better than I do, is it the money? She likes his money. No, she likes him, lights up as soon as she sees him; looks like a damned Christmas tree. Loves him, calmly accepting the two lives. Damn, damn, damn, Luis.

The twinkling lights of civilization appeared in the cypress woods. The big mileage signs were posted closer together, forty miles to St. Petersburg. The morning traffic of bread trucks, beer trucks, and early workers headed toward the city. The dawn came fast. She rolled the window down. The humid air had made her hair curl, but Luis loved the curls, to lace his fingers in her hair, to comb it with his hands, to twist the locks around his fingers, watching the springiness. She looked in the mirror, then adjusted it to see her complete reflection. Tiny tendrils outlined her face. She pushed up one side. Oh well, Luis here come the curls, even the Florida humidity is under your command.

Sadie had given her the directions. The sun was now bright enough to read them. She turned onto the causeway and rolled down the window. Ah the smell of salt water. Summer in winter, god Florida is great. "Luisa, wake up. We're here. You'll want to brush your hair."

Luisa rumbled around under the beach towels, then sat up looking around. "Where are we, Mom?" She climbed over the front seat and slid down into the passenger side of the car. She was bleary-eyed, trying to get a glimpse of the beach between the motels and restaurants that lined the St. Petersburg beach. Jill drove slowly looking for addresses.

"According to these directions, we are almost to Sadie's hotel. You can help me look for it. It's on your side of the road and it's big and pink, she said."

They spotted it easily when they were still two blocks away. They drove into the parking lot. The old hotel was elegant. Sadie had told Jill the whole history of the place, the winter home of many mobsters during prohibition.

The dark wood in the lobby and the unique musty smell of Florida met them. Early risers emerged from the elevators, walking to breakfast. Jill pushed the button to go to Sadie's room. "Just come up as soon as you get here," Sadie had instructed. She knocked on the door and almost instantly, Mike, holding his beach towel and plastic bag filled with buckets, cups and shovels opened it.

"Come in Luisa, we're going to breakfast, then Dad said he's showing us how to build the 'ultimate' sand castle. Sh-sh, Mom's asleep," Mike said softly.

Jill walked into the darkened room and hugged Michael. She whispered, "Hello. Our stuff is in the car, Luisa you want to change your clothes?"

Luisa headed for the bathroom. Jill walked to Sadie's bed and jumped on the mound that was Sadie's body.

"Get up, you hussy! Your best friend has arrived!"

"Shish! Before I kick your butt!"

"Sadie, the children," Jill said, laughing at disturbing the original morning bear.

"Come closer, witch. I have a message and I don't have enough energy to sit up," Sadie talked under the covers in a muffled voice.

"Mom, I'm ready," Luisa called from the bathroom.

"Sure, here's some money. Do you have a place to put it?" Jill said.

"Come on Jill, she's the guest of Big Mike and Little Mike. I don't think she needs money," Michael said.

"Michael, stop by the girls' room and make sure they have everything they need. TV goes off in one hour, when I get up. And tell Tanya to take them to breakfast, and sign the check with her room number. Traveling with children requires patience and imagination," Sadie growled.

They left, leaving Jill and Sadie alone in the room. Sadie sat up as soon as the door closed.

"Oh my god Jill, that man loves you so much."

"Michael?"

"No, dummy, Luis. You just don't know. But I promised not to keep you. Look over there by my purse. There should be a key."

Jill rummaged through the change, ash tray, travel brochures, Sadie's bra and a notepad. She held up a key with a green plastic tag hanging on it.

"Yes, that's it. Don't worry about Luisa. We'll be at the beach or the restaurant whenever you get...finished."

"Shut up, Sadie. Go back to sleep. But I do want to hear what you all talked about. I'm glad you always make *me* the center of *your* conversation."

ﯼﷺﯼ

Jill unlocked the door, not sure what to expect. Sadie's room was too dark to know what the rooms looked like. Cracking the door, a burst of sunshine, a gentle breeze and the smell of coffee greeted her. She gingerly stepped into a suite of rooms, a living room with sliding glass doors that led to a patio. Thin sheer drapes wafted in the Florida room - a wicker love seat, and wicker tables, everything in white, chartreuse and turquoise. Summer. It was quiet.

"Luis," she called in a hushed voice.

213

She closed the door behind her and walked past the couch to a door that led from the living room. On her right two china cups sat on a small kitchenette counter. She walked to the door and peeked in, but did not see him in the bed. The sea's scent from the opened sliding glass doors and Luis's cologne filled the room. The bedding was mussed, the sheets in a soft sculpture pile. The unmade bed looked inviting. She visualized a naked Luis on the sheets, and smiled. She laid her purse on a chair and kicked off her sandals. The partially opened bathroom door let a thin shaft of light illuminate the bedroom. She gingerly pulled it all the way open.

"Gringa." Luis stood naked at the vanity with his face covered in shaving cream. He turned toward her putting his razor down on the edge of the sink. "How do you want your Colombian? With or without cream?"

But she couldn't answer because he grabbed her and pressed the shaving cream all over her face, kissing her, squeezing her. She tasted the soapy foam and tried to pull away, but he hugged her tightly. He stopped and took his hand and wiped the cream from her cheeks and mouth. He laughed and she scooped it off his face and rubbed it in his hair. They laughed and he grabbed her hand then pulled her into the shower, he did not let go as he let the water get warm.

"No, Luis. No!" She tried to get away from him, but he drenched her in water. "Luis, let me take my clothes off. You can't take a shower...I can't take a shower dressed."

He stood with her unbuttoning her sundress. Her nipples were hard from the stimulation of the water. He unhooked her bra and slid her wet panties off, then he kissed her again and again as the shower sprayed them, washing away the shaving cream.

They dressed in the hotel's terry robes. Luis poured coffee and they sat at the glass topped table on the patio. Luis had one shaved patch on his face. Jill smiled at the whiskerless strip, "I think I like my Colombian with cream."

"You like your Colombian period. Your husband cannot know what to do with you or you'd be worn out."

"If I lived with you, you'd wear me out, is that what you are saying?"

"You'd be trying to find places to hide from me in the compound, saying, 'No, Papito! No! No!'"

"Let's try it."

Luis put his cup down and stood up. He walked to the dresser and pulled a cigar from a leather case. He clipped one end licked the other, and the length of the cigar. He took out matches and slowly puffed until it burned slowly. He walked to the patio's sunny deck that opened to the ocean. Jill went to the bathroom. She wrung out her cotton dress and panties and bra. She took them out on the patio and draped them over the chairs and adjusted the chairs to get the maximum amount of sun. Luis watched her, then turned toward the Gulf. She walked to where he stood and leaned against him. He puffed and chewed on the end of his cigar. He spoke not looking at her, only at the open sea, "Gringa, they are your parameters. Your parameters."

She dreaded this conversation because she hated the word. He used it derisively with her and had almost from the moment she first used it.

"You know nothing of the pain…to constantly say goodbye to her, to not share life with her. She comes home from school with papers and stories of her day, cheerleading? I don't see her games."

He turned to face Jill, his back to the railing. He stood with his robe open only to his navy silk boxer shorts. "I was sliced, an attempt to cut me half," he took a dismissive wave at the long scar that marked him from his neck across his stomach, "but this separation is more painful than anything I went through with this cut. And always I ask myself, is this right? Or is this heartache for nothing?" His shoulders dropped and he focused on her.

She backed away from him and walked a short distance to another area of the small patio. She drank her coffee. The sea smell exhilarated her, the negative ions, Sadie, inhale. The beach was several floors down from where they were, but she tried to see if she recognized Luisa, among the small bodies splashing in the ocean. His presence filled the patio; the sea air did not displace his words, her words.

Luisa *our* daughter, he wanted normal and yet says no, to his home, and Caylor…her face flushed and the anger simmered up, heating her skin, "I have no scar to show for my sliced life. You left me standing in a tomato field. You should have taken your knife and cut me in two right then, half to Michigan and half in Indiana." She walked and stood squarely in front of him, "But I healed. The scar is still there and when you walk away, you who gets on a plane and goes, you who says, 'No, not yet. No, not now. No, not to my home.' Slice! Slice! Slice!" She waved her hand slashing the air between them like a machete wielding bandit. "Luis, you cut me again and again and again. I wonder sometimes why do we continue this? Where is it all going? Where?"

"And what would you have done? Married your Mr. Bancroft?

Jill's eyes widened, "What did you say?"

"Maybe I should have let the basura (garbage) live. Maybe you should have let *him* take your virginity!"

Smack! Her hand hit the side of his face. He grabbed her hand and tossed it down like a Raggedy Ann doll; it felt limp to her, then he turned his back to her.

She stood planted shaking. Bastard! Bastard! Bastard!

"You have things to say, Gringa, say them," he spoke with his back to her staring toward the beach and the Gulf.

She walked back into the bedroom and sat on the edge of the bed, breathing short exaggerated breaths, biting her lips. Bastard. A tear rolled down her cheek. "Let him live…" What is he saying, not saying?

Luis walked in and faced her. She looked down at her feet and the carpet. The pile was very short, turquoise like the splashes of flowers on the bedspread and chairs. He reached under her chin, firmly holding it in his palm. She closed her eyes.

"Let me see the mahogany when I talk to you." She opened her eyes. His face, the face she recognized and hated because he sneered and hissed with the deep frown, eyes of ice, your soul is a goddamned refrigerator. "Gringa, Gringa, Gringa, you are a teacher. You teach your students to listen when you talk. You ask them if they understand. You answer their questions, si?"

Jill closed then reopened her eyes.

"Today, tomorrow, for all these days that I'm alive, you belong to me. You're listening? Is there something you don't understand? Questions?"

He took his hand away from her chin and took his robe off. He removed his boxer shorts. He sat beside her and kissed her neck under her ear, then he lifted her hair and kissed the nape of her neck. He wrapped his arm around the front of her body and pushed her back on the bed. He put one leg over her and leaned on his arm. He teased her body with his hand. Jill lay motionless. He kissed her. She resisted. He coaxed her mouth open nibbling her lips. He whispered, "Papito is going to take the Grandma Caitlin fire out of you."

She turned towards him, "Luis, I hate you." He rolled on top of her and pushed his tongue between her lips, in and out as he lay between her legs. She slowly responded in tandem.

216

"Come Caitlin," he whispered in her ear.

She heard herself say his name, "Papito" as she pushed against him, then she wrapped her legs around him, "Papito."

"Finished," she thought of Sadie's phrase. The sky had clouded and the breeze was cooler. She was wedged in the curvature of his arm. She turned on her side, pressing tightly against him in the chilly room. He stroked her hip, tapping his fingers on her bare buttocks. She traced his scar and twisted his salt and pepper chest hairs in one of her fingers.

"Gringa, you asked, 'where?'"

"I don't want to talk about that."

"No, you can know *where.*"

"I want to know what you meant when you said, 'let the basura live'?"

"I apologize. I should not have brought his name into our …discussion."

The muscles in his chest tightened slightly, "Luis, Jim Bancroft is dead. I don't know what happened." Luis was silent, looking at the ceiling.

"Silence?" she sighed. "I think you, too, have parameters. I'm going to see if my dress is dry." She walked to the patio and to get her dress and underclothes "Luis, I need things from my car."

"Call the bell captain. They'll bring your things," he said and picked up the phone.

She talked to the front desk then walked to the kitchenette and poured coffee. She carried Luis's cup to the bathroom. He had reapplied the saving cream, "Come here, Jill, sit down. I have something to say to you before we meet them all for lunch."

Jill preened in the mirror, retrieving her brush from her purse. Luis rinsed the double-edged razor in hot running water. He pulled the blade in parallel strips across his cheeks and chin, "Gringa."

She cleaned the extra strands of hair from her brush and put them in the wastebasket. She returned the brush to her purse, and then slid up on the vanity counter, facing Luis with her back to the mirror. "Señor Ochoa, you have my undivided attention."

"The surest thing there is, is we are riders,
And though none too successful at it, guiders,
Through everything presented, land and tide…
And all *our* blandishments would seem defied,
We have ideas yet that we haven't tried."

"Señor Frost?"

"Si. There is no 'where,' there are only ideas we have yet to try. And you may ride or you may guide, but, my gringa, we will do all of it as a dance. You may choose the waltz or the tango, but you picked your partner in a shed." He reached and pinched her nose between his knuckles. "Now, we need to find *our* daughter."

Jill scooted off the counter, "I suppose some days it will be the waltz and others the tango. One of us will lead and the other will follow."

"The cha-cha."

She shook her head and left the bathroom with her coffee cup.

Luis soaked a wash rag in hot water and held it against his just shaved face. He rinsed his face in cold water, then patted himself dry. He reached for his after shave from an unzipped leather travel bag. He splashed the Aramis on his face, poured some in both hands rubbing them together, then up and down on his chest, over his stomach and down to the crease where his legs met the trunk of his body. He viewed his image reflected in the large mirror that covered one wall. The scar, a half-inch welt, divided his chest neatly from his clavicle to the upper edge of his pubic hair. He touched the top edge of the hardened flesh at the round corner of his collar bone. He pushed the button of scar tissue, the place of the initial insertion of the knife, the bridge or was it the tunnel to the darkness?

The blackness of everything surrounded him. There seemed to be no sky. Or was there sky with no stars? A universe of endless darkness, black and cold, he felt iced, to the center of his body, his back, his legs. He pushed on the ground with his hand to rise, then his fingertips touched the warm liquid that he knew was his blood. He tried an easy push, a foot, a hand pressed against the ground, to start to walk, but the ground clung to his back, the back of his legs, his palms, only the fingertips moved. He tried one shoulder, off slowly, then the muscles that had to work to pull him up, rectus abdominis, he thought, why a Latin name now? But then the burn, like the touch of white hot iron from a blacksmith's anvil, from his neck to a place deep in his stomach, and there was no light just the suffocating blackness, in a pit, he could not focus. He sucked for breath, but it smelled of sulfur and burning gas, a refinery's belch?

He awoke again in a white room, white figures floated in, stayed, looked, not at him, just his parts, his hand, his leg, the tubes

218

into his arms, the tube in his stomach. He wanted to move any of those parts, but his body was concrete. He woke and saw her, angelic, like Marlene Dietrich in the blonde pageboy and white beret and white wool double breasted coat, white, her face white and she talked. But to him? He wasn't sure and then he slept or wept, he did not know. He opened his eyes, but it all was white.

As he recalled it now in the mirror, years and miles ago, the smell of sulfur, the dammed Texas oil-patch foulness still registered. He turned from the mirror and walked to the patio. He breathed deep, sucking in the salt air.

"Luis, I have pictures from our trip to Bermuda, I left them on the seat of the car. I'll go get them. I'll be back." She walked to him and rubbed his arm, "I don't hate you, you know that."

"Many have spoken of the thin line that separates love from hate, I know. I listen with my feelings and you express those very plainly in every way you react to me. Your words are drowned by your actions. Te amo."

She kissed him, and then left the suite.

Another deep breath of fresh ocean air. He turned and stared at the clean Gulf of Mexico spread out in front of him, extended, connected actually to Texas.

She, Victorianna Smith Houston. Was her husband truly related to Sam Houston as he claimed? He did not know, but she carried the heritage, the rank of her husband and he was truly a Senator. She had been there when the call came through, and he had been there, but left quickly as usual when "the Senator," as she called him, returned from Washington. She demanded a warning and the Senator for his own reasons did as he was told. Luis knew the Senator had probably caught his wife one too many times, in other places and other times. She had raged at Luis and sometimes in her insanity had said that there were others.

One day he awakened to colors and now he could not remember if it were morning or afternoon, but there was sun and there were colors, bright yellow roses with green leaves in an orange vase. The nurse had blue eyes, sky blue eyes, red lipstick. The walls were light blue, the table brown. "Colors," he had said, "it is over." Then the doctor came in and grabbed the clipboard making marks, but when he grabbed Luis's wrist, Luis had heard his own voice, an almost strange voice, but a familiar sound. "Doctor?" It was his baritone and accented English.

The doctor nodded, he too, had heard the voice. He held up a finger to his mouth demanding Luis not speak. He unhooked the clipboard from the end of the bed and brought it with him, sitting next to the bed.

"Luis Ochoa, my instructions are to explain to you in detail what happened to you from your admission until this moment." The doctor's face had no humor. "...missed the femoral artery..." He was fifty-something, Luis deduced. "...missed the saphenous veins, the transverse abdominal completely cut..." He was bald and wore a maroon tie with a white button down collar shirt, a Hathaway man. When he thought "Hathaway," he realized that was Victorianna. He nodded at the doctor. The man had no upper lip and talked between his teeth. "...the liver and small intestine spared..." His nose was red and pudgy, his hands, his whole body round and squat. "...a certain soreness as the tissue heals, then scars. The cut was clean, the surgery cleaner, movement restricted by your own will power....millimeters of depth, to the interior of your lung cavity, the diaphragm and the aorta; the sternum saved your life, but will always remind you of this division."

A division? He had been sliced, left for dead, he assumed, as the doctor completed the report, "Before you leave Mr. Ochoa, we will talk again. Rest and rest, then we'll get you on your feet again. Tennis, isn't that what you like to play?" Tennis? How did he know that part? Victorianna. But Luis had not seen the doctor again. He was never able to ask him about the tennis remark or how he came to be at the hospital.

They removed the tubes. He'd finally sat up and they helped him to his feet. He used the restroom. To hold his penis in his own hand, his bandage was close to his penis, but it functioned, a blessing and a relief. He walked and showered, then the nurse came and said his clothes had arrived and it was time for him to leave. She handed him jeans, a belt, black leather, not too wide, his belt the one with the silver buckle, but new, so not his belt, just a new one exactly like the old one, and boots, the Luccheses, new, but like the old ones, burgundy tooled shafts, black foot, and full welted leather sole. They smelled of the mink oil used for tanning the leather. And the shirt, denim long sleeve, white pearl snapped pockets, silver tipped collar points, the same clothes, but never worn. On the stack of clothes a felt hat, his, no, exactly like his only brand new, a black

Stetson. He picked it up 7¾, his size. It was the 5¾ crown, 4" brim and cattleman's crease that he had always worn from Veracruz when Ramos bought him his first hat, to San Antonio, always. He picked it up; a letter lay under the hat. He opened it, reading the type, no incriminating handwriting, not Victorianna, she was a serpentine.

> Mr. Luis Ochoa:
> I have left. You'll understand, you're a wise man. We said everything we needed to say when the time was appropriate. Therefore, there is nothing to say now. Your name will grant you admittance to the safe deposit officer at the Lone Star Bank. The Senator has decided not to seek re-election.

And no signature, no need, he knew. He could not breathe deep, he hurt, but the bandage was a small strip of gauze he could now take care of himself. And he had left the hospital.

He was left alone by the bank officer to open the long metal safe deposit box. When the door was closed, he lifted the lid and there was one stack of neatly wrapped $10,000 bills, all tied with a red ribbon. He counted, one, two, three, Salmon P. Chase, ten, eleven...thirteen, fourteen ...seventeen, eighteen, nineteen, twenty... twenty unused $10,000 American dollar bills. "Thank you Mrs. Houston," he patted them neatly into a stack, then reached into the box and pulled out a brown envelope, tied loosely with a cloth string. He unfolded a deed with the seal and name of Royal Dutch Shell at the top and read "...the bearer of this deed, Luis Ochoa, has the legal right to...on the island of Curaçao at... to be held by him in perpetuity..." it was notarized and dated, September 12, 1959.

He stuck the cash in his boot and pulled his jeans down, covering the top of the tooled leather. He walked out of the bank. Walked out and away from Victorianna except when he smelled sulfur, and then the branding iron point split him open all over again.

Jill now walked back into the room and said the maids were ready to clean.

"Come here, Gringa." He reached and pulled her into his arms kissing her.

"No, Luis, stop. We must go, we have a daughter..."

"Jill..." Luis stopped, holding her face against his chest, the soft curls brushed her cheek, the ridge of the scar on her temple. She heard his heart. His tight grip held her still then he gently patted her head.

She loosened herself from his hug and looked at his face. Tears formed at the corners of his eyes. "Si, Señor Ochoa?"

"The slicing is over," he kissed her lips, then kissed her nose. She knew the kiss meant time to go. She wanted to reach inside him, but inside was covered in a metal suit like a medieval knight, so she hugged him as close as the armor would allow.

Part B

Chapter 11

The sky turned charcoal gray, and the radio station began the blizzard warnings at 10A.M. The outlying schools immediately summoned the bus drivers to pick up their precious cargo before the storm arrived. When the first flakes began to blow, Jill closed her garage door. Weathercasters said not the Blizzard of '78, when nothing moved for five days, but this storm of '79 had entombed her farmhouse. They had called the farmhouse home for fifteen years, but it still did not hold her heart. Her country road officially closed only two hours after the wind and snow began their onslaught.

When life almost returned to normal, Caylor residents breathed a sigh of relief, and then it started again. The frozen ground was already covered in ten inches of snow. The second storm found most people better prepared. Jill had stocked her pantry and decided to keep it that way. Just in case. Jack chopped extra logs and stored them closer to the house for use in the fireplaces and her study's wood burning stove.

Crystal clear February air, crunchy snow, bright blinding sunshine were the aftermath of the three day blizzard. Watching the beauty the bitter cold wrought, Jill now sat bundled in a hand knit sweater, a Christmas present from her sister-in-law. In her long underwear and fuzzy deerskin slippers, she enjoyed the serenity. First the snow, then the temperatures dropping to zero and minus zero, guaranteeing no snow melts for awhile. "Here to stay," she could hear Henry's voice describing this type of weather. He and Lillian had escaped the blizzards by spending winters in Bradenton.

She looked out across the flat cornfields devoid of life. Stretching as far as she could see were white snow waves formed by the wind blowing across a crystalline surface. The essence of being inside from the inclement weather went with her mood like the marshmallows and hot chocolate she drank. Her special room allowed her to escape into private thought a long way from the snowy fields of Indiana. Luisa graduates in June and then to college, Ohio University, and then…Jack, you will be in this farmhouse by yourself. She sipped her cocoa.

Opening a locked desk drawer, she pulled out her pictures of the past three summers in Italy. The photos brought her summer flooding into her study. Italian dreaming on such a winter's day…sorry Mamas and Papas, but I'm going to summer in Italy. Sadie visited every year for the three summers she'd been going. She stayed a couple of weeks, switching daughters, first Claudine, then Kate, but always with Mike. They shopped and found antiques in Florence and Lucca, although the house was filled with paintings, frescoes, and tapestries. "Amazing," Sadie said in every room.

With acres of grape vines surrounding their villa, Luis took a keen interest in the entire process. He explored the villa's wine cellar, dusting off bottles and opening them for tasting with the vintner. Last summer she'd managed to get a picture of him dressed as the vintner who worked their land. He wore a well abused straw hat and a linen shirt covered in grape stains and baggy pants over leather work boots. He smiled and she snapped her only picture of him. He shook his head when he saw it, but said, "Okay, you may take it with you."

Gently rubbing his body in the picture, she liked the vintner look. Could she make him come to life? Right now in her study? And keep her warm? Villa della Principessa her heaven. The vintner even named a wine for the villa, "Principessa." Luis was a gentleman farmer in Italy, and she imagined the same farmer in Colombia, "El Campesino." He insisted he farmed in a war zone, then described an atmosphere of gun toting bandits. It sounded like a fantasy. She looked quizzically as he painted the picture.

"Really, Jill."

"Are you some kind of Che Guevara with bullets strapped to your chest?"

"No, not like Señor Guevara. Another CIA victim in Bolivia! Bolivia our neighbor, 1967, he was killed. CIA, Gringa, your United States, like some sickening plague they appear everywhere."

Mr. Angotti, "El Banquero" (the banker) visited occasionally driving from Rome. He always brought a more beautiful woman than the one he brought before. Luis and she laughed at the progression of beauties, wondering when he would run out of women. Luis and Mr. Angotti would disappear into Luis's office as Jill sat and entertained the woman of the day. Jill practiced Italian with most of them; on occasion he would bring an American woman. Sometimes they had Jill join them to use her signature as a witness to their transactions. Mr. Angotti had friends in London, New York, Zurich and of course, Rome. Often the documents were written in Italian.

She was getting more proficient in Spanish. At lunch Luis expected her and Luisa to speak only Spanish, and assured them that most Italians could speak Spanish with them. He tried Spanish or Italian conversations, but they often ended in laughter as the women inserted Spanglish and Luis frowned, referring to them as "Jankees."

Jack in the end went along with her absence, and she never asked him what he thought. Her planned speech was adamant, Henry left her money to travel and spending an entire summer in Europe would be educational for Luisa. After his initial objections about the length of time, she promised to be home to can the tomatoes. He worked more and did the garden himself. At the end of the first summer, she said they were thinking of renting a villa for the next one.

After the second summer, he really seemed to like his bachelor days. He lived alone for a long time before they married, so she assumed he was able to do whatever he did all those years. He did miss Luisa.

Hawk had driven up last summer for a few days. Jack said he could stay with him because the other two boys mostly hated him. He said he wanted to see the farm one more time before he died. He was also going to drive to Iowa and try to see Chick before heading back to Florida. He told Jack he had been diagnosed with cirrhosis of the liver and the pain would soon be intolerable. Jack said the disease did not keep Hawk from drinking the whole time he was with him. He'd removed a picture of Lillian from one of Jill's photo albums and Jack didn't notice until he was gone.

She now stacked the villa pictures together, put them in their envelope and carefully locked them back in the drawer. From another drawer she pulled out the Christmas letter from Mo. Her annual Christmas letter. Jill had placed it on the stack of letters to answer *after* the holidays. After? Two months after she'd read Mo's letter, but its enclosure she left unopened. Had she left it thinking it would go away? No, every time she sat down to write she would think of something else to do. Now with the blizzard it had been long enough. She took the letter out for the umpteenth time. Opened it, reread it.

December 1, 1978
Dear Jill,

Surprise! This is a Christmas letter just for you. I'm not sending you the usual PR memo from the State Department McClendon's. I have been worried about you this year. I don't know why, maybe my intuition antennae are extra sensitive because I'm pregnant. Ha! Yes, it's true. I told Stewart we had to do something soon because no one believed anymore that I'm still virgin. Please. So we finally consummated this marriage and we'll be the proud parents of a boy. Yes, I already know because they have this diagnostic test, amniocentesis. They said I was too old not to. I had been telling Stewart the same thing. They were afraid of Downe's syndrome since it is my first. They said late-in-life babies often have this problem. Late-in-life!?? Aren't we still young? I know I am. I will only be 35 when Stewart IV is here. I'm excited; you can tell I'm sure. And I wanted you to see the pictures of me with the big tummy. I owed you that after all those miserable months we spent at 1254 Butler. So put me on the refrigerator and laugh to your heart's content.

Can you call me? I need to laugh, we need to laugh. And plus I'm worried. Are you okay on the farm? It never seemed to suit you, and your husband, I don't know, he never seemed to make you smile like Hector. I guess we all are lucky if we even have one Hector in our lives. I may be biased because I loved Hector and you together. I remember.

Also you've noticed, may have read first, the enclosed. He sealed the envelope and said, "FYEO" (For Your Eyes Only). He emphasized that for my nosey-self. He was through here at Thanksgiving. You know Dad, always on his way to

228

someplace. I made him swear he wasn't trying to sneak onto your farm to whisk you off. He promised and said he sent it through me not to arouse any suspicion. He is always acting with his mysterious bullshit. I guess you already know that part.

Have I already said, please call? Stewart is nervous about fatherhood, but I told him to take one of those posts in Africa and leave me alone. (Reverse psychology, you know?) He says he'll quit first. He just wants to see me scream. I have been practicing cussing him out.

Please tell Sadie hello and give Luisa a kiss from her Aunt Mo. I wonder how your affair is coming along, or is it still ongoing? We always hear from T.J at Christmas, he has been re-elected to the U.S. Congress, I think 3 times. I am happy he made it; he wanted that for so long.

I love you and Merry Christmas.

Love, Mo

P.S. Baby is due around March 27

She folded it and put it back on the stack. Now. Open the enclosure.

Every Christmas it had been the end-of-the-year letter. Mo would tell of all the places they had been, all the places they were going. Jill wanted to write of the countries she had seen with Luis, about Luis period, but the relationship was more like William's M.O. – hush-hush. In the P.S. that ended each typewritten holiday letter, Mo added what the Colonel was doing.

And next month? Oh Mo. So exciting, I need to call, but she would hear my voice and know or at least ask. Beautifully pregnant, long blond hair and barely a baby showing. Amazing like always. And the cute maternity dress, I was wearing hand-me-downs from my sister-in-law.

The small envelope had only her name on it, "Jill," but in his handwriting. She smiled. It had been so long since she had seen it, the first time, when? All those years ago at State, so exciting, but scary. William had eventually remarried, then almost as quickly divorced and now had a live-in girlfriend. In, where? He was in and out of California, in and out of Washington, D.C. He did work for the CIA mostly, but always had his foot in the Air Force. It was fuzzy and Mo used only one sentence once a year, so what was that? Fourteen years and fourteen sentences? She had enough going on in her life that one sentence once a year was sufficient.

All these years of Christmas card letters from Mo, he never sent a message. When they were in Chicago, she didn't ask Mo directly what he did or where he was doing it. William was elusive as usual. He was a rogue. William, may I be wistful, just for a minute? We laughed, shared intimate feelings and had great sex, but life is much more than that.

She opened the envelope, then put it down and walked to her wood stove. She pulled another log from the brass bucket, placed it into the fire, and then walked to the window. The steam covered the small squares of glass. Finding a cloth she wiped the windows clear, only snow, blowing but not falling.

17 November 1978
Caracas, Venezuela

Oh, William, why there? Why goddamned South America? Mo said her house at Thanksgiving. What? You wrote it then brought it? Questions? Yes, I have many questions.

My taboo girl,

She heard the Temptations, "I've got sunshine on a cloudy day, when it's cold outside, I've got the month of May...I guess you'd say, what can make me feel this way...my girl." Okay let me see what you have to say.

I think of you always in those terms. Please
forgive an old man this small impertinence. As you can
see, I'm still not settled in one place. I do better, but
they call me and I cannot resist this summons to
remove myself from retirement, to speculate, analyze
or listen. Whenever you want to join me, if the
cornfields become unbearable there's an old Colonel
who could enjoy the company of a frisky farm girl.

So you lied to Mo. No, William I cannot join you.

Propositioning you is only the secondary
reason for this missive. I felt as if I needed to write and
tell you of some piece of secure information that only

mattered to one person in the world – Jill Havlicek. As the files are being gleaned for the exact reports of our Police Action in Southeast Asia, I took advantage of my position and researched your young man's name – Hector Andujar. There has been an outcry that men are lost in the jungles and we have abandoned them to their own private hells of survival. I know this anxiety applies to anyone who lost a loved one under "unusual" circumstances. Lt.Andujar was based in Pleiku, but his unit was more often in Laos where they didn't belong than in Viet Nam. He died on a mission there. His body was carried back into Viet Nam by his Special Forces unit, a renegade bunch. I'm sorry for any pain this memory may have caused you, but I would stake my reputation, the military one, you know the other one, on it. I want you to close the book.

William, we talked about this four years ago in Chicago. I knew what you said then. Now this. I don't understand. She sighed. Are you saying, what you are saying? Or are you saying something else? He knows I closed the book. Do I open the book? I think the pages are blank. The military is still lying to us about Viet Nam and there are hundreds, thousands still missing in action. I don't know what he is reading, the military intelligence? Andy assured me in Hawaii that military intelligence is a joke. I cannot go to the jungles of Viet Nam and look for Hector. I have made peace with all of that, William. This is what? The third time or so he has tried to tell me the "secret" information that confirms the "death."

Finally, for entirely different reasons and in completely different circumstances, I have run across the name Luis Ochoa, again. There must be many in this part of the world, but this particular one spent six years in the United States, 1954-60. I hope you took my advice in Chicago and researched coffee futures. If you are interested in any of the information I have come across, please write me via Madeline. I am very much aware of the adage, "Let sleeping dogs lie," but I wanted to present you with the choice or the dog whichever you prefer.

231

I have not changed my original advice to you
in Chicago...be careful.
Always, William

No, William, I don't know what your motivation is. I don't know what you want me to do about any of it. Protect me? Trust you on this? Luis has explained to me many times about the CIA and how they try to turn democracies into dictatorships allowing U.S. corporations to continue their enslavement of local populations. What could the CIA possibly know that I don't know about Luis, what? That he operates a coffee farm in the middle of a war zone? A war zone that is aided and abetted by the same CIA. No, William, I don't know what you know, but I really am not interested. I need to close the book on you, probably.

She heard the phone ring, but knew her teenager in residence would answer. Luisa knocked on her door. "Mom," she opened the door quietly. "It's toasty in here. You won't believe this, but Papa is on the phone. Dad went out to get a couple of more logs, so he didn't hear the phone. Lucky you."

"You are so funny. Why are you taking after your grandfather, now?"

"Because he is no longer here to tease you, someone must."

"Sadie is enough. Go! I have to get on the phone."

Luisa left, closing the door behind her. Jill picked up the phone gingerly, musing about the reason he was calling. She hoped he received the letter she'd mailed him, but didn't know why he was calling at this moment. She looked at the clock; it was in the safe time zone. Jack would have been at work except the snow prevented anyone from going anywhere. Luisa would not allow Jack to pick up the phone for any reason.

"Ah, Buenos Dias, Gringa."

"Luis, it is freezing up here. We had the worst storm..."

"I know. I read the paper. I watch the television. I wanted to make sure you were not killed in an avalanche and to see if you needed to be rescued."

"Avalanche, no, you need a few mountains. Rescue, please, si."

"Si, I will send the helicopter to pick you up. You must make a fire outside so Andy can find you."

Jill was curious about the call. "You were concerned about us?"

"Si. You're surprised. I made a New Year's resolution, Gringa."

"Really. What could that have possibly been?"

"To call more regularly. I need to check in on my gringa. Is everything okay? I worry about my Jankee wife...."

"What? Luis, it's me. Gina called my number. Your Jankee wife? Do you have one of those?"

"I am on my way to Africa and I was hoping to take my Jankee with me. Coffee futures are up. I am meeting with some coffee exporting chiefs. We have not been to Africa. Will your school let you come?"

"Stop. I can't go out my front door. It's snowed shut."

"How's my daughter?"

"She winked and grinned mischievously with this conversation because Jack is home. The snow kept us all here. I'm tucked in my study. I was looking at my pictures in Italy. My favorite vintner."

"Jill, I received your letter." His tone changed to his usual seriousness. She could see his face, frowning.

"Thank you for calling me."

"We cannot talk on the phone. This will not happen again. Entiendes?"

"Yes, no, no I don't understand. We can't talk on the phone, when can we talk?"

"Africa?" Luis said.

"Luis...why did they come to my school?"

She bit her lip recalling the fear the two men in suits elicited when they told her they were looking for answers to some questions about Luis Ochoa. She should have told them to call William; he seemed to have all the answers. She hesitated long enough for them to threaten her in a back-handed way, "Does your daughter know *who* her real father is?" She cringed, recognizing her question of the last nine years. Who is Luis Ochoa?

She sensed immediately that these two men were enemies of Luis and that was enough reason to protect him, but protect him from what? In the middle of Indiana? But questioning her in the parking lot, as she was ready to leave school, was wrong, and she had to stop that practice. Southeastern was too small for strange men to come and go unnoticed. And so the letter, but now the phone call. His joking about the weather was only a piece of the reason for his call.

"Gringa, you have choices, fly to Africa today, Curaçao next week when I get back, or your spring vacation in two months, but *not* on this telephone. Jill, one more thing, the vintner, he needs to go to Siddhartha's."

"Please, Luis."

"I apologize for that over which I have no control. Gringa, I promised to take care of you at your parents' funeral. No harm will come to Señora and Señorita Ochoa, ever. Hasta que la muerte nos separe. What kind of coffee do you drink?"

"Unlike Sadie, I do not get L.O., Ltd., so I buy Maxwell House."

"Terrible. The Coffee Federation will send you a gift. Check Siddhartha's mail. Next week in Curaçao? A long weekend. I must go, to Africa. Adios."

She hung up reluctantly. Again, no answers to the questions. And she had not told Sadie about the men who identified themselves as Drug Enforcement Agents. They were the types she read about in the newspaper or saw on the news in places like New York, Miami and Panama. She rubbed her finger across William's envelope...and Venezuela. She knew now that Luis was familiar with these men. He was only angry, not surprised.

The wind whistled outside the windows with each blast, the leafless lilac bushes tapped on the glass. No matter how they tried, they could not completely seal the cracks and crevices in the old farmhouse. Jack talked of one day replacing all the windows, but each summer opted for fresh paint and calk instead. Probably if Henry were around to encourage and assist him, he might have done it.

There was a muffled knock on the door. She turned from the phone and the rattling windows to the door, "Yes, come in."

"Honey, I made fresh coffee. Do you need more wood for your stove? It is toasty in here."

"I think I have enough logs."

"Are you okay? You look kind of sad. Luisa said you were talking to Molly from school. Bad news?"

"No, no. Just talk about snow days and what we were doing. She was talking about her son Dean. He is in college, a junior, I think. Anyway, she said it gets so quiet around the house when it is just her and her daughter, Jan, especially on days like this. So then I started thinking that next year, our house will be empty, Luisa will be away at school and it will only be the two of us. I miss her already and she hasn't even left."

"Come, let's go where she is and you two can argue, then you'll know why you won't miss her so much. She is making chocolate chip cookies to go with the coffee."

"Without me? No! She took that Italian cooking class last summer. Now she thinks she knows her way around the kitchen."

"Really, Honey, she does quite well in the kitchen. She is growing up. She'll be on her own, soon. She seems to have picked up a lot from all your wonderful trips."

"Yeah, maybe too worldly. I may need to go with her to college and take care of her…"

"Jill, come let's get some cookies and coffee. You've been alone long enough."

Every window she looked out, she saw endless white extending to the horizon, not an African panorama. He did not even say where in Africa, Dahomey, Niger, Ivory Coast, Ghana? Just Africa. A long weekend in Curaçao, can I think about the Caribbean and trade winds? Sadie help me with this.…

The phone interrupted her planning.

"Mom, Sadie."

I thought her up, or speak of the devil, "Hi, Siddhartha."

"Hi, Gringa!" Sadie imitated his accent.

"Funny, Sadie, very funny."

"Did he call you? Don't ask, you know he had to get my opinion before he called. Is everything okay? He sounded unusually friendly."

"Sadie, we have to talk, but after the blizzard. I have a house full of people."

"Okay, okay, I'll send Michael out in the dog sled to pick you up."

"No, but call Michael's uncle and tell him not to forget to plow in front of the farm."

"But of course, he'll expect you to vote for him when he runs for mayor again. My curiosity will have Michael plowing you out if it comes to that. Luis did not approve of my brand of coffee and said he would send a replacement."

"I heard, but I'll be in as soon as Mother Nature let's me come out and play."

"Jill, you sound a little reticent. Are you okay?"

"Everyone is home here."

"I know, which reminds me, Mike wants to talk to Luisa. Sweetie, keep your chin up you know old Sadie is here for you."

Jill peered over Luisa's shoulder, Luisa who was now two inches taller than her mom. Her almost eighteen year old was dropping the golden brown dough, filled with chocolate chips and walnuts on the cooking sheet. Jill sneaked under her arm to steal a raw cookie ball. Luisa tapped her mom's knuckles with the wooden spoon, but Jill snatched it from her. Both laughed as Jill threatened to hit Luisa with the dough covered spoon. Jill thrust the receiver in Luisa's direction.

"Here Luisa, Mike wants to talk to you. And don't try to figure out a way to get into town, not today and not tomorrow."

"Oh, Mom."

"I'll just finish these cookies. Shoo-shoo."

Jack had stoked the logs in the kitchen fireplace. His coat and boots dripped by the door where he had brought in more logs. He sat at the kitchen table reading through an old stack of mail. He picked up the church newsletter and began to read aloud:

"'Mr. and Mrs. Grayson say thanks to all who helped with the winter coat collection for the Henderson Home in Tennessee.' Jill wasn't that what you did with my favorite insulated jacket?"

"You never wore it. It had dust on it, hanging in the basement storage."

"Okay, okay. But did you give them any of the closet full of coats you have in the front bedroom?"

"Jack, just keep reading and be happy for the poor folks in Tennessee who are now bundled up in your coat."

Jack shrugged and continued to read silently. The aroma of chocolate chip cookies enticed Luisa off the phone. She poured a glass of milk, and then excitedly talked of her conversation with Mike. "He's trying to decide if he wants to go to Haiti for spring break with the youth group. Mom, he wanted to know if I wanted to go. What do you think?"

"Jill, the newsletter says the youth will be working at the Grace Mission Hospital." Jack pointed to the paragraph in the newsletter. "They've been asked to help with general maintenance and washing and feeding the small children. They will visit the mission, the tuberculosis sanitarium and the mission school. They fly from Indianapolis to Miami, then on to Port-Au-Prince. The deadline for registration is February 15. It sounds like a great experience, like the one Henry and Lillian went on down there."

"They were there two months and built a church up in the mountains," she said, dipping a cookie in her coffee.

"Henry always swore by the experience. He said it was the best of his life. You know the people he met still get in touch with you. Luisa could work for a whole week that might be a different experience."

Luisa picked up the wood spoon and shook it at him, "Thanks, Dad. I don't know if I want to go. I'll have to call Jan and see if she wants to go. What do you think Mom?"

"I wonder if they need an adult chaperone. Who does it say to contact?"

"Reverend Bradstreet or Myra Sayers." Jack said.

The family discussed the pros and cons, but the ultimate decision maker was on his way to Africa. Spring vacation was reserved for Luis and his family.

ᚱᛖᚱ

Most roads were cleared and the snow melted. Caylor residents returned to their regular activities within a couple of days, depending on how far they lived from the city. Jill thought two solid days of Jack in the farmhouse was more than enough. He followed her around making sure he couldn't do something to help her. He sounded like a yes man, "Yes, Honey. Yes, Dear." Locked in her study she'd been able to catch up on grading papers.

Her first day back at school, Sadie called the school office and left a message with Molly for Jill. "'Urgent,' she said. Jill, you *must* stop by her house on your way home. Why does Sadie always think her messages are urgent?"

"You know her Molly, maybe she's pregnant."

"Don't wish that on some unsuspecting child. She already has three." They laughed.

When Jill repeated her conversation with Molly to Sadie, she threatened both of them, saying "Wait until I see that Molly again!" Sadie served Jill coffee in her favorite hand painted pottery mug.

"Sadie, this coffee tastes great, oh, the commercial voice. You find the best tasting beans, at Kroger? Or did Michael bring it home with him? Tell me. Expensive, right?

"I don't know; mine was free."

"Okay, I apologize. You're not pregnant."

Sadie handed her the empty can...

"'El Campesino 100% Colombian,' Sadie why do you always do this to me?"

"I told you urgent. What else could I say on the school phone? But here is the best part."

Sadie reached into her pocket and pulled out two leather bound booklets.

"Buenos Dias, Señora Ochoa."

Jill opened the cover only to see a picture of herself. The information read 'Jill Havlicek Ochoa, citizen of Colombia, residence: Cartagena, Colombia, Birthplace: Cartagena." The physical information was correct, height and weight. The birth date was accurate and the picture looked like it was taken moments ago.

"Sadie, what has he done? No, what is he planning? And here," Jill handed the picture of Luis the vintner to Sadie, "He said for you to keep it."

Jill took a drink of her coffee and slowly explained the visit by the drug agents, badges, guns, and all. "They reminded me of a James Bond movie, at my school in the parking lot! He scares me sometimes. Sadie, when I talk he sounds like my questions are insignificant. He says everything is okay. I wanted to ask more questions, but he said 'not on the phone.'"

"You know I think of him as an international man of mystery. I guess James Bond," Sadie said.

"Oh, he is off to Africa, but I have to talk about Haiti, you know our kids are planning that trip?"

"Yes, Mike is excited about it. Missionary work on his Spring Break? I guess I better pay closer attention to my pin ball wizard. I do think it would be good for both of them. Did you say yes?"

"We always do Spring Break with Luis, so I have to run it by him. Luisa pretty much tells him what she wants to do, so I suppose...the kids are going to Haiti. But Sadie, Luis said next weekend in Curaçao, a long weekend. Can we make that happen?"

"We can do anything we set our minds to? Fly out Friday after school. Arrive Curaçao Saturday morning. Leave Curaçao on Sunday morning. Be back for school on Monday. A plan, si?"

٣٤٣

After their abbreviated Curaçao weekend, she now sat by herself in first class staring at the turquoise Caribbean Sea. Incredible. She drank wine at 11A.M. How had they managed? Her thoughts swirled like a kaleidoscope.

He picked her up and drove to his house, no Caz. And when they arrived, no Connie. He explained they only came if he were going to be there longer than three days. He carried her bag to his room. She shook her head, "At least this trip we can sleep together."

"Or your own room if you would feel more comfortable...." He laughed.

She walked through the living room feeling the trades, listening to the whispering slats. The muffled swish-swish-swish took her back to nine years ago. She picked up framed pictures he had placed on the alcove shelves where the cups had been. They were the ones she'd taken on her first visit. He also framed her prom pictures from high school.

"Luis, you framed these?"

"Yes, I told you a special place." He leaned down and kissed her.

She gave him Luisa's senior picture. He smiled proudly. "I want so much to come to her graduation, but I don't know....travel in and out of your United States...is getting so difficult."

She held her senior picture next to Luisa's, "Do you think we look alike?"

"M-m, there is a Ochoa all over that face, but her eyes...yours."

Connie had come, cleaned and put some breakfast food in the refrigerator. They spent most of the day talking and talking. There was no phone, so no one interrupted them. They sat by the pool, swam naked and talked.

Over a cigar and absinthe late on Saturday afternoon he started. "Welcome to Curaçao. No. Welcome to my world, and Señora Ochoa *your* world. You look at me. I know sometimes my answers leave you with more questions." He stared at the sea, not speaking, the crash and ebb. The water exploded and then quickly calmed. Again and again.

She put her hand on his arm, "Luis, is it time, is it the now you always speak of when you say 'Not now?'"

"We are getting close. Luisa needs to graduate from her school with her friends. As much as I want you to stay with me at this moment,

I have to say no, not now. For Luisa, si? But we're close, so close," he shook his head.

She was not sure what those words intimated. He had said he wanted to keep her with him; he wanted to "insure" she was safe and didn't want her to be alone in Indiana so far from him. He said in only a few months Luisa would be eighteen and it would be "time." It would be the "now."

"With your new passport you can go to Cuba. Do you want to go the next time I need cigars? But Gringa, Africa is an amazing place. We must go next summer."

"Luisa would love that. She has such compassion for animals. She's argued with her farmer uncle, Beau, about killing animals to eat. In her English class, she wrote a paper about vegetarianism."

"We'll definitely go and take David. I want them to meet, brother and sister."

Layers and layers of Señor Ochoa. And something about the peeling, the revealing frightened her, no longer could she use her imagination to fill in the spaces. As he talked, he held her hand, leading her through his farm life. She heard Henry's voice, "Yeah, leading you Princess, right down the primrose path." To where, Dad? A dangerous place? Or a good place?

Luis said he wanted to tell her many things, but could not jeopardize her in that way. "Information in the wrong hands can be deadly. The pursuit of the information could cause you and my daughter..."

"Deadly..."

"No, no, a certain risk to your safety." He sighed.

"It wouldn't do any good to ask what the hell you mean, I guess."

"I want to weave these threads..."

"Deadly and risk? It will be a helluva blanket. Luis, try. I'm going to Indiana tomorrow, I can't look at Luisa and think deadly and risk."

And so he explained that his mountains had become a battleground between several groups of "concerned citizens," he called them, some were U.S. citizens others were Colombians. Each group had its own reason for wanting to be in his mountains. He had a huge hacienda, Saldana, dedicated to growing the best coffee; other parts had been turned into cash crops.

240

"Remember this phrase, Gringa, cash crops. Cash crops pay for all the other crops; if coffee futures are rising or falling, cash crops insure income, security." He put his finger over her lips, "Cash crops. Use that phrase and only use it when you have no other choice."

"Jeezus H. Christ, Luis, what are you saying?! Or should I say, *not* saying? I am so confused and creating pictures of soldiers in the mountains and you. I know what cash crops are, I teach history for criminey sakes. You make yours sound mysterious, deadly, risky?"

His answer was to hold her and kiss her, squeezing her in one of his I-can-hear-your-heart-beating hugs.

Luis had decided they would eat in Willemstad. He held her hand walking to the restaurant. Feeling her, she thought, so he would know her reaction to what he said. There'd been a Cuban band and a dance floor. The cha-cha and Latin limbo she called it, but he said salsa and mambo. He promised there would be only laughing, dancing and dinner. Her favorite with him. He relaxed with the many tourists who shared their dance floor. She'd wanted to stop the clock and stay in that moment, but repeatedly...cha-cha-cha.

On Sunday morning, after making love, after they talked on his soft sheets, after packing her few things, he roasted his coffee beans and made the exquisite coffee she remembered. They ate toast and eggs and laughed, recalling Luisa learning to say heuvos.

She now finished her second glass of wine as the pilot announced they were preparing for their descent into Miami. An insurance policy to protect him from the vagaries of the world market? Mr. Angotti was helping him with other insurance. Mr. Angotti called them "financial instruments."

"Two phrases for insurance, Gringa, cash crops and financial instruments."

He did not trust any of the "concerned citizens" that operated in his mountains. They were all "basura" as far as he was concerned.

He spoke of Saldana, the complex of mills and drying pens, a clinic to take care of his workers. He explained the life of the trees and their need for constant maintenance and his refusal to use machines when handling the berries. His workers were paid wages they could live on and not starve unlike his own migrant experience and the dismissive attitude of those who hired him to work their fields. All of his work scarred him. He knew of cuts and pain and being unable to be treated or even given time to heal. He wasn't a slave owner, so people came to him to work and stayed. They had their own housing and small gardens. But the price of their end product was determined by greedy "basura" who bought and sold on the New York coffee exchange.

"Disgusting how much control they have over the ordinary lives of workers thousands of miles from New York. Always new places opening fields of coffee trees, Guatemala, El Salvador, Panama and Brazil's deforestation, constantly ruining rain forests in the name of survival.

"When prices went up in 1975, only four years ago, everyone wanted to grow coffee. Ah, Gringa, the theory of supply and demand. We destroy ourselves and seem unable to band together to insure a consistent supply. And so I must diversify to survive. I surrender some unused land to other types of crops, cash crops. I also allow other places to be used. To be in the ongoing supply versus demand cycle forces me to expand. I cannot store my crop for future use, like canning tomatoes or at the villa where it is made into wine and bottles get dusty in cellars. If I could control all the parts of production...ah, General Foods, or Procter and Gamble, but I cannot, so I move on and make other investments. You mentioned coffee futures, what is the future of coffee? I don't know, but I am trying to create the best beans for the finest end product and market it that way to potential buyers. I am hopeful, but still I must do other things. My country suffers under the volatility of this New York market place and all those who want to be campesinos."

"This reminds me of Jack and his brothers' conversations trying to decide which crops to plant and where, soy beans, tomatoes, corn."

"But your government assists them, paying them to grow or not grow, supporting their prices so they do not suffer from the vagaries of farming. My government has tried this method, but gone deeply in debt."

El Campesino, she thought. He promised she would see it all "soon," the many parts of the coffee production. It fascinated her; his description of picking, washing, drying, bagging and shipping. He tried to protect the land from which it all grew, guaranteeing it would grow the best beans. "All the beans are picked by hand on Saldana. Just like your tomatoes."

"Luis, you came to pick tomatoes."

"Si, to pick you Gringa. I prayed long ago..."

He looked at her, then looked away, finally crossing himself and saying, "Gracias a Dios, Amen."(thank you God)

He did say, "We'll talk in Haiti. Luisa as a missionary? She will have to speak French. I think mission work is like her mother in this way." He smiled and pinched her nose.

When she left, he held her so tightly she cried. She thought of telling him about William, but did not find an appropriate time. His rants against the CIA guaranteed an outburst. And then it would be questions about why she was still hearing from someone in his most hated organization. So, no, she could not really have that discussion. "Bob Smith" had caused the terrible fight between her and Hector. A woman of her word? Honesty, the complete story? Yes, Luis when the time comes, the now of your promise.

They were in their own cocoon miles from their homes, but home with each other. He had opened up in a way he'd never done before. He told her it was getting close to when she would be *his* wife. Registering that phrase, "his wife," her mind, the synapses started popping and spinning, Señora Ochoa, not the pretend wife on vacations, the real wife, in real life, a legal status. The twists in conversations she would have to have became a bowl of linguine between her ears. Would she move to Colombia? His wife in Caylor? No. But Luisa would be in Ohio going to college. No. Each scenario looked like a neighborhood "after," after the strong winds knocked trees into homes, cars smashed, telephone poles broken in two. No. Out of the cornfields? No more papers to grade? No more pretending with Jack?

She should have ordered vodka on the rocks. Sadie? Was it a good day to ask for a divorce? Luisa would be in college in six months. Six months and three of those they would be in Italy and now Africa. Maybe she could stay at the villa and send Jack a note. A bottle of wine, sitting at her desk, in the dusty rose room, "Dear Jack..." She would have to tell Southeastern now, right now that she would not be returning. Luis did not say when, only "close" and "soon."

"Gringa, you must accept that I protect you in not answering all of your questions, it is your insurance policy, as are your new passports. I know I ask much of you in this conversation. Please think about what I have said and always remember hasta que la muerte no separe." (until death separates us)

Who is Luis Ochoa? An insurance agent?

Sadie would be waiting in Indianapolis and what could she say? Luis had asked again if she trusted Sadie with her life. She did. Could she even have a life if Sadie weren't in it? But Sadie needs insurance, too.

The snow still covered Indianapolis. Her tray was in the upright position, her purse tucked under the seat in front of her. Was it the weight of the plane or the world she felt? Okay Sarah B., a weekend away from Caylor in Curaçao, of just being, being with Luis. In nineteen years, he continued to complete her as if it were their first time in the shed on the straw. Could she get insurance for that?

Chapter 12

"Mom," Luisa yelled down the stairs.

"I'm coming. I just took your clothes out of the dryer. And I'm bringing this letter from Reverend Isbell."

"I know what it says, 'don't pack much' and something we can 'wash out by hand.'"

Jill climbed the stairs with a laundry basket of shorts and tops. "It sounds pretty treacherous, Lo. He says the Grace Mission is always mindful of the powers that be. I'm looking forward to the trip, but…"

"Mom, we'll be okay. Reverend Isbell is there all the time. Let me have those clothes. What did Aunt Sadie say?"

Jill sat down on Luisa's bed amongst a coverlet of clothes and an open suitcase.

"She is convinced you talked Mike into going. Michael wanted to take him to baseball Spring Training in Florida, but he is going to Haiti to do 'mission work.' She also said Baby Doc is very scary. She watched some news show and they said it was dangerous, and not recommended for travel. And why couldn't you go to Florida like other teenagers at Spring Break?"

"Oh, Aunt Sadie, Mike is the one who kept asking me about going. It's an adventure, right Mom? That's what you always tell me when we go to meet Papa."

"'Dear Youth and Chaperones,'" Jill held the letter from Reverend Isbell, "'You'll be seeing and experiencing sights, sounds, smells like nothing you've had before. It will be challenging, but rewarding...'"

"I read it, Mom. See, an adventure, right?" Luisa picked pieces from the basket and threw them in her suitcase. She held a piece up to her face then tossed it on her bed.

"'Please come with an open heart and remember Jesus' command that, 'in as much as you have done it to the least of these, you have done it unto me.' I guess we'll know when we get there. All the missionaries from there said the Haitians are in need of anything we can give. Did you get all your stuff out of the basket? I have to go pack."

"Mom, don't forget to pack light and..." and they said together laughing, "wash out by hand."

Jill and three other mothers joined the group as adult chaperones with no real explanation of what their duties would include. The days seemed never-ending with another floor to clean, a pot of oatmeal, or a huge pan of pasta to fix. There was no pantry filled with her canned tomato sauce for spaghetti. She heard Lillian's voice, "Make do, Jill, make do. All are not blessed like you."

Jill and the other mothers were helped in the kitchen by the Haitian assistant. She wore a house dress that was immaculate in the mornings and stained by the time she left in the afternoon. Lillian would have been so pleased because the thin woman with a white rag neatly tied around her head "made do" in the barren kitchen. Jill watched as she mixed up a very spicy sauce. She stirred in onions, peppers, vinegar with a red sauce. "I make it at home. Special recipe." She told Jill when asked, then smiled and winked.

The youth group stayed busy from morning to night, scrubbing walls, washing rags used for dressings, and sterilizing medical instruments. Reverend Isbell posted jobs every morning. They picked an item and then checked it off. Jill watched when they cleared a lot next to the mission building in preparation for the next work group. Her daughter pleasantly surprised her as she jumped into the hard sweaty job. They stacked the broken planks and pieces of metal that had littered the space.

They fed the orphaned babies in the nursery. The youth ate the same meals as those prepared for the people they helped. Their lunch was sparse, a piece of bread and some clear soup with a few vegetables.

Jill now stood at the sink washing and drying dishes after lunch. Luisa walked in from the back yard area holding a dry dish towel from the clothes line. They took their turn to do the lunch clean-up. They'd been assigned this task in the morning. The kitchen's open door and large window provided light in the cinder block room. Water was heating on the stove to sterilize the washed dishes. "Luisa, has Mike said anything about being hungry?" Jill asked.

"No, nothing at all. I'm surprised because he eats like a horse at home. Mom, this morning I was outside hanging up clothes and I saw a tiny girl sucking on a used ice cream stick. She chewed on the wood, I think trying to get any left over ice cream that had soaked into the stick. How long can they live without eating enough?"

With no screens on the windows or door, Luisa kept putting down the dish towel, and swatting at the flies.

"I don't know, Honey, I don't know. But you heard Reverend Isbell ask us to go home and tell of the extreme needs, and not so extreme like screens. Screens." Jill shook her head, then using pot holders picked up the large pot and poured boiling water on the washed dishes.

"If Papa isn't mad that I'm not spending spring break with him, would you ask him if he could do something?"

"I think you do better with him than I do, but I'll let you know his mood after I see him tomorrow."

"I want to see him, but I want to be here. Oh mom, just make him understand." Luisa kissed Jill on the cheek.

Jill shook her head, "Reverend Isbell told us we would carry Haiti home with us and we would leave a piece of our hearts here. You're beginning to sound like that."

Each evening the teenage helpers examined the critical differences between the distinct cultures of their own American middle class lives compared to those around them. They sat in the kitchen area at an aluminum picnic table. Mike and Jill sat on overturned plastic buckets. Reverend Isbell had a bar stool next to the stove.

"No McDonald's or Wendy's. Actually, it seems a universe away," Ginny spoke as the talking stick was handed to her. Each youth volunteer was asked to speak of their day or their reaction when they received the stick.

Luisa cried, "It's so hard to think we could go to Target and get so many things they could use down here. And what happens the day after we feed them? Do the children go back to eating almost nothing? And their clothes? I have a closet full of things I don't wear."

Luisa held a month old baby that had been left by a young mother, younger than herself who told Reverend Isbell she could not feed her baby. Luisa asked one of the Haitian workers to wrap the baby on her front in a traditional native carrier. Jill helped her and told the story that that was how she carried Luisa; she did not fill in the part that William had shown her how to wrap her baby.

"We sleep under mosquito netting, but all those people living in the metal huts, have nothing like that. It's only mosquito netting. Christ Almighty, Reverend Isbell, we surely can get mosquito netting down here." Mike spoke, then passed the stick to Thomas, tall and thin, with long hair and an earring. He had kind brown eyes. Luisa told him they looked like the eyes of Jesus in all the pictures.

"Reverend Isbell, do you need us or do you need our money? I want to stay, but is it better I go home and collect money for the church to send here?" Thomas asked, then handed the stick to Reverend Isbell.

"There is a big difference between your world of affluence and the people who are so desperate. Each of you will think of this hospital mission and make a decision. I think I was about your age, Thomas, when I decided my personal journey would include helping others. I just didn't know how or where."

"One week is not enough time, Reverend Isbell," Jenn said. Jenn came with the Caylor group, but she belonged to the Methodist church in Swayzee. She wore her blond hair in two long braids and tied a kerchief around her forehead, like an Indian band. Jill said she was their own mission flower child in her long Indian print skirts and halter tops. Luisa told her when they went back to Indiana she hoped Jenn would call her.

After five days, Jill headed out of Port-au- Prince in Reverend Isbell's borrowed jeep. Henry's church building was up in the mountains away from the major city, so too, Luis. He said he would be up in Petionville and wanted to see her and go to Henry's church with her.

"I never met your father, but I would like to know him through his work," he'd told her on their last conversation before she left Indiana. "Craftsmen create works with their hands. Building a home is creation, a concrete showing of his work and skill."

"He has homes all over Caylor, but not a church. He would be so happy to know I'm visiting this place. And that you are going with me."

The filthy streets of the city suffocated the Midwesterners. People crouched on dirt curbs with wandering dogs and goats, and begged. So many people lived in the streets or on top of each other in squalor. Inching up the dirt and paved road, she saw fewer street people and children.

She drove unable to concentrate on anything. Haiti had been as good and bad as Reverend Isbell wrote in their welcoming letters. Baby Doc's personal police terrorized people with machetes. The kind faces of those suffering in dilapidated conditions, faces that should be angry, smiled at her. Haiti, 1979, she would write that entry in her journal at home. Maybe read a book that explained more fully than Reverend Isbell how Haiti came to be like this.

The wind blew dust through the open air jeep. Uncollected garbage and sewage permeated the air. Goats stepped in front of her car, and children held out their dirt covered hands. Their big bright eyes broke her heart. Grown men smoked cigarettes and laughed, but tried to signal her to slow down. Broken bike parts and used tires formed a shoulder of some sort on the street. Dirt roads, intersected paved streets. The street names were in French if there happened to be a sign at all. The sidewalks were broken concrete remnants of what had been. Stacked houses on the hillsides were balanced so precariously they could fall if rain or earthquakes rumbled through. So many people in such need of housing and food, let alone education. Where are the teachers? The schools? My students just don't know how lucky they are. Is there any way I can teach empathy?

When requesting the use of Reverend Isbell's jeep, she hadn't mentioned meeting Luis at a mountainside hotel. The road twisted uphill, but she viewed a radical change in environment. As she approached Petionville, she saw large mansions built on the sides of the mountains. She tried to reconcile the impossible. Haiti, why are your poor so poor, and your rich so rich? It is wrong, but can it be righted? Is that even a word, righted? God, help this country, please, in Jesus name I pray. Amen.

The map Revered Isbell drew depicted the exact route she was to take to the hotel. He told her the concierge at the hotel would provide a guide to the countryside to see Henry's building. She pulled into the hotel parking lot. A valet opened her door and told her, "Please register, ma'am, and we will take care of your bag and park your car."

Her shirt was simple light weight gauze that looked permanently wrinkled. She wore draw-string pants that could be washed and worn damp, if necessary. In the windy jeep, she had tied a scarf around her hair. She now pulled it off, as she walked into the hotel. She took one look at her reflection in the elegant lobby mirror, and saw him in the mirror, then turned. He hugged her sweeping her up in one gesture. She kissed him.

"You look eighteen all over again. Where is my other almost eighteen year old? I have a surprise for her," he spoke cheerfully.

"Luis, oh god, it is good to see you. Just one more hug, please? I feel like I have been in hell."

He squeezed her tightly, and she collapsed in his arms and cried.

"Gringa, what? Is Luisa okay?"

"She's so..." she inhaled and exhaled slowly, "involved in the mission; she didn't want to take a moment away from helping those children. She said, 'Tell Papa I am sorry. I will see him this summer.' She said she thought you would understand."

"Let's go out onto the balcony and see the beauty of Haiti."

"Beauty?"

"Si."

"The only beauty I've seen is the kindness in the eyes of those wonderful and terribly destitute people I've been talking to for the last four days."

"This country has such extremes. We cannot solve the problems of Haiti. I often ask myself why such a short distance from your United States and yet they let these people live like this."

They drank iced pineapple juice with rum and held hands. Could he keep the pain and desperation away? "Please just talk to me. I want to hear your voice. I want to know my world includes you."

"Gringa, you need to eat."

"I can't right now, with hungry children staring at us; no, not yet. The rum is perfect."

The mountains and trees of Haiti dominated the horizon. Mother Nature. Jill kept looking up, always up, to look down would bring the gut wrench of the reality she left. "Luis, I've tried to not cry in front of the teenagers. But it is so frustrating so much to do and who is helping? Not enough from the United States as you say."

"Gringa, you and your good deeds. I know you want to change the world, but it is a big job."

"But they will die unless we help. They will starve or get sick....Yes, I guess I do want to change something. The world? That's a pretty big mission. Will you help me?"

"My hard-headed Jankee, if your United States won't, I'll do what I can. But if we are bargaining, then what will I get?"

"Me?"

"I can take you with me?"

She smiled and clinked his glass as if toasting. The cold rum relaxed her. She stroked his leg, arm, and the hand holding his drink.

"Luis, I don't know why I wasn't better prepared. Dad said the poverty was unbelievable, but that was years ago." She finished her drink and then stood.

She pulled him from his chair. "I need to soak and wash away the smell, the taste, the dust. Come. Let's go, I want to take a bath."

They went to their room, and she filled the tub with warm water. Luis volunteered to wash her back. She pulled him into the tub with her, drenching his clothes. They laughed and played. He took his clothes off and they splashed as if they were three years old in a backyard wading pool. They sat in the tub, and she traced around his nipple. She lay facing him on his stomach; his legs were spread and bent. The water sloshed around them. "Luis, you always tell me *I* made a decision in the shed, to make you a part of my life forever."

"Si," he plunked suds on her hair.

"When did you decide that you wanted me, what do you say, 'Luis owns Jill?'" She pronounced the "J" sound as a "Y" imitating the way he often said her name.

"Your Spanish accent is like a gringa."

"No, tell me when."

"Three stages like the rocket boosters at Cape Canaveral."

"The first stage?"

"Your first day of work at the camp."

"I didn't meet you on my first day!" Jill said.

"I know, but I *saw* you."

"Where?"

"You were pulling up in your VW. Didn't you have a name for it?"

"Imogene."

"Si, Imogene. I was coming around the side of one of the shacks. I'd heard the car and came to see who it could be, then there you were. Well, really I saw your ass first," he paused to slap her butt in the tub his movement sloshing the water. "You were bent over in the back seat and I heard you cuss, 'Goddamned Sadie.' I thought a church worker who cusses, maybe someone not obsessed with saving souls had arrived."

Jill laughed, "I cursed that goddamned Sadie? That makes sense. And then what? Still Stage one?"

"You stood up and hit your head on the door frame and cursed again, 'Oh shit!' you yelled. I had to cover my mouth to keep you from hearing me laugh."

"Luis," she pulled his chest hairs.

He pinched her nose, "But you stood there rubbing your head, your breasts were standing up in your tight shirt and the sun shone on your hair. I thought 'angel hair,' strawberry gold in the bright sun. Your face was sweaty. Curls stuck to your forehead. I wanted to walk out from my spot behind the shack and lick your face."

"You can lick my face now."

He leaned forward and licked her nose and her upper lip, then kissed her. She pulled away, "Stop Luis. I want to hear Stage two. Let's get dried off, more rum, and then stage two."

"Other things before stage two…?"

"Rum. I want to hear this story, you've never told me before."

"Okay, rum and a cigar."

They dried off and wore hotel robes. The room had a small refrigerator for the pineapple juice.

"Let's order room service. We can watch the sunset and wait for our food." Luis called, and then they walked to the patio.

In the peach sunset, Luis lit his cigar. They sat on the patio of beige marble tiles and white wrought iron tables and chairs with bright orange and red seat cushions.

"Stage two, Señor Ochoa."

"Easy. The four-way stop on your bike. You wanted me then; you rode your bike in the heat on a Saturday morning, just to find *me*. I think you wanted me when we danced, but when you rode your bike and looked surprised to see me; I knew we shared the same feeling. When

252

you kissed me in that truck, you gave yourself to me. Sold. I owned you."

"No." She leaned across the table and slapped his arm.

"Si, Gringa. I said you gave yourself away in those sexy clothes. Sold to the Colombian coffee farmer, like a bag of green beans on the open market."

"Okay, stage three, but you already had me you said."

"Stage three. The night before...when the rain storm started. You came to work, and we sat on the porch on baskets. Remember the heavy storm the night before?"

She nodded and took a drink of her rum. The thunder had awakened her in the night. She listened to the crack as if lightning had struck a tree in her backyard.

"Little Milagros woke up crying, scared to death. She called me, 'Papa Ochoa, Papa Ochoa." I put my shirt on and went to her cabin. She laid her head on my shoulder; she held on tightly. I patted her and talked to her. I asked her to think of something she liked. She said, 'Mi maestra.' I said, 'Why?' She said, 'Papa, she is an angel from God.'

"An angel? I asked and Milagros said, 'She is beautiful Papa. She has angel hair and she is white like the Virgin Mary.'

"I cradled her in my arms until she fell asleep. But I was awake and lay on the floor listening to the rain beat on the tin roof. McKinnsey did have waterproof cabins for us. Milagros's description reminded me of the prayer I'd repeated many years before, and I knew on that rainy night... God had sent you."

"Luis," she cried, "hold me like you held Milagros. I want to know I'm safe for the moment." And he wrapped his arms around her, squeezing her against his chest.

ܬܨ

She awoke to find him poring over a large blueprint he'd stretched on a table in their suite.

"Gringa, I have ordered coffee. Come, I want to show you my special surprise that I have been working on for a long time."

The sun was coming in through the patio. "Ah, another hot humid day, I wonder how Luisa and Mike managed at the mission? I'm supposed to be chaperoning."

"Our daughter is very grown up. I think to leave her alone will be good for her."

"I know, too grown up sometimes. Okay, I'll trust her to be fine. What do you want to show me?"

"Remember…oh come let me show you." Luis pulled her out of bed, and led her to the blueprint. She flipped the outsized blue pages, the exterior front, the inside floor plan. The heavy pages took up the entire table. She turned the architectural drawings back and forth.

"It looks like a Spanish mission school, early California, Father Junipero Serra."

He turned to page two, the main building, was surrounded by an expansive arched patio. The upside down 'U' shapes were supported by round posts cemented in flowered concrete squares. The architect had drawn urns with flowers and a tiered fountain, centered in a semicircular driveway. Two tall heavy doors with long iron hinges were in the middle of an arched opening. Above these wooden doors was drawn in curved letters following the arc of the doorway, "Abrazar a Los Niños."(Hug the children)

"Luis, what is this?"

"Gringa, you told me you wanted two things…remember?"

"It has been nineteen years, the gray elephant?"

"Before you had children…"

"I wanted to see the world and…" they spoke together, "hug the children."

"Oh Luis, what is this building?"

"Your orphanage, Gringa. I want you to fill it with children and you can hug all of them every day."

"Oh my god. Is it built?"

"Being built. And you can thank David when you meet him this summer. He wants to go on safari with us. The Ochoas will all be together. David found a safe place for your orphanage. You can figure out how you want to run your business, the hug business."

"When? Luis, when?"

"When you are ready. The building will be finished in September. Five months from now."

More rum? She thought. For breakfast, maybe vodka in my orange juice. Well Sadie, is this a good day to ask for a divorce? She wished she could roll up the blueprint and show Sadie. September? The boxes on her calendar were filling up. Which one would have the capital "D" written on it? Let's see, Jack, I'm moving to Colombia to run an orphanage. She let out a heavy sigh, then hugged Luis. "It is amazing. Goddamned amazing. Oh Luis, will you ever stop surprising me?"

"'We dance around in a ring and suppose; But the secret sits in the middle and knows.'" He pinched her nose and carried her back to the bed. "Before they bring the coffee…"

ᚱᚲᚱ

They bounced along a dirt road to the small village where Henry and Lillian had visited years before. Her parents had brought home a map to the church. She kept looking up at the beauty that was Haiti, the Caribbean island that did not boast of perfect winter getaways to sunbathe and romp in turquoise water with white sand beaches. The people tried to escape and routinely drowned in decrepit ships coming to America. If by chance they made the six almost seven hundred mile trip, they were not allowed to stay; instead, they were returned to Haiti, unlike their Cuban counterparts who were given asylum and a pathway to citizenship. She wrestled with the inequity of it all.

"Luis, it is so unfair. The politics of Haiti and the United States…."

"Jankee politics? Hypocrisy! Jill, it hasn't changed. Remember your Jankee golden rule…."

"Do unto others as you would have them do unto you."

He chuckled and shook his head, "He who has the gold rules."

"Luis, you have some gold. Can't you do something? The children at the mission are in such desperate need of milk and cereal."

"What would you like me to do? I cannot make bread and fish. Coffee is not helpful for hungry children. What is the man's name in charge of your hospital?" Luis said.

"Reverend Isbell."

"Who was the reverend at the tomato farm?"

"Reverend Newsom."

"Ah, si. Do you think Reverend Newsom knew I took the virginity from his best volunteer? The woman who wants to change the world." Luis teased her.

"Stop. You know he didn't have a clue. Do you think Reverend Newsom ever had sex?" The thought amused them driving alone in the Caribbean island's back country.

"Luis, I have to be back at the mission hospital by Friday afternoon at the latest. He will worry that I have been kidnapped by some crazy Tonton Macoute."

"You have been kidnapped but by a crazy Colombian. And I will call with the ransom message. Jill reach into my pocket."

"I don't like reaching into your pockets. I never know what I might find, perhaps, Haitian primo."

He laughed at her reference, explaining he had only a surprise and indicated the pocket on his jacket she should open. "And get a cigar out of the other top pocket."

With trepidation she pulled out a folded envelope, "This?"

"Si, now the cigar."

She held the blank white envelope, "What now, Luis?"

As he twisted open the yellow aluminum tube holding his cigar, he said, "Open it! It won't bite you."

Lifting the flap of the envelope, she discovered an old newspaper clipping. Unfolding it delicately to protect the tattered creases, she let out a gasp. "Mr. and Mrs. Havlicek are pleased to announce the marriage of their daughter...Oh my god, Luis where did you get this? How did you get this?"

"Keep looking, Gringa, you will see."

She removed a small folded note. Opening it she read aloud,

"*'Dear Señor Ochoa, Enclosed is a picture and information regarding the young woman you asked about. I hope this answers your questions. She inquired of your whereabouts the following summer after your crew had contracted, 1961. Of course, no one knew anything. Your steward in Christ, Ned Newsom.'*"

"Luis when?"

Before he could answer, she pulled the small envelope that bore her name in phonetic spelling. "*Jill Hablachek.*" It was still sealed. She looked up at him. In the windy jeep her hair lashed her face and mixed with her tears.

"Open it, Gringa. See what your Señor Ochoa had to say fourteen years ago."

The old paper felt fragile in her hands. Gingerly she unsealed the yellowed envelope. His thick handwriting had become familiar to her over the years.

"Look at me, Gringa. I want to see your face. For so long, I thought about how you would react when you received this letter from me."

"*'March 12, 1965'*?" She looked at him, "Four months *before* I married. Four months, Luis? Before? What might have been...?"

"Si, Gringa. Our timing was terrible, but we had destiny on our side." He reached over and massaged her neck, then rubbed the back of his hand on her cheek. "Please continue."

"*'Mi Maestra,'* I can't read this Luis, I'm crying too much. Yes, that is the face you would have seen, me crying because you actually came back in my life. Crying as I held the paper. I need a handkerchief."

"You have to reach in my pocket. Blow your nose. I can't remember what I said."

"*'Mi Maestra, I have not forgotten you. I promised to take you with me, and I have. I wear a gold band on my left hand and have for the last five years and will continue until we meet. My time with you, having you, only made me want you more. I do not know if you have thought of me, but I would like to correspond with you. I have included my address. I will be waiting to hear from you. If you write, I promise to fill in the spaces with answers. You always have questions. I think of you as my little gringa. Hasta que la muerte nos separe. Siempre, Luis Ochoa.'*

"Luis, it is so sweet, but four months before I married....Our lives would have ..." she cried, then leaned over and kissed him on the cheek, "You knew Reverend Newsom's name all along. Why didn't Reverend Newsom send this to me?"

"I don't know. Your marriage? His marriage? Marriage? Don't they say let no man tear this asunder, as if they know God's will."

"Now tell me about this."

"When I completed my new home in the mountains, I moved things that had been stored and found this envelope. I knew I would see you here and now. I remembered how much I wanted to get in touch with you at that time. When I returned to Colombia, I had so much work to do at Saldana, so much. I hoped you would stay right where you were, not traveling to see the world trying to hug children except, of course, *our* daughter."

"Our daughter?"

"When I read the part about 'Luisa,' I just knew... as a flower girl, she had to be... I added it up, the years... she was mine. I cried, a daughter with you, my gringa in the middle of Indiana."

"Those damn cornfields..." Jill shook her head.

"It took another four years...but it said where you were. I prayed to our Heavenly Father, to keep you right there. In stage three, I knew you were given to me by God, and now knew you were still there. My letter to you was never opened, not by Reverend Newsom or me. This seemed like the time to show you."

Jill cried again releasing all the tension of Haiti, the pain of her love for Luis Ochoa, and how her life could have been.

ᴙξᴙ

The villagers remembered "Monsieur Havlicek" as they called him. They hugged his daughter and snapped pictures of Jill and Luis by the small cinderblock church Henry built. Strange, Jill thought, in ten years of meeting, they had not taken pictures together. But here in this hillside country village? Were they safe? Was the woods impenetrable?

They drove back to the hotel. Luis talked her into eating a decent meal before her return. She drank a coffee liqueur. She wanted to stay, but she also wanted to talk to him again about the visit from the Drug Enforcement Administration.

"Luis, I would like to ask a few questions, just a few, about those men who came to my school. I know we talked in Curaçao, but please let me ask."

"Si. They are basura."

"I don't know that. I didn't read that in the book at the library, but your opinion comes from what?"

"They will not bother you again."

"And how do you know that? You just say it like a snap of the fingers. Zap! An entire U.S. government agency – gone!"

"Si. Jill, they are involved with the government of my country. I'm involved with the government of my country. Our paths cross."

"But I'm not involved with the government of your country. I live in the middle of a goddamned cornfield, a few thousand miles from Luis Ochoa and Cartagena."

"Gringa, you will not like what I tell you because although, I speak English, I speak of something you know nothing of. My monitored movements are part of my job description. American spy agencies like to know the color of my underwear, but only my gringa knows."

"The color of underwear? I worry about Luisa, is she safe? I mean they won't try to talk to her? She is almost eighteen; they might think they can talk to her. It scares me Luis."

"Jill, no harm will come to our daughter, no frightening questions. She knows nothing and is of no interest to them. You are a question because they don't know what you know, and what you do know…it is too much. But to see you, to love you, I have *no* choice. Entiendes?"

"I understand your English, as you say, but I do not like what you are saying."

They finished their dinner and walked to the front of the hotel. The late afternoon cast a golden glow on the white stucco walls of the building. Jill picked at the buttons on his many pocketed safari shirt, "What is Luisa's surprise?"

"I wanted her to know that I tried to find her mother."

"She knows you love her."

"Did you tell her she has a Colombian passport?"

"No."

"Tell her." His tone was stronger than she had heard in their twenty-four hours together.

"I don't suppose you will explain why Luisa needs to know. Luis, why? Why do we have Colombian passports?"

"You need them"

"We have American passports that allows us to go most places."

"Except one," he said, holding up his index finger.

"One?"

"Bring them this summer when we travel as a family. Jill, I will be closing the account in Indianapolis. I want you to go there as soon as you get back and withdraw whatever is in there. Keep the money as cash. Do not deposit it in your regular account. If possible, keep the cash in a safe place at Siddhartha's."

"And no explanation…." she shook her head, "You are starting to scare me with this conversation."

They stood by her borrowed jeep. He hugged her, "Ti amo."

"Will you ever tell me who you are?"

"Timing, my gringa, is everything as you have seen with my note to you all those years ago. You are the mother of my daughter and for now that is enough of who is Luis Ochoa; maybe even that is too much."

"Luis, sometimes I feel like I am fishing bare-handed with you. I reach in to catch something and you wiggle out of my grasp."

259

"Gringa, to be successful when you go fishing, always use a pole and the right bait." He smirked.

She drove again along the narrow roads and sorted or tried to sort what Luis had said: passports, money, orphanage, and then to the Haitian mission. She had asked Luis if he wanted to ride into the city, but he said he preferred another route with a business associate. She smiled when she recalled his conversation about the coffee gift to Sadie.

"You see how easily we marry in Colombia? You did not have to be there and now you are Señora Ochoa. Do you want me to kiss the bride?"

The city of the destitute, Port-au-Prince came into view. And she thought of Jesus' comment that the poor will always be with you, challenging Christians to complete the never-ending work. Her grown-up daughter had taken up the vow of service to the least of these. She was proud of her and would tell her. Tell her and Mike. They worked so hard.

Luisa and Mike. He was three years younger, but they talked often on the phone. She and Sadie thought maybe she was helping him adjust to high school, although he was physically bigger, taller by three inches now. He was going to be tall like Sadie, but built just like T.J. And when they were sure no one heard them, she and Sadie said that very thing. If Mike were suspicious at all, he never said anything about it. Mike and Luisa were actually the same color. She and Sadie speculated that maybe there was something at Caylor High School that made them feel like compatriots. Luisa would be going off to college without having to leave "the love of her life," no need to break up. She'd been invited to the Stardust Balls and with nice boys, but she always shrugged saying, "No, Mom, he's cute that's all."

Finally, Luisa had done the rebellious thing of asking Mike to take her to Senior Prom. She and Sadie shrugged it off admitting and laughing that they too had been rebellious. They ended their conversation with a toast, "the apple doesn't fall too far from the tree."

When she arrived back, Luisa was noticeably relieved. She feared the worst, but Jill explained that away from the squalor that was the mission environment was an enclave of wealthy Haitians.

"What did Papa say? I mean was he very angry?"

"With his daughter? No. Actually he was relaxed. I think he took one look at me and knew we needed to have a friendly time, nothing harsh. We saw your grandpa's church building. They remembered him with fondness. You must go."

"Next time. I do want to come again to this mission to help. Mom, I don't know how to really say this, but when I see these babies it makes my heart hurt in a way I didn't know it could."

Jill thought she took to the children as if she were a mother. Her seventeen year old all grown up in that situation, not talking about clothes to wear, or hair-dos. She'd adapted to bathing with a wash rag and cold water in a bucket, a radical change from her habit of one sometimes two showers a day. Among the teenagers there was no talk of who was dating whom, or if someone was going to ask her out.

"When we get home and have had some time to think about this week, I will talk to you of your papa and his many surprises. It has to do with children. Oh, Luisa, you are getting so grown up, and getting ready to leave me…"

"Mom, no tears. I want to tell you what happened last night. I spent much of the night awake with the baby Angelique and Mike."

"Reverend Isbell let you in the nursery at night? Where was the night nurse?"

"Well, Mike and I sneaked in, then when she cried I just picked her up and we sat in the kitchen warming her milk. Reverend Isbell was asleep. But Mom, Mike was so sweet, he changed Angelique and talked so serious."

"Serious? Siddhartha's prankster, the pinball wizard?"

"I know, but listen to this. He said he was thinking that maybe he would like mission work, doing what Reverend Isbell does."

"The macho football player? Sadie will blame me if he doesn't play football in the NFL."

"He sounded like he meant what he said. I don't know, Mom, maybe we shouldn't say anything to Sadie. It may be this place. It works on you. I think if we weren't leaving in the morning, it might be hard to leave. I don't know how Reverend Isbell does it, but I think after holding Angelique, it would be hard to turn my back on the pain. The children, what did they ever do to suffer so much?"

Jill hugged her baby who at the moment resembled the young adult woman she always hoped she would become.

ﺭ§ﺭ

261

In downtown Cartagena Luis sat at his desk on the upper floor of his office building. He cast a glance at the panoramic view of the Caribbean Ocean and the old Spanish settlement founded in 1533 by Pedro de Heredia, a conquistador. Luis understood Pedro. He now controlled a large piece of the old Spanish empire. The world appeared at his fingertips: a small TV screen recessed in his desk monitored the office reception area, the entrance and exits to the building, and the roof where his helicopter was parked. The security was hidden, but extensive, every nook and hallway watched. He wore his jeans and Lucchese boots; it was his itinerant field hand look. He made commands all afternoon. Life was back to normal for a moment. What was normal?

He read the newspaper lying on his desk. It proclaimed, "New pact between America and Colombia," exchanging cash outlays for soldiers to help combat guerrilla units operating in the coffee fincas, with a proviso for drug eradication.

"Gina, get Jairo on the phone. Tell him I'm back and I'll be ready to pick up my check from Uncle Sam after the cabinet meeting," Luis barked, as he picked up the mail on his desk.

Gina walked into his office, "Luis, Luisa is on the phone."

"Hello mi hija! Cómo estás?"

"Hola! Papa. Muy bien," Luisa spoke, then laughed, "You know Papa my Spanish, but I have something to ask you..."

"Ah, like your mother in this way?"

"Maybe."

"Did you have a safe trip home with su Madre?"

"Yes, I'm sorry I didn't see you in Haiti, but next month we will be in Africa. I'm so excited, thank you, Papa."

"You called to talk wild animals on the savannah?"

"No, Haiti. The mission where I was... they need money to build a kitchen and..."

"And, let's see your mother and her 'good deeds.'"

"Papa, I want this to be my good deed, maybe my graduation present..."

"A present...no you will have a separate present, but I will do this for my angel. I made a promise long ago and it is time to fulfill my promise. Please tell me the details."

Gina brought in coffee and told him Jorge was on the phone.

"Luisa, I must take another call. I will see you next month in London, our first stop to Tanzania."

"Thank ...gracias Papa."

He chuckled. Then pushed the button on the phone to pick up Jorge's call, and frowned as soon as he said hello.

Jorge talked in terse spurts. "The problems have spilled over! Now Campesino! Into an adjacent village? Retaliation! It must stop.... The last death blast took out six men and one a damned gringo. A gringo! You have to go and solve this! Now!"

"Jorge, I'm going to see Jairo tomorrow, we will discuss this problem, again."

Luis hung up knowing that he was in the crosshairs of government vs. government, Colombia and the United States. Again and again, depress the price of coffee, increase the price of coffee. Control governments in other countries to make sure coffee prices stay low, low for whom? The consumer? The American worker? No, for General Foods and Procter and Gamble. Jankee corporations must make the money. He grabbed his briefcase, and left the office. Normal? Yeah, normal. Welcome home.

ɤξɤ

Luis attended President Jairo Humberto's Cabinet Ministers' meeting. As director of the International Agriculture Department and the National Coffee Federation, he had to constantly forge links between foreign businessmen and Colombian CEO's. His job also consisted of milking American government payments. They had to think their gringo money was being well spent. The influx of cocaine into the American cities had made this charade trickier. Raymond Sandy was his asset in getting the visiting Congressional groups off his back.

President Humberto said, "Luis, they want helicopter rides over the cocaine fields. They want to see progress being made in eradication. Can you provide this 'guided' tour? You work in the field," the President's words were persuasive. Luis knew to show-them-only-what-needs-to-be-seen tour. "Now Luis about the man killed on your finca, the man working for the DEA...the American Attorney General is talking of an investigation."

"I'll be going up there tomorrow, sir. The DEA recruits scum," his anger seeped into his voice. He wanted to know why his own army was the only one operating. "Where is your army, Jairo's ? Whose side are you on?"

"We know, El Campesino, but answers. The Yanqui's want answers. Right now they are looking at your fincas. Come back with answers." It was a presidential directive; however, it had been spoken in the privacy of presidential quarters.

"The goddamned Americans, they have the CIA chasing communists, the DEA chasing coca farmers, is it possible to throw them out? Revoke their visas! I'm a businessman, sir, a humble coffee farmer. I hate dealing with them. They have no honor, only hubris!"

"Answers, Luis. They are only interested in what exactly happens in those mountains of yours."

"So they can tell another lie to their people?!"

"Answers, El Campesino." The president stood up and shook Luis's hand.

Chapter 13

This June morning the doves cooed softly in branches of the large oak tree. In Jill's fourteen years at the farm it had grown several feet taller and much larger around. At the end of the porch, tiny hummingbirds fed from their feeder. Jill sat in a wicker chair and wrote in her journal....

Once Upon a Time, nineteen years ago, in a shed, a princess stumbled, no, hesitantly found her prince, actually a migrant worker, okay, a crew chief for migrant workers....she referred to the shed as a manger, and he vowed to be with her until death separated them. Unfortunately life separated them and a few other princes showed up trying to take his place. He, the prince of the shed, had won her heart, but she spent fifteen years trying to make it to his castle. His castle was thousands of miles and several countries from her home which was located much closer to the shed, only a few miles of cornfields and soy bean acres away.

The Prince, Prince Luis, preferred the name Papa and the Princess, whom he called Gringa, had a bambino, la Niña, whom the Princess named Luisa.

Jill stopped writing and watched a tractor stirring up dust clouds in the distance. The puffs left a haze on her otherwise sunny horizon. She reread what she'd written and smiled contemplating the felt squares required to make this story come to life, for whom? Her grandchildren? No, not yet. Luisa was leaving in three months for college. So grown up at eighteen. Would she find her own prince and write her own story? Her la Niña was at church camp along with Mike and Jenn giving a presentation on their Spring Break trip to Haiti.

For the moment, when her husband, really a true prince in so many ways, was at work, she could sip her iced tea until time to meet Sadie and the attorney. Luis had instructed them to file the paperwork to give Sadie 'Power of Attorney' over Jill's affairs. Goddamned Prince Luis, never stopped running her affairs, life, love.

She needed to finish the journal fairy tale and pack for Africa, and the summer in Italy. Luis had promised a special two week trip in August at the end of their vacation. She wrote "and they lived happily ever after," then closed the journal.

ᴙξᴙ

She and Luisa sat on the plane to Majorca, Luis's end of the summer surprise. The Mediterranean spread out beneath them. August came too quickly. She had committed to one more year of teaching to be close to Ohio if Luisa needed her. Although, as Sadie had refreshed her memory, she recalled a freshman year that did not involve Lillian much and was really tough. She and Luisa had been having sex education discussions for a long time, but with no serious relationship, they were moot. Luisa wanted to go to college and figure out what to major in that would allow her to be most helpful to those in need.

Luis reminded her several times that the orphanage building would be ready, next month. Next month? September. When was a good day to tell Jack she wanted a divorce? How many glasses of wine had she drunk trying to figure out when? Luis said, "He's your husband, you make that decision."

Sadie said, "Sooner rather than later. Let him lose both of you at once, Luisa to college and you to Colombia."

The summer had gone…where? Africa with the four of them in June. They took pictures of sleeping lions and bathing elephants. David and Luisa resembled each other and she kept trying to match their features to see Luis in each of them. She decided their noses, cheeks, mouth, the lower half of their faces were shared. Luisa had a female version of the Ochoa nose. Luis stood in between them an arm around each. He made her keep all the pictures at Principessa. Principessa? She wanted to stay. When they returned the next summer, the attic would be finished. The previous owner had used it for storage, but now it housed dust, spiders and broken furniture. She and Luis talked to the architect who had worked on the first floors. On paper it would be guest bedrooms and organized storage without the bugs.

"Mom, what do you think those islands are?"

"Where Honey?" Jill peered out the window viewing the Mediterranean from 25,000 feet.

"See them down there?"

"I don't know maybe Corsica or Sardinia."

"Remember when I was twelve, and we went to the Azores?"

"Yes, they were amazing," Jill said.

"I think we need to go there again. There was that cute boy. Remember his father was a fisherman? Papa said a fisherman was a good man, 'a farmer of the sea.' Now can you see me marrying a fisherman? Papa is so old-fashioned, but I'm not sure I want to marry anyone. I don't know. What would he think if he knew Demetri still writes and talks of marriage?"

"I don't think your papa is interested in your marrying anyone, ever. He is much too protective. Of course your grandpa never approved of much of what I did. Anyway, Honey, you have a lot of time, first school, then work, then…"

"Mom, I know, but there is Haiti. I can't forget. Mike and I had a long talk that night we stayed up till sunrise. He said something… it really shook me up….He said he wondered if Michael were really his dad. I looked at him like he was crazy. He said his color was not quite like his mom. He's darker. He made me promise not to say anything, but I wanted to see what you would say."

"I guess I would say, maybe one day he can talk to Sadie about that, you know, if he has questions."

"Mom, what kind of answer is that? You know Aunt Sadie better than anyone, anyone! Is he like me? I mean we talked about it, Mom, if you and Aunt Sadie did the same thing."

"Same thing?"

"Yes, let another man raise us, a man we thought of as our dad."

"Luisa, you knew long ago. Sadie was married to Michael when Mike was born."

"In Germany, right?"

"Yes, at the base."

"Mike says Aunt Sadie never gives details of that day he was born, July Fifteenth, the day after Bastille Day. We went last summer, remember?"

"In the wee hours after Bastille Day, July Fifteenth. Sadie and me... in Germany. Michael had to leave to go back to Washington, DC. I stayed to help her. You stayed..."

"I know that part. Mike and I also talked about what we could do next in Haiti. I still dream of Angelique. Maybe next summer we'll volunteer for a month, not with the church just go to Reverend Isbell's mission. Maybe even join the Peace Corps."

"The Peace Corps? Mike has to finish high school, you need to start and finish college. A lot can happen in those years, a lot." Jill stared at the sea below. She must talk to Sadie; let her know what was coming.

"Papa helped the mission; he gave that money to complete the kitchen."

"Well, the church newsletter said an anonymous donor, 'a returned favor for a coyote in Texas.' The message is cryptic, but then Luis is mysterious."

"Mom, he couldn't really say his name. Luis Ochoa? In our church paper? Dad would have a cardiac arrest if he saw that name. Anyway, I asked Papa. I said for my graduation present, but he said no, I would get something special. He asked me what I wanted."

Jill nodded. "You didn't say a horse?"

Luisa laughed.

Luisa's inquisitiveness and assertiveness engaged her papa in subject areas Jill feared to tread. Luisa called him and asked for money; Jill spent it modestly and hoped he would understand.

The islands jutted from the dark water as they descended into Majorca. She mused about their walks along isolated beaches, waves crashing, even at the Azores. At those times between the sea and sand, she seemed closest to getting her question answered - who is Luis Ochoa? And now Mike is asking, "Who is my father?" Yes, Sadie, here we are back at SNAFU, situation normal all fucked up.

"Mom, what does Papa think of Ohio University?"

"I think he is okay with your choice. Last summer he tried unconvincingly to say you should go to college in South America."

ﺭﻐﺭ

On the hot August afternoon Luis stood outside his air conditioned office, staring. The Caribbean stretched out in all directions. The early Cartagenians built a great wall right at the sea's edge. This view of the old town and limitless blue sea was the selling point for his office space. The small deck area outside his office allowed only for standing and...he pulled a cigar from his pocket. The equatorial breeze blew the smoke into a dissipating vapor. From a small table he reached for a pair of binoculars. A large ship steamed toward the Cartagena port. Liberian flagged.

I hope Jill decides that next month alone in Indiana is enough and she'll leave Jack. I wish I could tell her to do that, say something, do something, but I've told her the timing is her decision. The ocean licked against the great wall and today the waves broke gently on the beach. Cartagena, Colombia, home, well one of several. Peace. Is it the peace before the storm? What does Jill tell me, I throw thunderbolts? He chuckled. Zeus. She may have other names when the next one comes.

Gina tapped on the sliding glass doors. "Sir, they are ready for you. Andy just called down from the roof."

Gina watched him; he knew she read his movements to manage his moods.

She said, "You'll be up there in maybe forty-five minutes or an hour, Andy said. Good Luck."

"With what Gina? This flight up to the mountains? Every time I go there, it is another damn problem and it has nothing to do with cleaning, drying or sorting coffee beans. I keep thinking it will be over. Mr. Angotti met with me several times this summer and it appears that New York is going to come through for me, and it won't be on the damn futures market. Angotti is calling it hedging. I'll leave it up to him. Let me get out of here, the mountains and then Majorca."

269

"Are you ready, sir?"

"As ready as I can be. I thought I would tell her when we were together in Italy, but the time was short, then Siddhartha came and they all left for Venice...I have now run out of time. The house is ready, the car, the school, the orphanage... Jill... it won't be easy." He shook his head, knowing his hard-headed Jankee would object, fight, and then the Grandma Caitlin reaction.

"You know her better than anyone, sir. I know you better than anyone; I put my money on you."

He smiled slightly and gave her a thumbs-up. "I'll call you, Gina. I don't want to talk to anyone. Two weeks in Majorca and two weeks away from the mountains, the war. Adios."

The helicopter ride took him into the heart of the Cordillera Central Mountains, to the camp. He needed to have only one more conversation with David and take one last look at Saldana. The helicopter took a circuitous route to a clandestine landing strip. Men covered in sweat and rounds of ammunition came out to greet El Campesino. The heavy weapons required to fight with the guerilla army of desperados. Fuerzas Armadas Revolucionarias de Colombia, FARC, false, goddamned Colombian Communists. Armed and destructive, killing people and calling themselves the Peoples' Army.

Land distribution? Always trying to take *my* land. Killing or scaring the hell out of *my* workers. Why? Kill them to protect them from me? The dead peoples' army, filling the rivers with blood and dead bodies! And the damned Raymond Sandy, useless American CIA.

The helicopter engine stopped. Luis removed his ear muffs. He shook his head, "Andy, I am..."

"I know, sir. One day... the war ended in Nam and one day this one will end."

"Reading my mind again, Mr. Marshall?" Luis smiled.

"It's the body language, boss. I see it the closer we get to this place, like some actor changing his clothes in the dressing room and getting ready for the stage."

Luis climbed out of the chopper, grabbed his briefcase, and then adjusted his gun in his waistband.

"Papa," David rushed to greet his father taking his hand, hugging him. They walked briskly ducking the helicopter blades. David was built like his father, thick through his upper torso. His hair was dark and wavy, but his dark brown eyes were like his mother's. When viewed from the back, father and son could be twins, David only half an inch shorter than Luis.

They walked into a small comfortable office. David had charts strewn across the table, the charts Luis requested. Luis perused the "x's" marking the most current hostilities and the "o's" indicating the coca labs. And then the "y's" where the CIA trained their special forces. He quickly saw what he wanted. "David, have these people been paid?"

"Yes and no, sir."

Luis puzzled, demanded, "Where is Jorge? Is he there now?"

"Yes, it is as you said."

"There are too many 'x's' too close to the village. What is the status of FARC? What are they saying to my people, promises or threats?"

"Papa, you need to call Jorge, he is right there, waiting on your call."

"David, I want you to go out there and tell him this: I want the village rebuilt whatever FARC promised, assure them more, whatever they threatened, I want it stopped. FARC will not be on my property! They need to understand they are trespassers, and trespassers will be killed."

"Yes, Papa, Jorge knows, we all do. Your men are out there every day. When will Jairo help us out?"

"I hope when I tell him. The planes will be here in the morning. Are we ready?"

"Yes, sir. Jorge will be in Bolivia tomorrow afternoon and with Cara De Pina on Thursday. Relax Papa, you will be back in two weeks. But you're bringing her home?"

"She'll be here. *Cuida mi gente.*" (take care of my people)

Luis and Andy boarded the chopper and headed back to Cartagena.

ᴚξᴚ

Jorge looked at maps of x's and o's and y's. Every day the same maps it never stopped. His "office" was a tent in the outlying area of El Campesino's finca. Sand bags surrounded the canvas half-way up. The generator enabled light and a refrigerator. A heavily armed man outside the tent allowed him an ability to sleep.

The bullets, the tracers, and the bursts of gunfire defined these outlying fincas. "Why did they insist on seizure by force?" Jorge asked himself the question with no answers. It ruined the crops. The farmers didn't want to risk losing their lives. Without their farms, vegetables for their tables and coca leaves for El Campesino, they would have no lives - they were farmers and soldiers involved in civil strife that had no meaning. They loved El Campesino. He took care of their problems, even a doctor and a clinic.

The coffee production was good, but the labs hidden in their fields gave El Campesino the real fuel. The business of the Colombian mountains was the cash crops of coca leaves, chemicals to process them and the men to make the mixture into the kilo bricks so prized around the world. The coca business, El Campesino tried to end it and then pursue it and then end it in favor of his love, coffee. The FARC wanted to control the labs to make the money for their revolution or to be paid a high price to stay away. El Campesino was not willing to do either instead choosing to kill them and protect his small farmers that picked his beans and grew the coca.

He and El Campesino had had this conversation many times, over coffee and assault weapons, over absinthe with ice and Cuban cigars, but no matter the scene of their talks it came down to the basics. There was coffee the social drink, bringing people together to solve problems, talk of love, plan futures, listen to fine music, then there was the cocaine. The drug that killed so many in its making, killed so many in its transportation, killed so many in its use. Did any of that make sense? They did not reach conclusions or answers to the insanity.

Jorge looked at the beaten man just brought to him by his body guard. The blood was dried on the peasant's dirty shirt. His blood crusted on the side of his face where the guard had crushed a cheek and ear with the butt of his gun.

"Scum, donde?!" Jorge cursed at him, "Scum! Quen!"

Two more men came into the dimly lit tent. Jorge scowled, "More scum? Now tell me *where* is your camp? *Who* is in charge?"

The limp body clung to life, the head resting on the chest, the leg twisted, contorted in a direction legs cannot go. Jorge kicked him in that leg. His whole body flinched with the pain, but he was unable to scream. Jorge reached for his gun, complete with a silencer, and pointed it at one of the other soldiers just brought to him. "Scum! Donde?!"

The man's eyes wide, begging, "No, please, amigo; please tell him Carlos, tell him! I know nothing. I swear. I know nothing."

The beaten form on the floor looked at his buddy, not speaking as Jorge pressed the gun to his temple. "Donde? Scum! Donde? Donde? Uno, dos…"

Carlos struggled to whisper the words, "Hernandez, plot #16."

Jorge turned to the other men from El Campesino's small military force. He ordered, "Alberto, Juan come with me! Diego, Jesus, take care of them!" He pointed his automatic rifle at the beaten man on the ground and the second one standing.

Hernandez plot #16 lay on the edge of El Campesino's farm. It was some distance from the coca labs and much farther from Saldana, but constantly contested. It also produced some of the best coca.

The heat was oppressive; the mosquitoes hummed, then silently took their blood. Stealthily the men moved in a circle around the small tent. The glowing light from the kerosene lamp cast shadows against the canvas. Several men sat huddled inside. Jorge listened long enough for the American intelligence man with him to hear what was being said, then nodded toward Jorge. Jorge quickly pulled the hook from the hand grenade just as El Campesino's men dispersed into the jungle mountains. The explosion blasted the thick night.

The burnt tent scattered in small pieces. Jorge and the others entered the smoky mess and looked for weapons. A metal box was half buried, but the marking clearly visible "Medusa." Jorge ordered the weapons brought with them. One more FARC camp, then the perimeter would be cleared. Medusa, the elusive, paid these men to do his bidding. Now confirmed. He would let El Campesino know as soon as he returned to the cinderblock building he called his headquarters. He'd come such a long way from when he and El Campesino had first met at a National Coffee Federation meeting.

What would become of their beloved Colombia? She seemed only to fester and smoke and destroy herself. They both built huge fortified haciendas in Cartagena. El Campesino hired him out of friendship and for his many years in the Colombian Army. And why hadn't Jairo sent any men out here to protect the coffee and the peasant farmers? Their minimal livelihood was so quickly destroyed by these marauding bands of guerillas, their quality of life ruined as the FARC created a state of fear.

ϡξϡ

The mountains of Majorca were blanketed in heavy tall ponderosa pines and juniper. Scraggly oaks lined the winding gravel road to the private residence that would be their home for the next ten days. The sea surrounded them. The house sat isolated on a mountain slope overlooking the Mediterranean. With stone floors, antique Castilian furniture, heavy wood doors and windows that opened to sea breezes and desert fauna.

Luisa was headed for college and Jill was going to divorce Jack. Yes, it was finally a good day to get divorced. Sadie had made an appointment with a high school classmate who had become a lawyer in Kokomo. She knew Jack would hire someone from Caylor. It would be the white water of rafting, then she could take a breath and spend the rest of her life with Luis. She shivered at the thought. Fourteen years with Jack, but no, Lillian, I cannot do another day. I have to follow my heart. Please talk to Dad; I know you are sitting up there on some heavenly porch swing watching my life. How many times have you reminded him that I am *his* daughter?

She dressed now to take a walking tour of some of the cathedrals. In her continuing art collection vocation, she had read of local artists in her guide book. A lunch in town, some Spanish wine, and then walking the streets of this historic island. Luis and Luisa had gone horseback riding.

Luis scheduled the day to spend some time with Luisa alone. After their African trip, the three of them, David, Luisa and Luis had all taken the train to Zurich from Florence. Luis said Mr. Angotti had arranged to meet them in Switzerland. Luisa came back with stories of serious men talking in low voices and signing her name to pages of…oh, she was not sure exactly.

Luis said, "She's eighteen, Jill, and she needs to have her name added to certain accounts already set up for David."

"Luis, why?"

"The account in Indianapolis is closed and Luisa needs to have access to money, in case."

"In case of what? Is it a trust-me-on-this-Gringa, event?"

"Si. Insurance, as we discussed, only this time for my daughter."

And now today, his insistence that they be together. He kissed her goodbye, then said, "We'll have much to discuss over dinner. Find a place you like, some Spanish wine and we'll see how it compares to ours. And a good view of the sunset." He smiled and used his fingers to massage under her chin.

They always had lively discussions at dinner, but something, was it in his tone? She shrugged, sometimes she nicknamed him her "international man of mystery." He laughed when she told him and said, "Bueno."

He surprised her frequently. Sometimes an exquisite piece of jewelry or art, sometimes a statement of insight into him and his reasoning. Her day was planned and dinner would be dinner.

Jill grabbed her straw bag and headed to the garage. A couple of scooters were part of the rental. She cruised down the twisted road to the cobblestone streets of Palma. The island had been fortified for thousands of years by empires needing shipping lanes. Pick an empire, English, Turkish, Spanish, Roman and she could see the art work and architecture they left on the island. Their own villa had been built with the huge stones designed to keep invaders from claiming the place. She pulled a tourist pamphlet from her bag, marking her route to the giant stone stairways of forts, outposts and cathedrals.

They had only two more days in this nurturing place. If she had a novel to write, she might come right here and imagine her characters, but school was starting soon and she would tack up Majorca postcards on her bulletin board. Was this her last year? Divorce Jack and finish the messiness of all of that. And go where he is....

"Yeah, Luis, bueno."

𐤃𐤔𐤃

Their bed was oversized. Jill watched him sleeping comfortably between the lace-edged sheets. His mussed curls and thick hands, scarred from years of working, "Who are you Luis Ochoa?" she asked herself. Vulnerable in his sleep state, but she knew he could sense her movements, even if she quietly left the bed. He slept alone in Colombia, so when they were together he was aware of her close presence.

He opened his eyes. She smiled. He used his arm to throw her on her back, "Do you want me, Gringa? Is that why you smile? You want your Papa? Tell me." She pushed on his shoulders as he rolled on top her.

"Tell me, tell me you want me."

"I want you Papa." She wrapped her legs around him as he pressed against her, responding to his familiar movements. Familiar, but so seductive, whispering she belonged to him, to hear his voice in her ear as he kissed her neck down to her breasts. This moment, these moments she cherished and replayed when she fell asleep at night next to a snoring Jack. She imagined the time when only Luis would snore next to her *every* night.

Luis rose from the bed and poured coffee. He carried a cup to her. Every morning in their living area, a breakfast tray was left as they both slept. The staff quickly learned their schedule for waking and sleeping.

"For you, Gringa. We need to talk." He pushed a wicker chair across from where she sat on the bed. "Last night over dinner, I wanted to talk, but Luisa kept talking of riding horses. She loves to ride. Do we need to make a stable at Principessa? No, she is only there in the summer. We could borrow a horse from someone. Tony, the vintner has a couple." He let out a breath, "Luisa belongs to me now."

"What, Luis? She has always belonged to you."

He put his finger on her lips; his eyes fixed on hers. Cold and intense.

She pushed his hand from her mouth, "You're scaring me, Luis. It's that look. Your I'm-about-to-tell-you-something-you-won't-like look."

"Zeus," he said.

She put her head down. He reached under her chin and lifted her face. A tear rolled down her cheek as she held her lips tightly closed.

"When we say goodbye, tomorrow, I'm taking Luisa with me. She will go to school in Colombia at the University of Santiago. We discussed this yesterday as we rode. She kept saying that she wanted you to come with her. I do not want you to speak until you think about what you want to say. You may come with us tomorrow. You may visit, but Luisa will no longer live in the United States."

"No! Luis, no! I don't have to think about that...no! My baby? No!"

The tears streamed down her cheeks, she wiped them with the back of her hand. He moved from the chair, and sat next to her on the bed. The room's lace curtains fluttered with a slight wind. She breathed spastically, "You make love to me, then you tell me this bullshit. Go with you? You know I can't go with you...last spring, Haiti, I could have told the school I wasn't returning, filed for divorce....Luis, now I

276

go back…and my baby?… How will she possibly survive where no one speaks English? She doesn't know anyone!"

Jill rose from the bed and walked to bathroom to get Kleenex. "Do I have a vote, can I say no?"

"No. She will know Spanish and she will attend bilingual classes. The faculty is bilingual. It is her birthright, to be a citizen of two countries. My house workers have been practicing English for years, waiting for my Jankees to come home with me. She has asked to go with me for the last how many years?"

"I think you know she wanted to visit, not to stay. Will she live with you?"

"She will have her own place at school, and while she learns Spanish she will be at my home in Cartagena. I have to guarantee her safety."

"What the hell does that mean? You're taking my baby to a place that requires you to say 'guarantee her safety.' You say it is a war zone in your mountains, and you want to put your daughter in a war zone."

"Jill, you insist on talking of these things that have nothing to do with your life."

She paced in front of him, pointing with the Kleenex in her hand, "No, not good enough! I don't understand your parental responsibility. I want to know where she will be and that nothing, I mean nothing, will happen to her. Taking my baby to Colombia has everything to do with my life."

"I want you to come with us, to complete what we started. The tomato harvest, I was leaving Caylor and you too. I told you then that we were joined forever and we are," he took her hands in his, "Gringa, I have always wanted you. You insist we live separately."

"Bullshit!" And she pulled her hands from his. "You insisted! This separation is your life, whatever that is. I don't know who the hell Luis Ochoa is, it stands between us. Always. I ask, you hedge, you leave, you close me out. I have accepted those conditions and yes, stayed happily on my little farm in Indiana. I'll take part of that blame, but we need to share it."

Luis closed his eyes, and then reached to pull her next to him. He held her against his chest. "You're right, Gringa. It has been an arrangement of convenience. My country is a dangerous place. Politics and farming make me a target."

277

"For whom?" she stiffened and inched away from him, "Why would you be in danger growing goddamned coffee?"

"It's more than that. It's not what it seems. You know the men that came to your school? I do business with men who want to eliminate me."

Jill leaned back to him and then squeezed him. "Eliminate? What are you saying? Kill you?"

He nodded.

"Stop Luis! Stop that talk! You are here in Majorca with us. We can go right back to Principessa."

"Not so simple, Gringa. I don't run from the basura, I don't hide from the scum. Run me out of my country? El Campesino? No. Their threat is my challenge."

She stopped hugging him and walked to the outer room to retrieve the coffee pot. She poured them more coffee.

"Here, Luis," she handed him a full cup. "This conversation," she pulled his arm, "let's go outside, smell the sea. Coffee and sea air, Mother Nature's healing formula."

They walked outside to the balcony and leaned against the worn concrete railing.

"Destiny intervened in our lives that August harvest in Indiana," Luis spoke, drinking his coffee. "I have tried within your parameters as you call them, but now that part is over. I want you to leave Jack. Now. It is time for *us*, now, Gringa. I want you to take care of my home, rub my shoulders when I come home from work. I want you to run your orphanage. You've never belonged to Jack. I have played this separation game as long as I can." He paused to rub her shoulders as he spoke, then held her against him. "Luisa is ready for this change; you can talk to her. I promised that I would have talked to you by lunch time. Come. Let's get dressed. We need to go to Palma to the place you told us of last night."

"Lunch? Will a bottle of wine make this better?"

"You and Luisa, out of Indiana, with me, finally in Colombia...No, not even wine could make that better."

She walked to the closet and picked out a dress, white with little yellow and red flowers; it had little buttons up the front. She plucked her red straw hat from a hat tree. Red, her tribute to Grandma Caitlin.

٢٤٢

The restaurant in Palma was filled with people from all nationalities. The abused cedar furniture was cushioned with sand and rose colored pillows that matched the overhanging bougainvillea. Fallen bougainvillea petals danced across the stone floor. Jill sat subdued, trying to swallow each bit of her fresh gazpacho. The ambience between father and daughter continued without her. The short distance between them belied the expanse in her heart.

"Señor Ochoa. Here in Majorca, what a pleasant surprise," the male voice unfamiliar to Jill startled her. She turned and stared at the sandy-haired man. He looked familiar to her, the nose, the lips, something she had seen before. His eyes glanced toward her, then quickly turned away. Luis rose to greet the stranger.

"Raymond Sandy, what a small world. Let me introduce you to my wife Jill, and my daughter Luisa, both Americanos like yourself." They laughed.

"Ah, Luis, you have hidden talents. What a beautiful family. Buenos Dias, Señora and Señorita Ochoa."

"How do you do Mr. Sandy? It is nice to make your acquaintance," Jill said. The smile, how did she know him? His name is Sandy and his hair is sandy. He was tall, youthful. Twenty? Late twenties? He wore an open collar shirt and khaki's, sandals. His lips, something about his mouth.

"Luis, are you busy or could we meet for a drink this afternoon?"

"Two P.M., but only briefly. I have two demanding women to keep happy." Luis ended the conversation. Raymond Sandy walked away.

"Luis, he looks familiar. Has he been to Principessa?"

"No."

ᴙξᴙ

Raymond Sandy, sat stirring his bourbon on ice with a maraschino cherry, "And so you see Luis, we know it is Mitsotakis, but we need someone who knows him personally; you do." Raymond Sandy drank the bourbon in one gulp.

279

"This is my vacation with my family. What have gringos done for me? The coffee price is too low. I'm going broke on my investment."

Raymond Sandy ordered another bourbon, "Investments...not my line of work. Favors, Señor, now that is my business, your business, the meeting...no one knows. I could order bourbon in many places."

"Si." Luis drank his absinthe, then pulled a cigar from his pocket and offered one to Raymond Sandy. He shook his head.

Thank god, Angotti was getting him out of this business with the basura Jankees. His money was with the Italian. Maybe he and Jill would live off the interest of Angotti's financial instruments. I did not sell you my soul, Raymond Sandy; one day we will never have to see each other again.

"I will do this, Señor Sandy. Now get the hell off this island!"

Chapter 14

Jill stared at nothing and masked her face with a Kleenex. The service in first class kept her in wine as needed. Luisa had held her mom a long time at the airport.

"Mom, this is what I want to do. It is time. We've talked about my leaving home and going to college. I'll be with Papa."

"Honey, I'm coming, but if you change your mind at any time, we can go to Italy or we'll figure out something."

"Oh, Mom, we've known this would happen. Just tell, Dad, Jack, oh think of something. I love him Mom, but he will feel betrayed. I can't make him feel any different. You must try."

Jill nodded and accepted her baby was grown and in a few weeks would leave her to go to college anyway. Her school was now in Colombia. And Luis had a special place for Jill, an orphanage to care for children. Luisa would actually see the facility when she arrived in Cartagena.

When they made love last night, the last time for how long? She didn't know, but his response to her changed. When she wrapped her legs around him not wanting them to be physically separated, he stayed on top of her resting on his arms and allowing her to hold him locked in her legs like a Celtic knot. And slowly, slowly he became limp inside her. He kissed her, "Not much longer, Gringa, and we won't be separating at the end of summer. *Hasta que la muerte no separe.*" (Until death separates us.) I wish you would come with us now." He didn't let her up to get a cleaning cloth, just gripped her against his chest.

Did she even sleep? His chest pressed tightly against her back. She closed her eyes to feel his soft chest hairs, he smelled her hair and used one arm to lock her against him. His soft penis pressed on her butt. Could they just stay this close? Not waking up, skeletons to be found by an archaeologist in some distant century. Who was this couple locked in love? And why?

The captain announced their descent into Indianapolis. No, not yet. Her thoughts seemed like some fantasy, but she had seen the blueprint for the orphanage. And this time she made him sprinkle his cologne on his handkerchief so she could take it with her. She pulled it from her purse and sniffed it, then placed her bag under the seat in front of her for landing. So now, Jack, I will tell you. Jack. She would never have to have sex with him again. No pretending, no faking orgasm or enjoyment. It is over Jack. Easy to sit here in a plane and say, but how? Thank goodness Sadie would be picking her up. They could stop for Bloody Mary's and figure out something, a plan.

She took the escalator down to baggage claim and there was Sadie, waving like she had not seen her in years. Well, it could have been; so much had changed in just two weeks. Sadie had flown out of Italy with Mike, Claudine and Kate just three weeks ago. Was Jill still on Europe time, vacation time, thousands of miles from cornfields? Canning tomatoes? Before or after I say Jack I want a divorce? Yes, it is a good day to get a divorce.

Jill collapsed in Sadie's hug.

"Where is Luisa? Mike wanted to come with me, 'practice driving' he said, but he has football practice. You know Coach Hamilton would be happy to throw them off the team if they miss one practice? Luisa, is she coming..."

"No, never. She stayed with him Sadie."

"Oh, jeezus, Jill, what is happening here? Divorce?"

Jill nodded.

"Well, it's time, been time, you know that."

"Sadie, you don't seem so surprised..."

"Well…I did get a call. Luis said you would have some news and please be on time picking you up."

"I can't go home. Jack will be devastated. It is his daughter, no matter what Luis says, he raised her, took care of her when she was sick, provided…oh god, I feel so guilty. Am I going to hell?"

"First, there is no hell. Some crazy popes made that up to scare people into giving them money. And second, Jack? You almost sound like you love the man. Now that is a surprise. You do want to divorce him, right?"

"Yes, but…I don't want to hurt anyone, deliberately, you know that. I kept asking myself on the plane what Henry would say?"

"Henry only wanted one thing for you - to be happy. He did everything to ensure you knew that. He even protected you in your old age. He is the only one I know who would set up a trust for someone when they turn sixty years old. He must have figured one of these men would be there for you, or at least you could attract another man, if need be, until you turned sixty." Sadie laughed.

"Why is my tragedy such a joke to you? My husband is about to kill me and you laugh. And besides all that, there is Mike."

"Mike?" Sadie stopped midway to baggage claim.

Jill told her about the conversation she and Luisa had flying into Majorca.

"Oh Sadie, what am I going to do?"

"I guess I should say the same thing. How about honesty? You need to explain it all. From start to finish. I need to explain it all. No, Mike will not understand, not yet. But Jack deserves the truth."

"Hector told me it is hard to improve on the truth. I agree, it is too much for a sophomore in high school to think about who his father is and how that all happened. But Jack…I have to tell him."

"Yeah, let him know what a deceitful temptress you've been all these years."

"Sadie, you tell him for me."

"Whoa, I am the best friend who takes care of one Latin lover, it is enough. I would and have done a lot of things in the name of this friendship, but telling Jack, 'no.' You're on your own. I have become the banker of record and the power of attorney; I will be answering questions, right?"

The drive from Indianapolis to Caylor went too quickly. The tomato fields, and soybean rows, corn as far as she could see, August, Indiana, another summer completed. Where will I be next summer? Oh, yeah, Dad, don't tempt the hands of fate. They drove with the windows down; the locusts had started to buzz. Maybe Jack will throw me out before I have to can all those damn tomatoes, and can for whom? Jack. No. I'm done, Jack.

"Jill, did you remember that we are to work in the church booth at the county fair tonight? We are supposed to be there from seven to ten. I know, did we really sign up for this shift? Jack won't expect you until late. Maybe you can sneak in and tell him in the morning."

"I can't. You make it sound so simple. I can't tell him the truth. No, the truth won't muster with old Jack," Jill said.

"Yeah, but what other choice do you have? A story couldn't be this good, there is no 'they lived happily ever after,' they didn't even live happily before."

ᴙξᴙ

Jack awoke to an empty bed. He went downstairs and fixed coffee. She had the fair duty, maybe she spent the night at Sadie's no her bags, where are her suitcases? He walked out of the kitchen; there they were in the hall, just two. Didn't they take six for the summer? Luisa probably took hers upstairs, or did she stay at Sadie's? Jill must have slept on the couch in her study. He carefully opened the door, knowing the old hinges squeaked when opened. Her study was as she left it except for all the mail he had put on her desk.

The kitchen was quiet as the coffee maker hissed and then dripped. Her favorite cup a ceramic brown and gold design from one of her students last Christmas. Her students? Finally, she'd be able to stay after school as she had lamented so many times after picking up Luisa. The two of them now, what would be different? Later at work for both of them, then more TV probably. Maybe she'd have time to read all those novels on her shelves; she bought them to read on her vacations, but then never took them with her. I guess she had other things to do. He poured her coffee with a spoon of cream. Now to wake her and Luisa and hear their newest summer stories. Maybe she slept in the guest room so not to disturb me if she and Sadie drank too much. He walked back upstairs with her favorite mug. I wonder if she will be happy that I talked Mary Ann into canning some of the tomatoes. She may not have to can tomatoes, only the two of us, how many tomatoes will we eat? Dinner for two? It will be quiet around the table.

284

The guest bedroom door was open and the bed was still made, throw pillows untouched, "Home is where your heart is." His heart was home, but where? He opened the door to Luisa's room, Luisa would be sound asleep. His daughter never woke at this hour and she would definitely have jet lag flying in from Majorca. Only a few more days and she'd be leaving for her new room at school. He inched the door open. There was Jill lying on Luisa's bed, staring at the ceiling.

"Jill…"

"Hi…" her voice, he thought not so happy.

"Luisa stayed with Jan after the fair? I know they were supposed to help…Jan has been calling, she kept saying Luisa would be home this week."

"No."

"Sadie has kidnapped her a few times. Here Honey, I made you coffee." He handed her the mug.

"Jack, sit down, please." She held the mug and took her finger and traced the tiny squares of the lavender quilt Lillian had made so many years ago. She followed each tiny stitch on the white appliquéd lace, then sighed heavily. "I want to tell…sorry wrong words. I have to tell you many things, most of them you won't like."

"Jill, did something happen to my daughter, is she okay?"

"She's fine."

"I don't understand, Honey, what?"

"Just let me talk. The beginning or the end? Dad always said, 'Start at the beginning, Princess, then we'll both be able to work on the end.'"

"What does Henry have to do with Luisa?"

"A part, but let me start at the beginning." Slowly her words came out on top of each other, building a story. She cried, but he didn't want to hold her…ten years ago…a visit at her school…Luis Ochoa…she wove the story of the man who had come between them. Luisa's father.

"We've been vacationing together…all these years. Henry helped with the money. He knew. Mom and Dad both knew, Sadie, Michael….Luisa."

"You've been sleeping with him? Your dad knew you were sleeping with another man? Not Henry, you are making that up. Not Lillian, you just said that because they aren't here! You're a liar!"

"Jack, it is the truth, it is all true except my commitment to you…"

"You're a liar! A liar!" He threw his coffee cup against the wall.

He didn't want to hear anymore of the horrible sickening love affair with a migrant worker. The past had never been left, he had kept his promise, never, never did he bring that man's name into their conversation. She never loved him, only this man from where? A broken down truck in Texas? It is where they all came from and traveled to, no home.

Luisa? Not his daughter, yes, his daughter, but she's mine, she has my name, Luisa Jones. This is her room, her bed. She's going to college next month. They'd paid her tuition...

"Luisa? You made her lie with you, you made her tell this story....My little girl... not a liar like her mother! No! No! No!"

He ran from the room. He couldn't look at the evil lying in Luisa's bed. She had destroyed his life, a liar! He wanted to shake the devil who had shown up, shake her and get his wife back. The she-devil needed to leave.

He ran out of the house toward his tool shed... the envelope from Colombia...Sadie a part of the deceit...Henry....Lillian...all these years...never said his name, never a mention...of Luis Ochoa to Jill. He'd kept his promise to the liar. The sweat dripped from his face, he paused to rub his forehead and bent over, his chest hurt. He sucked in air and tried to talk, then his left arm, he could not feel it...take a breath...the wall. He slid down, "Ji..."

Electronic monitors, a light blue room, Beau stared at him, and there was Jill. He closed his eyes; his wife had come back. He tried to smile, but he couldn't feel his face, not quite.

ᴙξᴙ

The flight to Greece had not been on his agenda. Luis wanted to fly from Florence to London then home, time to introduce his daughter to her homeland. But Raymond Sandy made this circuitous route necessary, requiring him to introduce her to a different set of his business acquaintances.

Luisa had surprised him with her reaction to leaving her mother. "Papa, it will be okay," she kept repeating as they rode horses in Majorca. "Mom will come. She owes it to Da...Jack. I know you frown at the mention of his name, but he is a part of our lives. And yes, Papa, I do love him. I love him and you. Love isn't a finite amount, because you love someone this much doesn't mean you love someone else less. Please understand. Please, por favor, there I'm learning Spanish." And she had nudged her horse to take off in a gallop.

Watching her dust, he had to smile. She was impulsive like her mother; he recognized that quality at an early age and over these last few years he saw himself, the determination to try new things and meet new people.

Jill's sadness was the hardest to bear. He had listened once again to her parameters, "settle accounts, her trust inheritance, the divorce and the farm," all legitimate concerns that had no relevance in his world. As her plane left for London, taxiing down the runway, he had his arm around Luisa, but his heart hurt, something was wrong. Intuition was Jill's forte, but letting her go…he wanted to have his arm around each of his Ochoa women, heading to a world he controlled. Impulsive? Yes, but not to leave her Hoosier world behind so suddenly. Maybe at eighteen to get in a broken down truck with a migrant, but at thirty-six…she needed to…her parameters.

Raymond Sandy *was* taking them to Athens. Luis would present his daughter to the confluence of Mediterranean power. Raymond Sandy threaded their way through Athens to a street of boutiques, and then the three of them, shopped for Luisa. Raymond insisted on a tiny black dress. Luis preferred the long burka of Muslim women, but knew his protective father response held no sway with his young adult daughter. After a tough negotiation, they settled on a fitted chemise, short above her knees, capped lace sleeves, and with Sandy's urging, a dainty teardrop shaped diamond on a white gold chain, and a narrow white gold bangle bracelet. The shoes were black leather, and Raymond Sandy had picked them out. "Too high, heels," Luis had objected. She had her mother's cheerleader shaped legs, now exposed and accented.

"I'm curious Señor Sandy, where did you learn this fashion advice for women?"

"My mother, New York City." He winked at Luisa as Luis frowned.

To see his little girl change into a very attractive young woman was a nightmare. Damn Raymond Sandy, making this transformation, another reason to hate the CIA.

In her fitted dress with her long dark curls hanging softly on her shoulders, they walked into the elegant dining room. As soon as the three of them stood in the door, they garnered attention. Luisa held her hand on his arm, but he knew he would walk away and let her stand alone.

The tables were set formally in crystal and heavy blue painted china with gold trim. The gold dinnerware matched the gold chrysanthemums on every table. Each engraved gold napkin ring held a white linen napkin embroidered in the same style as the ring - a large garish "M." Waiters dressed in white, wearing gaudy gold lamé vests carried gold trays with glasses of champagne, also a warm gold color.

Raymond Sandy talked to Luisa.

"These men have so much money, they use it to light their cigars."

"Why would they do such a stupid thing?"

"I guess to let everyone know they can."

"What you just said doesn't make much sense," Luisa said.

"You're right. Most of what they do makes no sense, but it makes them a lot of money. And that is how they achieve respect in their world."

"Have you been to Haiti, Raymond?"

"Briefly. In and out, which is the way I see most places."

"Who are you exactly? A friend of my father's, or a business associate?"

"Both maybe, depends on his mood," Raymond said and smiled.

Luis watched every move Sandy made. His sole responsibility was to make sure Luisa drank no champagne and no one spoke to her unless Luis introduced her first. Sandy walked with her if she moved, and Luis stared if they talked too much to each other.

Luis and Raymond Sandy wore white dinner jackets and slacks.

Luis walked to up to Luisa, "How do you like this party?"

"I'm just watching, Papa. I do like the white suits. You look like…"

Sandy interrupted, "We look like walk-ons for Casa Blanca."

Luisa laughed. She had a cheerful and infectious laugh.

Raymond Sandy making her laugh? No. He shook his head familiar with the French phrase that if you made a woman laugh, you had already bedded her. No. Luis shuddered at the position he had put her in, goddamned CIA.

On the flight to Greece, she had asked many questions mostly the "who" and "why" of their trip. He chuckled and said she must listen to the conversations at the party, then many of her questions would be answered. He identified the people in the reception as business associates.

The host, Mitsotakis, was effusive, stout, tan and dressed in the white formal attire required of his guests. Some spoke Spanish others Greek or Italian. Luis translated as needed and he instructed Sandy to also translate. Sandy knew Greek. The mixed crowd of government officials and international CEO's acknowledged Luis. He introduced Luisa as his daughter and Raymond Sandy as her escort and translator. Mitsotakis moved from group to group tracking who was standing with whom. Luis knew this was his method of determining who was actually doing business with whom.

"Ah, my friend, El Campesino. This pretty woman you brought with you, where did you find her? Not in those mosquito infested mountains…"

"You should visit my mountains, and see how Mother Nature has blessed Colombia, Mitsos," Luis said.

"And leave this magnificent blue Grecian Sea? No, I'll leave those mountains to you." Mitsotakis shook his head, smiling.

Luis introduced Luisa and Sandy to the fun-loving Greek who had done Luis' shipping for many years. They continued laughing at past exploits of docking in a harbor that was unable to unload anything; of coffee that sat so long waiting to be received it increased in value. When Mitsotakis mentioned an evening that they shared drinks and women, Luis walked him away from Luisa. He ambled over to a few OPEC ministers who greeted him warmly. Mitsotakis transported much more oil than coffee, but all were his friends on this evening.

Luis wanted to be closer to monitor the conversation between Luisa and Raymond Sandy, but he also needed to be a part of these other conversations. Luis moved from OPEC ministers, to arms dealers, and then back to Raymond Sandy and Luisa.

Raymond Sandy was tall, built like a soccer player who could easily take care of any unwarranted advances. But Luis stared, knowing the biggest advance could come from Sandy himself. He was at least ten years older than his daughter. He shot a stern glance at Sandy then went to join his friend Fulaij.

Luis recognized Ahmed Fulaij standing by himself. They had not talked since their last interaction- importing arms into Colombia to enable his men to carry on the business of his mountains. Fulaij spoke quietly in the spirited party chatter. He wanted Fulaij to meet his daughter and signaled for Sandy to bring her over to where they stood.

"El Campesino, a surprise. Are you here for business or pleasure?"

"Business, it is hard to avoid when Mitsos has a party. I want you to meet my daughter, Luisa Ochoa."

"How do you do, Miss Ochoa? Such a beautiful young woman, mountain grown like your wonderful coffee, Luis?"

"No, she is beautiful like her mother. I can't claim any responsibility. I am just a rough cut campesino. She will be studying in Colombia, but as an American."

"Thank you for the compliment, Mr. Fulaij. My mother is American from a state called Indiana."

"Oh, yes, I know Indiana, a great agricultural state." He turned to Luis and continued, "I didn't realize you had such a strong connection to what do you call them, 'Jankees.' But you are a man who is always a mystery, like the veiled women of Damascus; we never know what we don't see." He looked at Luis and nodded.

Cartagena was thousands of miles from Mitsotakis, but Luis knew Mitsos would call in a few days inquiring of his American friend, Luisa's escort, Raymond Sandy. Americans were unwelcome on Mitsos' isle. They wanted to control the politics of the eastern Mediterranean. The Greek shipping magnate only tolerated Sandy's presence because of Luis. But the *raison d'être* of the American stranger to Mitsos' group were inevitable. In this conclave Americans' presence needed to be explained; suspicious minds would want to know.

Luisa impressed him in her debut with the power brokers that would become her milieu. Spending summers in Italy had helped her immensely. She was comfortable in the presence of people from all over the world. And she was curious; he'd encouraged her to learn more about every place they went. The trip to Zurich with her and David surprised him. She walked into a Swiss bank as if she had been making that trek all her life. Mr. Angotti was impressed with how much Italian she knew. She was serious, calm, and too relaxed now with Raymond Sandy. Meeting Mitsos' was a surprise for all of those brokers. He knew they would talk of the young American woman, Luis Ochoa's daughter. Fulaij was right, he did have surprises.

Now they sat in first class 35,000 feet above the sea headed for home.

"Papa, I have a question. I know you said if I listened I would have my questions answered. This one, I don't have an answer. Remember when your friend Mr. Mitsotakis held my hand to kiss?"

"Si."

"He had a ring on with a gold etched, Medusa. I learned of the snake-haired lady last year in Greek mythology class."

"Si."

"Well it made me think of something else, a while ago. When we had our private cruise, after Grandpa and Grandma died…"

"Si, Luisa, what?"

"One afternoon, Demetri took me way below the deck to show me some 'treasures' he had been picking up in his travels."

Luis frowned.

"Stop, Papa. I want to tell this story. Anyway, I looked at his stuff, but we sat on these long wood boxes and each one had this same picture, the snake-haired lady. I never thought about it until I saw your friend's ring."

"Are you sure of this, Luisa?"

"Yes, I wanted to ask Demetri, but he talked and I forgot because he…."

"He what?"

"Papa, don't be mad, but he kissed me."

"And what did you do?"

"Oh…I kissed him back, but then I was scared and said, 'Let's go.'"

"And?"

"And that's all."

"I should have thrown him overboard when I had the opportunity. I told your mother, I told her no, not that hard-headed Jankee, pen pals and all that nonsense."

"Papa, Mr. Mitsotakis doesn't like you, does he?"

He shrugged, "Luisa, he is polite to me, he transports my coffee beans. He respects me and knows people important to me. We do business together, share a cigar, a business relationship."

"Mr. Fulaij, now he was so respectful of you. I think he was genuine, not a phony."

"Not 'a phony,'" he chuckled. He reached over and patted her hand. She read them better than he thought. Now what did she think of Raymond Sandy. Oh well, Sandy was gone and Luisa was sitting next to him flying to Cartagena. My daughter going to her home.

291

David was waiting in the limousine. *"Mi hermanita Chiquita.* (my little sister) Hola."

They hugged. David's big bear hug was like her papa's. She'd met and become acquainted with her older brother when they all went to Africa. He wore his hair short and dressed in jeans and a windbreaker over a plain t-shirt. Many of her friends had older brothers in high school. Now that she'd met him, she wished he had been a part of her growing up years. He was thirty-three, so he would not have been around too much, but to know he was there if she needed him would have been comforting.

Africa was National Geographic. The lions and elephants close to their jeep tour, but her favorite was the cheetah. They watched as he killed a gazelle. She squeezed her mother's hand seeing the gazelle fight for life, but David put his arm around her and insisted she was witnessing the laws of the animal kingdom. She was happy her papa had chosen to take them all to view, learn and know what life is like for the wild African animals even as she flinched at this death struggle.

She listened now as David and Luis discussed business quietly in Spanish. She tried to understand, but they spoke too quickly. The tone seemed urgent.

David leaned over the seat, "Luisa, are you hungry? Would you like a cheeseburger and french fries? I remember you kept saying that was what you wanted when we were in Africa."

"Yes, please. We had something wrapped in a grape leaf and lamb on a stick at the Greek party. Then there was airplane food. Yes, a burger and fries would be great!"

"Luisa, you will be eating more rice and tortillas..." Luis said.

"Si, Papa, but right now..."

David pulled up to a small restaurant that advertised American food. He went in and picked up her burger and fries. As she ate in the car, David drove through Cartagena to take Luis to his office. She took bites of fries and stared at the brightly colored houses and high rise buildings under construction. Some of the streets reminded her of New Orleans, the people, street vendors with carts of fruit and paper flowers, shoes, so many exciting colors in clothes and food. She realized she looked like the people she saw, dark curled hair, and many shades of brown skin.

Luis stepped out of the car and said, "Luisa, don't ask David too many questions."

As soon as the door closed Luisa peppered him with questions, "David, Who is Raymond Sandy?"

"A business associate."

"Not a friend?"

"No."

"Does Papa own that building where we let him out of the car?"

"You'll know all of his real estate holdings soon."

"Do the people at his house speak English? When we were in Curaçao and the driver spoke only Spanish or…I don't remember the name."

"Papiamentu."

"Yes, that's it. Have you been to Curaçao?'

"Yes. How many more questions?" David smiled, shaking his head.

"Okay, one more, one more…if I go shopping, do people speak English?"

"You'll go shopping with someone who speaks Spanish and English."

They drove past enclosed areas with gates right next to the road. The farther they drove, a long time from leaving Luis at his office, the houses were separated by longer and much higher fences, with barbed wire on top of large stucco or concrete blocks. They eventually turned off the main road.

"David, one more, please, do you have a girlfriend?"

"Too many questions. But I must answer one you didn't ask. Papa is well-known in the government of Colombia. As a government official he is provided with security personnel."

"You mean soldiers or secret service men like our President?"

David stopped the car and two men dressed in green uniforms with short sleeves approached the car. David told her they needed to know exactly what she looked like. David left the car first, then signaled for her to get out. She had dressed in jeans and a loose shirt to travel the three plane rides from Greece hours ago. She'd pulled her hair into a ponytail, but now yanked the band holding her thick hair. David introduced her, then they both climbed back into the car. The gates opened onto the main entrance of wrought iron arches. They drove up a

293

winding road to a huge house, one story stucco with long wings, not like Sadie's house that was three stories tall.

٣६٣

Rushing by Gina, Luis walked into his office, "Sir, how was your trip? The Americans have been in and out of here all week. It seems a man was killed who was working both sides, and explanations must be made. Señor Sandy says he is at this number and will stay until you call. And Jill called and said she needed to talk to you and Luisa. Jack is in the hospital. He had a heart attack."

He grabbed the handful of messages she had for him. Gina called after him, "Mitsos has been in touch with us, he said, 'This goes beyond coffee' and you would know. And he said Luisa looked Mediterranean as if she belonged on a Greek isle and he was happy you brought her."

"He said he was happy…"

"Yes, Luis, he said he…"

"I heard! Get Jill on the phone! She is probably at Siddhartha's."

٣६٣

Aug. 31, 1979
Cartagena, Colombia
Dear Mom,

There is much to tell you. I know I've only been away from you for two weeks, but Papa has me doing all these things. It took me a week just to figure out how to get around "the compound" as Papa calls this place. I can hardly wait until you get here. It is huge like a hotel in some ways. There is just too much to say in one letter, but I have to describe my bed. It has iron posts at each corner and they meet like a circus tent in the center, and I have this lace stuff for mosquito netting that I close all around me when I go to sleep. Well, really it is Josephina who closes it when I'm ready to go to sleep.

294

Papa makes me learn Spanish. I have a tutor, Señor Rodriguez-Gacha, who comes every morning. Yuck! And he said I must translate this entire letter in Spanish for him to check my work this morning. Mom, please come. Papa is a perfectionist, but I love my brother David. He is so sweet. He was raised by his grandma; he calls her "Mamacita." She lives on the compound, but she is very old and frail. I spend time with her in the afternoon by the pool. She likes to watch me swim. The pool is a nice size, about the same as Sadie's. Gosh, I wish Mike were here. I miss you all so much. I'm looking forward to talking to all of you. Papa says school starts in one week and I must know Spanish. Buenos Dias, Madre. David knows English, but he talks Arabic, too.

How is Dad? I know he hates me. Mom, what should I do? I love Dad. Please tell him that, if you think he will listen. Papa says, oh, he gets angry if I say much about Dad, so I don't.

Mom, I'm calling Sadie's Friday afternoon, September 7. Papa says I can't call the farm. And I didn't argue with Genghis Khan (ha! ha!)You understand, Mom.

Jill and Sadie sat at Sadie's kitchen table. Sadie had made chocolate chip cookies for the girls when they returned from school. She served them to Jill with coffee. Jill brought the letter and read it to Sadie. Jill had cried when the letter from Luisa first arrived. "Sadie, why did I ever commit to teach this year? I want to go now."

"Now you get to be a nurse, remember? Jack needs you. Hey, maybe Luis will pay for a nurse, send someone up here from Colombia."

"Guilt is a helluva thing. Why am I suddenly getting a case of the guilts?"

"Because you haven't bothered to be sincerely regretful for all the things you've done wrong."

"Quit!"Jill said.

"I refuse to be part of your pity party. You'll be there in nine months and what? What about Sadie, have you even considered my feelings?"

"I'm coming for drinks whenever I get ready. Luis can afford it."

"Money is not a problem. Control is what you need to look out for. I imagine your leash won't be very long."

"Like I'm his pet? You are full of support today. When will Mike be here? Luisa will call soon."

"Any moment, he said he'd come home right after football practice. You know when you came back from Haiti, I had the feeling this young man had a crush on Luisa. Something was different. You don't think anything happened after the prom do you?"

"No, the connection seems…I don't know when it started, but I know something happened in Haiti, the night I wasn't there."

"This month that she has been gone, he has completely changed. He talked and talked about playing varsity football this year and getting a car. I asked him if he wanted to go look at Gerard's car lot; the new models are coming out. Michael promised him if he made it on the dean's list he could pick one. Jill, I could not get him interested. The boy is love sick. And it is one disease, I am very familiar with."

The phone rang; Jill looked at the clock, 4:30P.M. Right on time. Sadie answered the phone. Thank goodness she had a regular phone installed in the kitchen and only used the old hand crank one for decoration.

"Buenos Dias, Sadie," Luisa spoke. Sadie talked briefly, then said she would hang up so Luisa and Jill could talk privately. As Jill walked to the library to pick up the phone, Sadie said, "Are you going to be my daughter-in-law?"

"No, *Aunt* Sadie. What gave you that idea?"

"Oh, curiosity. I think your mom is on the phone. I do miss you, Sweetie! You can write me, too, not just your mom."

"But Aunt Sadie, where is Mike?"

"He knows you're calling and he'll be here. It was the last thing he said when he left for school."

"Okay, Mom, your turn. What do you want to know? Papa said you'd have a long list of questions and I should only answer half of them."

"Do you like it?" Jill rattled off all the questions about Luis's house, Luisa's everyday life, and then asked, "Where is Luis?"

"I can't answer that one, Mom. Don't try to think of another way to ask. Have I gotten any letters from Demetri?"

"Yes, what do you want me to do with them?"

"Put them inside the letter you send to me. Oh, Mom, I miss you so much. Papa has servants that do everything. I'm teaching Maria Santa Maria, his personal cook, how to make chocolate chip cookies. How is Dad? Is it my fault? I feel like my just disappearing...I never meant to hurt him."

"Not you, Sweetie, just me. I lied for many years and even to myself, I didn't love him as I should have. I took him for granted. He deserved someone who would have returned his love, a true love. I cheated him of that.

"But not you, not even for a minute, only me. I lied and asked others to do the same. I loved Luis at a very early age, yours actually, eighteen. You asked me long ago how I loved two men, and the words escaped me, but I loved only one. I cared for Jack, he was a decent man as your grandpa reminded me so many times. We will talk about love and men when I move down there.

"Jack took early retirement because he was getting too tired. I really think the farmhouse is too much for him, but he refuses to consider anything that I say. He is still very angry, but won't say that. He snips at everything I do. His family hates me, so I haven't talked to any of them since he left the hospital. It's kind of like living in hell."

"He hates me, too?"

"He won't let me say your name. I told him we need to look at apartments closer to town where it would be easier for him to manage. I wish this school year were over, but I feel so responsible for his pain. I just can't abandon him now."

"Gringa?"

"Luis? You're home? How is my baby?"

"Which should I answer first? Luisa? She is not a baby. You would think she has always lived with a house full of servants, but she misses your cooking. Next week she leaves for school. She will be able to call you at the farm from her place. I'm sending Josephina with her to cook, clean and do her wash. She doesn't seem to have these skills. Why?"

"Because she had me."

"I must go Gringa; your daughter tugs at my sleeve to give her the phone. *Te quiero y te amo.*"

"Mom, you know what he said?"

"It sounded like what he whispers when we are alone."

"Oh, Mom, he told you he wanted you and loved you. Is Mike home yet?"

"You mean this big sweaty football player, standing here waiting for me to get off the phone. I love you. Call me as soon as you get to your apartment."

⁊ξ⁊

Luis's pool was made of cream colored tile with a dark blue decorative border. The patio area of slate and tile was shaded with large palms and avocado trees. Mamacita sat in her wheel chair with a lightweight blanket over her lap. She smiled as Luisa swam. Luis in swim trunks dangled his legs at the edge of the pool. Luisa encouraged him to jump in, but he did not.

"Come Papa, let's race. Two laps back and forth, come on. You going to let your daughter challenge you without rising to the challenge? Come on Papa."

He jumped and swam to the far end. She caught up with him as he flipped to turn for the return lap. They arrived at the edge of the pool at the same time. Mamacita laughed.

Luis stepped out and dried himself off and coughed, then coughed harder. He shook his head and rubbed his hair with the towel. He donned a terry robe and held one up for Luisa, "Come, my fish. It is almost time for dinner. We need to talk about school next week."

"I want to talk about something else. Why did it take you so long to find Mom? She said she went to look for you every summer at the tomato farm, but you weren't there."

"The season ended as they all do, but when I returned to San Antonio, I received the letter from Mamacita. I had had many years of waiting. She wrote, 'Now, Luis, time to come home.' And I did, but..."

Josephina brought some mango punch out to them. They sat opposite each other at a glass-topped round table with metal chairs. The seats were canvas covered in the dark blue color of the border in the pool. Luis stood and walked to a bar at one side of the pool. He opened a box of cigars; lighting one he came back and sat down.

"But, Papa? You started..."

"It's a long story, but...okay no more 'buts.' When I left America, I was never so happy to leave any place except when I left Veracruz, but I knew...that a part of me stayed." He pulled deep inside to answer the pointed question of his daughter. "I vowed in the church at your grandparents' funeral to make you a part of this life, my life all the parts. What I do, my business…"

"And is Raymond Sandy a friend or business associate?"

He puffed his cigar. "Your mom always asks who I am. For you Luisa, you will know the answer to that question." He blew smoke rings, "But not all at once. I need you to be trained in business, at school and my business. David and you will one day…."

"Papa, I don't even drink coffee."

"Okay, let's start there." He stopped and signaled Josephina to bring two cups of coffee.

He wanted her to know him and his motivation for doing the things that he did. He accepted the imminence of his death. It could happen at any time, Luisa needed to know him and not the one-sided story she would be exposed to from his detractors.

"Your mother, who did drink coffee when I met her, had reached in, grabbed my heart. I have thought about this over the years because…what is the best way to say this…I have met many women. Many. I made a commitment to your mother and I am a man of my word. She did not know when we said goodbye that only time would separate us. But from the day we said goodbye which was the day you were conceived, I considered us bound. Time passed and I returned to her. But she was married…"

"To my da…Jack."

He frowned. "I know you are in pain over leaving Jack, but your mother insisted. No, I will not blame her; we both agreed staying at your Hoosier farm was best for you. Stability. We both wanted that most of all."

"Why do you want me here, now?"

"This is truly your home. You are Colombian."

"No, Papa. I am American and Colombian."

"Si, but you will…"

"Why do you say, 'you will'? I have a mind, I can make decisions." She looked at him frowning.

No one talked to him like this dark-haired young woman who sat facing him. He took a drink of his coffee and puffed on the cigar.

"Papa, did you ever think about quitting smoking. You know it's not good for you, tar, nicotine. Yes, I learned about all that in health. I heard you cough when you finished swimming. I think you need to think about it. Maybe I should say, *you will* quit smoking."

He shook his head and smirked. "Angel, I must leave and go to the mountains in the morning. David and Andy will fly you to Cali to school. I have business…"

"You use that word for many things."

Luis stopped. What could he say? She watched him, waiting. She took her finger and drew lines on the water condensed on her punch glass.

"I do business on several levels; each carries its own particular problems. In the mountains, I own vast amounts of land that are used to grow coffee. The people who work for me are constantly encouraged to revolt against el hombre de siempre. (man of always) The people who encourage them are scum, but they are violent. They only understand the bullets and guns."

"Papa, you carry a gun when you go to the mountains?"

"I must travel with a small army. You are familiar with war?"

"I have studied wars and seen many movies. There is a war in your mountains?"

"Si."

He knew he had just thrust his most sacred love into a scene that marked her. Her protection must now come from knowing, not ignorance. She could not fathom the depth of danger in her knowledge, but her education would come in the building blocks of experience, one piece after another in no particular order. As much as he would have liked the role, he could not be God.

Chapter 15

His beloved Saldana, he'd recently white washed the stucco and the wrought iron planters were brimming with bright red and yellow flowers. The wood window boxes overflowed with the pinkish red flowers he liked, but could never remember their name. The trees Mamacita planted years ago grew tall in the back area. The tile wraparound porch with his favorite wicker chair provided peace, but not today. Luis looked at the beauty of his hacienda with its well manicured lawn and imagined that this idyllic scene provoked the same kind of peace in Pearl Harbor just before. But beyond Saldana's well fortified walls was something evoking a scene from, what did Luisa say? A war movie.

He locked Saldana's metal gate fashioned like a medieval door and walked to his cinderblock headquarters. The war room building was reinforced with sand bags and situated a hundred yards from Saldana. He was surrounded by several armed men, all dressed in camouflage fatigues, some with assault weapons, others with just handguns in belted holsters. El Campesino listened as David explained the most recent event.

"Papa, they killed Jorge at the last raid, the last plot, the one where we have so much trouble, Hernandez #16." David spoke in rapid spurts.

"Any other details I need to know?" he glared at David, "Where are the government soldiers?"

"I've waited, but…."

"Jairo said he would have them out here!" Luis banged his fist on the rough drawing resembling a pirate's treasure map.

"We have waited for two days, Papa, nothing. We have sent twelve men out there and we have fifteen more ready to go with your direction."

"Let's go see for ourselves what the hell is going on! I will deal with Jairo when I get back!" Luis grabbed an assault weapon and ordered the men to grab rounds of ammunition from large metal boxes that were clearly marked "Property of the United States." Five of the men jumped into a waiting helicopter. Andy Marshall looked at Luis who climbed in beside him and waited for him to signal "time to go."

The helicopter trip was short. After landing, several more men forming Luis's small army met the occupants of the helicopter. As they approached the outlying area, Luis barked instructions, "Move out. Get anyone you can find! We need some witnesses! Someone who knows what happened!" He tried to be louder than the chopper.

The small community of farmers recognized El Campesino. They ran up to him, talking excitedly at once. Several pointed to where the guerillas had come from and then gone. Luis stopped when he saw Rafael. Luis had known Rafael for many years. They stood as friends and Rafael called him Campo, a shortened version of hombre del campo. (man of the country) He was dressed in a new shirt, pants and shoes.

"El Campesino, gracias." He waved his hand over his clothes. "My wife said so much good from El Campesino. She is cooking on her new stove."

Luis asked Rafael to follow him away from the others.

"Rafael, what has happened out here?"

Rafael spoke in a hushed voice, in English, as most of the others knew no English. "The guerillas had come to recruit the peasants get them to say where you were, '¿Dondé esta El Campesino?' then ¿Dondé esta Jorge?' over and over. Then the bullets to scare us.

Finally," and Rafael whispered in Luis's ear, "Diego got scared with the guns, he's young, Campo, and told them where Jorge was. Jorge fought hard and killed several of the guerillas. The others fled into the woods. Cowards. They yelled, 'Medusa,' Campo, but I didn't recognize them. Strangers to all of us here."

"We will find them," Luis said. "David, take them in the direction Rafael has said, find this basura with the large slash down his face, Diego," Luis spit as he said his name, "I want him brought to me!"

"Campo, the guerillas seemed only to want to kill Jorge, or you. They said, 'don't bother the peasants.'" Rafael took his straw hat off and wiped the sweat on his forehead, "Please, be careful. They asked Jorge, well, they said your name to all of us. We looked down, kept picking cherries."

David and two of Luis's soldiers went to Diego's small house and brought him to Luis. Over and over again, Luis demanded the name of the guerillas, until the man said, "Medusa." Luis shot him. He handed his gun to David, "I want this problem over! They will learn to stay off property that doesn't belong to them. Trespassing is forbidden on El Campesino's land!"

Luis boarded the helicopter. He and Andy flew alone to Cartagena, leaving the small army to help David. When he jumped from the plane, Gina was waiting for him. They walked hurriedly to the roof top elevator. She waited until the door closed, then spoke, "Sir," she paused.

He looked at her, "Gina, your face, what? I just left a goddamned mountain filled with basura! Say..."

She took a deep breath. "Sir, Jill called."

"Worried about Luisa, no doubt. Did you tell her Luisa's phone number? Luisa has given her that number. Was it something else?"

"She's at Siddhartha's waiting for you to call her." Gina looked down, allowing her long dark hair to cover her face.

"What?! What are you saying? What time is it there?"

Gina looked at her watch, "9:15A.M., Indiana time."

"Why isn't she at her school teaching? Get her on the phone, then call Jairo! And I don't care if he is in a meeting, or screwing his wife, I need to talk to him, now!"

٣٤٣

A knock at the farm door aroused Jack from a catnap in front of the nightly news. For a moment in his disorientation, he could not understand why Jill did not answer, then fully awake, he remembered she was at a PTA meeting. He opened the door to see two men in suits, looking stern and foreign on his porch. He had to use his best effort at speaking to ask who they were.

"Yes, who...are...?" His tongue was thick and he let out a breath.

"Is Jill Jones, here?" The question was curt.

"Who...who are...who are you? What do you want?"

"Can we come in?"

"Jill's not here, now."

They pushed past Jack.

"Wait..stop...what do you want?...Who are you?"

They looked over him, "When will she be home?" They walked into the hallway and stared at pictures on the wall. "When? We need to talk to her as soon as possible?" They pointed to Luisa's senior picture, "Luis Ochoa's daughter?"

Jack put himself between them and the wall where Luisa's picture hung. He turned and pulled it off the wall, "My daughter...."

"No, Mr. Jones, that young woman belongs to Luis Ochoa."

Jack started to shake and they continued to look at pictures as if searching for something.

"Who are you? It is time for you to leave. Jill's not here."

They paused in their scrutiny, "We're from the Drug Enforcement Agency. Do you know Luis Ochoa?"

He shook his head, wishing he had not ever heard that name, the man who stole his daughter. Jack haltingly asked, "What do you want with my wife?"

They relaxed slightly and told a story of a major cocaine dealer sought by the United States government for murdering a Drug Enforcement Agent. "We need to talk to Jill, ask her a few questions about her 'Latin Lover.'"

The epithet enraged Jack, but he bit his lip, afraid of making the wrong comment.

"The murder was committed when she was out of the country. The United States government has reason to believe she was in South America with Ochoa at the time. She could be indicted in the conspiracy for murdering a United States government agent, a crime punishable by at least life in prison."

Back and forth each agent added a piece of information.

"We may be able to change the indictment if we can talk to her. We need her cooperation. So when she gets here, please give her this card. If she calls this number, I'm sure we can answer all her questions."

They wrote the name of the local hotel where they were staying. "We are staying over in Kokomo, The Kings Crown Inn. We'll be there until tomorrow afternoon. Have her call. It will be best for her in the long run."

They walked out the door and Jack threw Luisa's picture on the stairway.

He put the card on the table as he sat down. His head pounded as he remembered the physical therapist's orders, "Stretch your arms, take big breaths, stretch your arms, take big breaths."

Jill pulled into the driveway, and tapped her automatic garage door opener. She looked at her watch. Nine. Thank goodness for the PTA meeting, it kept her away from the house even longer. Jack would be watching "Hawaii Five-O." Since the heart attack, Jack sat glued to the television, so she knew the schedule. They talked in brief terms as if speech connected them in ways they wanted to avoid. She left for school every day with a great sense of relief, a good eight hours before the forced conversations. The dreaded drive home suffocated her as each mile brought her closer to the farm.

The garage door plunked shut. She sighed audibly, "Rise to the occasion, Jill." She grabbed her bag of papers to grade, at nine o'clock? No, she yawned, to bed. Tomorrow is Friday; I'll grade them this weekend, something to do after spending some time with Sadie, the only sanity I have any more. Call Luisa from Sadie's and make sure Mike would be there. Why did Luisa make that requirement for their calls? A continent away and still wanting to talk to Mike.

Jill opened the back door and walked to her office away from the living room. She would check the kitchen and see if he ate the soup, she'd left for him to heat up. Maybe he will be asleep. I can go to bed and let him sleep. No, I need to make sure he ate. She tossed her bag on the desk and hung her jacket over the chair.

"Jack?" she spoke in a whisper as she walked down toward the television. She spotted Luisa's senior picture lying on the stairs. Strange. She paused and frowned, glancing at the wall where'd it hung, and then took the few steps into the living room. She heard the television and saw the reflecting light.

He stood up, his face beet red, then stumbled, but grabbed her shoulders and started shaking her. As he shook her, she stared, trying to speak, "Ja..."

His words stuck, but his anger exploded; just like the time when they left Hawk's trailer so many years ago.

He yelled "Luis Ochoa! Luis Ochoa!" over and over again. "You're a murderer! ...A murderer...you killed a...." His phrases became scrambled. His face contorted, he dropped her, then fell to the floor in a heap.

She screamed, "Jack, Jack, Jack, say something!"

He lay motionless. Was he breathing? She ran to the kitchen phone and called the emergency number tacked on the refrigerator. The hospital gave it to her when she brought him home after his heart attack. She returned to him, picked up his arm sobbing, "Jack, Jack say something."

She grabbed the couch afghan and covered him, then saw the DEA business card on the end table. The phone rang. She jumped, grabbing the card before running back to the kitchen phone.

"Jill," Sadie said cheerily, "did Jack tell you I called?"

Jill choked on each word as she said, "Jack had another heart attack. I called emergency. They're coming," Jill whispered, "Call Luis before you leave for the hospital."

ฯ๕ฯ

Gina came in and said Jill was on the phone. She closed the door and Luis picked up the receiver.

"Gringa, what happened?"

"Oh, Luis, the DEA, Jack, shouting Luis Ochoa, Luis..." she sobbed, the hiccup spasm of crying over a long period of time, "collapse...grabbed me, the ambulance...he shook me, shaking, shaking..."

"Jill, you are making no sense, put Siddhartha on the phone!"

Sadie explained in detail that Jack was pronounced dead on arrival from a cerebral hemorrhage. Sadie ended the story and now handed the phone back to Jill.

"Luis," as she started, Gina, walked in and they both said at the same time, "I tried to call Luisa all night. I couldn't reach her."

He stared at Gina, but spoke on the phone, "What, Jill?! What are you saying?!" He held up one finger to Gina, then signaled for her to come all the way into his office. "Jill, stay at Siddhartha's. I will call you back. Be strong, I will find her and have her call you. Jack, your husband, I'm sorry that this happened this way. Stay where you are, don't go back to the farm. Put Siddhartha on the phone."

There was a pause, "Yes, Luis." Sadie spoke.

"I don't know where Luisa is, but I need you to keep Jill safe, hidden, you know what I'm saying?"

"I think so. But here in Caylor, the hospital, her school, everyone knows both of us…"

"It won't be long, just until you hear from Gina or me. Si? I need you to be there for her. She cannot do this alone and I'm too far away."

"Don't worry, Luis. I will do everything I can to protect her, always have, always will, but sometimes you make my work very difficult."

He hung up and ordered Gina to get Mitsos on the phone.

"Jairo's on the phone," Gina said.

"Jairo," he said in a calm tone, then shouted, "The goddamned Americans! The DEA! The CIA! All the basura, I want them off my property, out of the Cordilleras! Jairo, get them out of our country! I can't grow coffee when they are killing my workers, threatening them! Get them out! Call your gringo friends! They killed my most trustworthy man! This fucking game is over! Do you hear me? I'm going to expose this whole international fiasco! My Mediterranean friends are ready!"

The tirade continued until Gina interrupted him, "Raymond Sandy was on line two."

"Jairo! Call me when you have sent your damn army up there, otherwise, the CIA is on the phone right now!"

He pushed the button for line two, "Sandy, you low-life son of a bitch, American scum…"

"Luisa!"

"What did you say?"

"If you want to see her alive, back off your war against our agents in the Hernandez," then Raymond quickly added, "not the CIA Luis, that is the message I was given to read to you. Not me, mi amigo, not me. I swear, the CIA, does not have a dog in your fight up there. I fucking swear, Luis, nothing. They picked me because in spite of our differences, the Director of the CIA heard from DEA and then said to me, 'help with this situation, you know the players.' "

Luis sat and stared out the window. I promised to keep her safe…"Okay Sandy, tell me."

Gina came in and said she could not get Mitsos on the phone.

He put his hand over the receiver, and said in a whisper, "Call Fulaij."

"Luis, they want you to stop killing their men wholesale," Raymond Sandy said.

"Never! They are basura that trespass on land that doesn't belong to them. They killed my…" Luis stopped, looking at a picture of David. They killed David's mother, her father, and now Jorge. How many years must this violence go on?

"Yes, I understand, but for the moment you must get a grip on yourself because they have Luisa. And only you have the key to her freedom. Think about that, Luis, you have the key to her freedom."

"I hate them! I hate them with all of my being. How can they take what they did not earn? I'll castrate all of them; let the vultures eat their eyes!"

Sandy explained they wanted five million dollars in cash, delivered to them personally by El Campesino, and they want his personal army to turn jurisdiction over to the army of Colombia and his friend Jairo Humberto. They would call Sandy when they had the place and time to meet him. Hanging up, Gina told him Fulaij was on the phone. Luis asked Fulaij for his help. He explained that he needed to house Luisa's mother. Fulaij said he had a place outside Paris that was well protected and she could stay as long as he wanted. Luis hung up and told Gina to call Jill and make sure she understood what she needed to do and she had no choice, but to leave for Paris at once and Sadie would now exercise her power of attorney.

Gina dialed the number and started to speak as Luis grabbed the phone, "Jill, listen to me, you must do exactly as I tell you, no time for your hard-headed Jankee talk, just listen. Siddhartha needs to drive you to the airport. There is a ticket on American Airlines to take you to Paris. You will be met. You don't need to pack, just take your money and your Colombian passport. Leave your American passport with Siddhartha. Entiendes?"

"I understand, I guess. Where is Luisa? I want to talk to her."

"She and I are not in the same place and as soon as we are, we will call you *in Paris*. Do not go back to the farm. Siddhartha must now take over her power of attorney."

"Luis, it is all so scary. Are you okay? I can see your face and worry is written all over it. What about Jack's funeral and my teaching…"

"Jill, I am getting ready to leave to go get Luisa. I need you to drive with Siddhartha to the airport, now, right now. By the time you get to Paris, we will call you. Hasta que la muerte nos separe."

He hung up then sat back in his chair. He pulled out a cigar, then removed the matchbox, tapping it on the desk top. He put them back into the desk drawer without lighting the tobacco. Okay Luisa, for you, less smoking. He chewed on the unlit cigar and picked up the picture of he and Jill, the only photo he had. They stood by the church building in Haiti. He rubbed his thumb over the image, oh Jill, it wasn't supposed to be like this. God, what was it supposed to be like? Maybe I should have just put her in the truck and taken her to Benton Harbor. I could have taken her out of Indiana right then. Raise our daughter together. She wouldn't have had to lose her love in that goddamned American war, Viet Nam; he wouldn't have been her love. No farmer Jack, like some stone around her neck all these years.

Gringa, a part of me all these nineteen years. Innocent, so innocent on many levels, trusting me with her only child. She was honest, intuitive, the perfect mother for my daughter. He had known that from the beginning when he saw her with the migrant children. She loved them; hugged them as if they were her own. She was patient, but she could release that Irish, "Grandma Caitlin," when need be. Parameters? When she protected those, he wanted to challenge her to see the red face and pouted lips. Goddamned tempting in all that anger. Oh, Jill, I love you so…do you know that? Have I told you enough? No one, no other woman…jealousy, no need, even though they keep trying. The money, always attracted to the money, she knew me as a migrant worker and gave herself to me. No, Jill, there is no one. She had proved her metal with the DEA, goddamned American terrorists, she protected me, a person she insists she doesn't know, but still loves. I must get our daughter. Thank god, Angotti sold my share of the Pakistani bank deal; the money will help in whatever is going on here now.

Gina walked in, "Jairo is on the line, sir."

The president ordered Luis to calm down. Luis explained the kidnapping of Luisa. Jairo promised to provide him with the army as requested by the kidnappers, then hesitantly mentioned he had been heavily pressured in the last few days with the American drug agent's killing. Controlling his anger, Luis told him the Americans could *"metanse en el culo!"* (shove it up their ass) He continued and his anger erupted all over again.

Gina gave him the only message he wanted, Sandy was on the phone. The arrangements had been made. Luis demanded to talk to Luisa. He waited momentarily while Sandy rang a number. Luisa answered. "Papa?"

"*Mi hija,* (my daughter) are you okay?"

"Yes, have you talked to Mom?"

"Si." And the line went dead. Luis hung up and rushed out of the office. He did not say anything to Gina, but rushed past her to the elevator and headed for the roof. Andy stood at one corner of the helicopter pad, smoking a cigarette. Luis signaled to him to get his bird flying. When he buckled his seatbelt, he told him, "Armero. You'll drop me off, then pick up Sandy! You have to remember where I am because my briefcase is empty. Sandy has the ransom money, compliments of Señor Sam, if I need it."

They were up and then within twenty minutes down. Andy lowered the helicopter onto an empty warehouse parking lot.

Luis yelled over the sound of the helicopter blades, "Stay close! I'm not fighting this goddamned war myself!" Luis said, then jumped out of the helicopter.

As soon as the helicopter left, a black SUV pulled up to where he stood. Two men jumped out, patted him down, then shoved him into their car. They tied a blindfold over his eyes.

He counted slowly trying to figure the driving time, not far, ten minutes at the high end. They walked him across crunching gravel, then up steps and through a door, a screen door he thought, as it slammed. They pulled off his blindfold. Sitting at a small desk on a plastic chair was a masked man who asked for the money. Luis patted the briefcase. The briefcase was empty. If Luis could not get Luisa any other way, Raymond Sandy should be outside waiting with the real US dollars.

The masked man explained in a condescending tone, "Your army killed Jose Castro, from the DEA."

"Goddamned basura whores!"

"You want your daughter, we're here to get an agreement. The murders will stop."

Luis said, "Get them off my land, they'll live longer! My workers are murdered! Where's my daughter?"

"You cannot bargain with DEA or us. And soon your American lover will be arrested for conspiracy in the murder of a DEA agent."

Luis stared from one kidnapper to the next. Three of them. One stood directly behind him, one stood by a door that led to another room, and the third sat in front of him with a small automatic pistol. The one in front of him spoke, "Where is the money? And we can make all this go away, Señor."

None of it was making any sense now. The DEA would not kidnap Luisa. But why would they threaten Jill with arrest? They weren't DEA, the words were nonsense. So who? Why? The CIA wouldn't give money to the DEA. No, something else....The man behind him and one by the door held Uzi weapons, the preferred gun choice of the FARC, but why the goddamned communists? Speaking for the DEA? Raymond Sandy may have been right. The ruse. Who then was up in his mountains hiring the FARC? Who wanted his coca trade? He would have that conversation later with Sandy, now he needed to get Luisa.

"The briefcase, the money, Señor!"

Luis had only a moment. He pulled the briefcase up slightly, making a move to give it to the negotiator, but he swung backward quickly, hitting the man behind him, knocking him down, and grabbing his Uzi. He shot him and then rolled faster, firing at the guard by the door.

The negotiator yelled, "Guillermo." Luis pointed the Uzi at the man's head and grabbed his hand gun.

The negotiator said, "Get the girl." He yelled at someone behind the door.

The door burst open, and the negotiator yelled, "No! Medusa! No!" Luis stared at his "friend," who pointed his Uzi at Luis.

Mitsos signaled behind him, pulling Luisa in front him, "I have no interest in your ransom money or your daughter!" Mitsos pushed Luisa towards the door Luis had entered. "Go Señorita Ochoa! Say goodbye to Señor Ochoa, the dog!"

Luisa brushed Luis's arm and ran out the door. Luis continued to hold Guillermo and inched closer to the door.

"Your hostage is dead. I don't care about him. It is you Señor, you traitorous dog bringing the CIA to my sanctum! Now you will pay for your disloyalty with your life. You embarrassed me."

311

Luis pushed Guillermo towards Mitsos, then pointed the gun at Mitsos. Shots came from every direction. Luis fell holding his chest. The Texas darkness again.

ϒξϒ

Jill paced the palace of her Paris host. It had been two weeks and no call from Luis and Luisa. She wanted for nothing in her suite of massive elegant rooms. The furniture was gold leaf with cranberry velvet upholstery, long gauzy drapes hung between layers of velvet and satin trimmed in gold fringe. Hard wood floors peeked between pink, gold and cranberry Persian carpets. Someone brought clothes that were the perfect size, underwear included. How did they know her bra size? But the clothes were cotton, comfortable drawstring pants and tunic shirts, perfect for sitting and reading books if she wanted them. Fulaij asked her to tell him what titles or subjects she liked.

She had a hard time sitting and not thinking, so difficult to concentrate. Sadie, Jack, did they have a funeral? Southeastern? She didn't show up one day. How did schools handle disappearing teachers? The same way if a teacher died, I suppose. And my students…I never said goodbye to anyone except…Sadie. What did you say? Southeastern would know Jack died. They would not expect her for a few days…oh, Sadie. Michael? Was he mad that this was their worst plan ever? Oh, Sadie, I'm sorry if they are giving you the third degree. I left you with such a mess. My life? Yes Luis, I trusted her with it, with ours, Luisa, yours, all of us. Only she knows Paris. Oh, God don't let them come to Sadie's.

She asked for writing paper. There was no calendar, so she tracked her days. She drew her own squares and tried to figure out what day she arrived and marked "x's" in the squares as she said goodnight to herself. In all the stress of leaving and waiting, she also drew a calendar for the last month and tried to remember the date of her last period; she had always kept track all these years from when the nurse admonished her at State's health care. Calendars? Why were the little white squares so important to her?

Her bed was gold leaf and way too big for just her; it really was a princess bed. With a cranberry velvet quilt and the softest cotton sheets she had ever slept on. When she closed her eyes, she imagined sharing the space with Luis. Could she have one on each side, Luisa, and Luis, safe in this cranberry room? She prayed for the safety of Luisa and Luis, but she could not call, only to God to protect her family. She was in Paris. Could she just get on the train and go to her villa? She knew how to do that. She had the money.

So many questions, why? Why Luis? Why can't I go to our Italian home? Fulaij did not allow her access to a telephone. He politely told Jill that he was unable to answer the many questions she must have about Luis and her daughter. Questions? Luis's tone had scared her. How much danger was he in, if they told Jack she was a murderer? What did they say to him? And God, Luisa....

She paced, picked up a book, but all the words started with "L." They ran together like some runaway train, no sentence stops, and words one right after the other making no sense. Luis, call me. Tell me everything is okay. She cried. "Be strong," he said.

Her host, Fulaij, an older gentleman, "Syrian," he answered her question. When they talked, his dark eyes were kind and serious, asking for honesty with her conversation. He constantly pulled his small gray goatee that extended from a white narrow mustache. She wanted to cry on his shoulder, but his professor of Mideast history demeanor prevented such an intimate exchange. He wore a long tunic and loose fitting pants and sandals. They talked over lunch, afternoon tea and dinner. They ate wonderful dessert cakes made of honey. The coffee was served in fine china. Fulaij held the cup with his delicate long fingers.

He was most interested in farming in the United States. He said he owned property in the Bekka Valley. His friend Señor Ochoa was a farmer in Colombia and they often talked of the joys and heartaches of farming. His knowledge of American agriculture amazed her. Jill talked of Beau's farm. Beau and Mary Ann? She never had time to talk to Beau about Jack's death, nothing. His family hates me. They may be happy I've disappeared off the face of the earth, at least out of their lives.

Fulaij hinted of a netherworld, but in such guarded terms. He was right in describing her anxiety. She complimented him on his graciousness and his precise English. He smiled explaining he had gone to English schools in Cairo.

"Señora Ochoa, do not worry. You are safe here with me. No harm will come to you. Sometimes events happen, but in our world we can protect you. For friends nothing impedes safety. Are you familiar with the chador cloak?"

"Chador cloak? I don't think so."

"It is the black cloak worn by our women. You will wear one when we leave the compound and the hejab, for your safety, Señora Ochoa. I see by your face this bothers you. As your host, I will deliver you as you came to me. It is the bond of friendship. You may take your clothes that we have provided."

She was happy he had said that because she had no clothes and had no idea where her next stop would be.

When the call came, Fulaij sent the cloak and head cover to Jill. The Syrian servant helped her tuck all the red-blonde curls safely from view. The only things visible were her large dark eyes which Fulaij commented could belong to a woman from his home.

They drove out of the gated compound and into Paris, then to the airport. The limousine took them to a private area reserved for those of Fulaij's ilk. The small jet seated eight people, but she was the only one besides the pilot on the plane. Fulaij boarded the plane wearing his own robe. It concealed a mechanic's coverall suit. He quickly removed his robe and then disembarked, he whispered to Jill, "Your husband is an honorable man, Señora Ochoa. It was my pleasure hosting you."

Jill trembled as the small private plane was quickly airborne. She had come a long way from her Hoosier farm. When would she talk to Sadie? There was so much to tell and so much to ask. The pilot only made one announcement, "Fasten seatbelt for landing in Nicosia." She tried to remember exactly where Nicosia was. She knew that somewhere someone planned each of her moves exactly. She kept her cloak on as she emerged from the small plane. David greeted her, "Hello Jill."

"David, where are Luis and Luisa? Where are we? What is going on?"

"Wait. Luisa said you would have many questions. We are going to join Luisa now. I'll try to explain as we drive."

The bullets, their damage was extensive, debilitating, but not fatal. Luis spent several hours in surgery, one bullet removed from its niche between the lung and diaphragm. The marksman saved his life by perfectly placing the metal explosive. In millimeters, the surgeon told David and Luisa to measure his life. The others damaged muscle tissue; he would need complete rest and a slow process of physical therapy. Brother and sister decided that the threat was not over and announced his death.

The limousine driver took them to a marina. David helped Jill, escorting her to a large waiting yacht. Boarding the craft, she was greeted immediately by Luisa. Jill was impressed with the change in her eighteen year old baby. David hugged each of them and returned to the waiting limousine. He promised to meet Luisa in Cartagena soon.

"Mom, we are going to a small seaport in Turkey, Bodrum. Papa has a strong heart, but he has been severely wounded. This is the first time we have been able to move him. He looks very ill and much thinner than you remember him. He was in surgery many hours. The doctor said if his heart weren't so strong, he would be dead. As Luisa explained the details, Jill cried, shedding her cloak. "But Mom, you must control yourself because he feels so responsible for you."

Luisa and Jill entered a large state room that in some ways looked like a hospital room. Jill haltingly approached his still body. She held his hand and kissed his sleeping face. Two small tubes taped to his nose fed him oxygen. His breathing seemed forced, but he breathed on his own.

She whispered, "Luis?"

The hazel-green eyes remained closed and she sat and cried, rubbing his hand.

The yacht landed in Bodrum and a medical van with a Red Crescent painted on the side, met them at the dock. Two very large men, dressed in white trousers, shirts and shoes, carefully removed him from the state room. They all rode to an apartment overlooking the marina and harbor, not far from where the yacht docked. The heavy sedation allowed all the movement with no protests from Luis. The apartment had been furnished with a hospital bed. Luisa said she would be staying for a week then returning to Cartagena. As the men left, leaving tanks of oxygen, one of them said in heavily accented English that the women should call if they needed help in any way before their next scheduled visit. They said he would wake soon and there was soup and tea in the refrigerator.

Jill and Luisa sat on the patio of the apartment looking out at the blue sea. A blue like no other, Jill thought. Mother and daughter sipped tea and discussed their immediate future. Luis would need to eat and walk on his own. He had medication. Jill stared at her daughter as if she were a stranger. When did she become the responsible-giving-orders person who sat across from her, drinking tea?

Luisa explained that she would be contacted by the man she met in Majorca, Raymond Sandy. He would probably be here in a few weeks to help with their return to South America. "Papa will wake up and want to make decisions about business, you, me, his farm, the orphanage. We will need to get him back to his corner of the world. But Mom, Raymond Sandy says you must get married, legally, not some passport that states something which is not true."

"Papa is Catholic; he will want to be married by a priest. You need to tell your Raymond Sandy to find a priest if he wants that to happen."

Luisa continued with the scare of men stopping her on campus, knocking down her security guard and putting a bag over her head. Andy Marshall came to the house where they kept her and brought Raymond Sandy. They were all shooting, but Andy Marshall grabbed her and carried her to a car as Raymond and David took Luis. They drove to the hospital. She and David stayed through Luis's surgery, one of them, Andy, Raymond or David was there with her day after day for a week.

"I'm going to call Mike. Is there anything you want me to say?"

"Everything. I want to talk to Sadie, need to."

"But Mom, you can't call yet. You may want to write a letter, no one can read them. I think for the moment it will be best. Papa had to get you out of the United States. He will tell you why because I don't know all the reasons for what he does. You know Papa is a merchant, coffee in Colombia, wine in Italy. He also has investments in New York, through Mr. Angotti. He does other things also. He must explain after you are married and when he is better Mom, when he is better. He runs a company that includes the coffee farms. As his daughter I am responsible on some documents for things that are going on. David is so patient with me, learning these things in the last two weeks has been like a college education."

Luisa wanted to know the details of Jack's death. She cried when Jill told her how suddenly he fell, right in front of her. She said when she talked to Mike, he could probably give her details.

"Mom, I talked a lot to Raymond Sandy in Greece at a party thrown by one of Papa's enemies. But Raymond can be trusted. When you meet with him, listen, please. I know you want to protect Papa, but Raymond will help you."

᛭ξᛓ

Luis slept and woke and slept and woke. She lay next to him and jumped every time his breathing changed even slightly. He was in a sleep state for most of the first week when Luisa was with them. The Red Crescent workers came every third day to help turn him, bathe, sit up and walk. Slowly he recovered. He mumbled in Spanish; she listened intently, deciphering the partial syllables.

Their Turkish hideaway had an open market that she went to every day, trying to find things for soup. She was in the market searching for ingredients and trying to get pricing from a woman who spoke very little English, when Raymond Sandy came up to her.

"Jill Jones, let's go for coffee."

She hadn't heard that full name for awhile.

"Or tea if you prefer…" he continued.

"Okay," she heard herself say to Raymond Sandy and to Luisa wherever she was.

Raymond identified himself as being involved with Luis for several years, and said that Luis regarded him as basura on a good day and much worse on most others.

"Jill, when I met you in Majorca you looked at me as if you knew me. And I want to say that you do. We met in New York many years ago at my sister's wedding. You were with my father, William Cunningham."

She shivered and rubbed the goose bumps on her arms. She stared at his face, the lips, yes, now I see, William. "Maybe we should have gone for vodka and soda. What in god's green earth are you saying to me?"

"I am Christian Cunningham. I am letting you know my real name; please do not repeat it to Luis right now. There is just too much information here that he is not quite ready for. It wouldn't be good for his heart."

"*His* heart? Jeezus H. Christ, I'm spinning here, Christian. Mo…does she know?" Jill trembled as she sat, staring at the "CIA scum" as Luis called him, but a handsome young man. William what have you done now?

"No, very few people…Jill, I will be coming to your apartment in a few days with an American priest from the Air Force base to marry you two. In order to protect you, you must be married, legally, not some passport from Colombia."

"But…"

"Please listen, I don't have much time. We need to get you out of Turkey as soon as possible. Luis has friends here, then he has 'friends' here, if you know what I mean. His Greek 'friend' tried to kill him because of me. Father and I were able to keep you safe for awhile, but soon you must leave. Greece and Turkey are neighboring countries. Luis has a lot of money, but he also has a reputation across many continents. We will be moving you to Buenos Aires, and one more thing...I was told to say 'what happens if you kiss a redhead in Buenos Aires.'"

"Oh, god, no...where did you hear, that?" She felt the blood drain from her face, again she was covered in goose bumps; she looked at her hands, no, who is this storyteller, some young man, not William's son, the letter, did I not read between the lines. How could this be? She quivered. Why a restaurant with nothing stronger than Turkish coffee, strong enough, but no match for...Hector, no. He was killed in Viet, Laos, but killed. No, Raymond, Christian he must stop. "No, no, no."

"Yes. In Argentina you can practice your Spanish. One final piece of information, in the United States, as you know, a wife cannot testify against her husband. There are agents looking for you to ask questions. The DEA has clouded this issue well, actually Luis's shipping friend, made it much too murky, a SNAFU, as Dad would say. You're soon-to-be husband is protected by people with a much higher pay grade than me. We have to get you this protection because he can only protect you up to a point. And my father says..."

"No, no. No, Christian."

"My father says he is there for you if you have any questions. Jill, he has been able to make this respite possible, also the move."

"What is he? Some guardian angel in my life?"

"Angel? Absolutely no way, my father, you know him better than that. Guardian, yes, he loves playing that roll for all of us, some progenitor of God. I think you also know another man like that."

"Can this all be true? I feel like I'm in the 'Twilight Zone' or an episode of 'Mission Impossible.'"

"Real, Jill, very real. I met Luis in Miami a few years ago; we flew to Caylor, Indiana to some fortress looking church. He was quiet most of the trip to Indiana, then on our way back to catch a plane at Grissom Air Base, he made me drive down some country road looking for a farm building. Mc...something, it was hard to read, a cow picture..."

Jill whispered, "McKinnsey." She blinked a tear away and took her napkin to tap her eye.

"Yeah, that's it, he spoke of destiny. It made no sense to me." He drank his espresso in one swallow and shook his head. "Whew!

When I arrive, Luis will be angry, perhaps you can mention I saved his life, but otherwise, it will be me and a priest."

"I have a favor to ask, when can I call my best friend Sadie?"

"I think Luisa instructed you to write, but I would also tell her as in 'Mission Impossible' to destroy the letter after she reads it."

"Luisa? You talk as if you know her, I mean much more, how much more?"

"You have an amazing daughter, yes we met in Majorca for the first time, then I was to be her chaperone at a party Luis took us to Greece. She was at home with all those Mediterranean power brokers. Men couldn't keep their eyes off of her, the long dark hair and touch of olive skin and she has that wonderful laugh, makes you feel so at ease. But just as quickly like her father, a frown on that sweet angelic face. Now talk of angels, she definitely…"

"Christian, you sound smitten. Aren't you too old…?"

He shook his head. The cold veneer of nothing but the facts and seriousness left his face. And he blushed. "Ten years."

"You have thought about it. Oh, you have a story to tell her mother." Jill turned her head as if waiting for a certain sound.

"When I told my father about her, he said, 'I changed her diaper…' then stopped on a dime and looked away from me. I have no idea where that came from. Looking at you, the way you smile…I won't pry, not today. But you, too, may have a story to tell."

"Probably not. Her father hates you, hates the CIA, hates the United States government even if they support him on some level…or saved his life and his soon to be wife."

He nodded, "Believe me, I know. But life is random, I tell myself. I never know what the day is going to bring. My mom used to say that to me, she probably still would if I called her right now."

"I met her, she looked like a cover of Vanity Fair."

"Yes, she works very hard to maintain that look. I must go, there is much to do and pretty quickly. I am happy to have had this talk with you. Father did say you were not like Luis and I would be pleasantly surprised. It has been a pleasure to talk to you." He stood and left her at the table.

William, I didn't have to call you, you sent Christian. Did you not trust me to call when trouble came down all around me? She wanted to order vodka, but in the Muslim surroundings, she continued to drink the Turkish coffee. Colombian would be so much nicer.

Luis groggily let her feed him soup. The middle of the third week, the men from the Red Crescent helped her set him outside on the patio. He walked, but slowly. The fresh sea air invigorated him. The seagulls dipping into the Aegean and crispy white clouds made their view spectacular. Bodrum was dry. It reminded her of Arizona and Majorca. When she walked to the market, she passed ruins of weathered rock buildings, pieces of ancient stone falling askew by the road. All of the ancient civilians had their broken memorials - the Ottomans, Romans, and of course the Greeks.

She now sat holding his hand; a pot of tea sat on the small table between them. She stood and walked into the kitchen to cut some lemon for the tea.

"Gringa?"

She paused, "Yes," she said, "Yes, Luis?"

"Where the hell are we?"

She carried the lemon to the small wood table that separated their lounge chairs.

"And what is this? Tea? I want absinthe and a cigar!"

His demands reminded her of when Luisa had a fever and it broke; she quickly returned to her normal rambunctious self.

"Luis, you can have neither. And you must calm down. Your heart was almost blown in half by the bullets. The doctor said you needed to rest, to heal."

He rubbed his bandaged chest, "More scars, but I don't remember this. I do remember that traitor Mitsos, trying to steal my...did I kill him?"

Jill gasped, "You must not get upset. Murder? Oh, god, Luis, we've been through hell. Just relax."

"I want to talk."

"Okay, but lower your voice. David made me promise to keep you here and keep you quiet. And no sex under any circumstances. I didn't even ask why he would give that piece of advice. Your son, I suppose he knows something. Or chip off the old block?"

"Damn son! Come here let's make another son, we don't need him."

She reached for his hand, touching his fingertips; she spoke softly, "Maybe we already have."

"Jill?" he whispered, "You said it so quietly."

"Luis, we have much to discuss, but now you must heal. Take it easy, slowly, and calmly as David said. All emotions foreign to you. Your daughter also said, 'No; nothing radical.' Amazing how she says it like you do."

"Let's call her and I will tell her no."

"We don't have a phone line for long distance calls, oh yes, you asked where. We are in Bodrum, Turkey."

He looked at her and touched his chest gingerly, then winced. "Tea? Okay, Gringa. I'll drink tea. I see now there is much missing in this story." He stopped talking to look at her. "I think it is time to tell you everything. But *I* must ask questions." He chuckled, but grimaced, pursed his lips, frowning as he gently patted his bandage, "No laughing, either, the chest is not ready. Basura!"

"Stop, Luis. I am losing my patience. I waited too long and almost lost you. Please talk… in a calm voice. I would say take a breath, but I know that must be most painful."

"Si. So where shall I begin? In my 'calm' voice." He imitated her higher pitch when he said calm.

"My dad always told me to start at the beginning, and then we could work on the end together."

"Smart man. We will work on the end together. Did he know what a wonderful daughter he made?"

"He called me his princess that should tell you. And he knew what a wonderful daughter you made."

He held the tea mug under his nose allowing the honey and lemon smell to float in his face. He sipped the hot aromatic drink, then looked over at Jill, and smiled, "A baby? I…okay, I'll listen." He sighed audibly, and whispered, "A baby."

She scrutinized his every move, "Maybe, Luis. I've been through emotional hell, and that could be causing my body to react differently."

She drank her tea knowing she had spent the last couple of mornings trying not to vomit and blaming the food from the market.

"I love you, Grin…Jill Caitlin Havlicek Jones, marry me now! Let's begin there. Any priests in this place?"

"Yes, there is a plan. Please, please listen and try not to let your anger erupt. You are here because some loyal people insured your safety, your life really."

Just as promised, Raymond Sandy arrived with a priest in tow. He stood next to the priest who came in Air Force dress blues, with a stole around his neck. Luis frowned and Jill squeezed his hand mouthing her admonition of remaining calm. He shook his head, and said, "Goddamned CIA," before the priest began the abbreviated service.

Jill wore a chemise dress, sleeveless, light weight cream silk with a lace insert in the scoop neck. She tucked a white flower behind her ear. When she shopped, she found an antique gold ring. "Worn by an Ottoman priest," the shopkeeper explained. She liked it and thought Luis would or could buy another one at some time in their future. Jill tried to buy clothes for Luis in the market and decided on loose and comfortable. His chest was very sore, so she picked a long tunic over baggy linen pants like those Fulaij had worn. After six weeks of not shaving, Luis had a full beard.

Luis told her they would have a proper wedding ring and a wedding and in a church when they arrived home.

The priest said, "Since it is your intention to enter into marriage, join your right hands, and declare your consent before God and his Church."

"I, Luis Ochoa take you Jill Caitlin Havlicek Jones, to be my wife. I promise to be true to you in good times and in bad, in sickness and in health. I will love you and honor you all the days of my life."

The green eyes, kindness, stared at her; no longer frightening as when she stood ankle deep in straw. He squeezed her hands tightly. She rubbed his "wedding ring," the one he had been wearing since he left her in Indiana nineteen years ago. Driving with Sadie to the airport, American Airlines to Paris, she had taken off her wedding ring from Jack and handed it to Sadie, telling her to bury it with Jack or whatever Sadie wanted to do with it.

"I, Jill Caitlin Havlicek Jones, take you, Luis Ochoa, to be my husband. I promise to be true to you in good times and in bad, in sickness and in health. I will love you and honor you all the days of my life."

They kissed. Raymond Sandy snapped a picture of them. October 25, 1979. She would start her own wall of weddings. Where would that be? With Luis Ochoa and that was all that mattered.

About the Author

 Jacqueline Hendricks grew up in Indiana. She received a BS and MS from Indiana University, but learned about life in Kokomo, Indiana a small town. She now lives in Boulder, Colorado, but insists Indiana will always be "home." She taught English, Journalism and Social Studies. She's published a non-fiction memoir, *Dear Joe Biden: 97 Months, A woman's Story of Six Years in Federal Prison as told in Letters to Senator Joseph Biden. 1990-1996*

[available at Createspace.com, Barnesandnoble.com, Kindle.Amazon.com and Amazon.com]